To Tempt the Wolf

TERRY SPEAR

Published by Sourcebooks Casablanca, an imprint of Sourcebooks, Inc.
P.O. Box 4410, Naperville, Illinois 60567-4410
(630) 961-3900
FAX: (630) 961-2168
www.sourcebooks.com

Printed in Canada
WC 10 9 8 7 6 5 4 3

I dedicate To Tempt the Wolf *to the veterans who have served their country, to my son, who will be joining their ranks, to my father, who had been a prisoner of war and retired with the USAF, to his uncle, who died as a prisoner of war, and to my mother and all other women who have also served their country.*

Chapter 1

SUCKING UP OXYGEN, THE FLAMES SPREAD OUTWARD, devouring thirsty timber and underbrush, perfect fuel for the firestorm. The winds picked up force, and Tessa Anderson's adrenaline surged again as she snapped the last of the photos for the magazine. The summer drought had continued on through the fall and winter, leaving the California forests desert-dry, and now either a careless camper or an arsonist had turned the woods into a fiery inferno.

What in the world was she doing risking her life to photograph this disaster?

Coughing, her eyes filled with smoke, she reminded herself she needed the money to help defend her brother. Then in the haze, the silhouette of a wolf appeared—gray, like the smoke, a phantom. Watching her. Stalking her? Wild animals knew better than to linger with danger threatening. Only a human would be dumb enough to stay put.

His uncharacteristic actions made her back toward her vehicle. Having been fascinated with wolves all her life, she knew his behavior wasn't natural.

A tremor stole up her spine. He looked just like one she'd seen before. The one who'd attacked before.

Snapping a picture of the wolf, she bumped against the passenger's side of her Escort. As soon as she fumbled for the door handle, he crouched, readying to spring like a coiled snake.

Heart thundering, she jerked her door open and jumped inside. Before she could shut the door, the wolf's hulking body slammed against it, knocking it closed. She jumped back.

Snarling, he bared his wicked canines. She scrambled over the console and twisted the keys in the ignition, her skin prickling with panic. Tires spun on gravel as she whirled the car around and headed for the main highway.

A half mile later, she came across a home in the direct path of the fire. An SUV was parked in the driveway. Its trunk lid was open and the back filled with boxes. Reassured that the occupants were leaving, she tore on past.

Her main concern now was returning to her brother's trial and praying he would be found not guilty.

Hunter Greymere shoved four more suitcases in the SUV while his twin sister rushed out of the house with another box of dishes, her face and clothes covered in soot.

The air was so thick with smoke, Hunter choked, fighting to draw in a breath of fresh oxygen. "Meara, enough! Get in the vehicle. We leave now!"

Black plumes of smoke spiraling upward indicated fire had claimed another of his pack member's homes and was growing ever closer to his own. Ash rained down like a light gray snow flurry. The smoke blocked out the sun, but the flames lit the sky with an eerie orange glow.

Meara shook her head and dashed for the house. "We have to get the safe."

Seizing her arm, Hunter pushed her toward the vehicle. "*Get* in the SUV! I'll grab the safe."

The look of mutiny on her face meant she would

disobey him. He didn't have time to make her listen. Running in a crouch so he could breathe, he grabbed the steel box from his bedroom closet and carried it through the hazy living room. He crashed into Meara, stooping low, her arms filled with another box.

"Out, now!" he growled.

The blaze crackled, incinerating the old forest and homes in its path. The emerald green woods, already rusty with trees that had died from insect infestations and drought would soon be blackened. And the home they had lived in for two hundred years would vanish in a roaring ball of fire. No time for regret now.

The super-heated gases singed Hunter's throat and lungs, and he chided himself for staying as long as they had. After climbing into the vehicle, he turned the fan on high, but the car was already so filled with smoke, his eyes and throat burned. Meara's amber eyes glistened with tears as she covered her mouth and nose with a wet towel.

"We'll be all right, Meara." Hunter gunned the accelerator and sped toward the highway that would take them to Oregon, nearly hitting a Ford Escape in the fog-like smoke in front of them. The driver apparently had the same notion, but was not driving fast enough for Hunter's liking.

"Hell, who is that?"

"Oregon plates. Some idiot human camping out here? Who knows."

"A woman? By herself?"

He peered harder into the smoke and made out a crown of flame red hair cascading over her shoulders. Intrigued, he wondered if her face was as enchanting as the waterfall of red curls. But then he scowled. She shouldn't have been here in the first place.

He followed her as she hightailed it out of his territory in an attempt to keep ahead of the eye of the firestorm, and *him*. And for an instant, he felt like a predator stalking his prey. "At least we got all our people out."

Meara didn't reply.

She didn't adjust well to change. Moving from the Scottish Highlands over two hundred years ago to the untamed California wilderness hadn't set well with her. But change was inevitable for the *lupus garous*. Meara had been lucky they hadn't had to move as much over the years as many of their kind, hiding the fact that once they reached eighteen, they aged only a year for every thirty.

"Where are we going?" she asked, staring out the window at the vast ancient pines that would soon suffer the fate of their steadfast companions.

"To Oregon. Uncle Basil called earlier this morning while you were helping others pack. He's retiring to Florida. The cabins on the Oregon coast are ours now."

"Florida? Are there any of our kind there?"

"Real red wolves on St. Vincent Island off the Panhandle of Florida."

"*Real* red wolves?" Meara snorted. "I didn't think he liked mixing it up with red wolves, *period*. But *real* wolves?"

"He said he found a pack of gray *lupus garous* near the Everglades."

She shook her head. "So what's he going to hunt there? Alligators?" She let out her breath. "I don't want to move to the Oregon seacoast."

Hunter didn't respond. It didn't matter where they

went. Unless it was back to their home in the woods, she wouldn't be happy. Not until she had time to settle in. Hopefully, it wouldn't take as long as the last time.

Hunter finished his shower at Uncle Basil's home, nestled in the woods overlooking the rugged Oregon seacoast, but couldn't get the smell of smoke out of his nostrils, and his eyes and lungs still burned. Nothing had gone as he'd planned. Not only was Meara refusing to speak with him— as he expected—but his people had mutinied as well.

As soon as he joined his uncle in the living room, he realized the day wasn't going to get any better. Not the way his uncle gave him a warning look.

Once Hunter assured himself Meara couldn't hear them from the laundry room, he settled on the leather couch. "So what *didn't* you tell me when you offered this territory for my pack?"

Uncle Basil sat on his suede recliner, looking like he had aged ten years since the last time Hunter had seen him, his hair grayer, longer, his beard shaggier, his amber eyes tired. Which meant his uncle must have had some real trouble.

"*You* have a problem you'll have to deal with. One of your neighbors has been taking pictures in our woods. It wouldn't do for her to catch you shapeshifting. I tried to buy her out, but she won't budge. First her grand-parents, and now she and her brother live in the house about twelve miles south of us on the coast. You'll need to make her understand she can't trespass on our land any longer. Of course, if your pack doesn't return from where they've scattered, it'll be just you and Meara enjoying the area in your fur coats. But when you lease the cabins to other grays, the risk will become greater. Up until recently, the place has been a safe haven for them, but this woman…" Uncle Basil shook his head.

Hunter knew damn well his uncle normally wouldn't hesitate to eliminate her if she could expose their kind for what they truly were. "You mean, the *woman* will be at risk." When Uncle Basil didn't say anything in response, Hunter swore under his breath. "You couldn't do it, and that's why you're retiring?"

His uncle avoided looking at him.

Hell, as if Hunter didn't have enough troubles to contend with. "All right. I'll take care of it. Are you going to have supper with us before you leave?"

"I already ate. Got a ticket on the next flight. I left a couple of salmon steaks out for you. Place is stocked with food so you won't have to shop for a while." Uncle Basil stretched his six-foot-two frame. "Looking forward to sunshine warming these old bones. Hips are bothering me something fierce. Figure the cold dampness might have something to do with it."

Then he leaned forward. "Your mother and father would have been proud the way you've managed to keep the pack safe all these years. Your people will return. Give them time. Just be sure and take care of the woman. Her brother most likely is going to prison for murder, but the woman's still a threat, unless she decides to move. Tessa Anderson's the name. Take care of it. And soon."

He stood and gave Hunter a fatherly embrace, then said his good-byes to Meara. Hunter waved as his uncle left in his old pickup, wondering why he hated to buy new vehicles as much as Meara hated to change where she lived.

Hunter walked to the picture window overlooking the Pacific Ocean and stared out at the gray day, the cold, fog, moisture—in stark contrast to the dry, burning heat and smoke of their abandoned home. Regret and relief warred with his emotions.

Meara slipped up next to him. "I don't like being here."

"You'll get used to it."

Knowing full well she wouldn't appreciate any attempt to console her, he headed into the kitchen and tossed the salmon steaks into a frying pan. He was determined to enjoy their newly acquired cabins, even if his sister didn't like it. Not that they'd had much choice. Settling with the insurance company would take forever and most of their savings were tied up in mutual funds.

"It reeks of fish here. How Uncle Basil could have ever stood it… I didn't remember why I hated this place whenever we visited. But that was it. The strong odor of fish and rotting seaweed." She opened a kitchen cabinet door, peered in, and then slammed it closed, rattling a couple of others.

"Eventually, you won't even notice it."

She opened another cabinet door and pulled out a can of spinach. "I want a mate! How am I going to find one way out here? You've made sure there are no other *lupus garous* in a four-hundred mile stretch of land."

So that was some of the trouble. Not that he'd had much luck finding her a mate in California either because she'd been so choosy.

"*That's* a bit of an exaggeration. Besides, when we

rent the cabins, the grays will come from all over the country and you can find a mate."

He hoped. Never having discussed Uncle Basil's clientele with him, he assumed his uncle advertised on the Internet and in magazines that would help draw a crowd from all over. All Hunter had to do was tweak the ad to let alpha male leaders who were without a mate know his sister needed one.

Hunter flipped the steaks, seared them for a minute, and then tossed them on the rose china that had been passed down two generations. "What did you want us to do? The arsonists destroyed the forests and moving north to Oregon was the best thing we could manage."

She didn't reply and he sighed. "So, five members of our pack moved into the vineyards in southern California. What kind of a life would that be? We're used to hunting in woods during our nighttime excursions. No other *lupus garous* live in the area, so no worry about encroaching on another pack's territorial rights. Besides, Uncle Basil decided it was time to retire and was glad to gift us the land and cabins. It couldn't be more perfect."

"So what's this *really* about? Uncle Basil never once mentioned he wanted to quit the business," Meara said.

"We were happy in California. He knew unless something like this happened we wouldn't have moved a foot out of there."

She peered out the window. Her spine straightened and her mouth dropped. "I'll be right back." She flipped her long, dark hair over her shoulders and headed outside.

He strode to the window and looked out.

"Hell."

It was *the* woman. Had to be. Tessa Anderson, the photographer. Petite, swallowed up in a white parka, she trudged toward their house with a camera strap slung around her neck. The camera bounced between her full breasts, which were accentuated by the snug fit of her pale blue turtleneck. Her jeans outlined curvy legs, and suddenly he had the most lascivious thought, wondering what was wrong with him at a moment like this, to be envisioning this woman naked with her long legs wrapped tightly around him.

A pink ski cap hid her hair, but her brows were red, her green eyes sparkled with fire, and her cheeks and pert nose were rosy from the cold. Full, sensual lips shimmered with pink gloss that begged for a man's caress. Her eyes garnered his attention again. Expressive, vibrant, full of life, yet a subtle sadness marred them.

Why was she wandering the woods alone when the night would soon cast her into darkness? Why here? Unless she had made friends with Uncle Basil and had come to see him.

Hell. No wonder he couldn't get rid of her himself.

Meara quickly confronted her, and Hunter raised the window to overhear the conversation. Even though *he* planned on talking to Miss Anderson, it didn't hurt for Meara to tell the woman the error of her ways. At the very least, giving Meara some control over their lands would make her feel more at home here.

Meara raised her hand to the woman in her path. "You're trespassing."

The woman's eyes narrowed and her brows knit together in a tight little frown. "Uncle Basil said I could take pictures out this way during the winter because he didn't have any B&B guests this time of year."

She had Uncle Basil's permission? What was the crafty old wolf up to?

"*Uncle* Basil?" Meara asked, her voice rising.

"That's what he told me to call him."

So, Uncle Basil had a relationship with the human female after all. Which wasn't like him.

"Well, his *real* niece and nephew have taken up residence, and Uncle Basil has moved to Florida. The rules are different now. Find somewhere else to take your pictures. *Don't* come here again."

The woman glanced at the house. *Looking to rescue Uncle Basil? Or maybe she hoped he'd come out and save her from Hunter's sister?*

Facing Meara, she offered her gloved hand. "I'm Tessa Anderson, a professional photographer. I live down the coast."

Meara folded her arms. "Then you must have plenty of photo ops on your *own* land."

Tessa stiffened and Hunter could see now the woman wasn't going to be easily persuaded. Her jaw tightened and her eyes flickered with inflexible resolve.

"Every area along the seacoast is different. And it changes as the tides pummel the coastline. It varies with the seasons also." Tessa tilted her head to the side. "Uncle Basil never said anything about moving. He isn't ill, is he?"

Hunter shook his head. He admired tenacious *lupus garou* women, but a human female like that could cause real problems. So *why* was he checking out her package again—the way her turtleneck caressed her breasts, the camera strap pressing between the sensuous mounds, outlining them further, and lower to the jeans accentuating her long, curvy legs.

Lifting his nose, he took a deep breath. Because of the shifting breeze, despite the smell of pines and the sea air overwhelming all else, he caught a whiff of the woman's scent—of peaches and… tequila and margarita mix?

His eyes widened a bit as he smelled something else, something that generated an age-old need—a desire so strong that it could only mean her pheromones were triggering his craving. *What the hell? She wasn't a* lupus garou—*didn't have their distinctive scent, yet sexually, she served every bit as much a magnet for a male* lupus garou.

His gaze fastened on her eyes, now narrowed a little, sharp and full of mistrust.

"Did he always keep you posted on his plans?" Meara asked Tessa, being her usual snarky self.

"I was supposed to have dinner with him." Standing taller, Tessa considered the house again. "Do you have a number where I can reach him? Or an address?"

Dinner? Had Uncle Basil forgotten? Or conveniently avoided it, which would explain his warning—although cryptic—about Tessa before he left. Hunter let out his breath in exasperation.

Meara snorted. "Leave, now, or I'll call the sheriff. Don't come back here."

"It was nice to meet you, too." Tessa glanced once more at the house as if to say she wouldn't be thwarted from seeing Uncle Basil. Her breath mixed with the cold air in a puff of smoke, she lifted her chin a little, and then whipped around, and headed back into the woods.

The urge to hunt the minx filled Hunter with a craving so strong, he had to remind himself she was a threat to their existence. If she'd been a *lupus garou*, that would be a different story. He would have shown just *how* interested he was and worn her down until she felt the same for him, if she didn't automatically. But a human like her was nothing more than tempting forbidden fruit—one taste would never be enough. Best to buy her out and remove the menace from the area.

Meara stalked into the house, saw Hunter at the open window, and gave a half smile. Then she frowned. "Don't you go getting friendly with that woman, too. Jeesh. I heard you and Uncle Basil talking about her. You know, the lower your voices go, the more I listen in." She shook her head. "No wonder Uncle Basil couldn't get rid of her. Sweet and innocent. Miss Red Riding Hood in a white parka." She raised a brow. "And by the way, as petite as she is, her boobs are silicone—have to be."

No way was the woman anything but the real thing, every bit of her, and he wanted to prove to himself they were in the worst way. Hunter shut the window. "You made Tessa Anderson suspicious. She thinks we've buried Uncle Basil in the backyard. So now *I'll* have to take care of it." And he would, starting tonight.

"*Hmpf.* What about the rest of our pack?" Her spine stiff, Meara stirred the spinach heating on the stove and refused to look at him.

"The seven who took off for Portland will return when they get tired of city life."

"So they moved to greener pastures, and we're stuck in Timbuktu?" Meara's amber eyes flashed with irritation, her lips turned down.

"We'll rent only to *lupus garous,* like Uncle Basil did. We'll entice eligible alpha males to visit, and you'll put them under your spell." He failed to understand how she couldn't see the beauty of the area. If she would just take a run with him in the woods, work out some of her frustration, she would feel better. "We're not a city pack. The rest will tire of it before long."

"And then?" She yanked out her chair and dropped into it, fixing him with another chilling look.

"They can join us here. Plenty of game for hunting on moonlit nights. Oregon has laws to protect wolves. We won't have any problems."

"I want to go to the city." She looked up from her salmon and although she kept her expression stern, her eyes glistened with tears.

Ah, hell. What *really* was the matter?

"A red pack already resides in Portland."

Her mouth parted.

Hunter clarified, "Leidolf is the pack leader. I met him last spring when you wouldn't come with me to see Uncle Basil. He seemed a nice enough *lupus garou* for a red. As nice as one can be when he's dealing with a gray pack leader, but he won't like it that some of our pack are encroaching on his city."

She folded her arms. "Fine. You're bigger than the reds. Push them out and we can start over there."

Leaning back in his chair, he studied his sister's stubborn expression. She'd always been so predictable, so agreeable. What was wrong with her now?

"Quit looking at me like I've lost my mind. I'm in my first wolf's heat and *I... want... a... mate! Damn it.* Don't you ever feel the pull? No, of course not. You have one-night stands with human women who want the same thing and then you're satiated, for a time."

But he suspected her first wolf's heat wasn't the only thing making her so unreasonable. Damned if he could figure it out.

"Of course I want a mate. Nevertheless, you know as well as I do the males outnumber the females in any given pack. If I can't find one of our kind..." He shrugged. "I'll have to find my pleasure elsewhere."

Not that he had been with a woman in a very long time, or was often with one. Running a pack took priority and searching for an eligible *lupus garou* female was impractical since he didn't have a sub-leader who could watch over his people in his absence. He couldn't even trust Meara for now.

"I miss Genevieve and the others," she said softly, avoiding looking at him.

So *that* was the problem. "They'll come back, Meara. Trust me in this."

"And I miss our home." She poked at her food, then she looked up at him. "You're right about one thing, dear brother. I should fetch a pretty important alpha male, don't you think?"

Important? Try more headstrong than his sister, or her mate would never have any say in their relationship.

Hunter gave her a small smile. "That's what I've been saying."

"So *find* me one." Her gaze sharpened along with her voice. "*Or else* I'm joining the others."

Hunter's twin sister was *his* to protect until he could find a suitable mate for her. Meara was not going anywhere without him. The pack would return. *Damn it.* And he wasn't about to chase after them.

Already past midnight by the time his sister fell asleep, Hunter threw open the front door and took a whiff of the breeze. Winter, pine, the smell of the sea. Fish. And sea kelp. Time to mark his territory, indicating he was taking the area over from his uncle, and check out Tessa Anderson's place. Not only that, but running through the woods—seeing them alive and green after the flames had devoured the California forests, leaving ashes in their wake—he hoped it would settle his troubled thoughts. At a wolf's pace, he would reach Tessa's home in a couple of hours, less if he ran. Although he needed to leave his scent along the way.

Painlessly, he allowed the change to come over him, stretching his limbs, feeling the power fill his legs and body. His face elongated into a snout, his curved canines extending until they were deadly weapons that could crush bone, if he'd felt in the mood for a hunt. A double coat of banded gray fur covered his skin, keeping out the bitter cold as he loped outside in his wolf form and headed into the forest, his black nails digging into the pine needle covered floor.

At once, he enjoyed the oneness he felt with the wild out-of-doors, instead of being an intruder on the land the way he felt when he was in his human form. Now, he was a predator, more in tune with the feral side of his nature.

Yet, he felt a trifle unsettled as he headed south on their property.

Maybe Meara was right. Moving was harder than he'd expected. Part of him enjoyed the newness of being here at his uncle's place a couple times a year, but part of him longed for his familiar hunting grounds.

Time to put aside regrets and concentrate on business.

While he was traversing the area for a few miles, the chilly, crisp air ruffled his fur, and the sound of the ocean crashed down below the rocky cliffs. The sweet fragrance of fir trees looming overhead mingled with the fishy odor of the ocean and the seaweed rotting on the beach, nearly masking the scent of a rabbit nearby. But then another smell came to his attention—not a welcome odor, either.

He twisted his head to the south. Male gray *lupus garous*—three of them—their smell wafting in the air. And not any of his pack either. *These* three shouldn't be here.

Listening for any sounds of them, he paused. *Nothing.* Yet the adrenaline surged through his veins, preparing him for the confrontation.

He had marked his territory well, brushing his tail and face against tree trunks and branches. Even his toes pressed against the earth left his unique scent, showing beyond a doubt he had claimed it, as his Uncle Basil had before him. What gray would be fool enough to trespass on another's lands without permission in the dark of night?

Meara! In her wolf's heat, she must have caught their attention.

Hunter sprinted back toward the cabin. The closer he drew to his quiet home, the more his chest tightened. The grays had been here and could still be here. The transformation swift and painless, he quickly changed from wolf to human form and stood naked on the front porch where the door was still wide open. His blood burned so hot, the cold didn't touch him. "Meara!"

The door to her bedroom was open. The smell of the

three males lingered heavy in the air. A deathly silence pervaded the place.

Hunter stormed into Meara's bedroom. She was gone. His heart racing, he roared, "Meara!"

Her bedcovers were tossed aside, but it didn't look as though there had been a struggle. Bile rose in Hunter's throat. Had the grays forced her to leave with them, or had she gone willingly? He couldn't be sure, the way the wolf heat—particularly the first one she'd had to experience—was making her so crazy.

Either way, they were dead men. Nothing less than a gray alpha male of his choosing would do for his sister. And no one would steal her away in the middle of the night without facing the devil over it.

His face extending into a wolf's snout and his torso and limbs changing as fur covered his body, he became a wolf once again and raced out of the cabin. He smelled the intruders' scent on the turbulent sea breeze and followed them as they headed south.

Once he found them, he would deal with them wolf to wolf, teaching them to take care when stealing a leader's sister.

Hunter's breath mixed with the air, an ice storm threatening.

Mile after mile he tracked the three of them and his sister. They were either so arrogant they didn't worry about him, or just too stupid to care. They left a trail a brand-new Cub Scout could follow—broken branches and clumps of fur rubbed against trees; two even urinated a few times as if taunting him—or maybe they had weak bladders.

He growled low.

When the sun illuminated the gray clouds, brightening the day just a little in the early morning hour, he sensed the wolves had marked this new territory for their own. Trespassing or not, he wouldn't allow them to stop him from freeing Meara and taking care of the menace.

Out of the mist, a blackened pine tree, like a soldier bitterly scarred, stood at the edge of a cliff that gave way to the ocean below. Like the forests devoured in flames they had recently escaped, except this silent soldier had been here for a very long time, the remaining forest again green.

Branches rustled west of Hunter, and he whipped around. Three hefty grays stared him down, their tails straight, the hair on their backs standing up. Hunter took a whiff of the breeze. They weren't the ones who had taken his sister. And there was no sign of her now. But the way the leader of this group crouched low and curled his lips back, exposing his teeth, Hunter had no choice. He wasn't backing down. If they were protecting the others who had taken his sister, they'd pay, too.

Fresh adrenaline charged through his system, preparing him for battle as he growled low, stiffened his tail like a flag of warning, and rushed the biggest of the three wolves, his muzzle wrinkling as he bared his killer canines.

The Oregon temperature was thirty-one degrees, but the knowledge Tessa Anderson's brother might not go free made it feel colder still. On top of that? An ice storm was imminent.

Her back rigid enough to cause it to spasm with the

building tension, she sat on the wooden bench in the courtroom, her fingernails biting into her palms. She clenched her teeth, fighting tears as she waited for the foreman to make the announcement.

She prayed she and Michael could return to their cabin on the coast and weather the storm like their grandparents had. Only this time, she feared her prayers would go unanswered.

The look Michael cast Tessa pleaded for her to save him from this nightmare. He appeared pale and gaunt in his black suit, the same one he'd worn to his last art exhibit in Portland. How had their lives turned so upside down?

She, who had always gotten her younger brother out of scrapes since their parents had died five years ago, felt like an avalanche was crushing her heart. She'd spent all her savings and some of their inheritance trying to prove his innocence and only wished the rumors that gold was buried on their property was true—and that *she* could find it—to use to help save her brother.

She let out her breath. Michael *was* innocent. *Damn it.*

God, please, *oh please*, find him not guilty. Set him free.

"Michael Anderson, on the count of first-degree murder of Bethany Wade, the jury finds you guilty."

Barely audible, the words melded and faded. The breath she'd been holding whooshed from Tessa's lungs, and her head grew fuzzy. The bright lights in the courthouse blinked out.

The next thing she knew, her head was resting in a stranger's lap and a man and woman were shaking her. "Miss Anderson? Miss Anderson?"

Her mind cleared and she looked around at a sea of

concerned faces. Her heart began racing again. *Guilty.* The jury had found her brother guilty.

The police were escorting her brother from the room in handcuffs.

She hurried to mouth the words, "I love you, Michael. I'll get you out."

His green eyes filled with tears, he gave her a slight nod. He knew she would try. No matter what, she'd exhaust every avenue before she let her brother rot in prison for the rest of his life for a crime he didn't commit.

A new lawyer, new evidence, appeals. Where could she find a good lawyer to start all over again?

Her heart encased in ice, she realized the only way to prove him innocent was to find the real murderer. Unfortunately, in the Oregon coastal community, the sheriff believed in only one suspect, Michael. Now that the jury found him guilty, no way was the sheriff's department going to look any further into the matter.

Her family's home, the townspeople, the community—all the things she held dear since her parents perished—now meant nothing. No one she knew had sat with her to offer solace during any part of the trial. She felt betrayed, isolated from those who had been her friends.

She stumbled to her feet. Her legs were like melted wax, but she clutched her purse and headed for the courtroom doors, her head held high. A weariness crept through her, as the adrenaline rush from her anticipation of the verdict fizzled into oblivion.

People quickly moved out of her way as if avoiding a communicable disease. Some of them watched her, their eyes narrowed in contempt, acting like *she* was the reason for the crime in their once secure and sleepy little community.

A tall, thin man observed her from the other side of the room. His dark brown hair curling about his shoulders, the angular planes of his narrow face, the way his shoulders stooped forward, made him seem somehow familiar. He shoved his hands in his pockets and glanced at the exit. But when his gaze zeroed in on her again, this time she caught his eye. He quickly looked away as if he couldn't decide what to do—approach and offer condolences or scowl at her, too.

Another of Bethany's relatives? He might have been. She'd been dark-haired, too, and tall and willowy. Plus tons of her cousins from back east were here for the trial.

Bethany's parents hesitated at the entryway as if wanting to say something to Tessa, but then, maybe thinking better of it, Mr. Wade quickly escorted his teary-eyed wife outside.

Tessa blinked back her own tears. But as soon as she left the courthouse, a lone newspaper reporter targeted her with a photographer in tow.

She groaned inwardly. *Rourke Thornburg.* Once an on-again/off-again boyfriend in high school who had tried to renew their relationship after she'd finished college and returned to the coast, now just an annoying waste of time.

As usual, his dark gray suit was impeccable and his manicured hair had not a strand out of place—making him appear like a big-time-news-reporter wannabe. From the high-school paper to this—his first big story in the coastal town—other than reporting the weather, new storm rolling onto the coast, or crab season's arrival.

She hurried down the courthouse steps and headed for her Ford Escape, hoping to avoid the inevitable.

Like a used car salesman with the deal of a lifetime, Rourke dove in front of Tessa. "Any statements, Miss Anderson, now that the jury found your brother guilty of first-degree murder?"

Taking a stand, she drew taller and looked Rourke squarely in the eye. "My brother is innocent. He loved Bethany. The murderer thinks he got away with the crime, but I won't give up until he or she has been brought to justice."

She shouldn't have said anything to the press. She knew it, but she couldn't stop the words.

"Do you think the sheriff's department is guilty of a cover-up?"

Out of the corner of her vision, she saw Sheriff Wellington watching her, his blue eyes hard as ice. "I think the sheriff only saw Michael's involvement with Bethany, overlooking the possibility someone else was the killer. I wouldn't say it was intentional."

"How do you propose to find the real killer, supposing Michael is innocent?"

"You'll be the first to know." She squelched the tears, unable to offer anything close to the truth.

Rourke knew her better. However, she also realized he wouldn't let go of the story. So what would he do? Report on her progress, sensationalizing her failures to bring the true murderer to justice to make a name for himself? She could see the report now: *Sister Seeks Killer to Free Her Brother. When Will She Recognize the Truth?*

Rourke motioned to the cameraman to quit taking

pictures and walked Tessa to her car, his hand supporting her elbow.

She wanted to jerk away from him, to show she wouldn't allow his attempt at placating her, but too many people were watching. For now, she had to be the proverbial pillar of strength for her brother. Anything less would show defeat.

"I know how upsetting this has to be, as much as you care for your brother, but the jurors were right."

Without responding to Rourke's remark, she unlocked her car door and climbed in. But then she reconsidered. Maybe, just maybe, she could solicit his help. Who else did she have? Nobody.

"If you really want to be a reporter, you might investigate this case yourself. Look at the guys who dug into the Watergate mess and how much dirt they uncovered. No one else did. Ever think you could put your talents to good use?"

A spark of interest flickered in his gray eyes, but he was far from being convinced. Like everyone else, Rourke believed Michael was guilty of the crime. End of story.

He leaned against her door and sighed. "All right. Here's the deal. You and I can get together over dinner, and you can tell me what makes you believe Michael didn't do it, other than the fact he's your brother."

"How about you look into it, and when you discover some other leads, you give me a call. Then we'll do dinner."

"Shrewd." Rourke offered a coy smile. "Not one person could verify Bethany was seeing some other guy. Michael made up the whole story. No evidence points to anyone else."

"Not if you don't bother looking for it. Gotta go, Rourke. Later."

Nearby, Sheriff Wellington gave her a warning look as if to say she had better not stir up any more trouble. Nevertheless, to prove her brother's innocence, she'd do whatever it took.

Mist covered the winding coastal road on the long drive home, and although Tessa usually felt comforted by it, late this afternoon it seemed gloomy, warning of impending disaster. The last time she felt an overwhelming sense of doom, she had learned her parents had died in a car accident earlier on a day just like this one, her last year at high school. She shuddered, despite telling herself the disquieting feeling didn't mean anything.

When she finally pulled into the curved driveway at her redwood home overlooking the rugged coastline, she couldn't shake the feeling that something wasn't right. A winter-chilled breeze played music on her wind chimes as the contorted pines stretching next to her house stirred. She glanced at the gray clouds. As cold as it was, if it rained, it would turn to sleet or snow or a mixture of the two soon.

She climbed out of her car, shivered, and locked the doors. The place looked foreboding now that her brother was gone. Not the welcome refuge it had always been.

She hurried into the house, the air as chilly inside as it was out, and rushed to change in the bedroom.

After laying her wool coat on the cedar chest at the foot of the bed, she turned on the floor heater, and pulled off her black dress. Black as if she were in mourning. Which she was all over again. The house seemed so empty without her brother's presence, his laughter, the sound of his video games playing in the background as he fought another epic fantasy battle before he settled down to paint.

Now, except for the howling wind and the waves crashing on the beach down below the cliffs, everything was quiet. Too quiet in the isolated cottage. For the first time ever, she felt—spooked.

There wasn't any other way to explain the reason goose bumps rose and the hair stood on end on her arms.

She kicked off her pumps, slipped out of her panty hose, threw on a pair of heavy socks, black denims, and a turtleneck. If she didn't quit imagining all kinds of horrible scenarios, she would lock herself in the house until the storm passed. She wasn't normally a cowardly person, but she had never felt so alone before, like she'd fallen into a parallel world where she had no family or friends. And now even her good friend Uncle Basil was gone. But she couldn't believe he'd leave so suddenly without a word. First chance she got, she was checking further into the matter.

An animal howled in the distance. A shudder stole down her back. *A wolf.* Had to be.

She peeked out the window, but didn't see anything except tree branches swaying briskly in the growing wind.

She wanted to believe it was just a dog. But she knew better. Wolves from Idaho's reserve had crossed the Snake River and were roaming the northeastern part of the state. Visitors to the Wallowa Mountains and the Eagle Cap Wilderness area had also reported sightings of wolves. She'd even snapped a picture of one near

La Grande and more recently, a hunter killed a wild wolf there. So why couldn't a wolf have made it to the Oregon coast?

Despite there not having been any sightings, she was certain a wolf had been roaming the area. Worse, she couldn't explain how she felt compelled to discover the truth, but on the other hand was afraid of learning any were living here. Neither her underlying fear of them or compulsion to seek them out made any sense to her. Except as she stalked them, she was sure they stalked her. Which was plain crazy. Or was it? She'd had more than one experience like when she'd been taking pictures of the California wildfire. A phantom gray watching her, waiting, an unnatural standoff between man and beast. And then the sudden unprovoked attacks.

She yanked on her snow boots. After slipping her favorite pink ski cap on her head, covering her hair, still pinned up in a bun, she threw on her parka and grabbed her gloves.

She had nothing to fear. Nothing—except the fact someone had murdered Bethany Wade, her brother was going to prison for it, and the real murderer was on the loose.

But worse than that?

She had challenged him—which would now be in the local newspaper, no less—that she would uncover who he was and clear her brother's name.

She glanced at the bedside table where she kept her gun and took a deep breath. "Firewood, or else you'll go without."

If an ice storm knocked out the electricity, she would be in a world of hurt. A quick walk on the beach to gather driftwood for a fire would have to suffice. She shouldn't have put it off so long, but all she had thought of lately was how to get her brother cleared of the charges. She needed a new lawyer. Someone who was a lot more determined. And a new private eye, someone who would find something that would help Michael, instead of just running up a bill.

After locking the back door—although normally she wouldn't have bothered, but she couldn't shake the feeling that someone was watching the place—she traversed the narrow and steep path through the woods and boulders down to the small sandy beach below.

From one of the mills up north, lumber floating on the current piled up on the beach, littering it. No sense letting the wood go to waste. She shoved some over on its side and considered how wet it was. *Very* wet. All of it would take too long to dry. But if she didn't hurry and the rain began, it wouldn't matter what she gathered—the wood would *all* be too wet to burn.

She trudged through piles of seaweed—hating the smell and unsightly mess it made as the storms churned it up on the beach—and made her way around a cluster of boulders where she spied a stack of wood. Far enough from the tidewater, it would have had more time to dry.

Skirting around to the other side, she figured the timber would be the driest there. But what she saw next made her gasp and her heart nearly quit beating.

The body of a veritable Greek god lay naked on his stomach, his skin, slightly blue, stretched over tightly toned muscles, his dark, wet hair draped across his face, his eyes sealed shut.

Not dead. Please, don't be dead.

Chapter 2

Before Tessa reached the man lying deathly still on the beach, certain he was dead, she thought one of his fingers twitched. Her heart went into overdrive.

Not dead. Ohmigod. He's alive. Maybe.

She rushed forward and pulled him onto his back. Big. Naked. Blue—she reminded herself. And badly battered—his face, body, limbs.

She yanked off her glove and held his wrist. No pulse that she could feel, although her blood was running so fast, she figured it overrode feeling his pulse, if he had one. Not breathing, she didn't think, because her warm breath was turning into puffs of smoke in the chilly air and there was none escaping his parted lips, full and sensual, but purple.

"Hello? Hello? Can you hear me?" She jerked her glove on, and then fumbled to remove her parka. Covering his torso with her heavy white coat, she tried to remember her CPR training. "Fifteen pumps to the chest. Breathe two times into his mouth. Then repeat. No, clear his passageway first."

With hands trembling, she crouched next to his head. His wet hair dragged the sandy beach, his eyelids sealed shut. She tilted his head back and made sure nothing obstructed his airway. Moving back to his torso, she pushed the coat lower to expose his chest—muscled, sculpted, dark curly hair trailing down to her parka, speckled with sand, the best shape she'd ever seen a man in close up—which meant he was too hardy to die on her. She prayed.

She pressed her gloved hands together against his hard chest and began compressions. Counting under her breath, she hoped to God he didn't die on her. If the wind and cold weren't bad enough, sleet began sliding down in gray sheets, crackling and covering everything in a slick icy sheen, plastering her turtleneck and jeans against her frigid skin. She worked harder, faster.

The blood pounded in her ears, blocking the sound of the wind and sleet and waves.

"Fifteen!" she shouted, and then moved closer to his head, yanked off her glove, and felt for any sign of a pulse in his neck.

No pulse, or so faint she couldn't feel it. And no breath. He wasn't breathing.

Her heart in her throat, she pinched his nose shut and leaned down to cover his mouth with hers. Before she could blow air into his lungs, his eyes popped open. Amber, intense, feral. Her mouth gaped.

With a titan grasp, he grabbed her wrists, flipped her onto her back and straddled her, the parka wedged between them as the weight of his body restrained her.

"No!" she screeched, right before he kissed her—pressed his frozen lips against hers, his mouth firm, wanting, pressuring with uncontrollable need—like a man used to dominating—sending her senses reeling.

Instantly, the cold left her, his body heating every inch of her to the core, her heart pounding. And in that moment, she wanted him—as insane as the notion was.

He lifted his mouth from hers and glowered at her for a second, his eyes smoky with desire. Speechless, she stared back at his chiseled face, the grim set of his lips, his dark silky hair curling down, dripping water on her cheeks. Then his fathomless, darkened eyes drifted closed and his tight grip loosened on her wrists.

"No!" she shouted, right before he collapsed on top of her in a faint, his dead weight pinning her to the beach.

"Hey!" she yelled, her hands on his shoulders, shaking him. "Wake up!" She couldn't budge the muscled hunk, but if she didn't revive him and get him to some place warm, he would die for sure. "Hey! *Wake… up*!" She pushed and shoved, trying to roll him off her. But he was too heavy—solid muscle and bone.

"Get… off… me!"

He moaned and lifted his head, his glazed eyes staring at her, his beautiful white teeth clenched in a grimace, but he didn't seem to comprehend.

"Can you move? I'll… I'll take you up to my house and call for help."

For the longest time—although it probably was no more than a second or two, but with the way his heavy body pressed against hers, it seemed like an eternity—he watched her.

Then he groaned and rolled off her onto his back. She hurried to recover him with the parka, yanked off her knit cap, and stretched it over his head. More heat was lost through the head than any other body part, she recalled hearing from a survival show. Odd the things that would come to mind in the middle of a crisis.

He observed her as the sleet continued to pelt them—an expression without feeling, icy cold like the storm, a face devoid of fear, unlike the way hers probably looked.

"Okay, listen... we're both going to catch our deaths here on the beach in this weather. We need to get you up to the house. Can you move?" She pulled on her glove.

His gaze drifted to her soaking wet turtleneck. But otherwise he didn't move or speak. Tugging at him, she finally managed to help him sit. She slipped behind him, wrapped her arms around his chest with her body hugging his, braced with her knees, and tried to pull him up. She couldn't budge him.

"You've got to help." Her voice exasperated—not with him, but with herself—her frosty breath curled around his ear.

He finally leaned forward, pressed his hands against the sand, pushed himself up, and moaned. The sound of his pain streaked through her like a warning. He was in bad shape and could still die if she didn't move fast enough, didn't do the right things.

As soon as he stood, he grabbed hold of her shoulder and swayed.

Her heart lurching, she seized his free arm. He leaned hard against her, ready to collapse, and a new thrill of panic swept her. If he pulled her down with him, she'd be where she was before, trying to lift the veritable muscled mountain off the beach.

She hung her parka over his broad shoulders and wrapped her arm around his trim waist. "Okay, it's not too far to climb."

Although it *was,* considering the injured man's shaky condition.

They stumbled up the rough path, and she glanced down at his poor feet, taking a beating on the icy rocks. Every step could be his last, she worried, while he clung to her as if his life depended on it.

Which it probably did.

When they reached the short path to her back door, she intended to rush him inside, call for help, get him warm—not necessarily in that order—but instead, she froze in place several feet away from the edge of the small brick patio.

The back door was standing wide open, the wind banging it against the house.

"I locked it," she said under her breath. "I know I locked it."

Despite the overwhelming panic that filled her, she had to get the injured man into the protective shelter of the house. With trepidation, she walked him the rest of the way, and once inside, she led him through the kitchen. No sign of an intruder. But her spine remained stiff with tension.

The injured man lifted his nose and smelled. He tilted his head to the side as if he was listening for the same thing she was—sounds of the housebreaker.

She hurried the man to the velour sofa where he collapsed in a ragged heap, his expression slightly dazed. She had to get him warmed up. But she had to make sure no danger could threaten them inside the house. Glancing toward the hall and the three bedrooms, she listened. No sound of anyone rummaging through any of the rooms.

Sleet continued to pour on the roof, the sound a loud roar, which could hide the presence of someone moving around inside. She grabbed the wool afghan at the end of the couch and covered the injured man's lap, the parka still draped across his shoulders and pink ski cap stretched tight on his head.

"I'll turn on the heat and get some more blankets for you," she said to him, without taking her eyes off the hallway to the bedrooms.

First, she was calling 911 and getting a knife for protection. She patted his shoulder. "Stay here. I'll be right back."

She didn't wait for his response. Instead, she hastened to the kitchen, yanked open a drawer, and pulled out her largest carving knife, although it was about as dull as her butter knives. Too bad she couldn't get to her gun. With weapon in hand, she grabbed her phone, punched in 9–1–1, and lifted the receiver to her ear. *No signal.* She tried again. *Same thing.* Hell, what else could go wrong?

Shivering in her wet, icy clothes, she shut and locked the back door. When she turned, she gulped back a scream. The battered man was standing in her kitchen, looking even bigger, taller, nude again, and still blue. He moved as silently as the cat she had once shared the house with until it took off for parts unknown.

"My god, you need to rest on the couch and… and I'll turn the heat on and…"

His indomitable gaze lowered to the knife in her hand.

Mouth dry, her heartbeat quickened. "I… someone broke into my house. I think."

Without a word, he stalked off, his step more sure, although he had to be in terrible pain, as bruised and beaten as he was. She followed him, her gaze shifting to his butt, firm, muscled perfection with every step he took. He glanced over his shoulder with a glower, but when he caught her checking out his derrière, his mouth curved up a hint.

Her cheeks on fire, she raised her brows and stood taller.

Realizing he couldn't dissuade her from following him, he grunted and moved forward, checking out her brother's room first. The navy velvet curtains flopped in the breeze, framing the shattered window. She sucked in the chilled air and stared at the jagged window, now a gaping hole into the black void outside. A shudder shook her to the center of her being. He could return anytime.

She examined the carpet closer. No glass, which meant the intruder had broken it from the inside, not outside to get in. This further meant he must have entered through the back door and hadn't escaped that way like she was beginning to think.

The injured man crossed the floor to the window, peered into the dark, standing in the icy breeze as if he was made of pure marble and the cold couldn't touch him. Then he turned, shaking his head slightly.

Her gaze dropped from his furrowed brows, narrowed eyes, and the set of his grim mouth to his ruggedly sculpted abs, and then lower to the dark patch of curly hair at the apex of his sturdy thighs and his incredible... *size*.

Her eyes shot up. He was injured, for heaven's sakes, and probably suffering from frostbite and a concussion. Yet, she swore lust clouded his eyes.

Ha! More likely the onset of pneumonia.

"Let me, uhm, get you some of my brother's clothes."

She hurried into the closet, grabbed Michael's fleece-lined navy sweats and a pair of his sneakers, and exited. The man was gone. She glanced at the wind and sleet coming into the room, wetting the beige carpeting. Wishing she could tack something up in the meantime, she knew they didn't have a shred of canvas. Although even if she did, it wouldn't prevent the intruder from coming back in that way.

Clutching her brother's things to her chest with one arm, the knife readied in her free fist, she rushed into the hall and nearly collided with the naked man. A gasp slipped from her lips before she could hide her unsettled reaction.

"You're going to hurt yourself with that." His words sounded husky and wearied. His colorless lips lifted slightly. "Or me."

The way he said, "Or me," sounded suspiciously like he didn't believe she could hurt him. As wired as she was, her hands trembled with the notion she might have accidentally stabbed him.

His icy hand touched hers, almost reverently. Was he worried she was scared to be unarmed? She was more fearful that she might have caused him further injury.

Despite how cold they both were, his flesh sent a volley of warmth sliding through her, his eyes never straying from hers. Heat, passion, and a knowing look as though he could read the way she was feeling showed in the glint of his amber eyes. And then he slipped the knife from her grasp, his fingers leaving hers and the cold returned.

He had to be chilled to the marrow of his bones. She was and she wasn't even nude in the icebox of a house, although wearing wet clothes had to come in a close second for making a body cold under these inhospitable conditions.

"No one in any of the rooms," he assured her, his voice cloaked in darkness, his gaze steady, penetrating.

Something unspoken tied them together, although she couldn't sense what. The way he considered her as if she was important to him somehow—not as his savior exactly, but more like his… *captive*, his *prey*.

Before her frozen mind made anything stranger of her reaction toward him, she shoved the sweats at his chest. "Here, get dressed and I'll—"

"Turn on the heat?" He cocked an arrogant brow, his lips neutral.

One of her medieval romance novels could have featured him as a brooding, striking—albeit a bit battered—hero. Or the villain. What did she know about him, after all?

"I would have already," she said, storming back down the hall, "if an intruder hadn't been in the—"

"The electricity isn't working."

She stopped, turned, and stared at him. It would be dark soon. And even colder. Hell, she hadn't even gotten one load of firewood from the beach yet.

Now, she was stuck in the middle of the ice storm with no electricity and no phone… *with* a total hunk of a stranger still standing in her hallway naked.

The man slipped her brother's sweatpants on, but the corded muscles of his chest were exposed, his skin tan, no longer blue, but bruised and cut. He yanked the sweatshirt over his head. "I checked the heater while you were getting the knife. Light switches, too. There's no electricity." He pulled on the pair of sneakers.

"Then I need to gather wood for the fire." Tessa shuddered involuntarily, both from the cold and her wet clothes. But also from the fact she would have to trek back down the hill alone when the prowler might still be out there hidden in the woods, watching, waiting.

The injured man swept his hair back away from his chiseled face, the planes edged in marble. "You need to slip into something dry. I'll get the firewood."

"But you… you were half dead."

"I heal quickly."

"Good." Her voice conveyed she wasn't convinced.

No one could heal that quickly—probably trying to sound macho to appease her. She took a deep settling breath and watched him deposit the knife on the tiled kitchen counter with a clunk. His hands were big and rough. Not an artist's hands like her brother's, but strong enough to pin her to the beach, not allowing her an inch to struggle. An annoying sliver of eroticism stoked a fire deep inside her, just thinking about the way his body had pressed against hers. He'd been delirious, for heaven's sakes, and didn't even realize what he had done.

"I'm going with you, just in case you begin to feel badly. You probably suffered from a concussion and should go to the hospital. But the road will be too icy and—"

He pulled the back door open.

"Wait! Let me get my parka, and I'll get Michael's field jacket for you."

She rushed into the living room, grabbed her coat from the couch, and pulled it over her wet clothes. The turtleneck and jeans clung to her skin like pieces of cloth soaked in ice water, and again she shivered. She would have changed clothes if he had given her a couple of minutes. But if they didn't get wood in a hurry, it would be soaking wet. Forget a warm fire then.

After retrieving her brother's jacket from the hall closet, she joined the stranger in the kitchen.

"I'm Tessa Anderson, by the way, and you are?"

His forehead wrinkled slightly and his jaw tightened. "Hunter's the name, although… I can't seem to remember anything else. My tumble in the ocean probably had something to do with it."

"You don't remember a last name?" Her skin prickled with fresh unease. A naked stranger without a last name washed up on her beach and no way to get outside help in the event he was unsafe—

"I'm sure it'll come to me after a while." He threw on the jacket and headed outside.

"Wait! Gloves!"

But he was already halfway down the trail. She grabbed a pair of her brother's fur-lined leather gloves from the hall closet and rushed after Hunter. As much as she didn't want to admit it, she was more afraid of staying alone in the unsecured house, than with chasing after a stranger. Even so, she sensed the driving power inside him, the danger inherent, something about him that made her think of—she wasn't sure.

"Wait! Here are Michael's gloves!"

Moving too fast on the icy ground, she slipped. Her heart tumbled and she threw her hands out to brace her fall on the rocky path. If Hunter hadn't leapt forward and caught her wrist, pulling her into his hard embrace, she would have landed on her face.

Heat suffused every pore, and the stranger showed more than a spark of interest. His gaze smoldered with passion as he looked into her eyes, lower… to her lips.

Her chest pressed against his, his heart beat as fast as hers, maybe faster, and for an instant, he didn't seem to want to let go, his arms holding her tight, lots closer and longer than necessary. More than that—he acted like he wanted to kiss her again. Although she knew the first time had to have been a mistake—a deliriously, delicious mistake. And for an instant, she envisioned the kiss. Possessive, demanding, and oh so hot. And she, too shocked to respond, but wondering if she had, how would he have reacted?

His gaze drew back to hers. His whiskey-colored eyes—like the wolf's.

A strange awareness crept through her—like she was looking into the eyes of a predator. But then he averted his attention and released her. "The path's icy."

"Right." As if she wasn't aware of the obvious. But that wasn't half as dangerous as what had just occurred between them.

So what *had* occurred between them?

Trying to keep up, she hurried down the path after him.

She didn't know him. He didn't know her. Hell, he didn't even know himself. Yet there was something about him that was driving her crazy. Almost like animal magnetism. Which really was nuts. She didn't believe in primitive sexual attraction, although her brother had always teased her that she would know when she finally met the right man—a sexual draw so compelling would exist between them, she wouldn't be able to resist.

That would be the day.

"You should have stayed behind." The stranger's gruff voice snapped her right out of her sexual fantasies.

He slipped Michael's gloves on and continued down the path to the woodpile where she had first found him.

A thank you would have sufficed, she grumbled silently to herself.

Even though he appeared to be all right now, his jaw tightened when he leaned down and lifted an armload of wood, and again when he straightened his back. As injured as he was, she wished he hadn't had to help. Gathering up as much timber as she would have in three trips, he returned to the path leading up to the house.

A little ways up the hill, he stopped, cast a glance over his shoulder, his dark brows pinched together, his eyes watchful while he waited for her.

She stumbled up the path with an armload of timber, miniscule compared to the load he was carrying.

He grumbled, "I told you that you should have stayed in the house."

"Yeah, well, we need all the firewood we can get if we're going to be stuck here without electricity. Besides, I do this all the time without anyone's help."

Although that had been the case only since her brother had been incarcerated. Otherwise, he had always been the one to get the firewood and do the other more manly chores around the place. At the thought she might not see him here again for a good long while, her eyes filled with tears and she sniffled.

But she wasn't going to sit in the house, worrying whether the stranger might reinjure himself on another trip to the beach or back alone. So he was stuck with her, whether he liked it or not. Besides, staying there and worrying about the intruder's return wasn't an option either.

He shook his head, yet the corners of his mouth turned slightly upward.

He walked the rest of the way to the house, moving slower this time, as if making sure she didn't slip again or fall too far behind. At least that's what she assumed. Unless he just hurt so much, walking was difficult.

They headed inside and he set his firewood on the rack. Taking the wood from her arms, he stacked it with the rest. Then like a good Boy Scout, despite looking too roguish to be one, he set up a perfect fire. Slowly, the flames began to crackle and throw off a curl of heat.

Crouching in front of the fireplace, he frowned up at her, his darkening gaze drifting again to her turtleneck. "Why don't you get into something dry."

"I'll be fine." She couldn't admit she was afraid to be by herself.

"Your clothes are soaking wet. You're shivering. The house is freezing. You're not fine. Lock the bedroom door, if you're afraid."

She clenched her teeth. She wasn't afraid of the veritable god. Well, maybe a little. She yanked off her wet gloves and parka, tossed them on the coffee table so they'd dry by the fire, and then returned to the bedroom and locked the door—as a precaution. She tried the phone; still no dial tone. She glanced at her bedside table. *The gun.*

She jerked the drawer open. Her heart skipped a beat. *No gun.*

Blind rage filled her. Feeling violated, she collapsed on the edge of the bed. If someone used the gun to commit a crime, the police would trace it straight to her. Not to mention she couldn't count on it for protection now.

How had the man known where to find it? What else had he taken? Nothing looked like it was out of place.

Focus—get warm and dry before pneumonia sets in. Shaking violently from the cold, she stood, peeled off her wet clothes, and dumped them on the floor.

She shoved on a pair of emerald fleece sweats, matching heavy-duty socks, and her fur-lined boots. Feeling a little warmer, she hurried down the hall and dumped her wet clothes in the dryer, her thoughts centered on the naked man.

Did he really have amnesia? Or was it just a ploy to keep his identity a secret? He seemed so dangerous, maybe because he was so powerfully built. Her brother and the men she had dated were scrawny compared to this guy.

She twisted the dryer dial to turn it on high. *No response.* Damn, no electricity.

Grumbling, she yanked her wet things out of the dryer and hung them in the shower to drip dry. But then a dark thought crossed her mind. What if the ice storm hadn't knocked out the electricity? What if the intruder had done something to it?

She hurried to the coat closet to check the circuit breaker, glanced in the direction of the living room and noticed the fire had caught hold, its golden flames throwing off some heat. But Hunter was gone. Her heart fluttered with fresh apprehension.

She rushed to the back door and saw him trudging up the hill with another armload of firewood as big as the first. Curbing her annoyance that he would sneak out and chance injuring himself further without her being there to rescue him, she glowered.

Even her brother couldn't carry that much, certainly not if he had had been injured like this man. He reminded her of a Highland warrior, his brow creased with determination, his face dark and brooding, his body hard and ready to win any battle no matter how much his enemy had beaten him beforehand. A kilt was all he needed to complete the look. A kilt, and nothing else.

He caught her eye and offered her a hint of a smile. Hell, she'd been ogling the poor man—again.

"Do you have anything in the house to eat?"

Walking past her while she locked the door, he smelled like the sea, pines, wind, rainwater, and a rugged outdoorsman. If they could bottle his scent, the cologne would drive women crazy. With a clunk, he deposited the wood neatly with the rest, shaking her loose from her insane thoughts.

"Uhm, let me check one thing." She returned to the coat closet and pulled the door open. She yanked on the light switch pull and then shook her head when the bulb didn't come on. When would she get it through her brain there was no electricity?

Before she could get the flashlight, he placed another log on the fire and said, "I already checked the circuit breaker."

He was way ahead of her. "You think the ice storm has brought down the lines?"

"Since your unwelcome houseguest didn't mess with the circuit breaker, that's what I assume."

She took a settling breath. If the intruder *had* shut off her electricity, it probably would mean he'd return.

Hopefully, this meant he'd only come for the gun. Unless he realized she was alone and would return later to steal more. The newspaper had covered the press on her brother's story for weeks. Everyone knew she was by herself now. Instantly re-chilled, she rubbed her arms and returned to the kitchen.

"I have a rack that we can put over the fire and grill some steaks," she offered.

"Rare." He walked into the kitchen, sure of himself, no hint that he'd been mostly dead a half hour ago.

Her brother's sweats would never look the same. Whereas they hung off her brother's slim frame, they hugged this guy's muscled body.

She tried to get her mind off the man's physique and concentrate on dinner. She had never attempted cooking anything in her fireplace. Would it work? Or be a total disaster?

"Garlic? Lemon and pepper seasoning?" Wishing it was at least defrosted, she pulled the meat out of the freezer.

"However you prepare it is fine with me. As long as it's rare."

"What do you think happened to you?" She handed him the rack for the fireplace.

"Not sure. My skin feels tight, like I soaked for hours in a tub of salt water, so I imagine I took a swim in the ocean."

"Did you want a shower?"

"Would you have enough hot water?"

"Probably not."

She seasoned the steaks and carried them into the living room. "I've got candles and flashlights in one of the kitchen drawers, if you want to get them for later."

It wouldn't be dark for another hour or so, but if the electricity didn't come back on, she wanted to be prepared before nightfall.

"I'll watch the steaks."

"All right. Medium. That's the way I like mine."

She returned to the kitchen and rummaged through the drawers, looking for the emergency candles.

"Is anything missing from your house?" he asked.

She headed back into the living room with an armful of lighting paraphernalia.

A shadow of dark stubble covered his square jaw, and his eyes looked haunted. No wonder, after all he had been through. His coffee-colored hair hung to his shoulders and dripped water. She needed to get him a towel.

"He stole my gun." She set two flashlights, two camp lanterns, and four candles on the coffee table.

The man's eyes widened. "You know how to shoot?"

"Of course. I have a concealed weapon license. Someone broke into our house a couple of times before because we're so isolated."

He flipped the steaks. "Where's your brother?"

Tears cascaded down her cheeks before she could stop them. "He went to prison for a murder he didn't commit." She grabbed a tissue from a box on the coffee table. Almost empty. Again.

Hunter studied her for a moment before saying anything. A hint of compassion showed in his eyes. For her? Or her brother? Or was she hallucinating?

"Have any proof?" He flipped a steak onto a plate. Barely cooked.

"No. He didn't do it. And I'll find the killer if I have to. Michael's girlfriend was seeing someone behind his back. What if *he* was the one who killed her? Usually the murderer knows the victim."

Hunter looked like he didn't believe her.

She cast him an annoyed look. After she saved his naked butt, the least he could do was *pretend* he believed her.

"I've got some rolls and canned asparagus we can eat cold."

She stalked down the hall to the guest bathroom, grabbed a fresh bath towel from the linen closet, and returned to the living room. "Here, to dry your hair."

He had a plate in one hand and was turning her steak with the other. She hesitated. If he'd been a friend, she would have offered to dry his hair. But he wasn't. Still, the house was cold, except for the part of their bodies directly exposed to the fire, and…

He tilted his head back and looked up at her, his mouth curving slightly upward. "Maybe you can towel-dry it. Icy drops of water keep rolling down my neck."

Rife with indecision, she stood next to him. The fire flickered light off his eyes, like a wolfish predator, tempting her to draw closer into his web of seduction. What was there about him that turned her insides into mush? No man had ever made her feel that way with just a look.

The thought of drying his hair seemed so… intimate.

Taking a deep breath, she moved closer, leaning over him, sliding the fluffy towel over larger clumps of his dark hair, trying to dry it quickly. To not get caught up in the feel of him, the way his body's heat reached out to her, the way he smelled so masculine, so intriguing. But then she separated his hair into smaller sections and wrung the shiny strands as dry as she could to prevent his getting chilled. He leaned his back against her legs, relaxing his posture, and she couldn't help wanting to melt against him, too.

He looked up at her, his expression half gratitude, the other half pure tantalization, his eyes clouded with desire. She cleared her throat, switched her attention to his damp hair again, and massaged his scalp.

"Hmm, your hair is a little wet, too," he said under his breath, his rigid body relaxing as he set the plate down and reached up and touched a wet curl dangling over her shoulder.

She swore the heat from his touch could dry her hair in a flash.

"Thanks, Tessa. That feels much better. Got another towel?"

"Uh, you're welcome." She touched her sagging bun, damp trails of curls trickling down her turtleneck. "I'm okay."

"Bring me a dry towel."

How could he sound so sexy when he commanded her to do his bidding? If it had been anyone else, she would have stood her ground. Her hair wasn't that wet; she was fine. But she headed for the bathroom and hung up the wet towel in the shower and grabbed a dry one.

On the way back to the living room, she dropped the towel on the leather footstool. "I'll get the rolls, first."

"I can warm them." He poked at her steak again.

"So… how do you think you ended up taking a swim in the Pacific in the middle of winter?" she asked from the kitchen.

With the package of rolls in hand, she returned to the fire and handed them to him.

"Haven't a clue."

"Without any clothes?" Her cheeks heated, just thinking about how he'd looked in the raw—male perfection, buff muscles, dark curling hair trailing down his chest, tantalizingly seductive, his stomach flat and his butt—which she would die to have—toned and provocative.

His mouth curved up slightly.

Even though he *said* he didn't remember anything, she had the distinct impression he knew more than he was letting on. But then again, what did she know about amnesia cases? Nothing, except about some isolated cases she'd read in the news.

"Who was seeing your brother's girlfriend?" He turned the rolls.

"Michael didn't know. And the police couldn't locate him."

Hunter gave her a skeptical look and served up her steak and the rolls.

"My brother couldn't catch her with him, but he knew she was seeing someone else." She took a deep breath. "I'll get the asparagus."

After she returned and served up the asparagus, but before he began to eat his meal, he scooted behind her while she sat cross-legged in front of the fireplace, as if they had known each other forever. His legs stretched out beyond hers way too intimately, caging her in, and yet to be able to keep her arms from being pinned, she rested her elbows on his knees. She had never known anyone she could get this close to so quickly and feel just right.

He removed the pins from her hair, gently, careful not to pull it.

"Your dinner will get cold," she admonished, feeling out of her element. No man had ever let her hair down and the experience was just as beguiling as the rest of his moves. "And if nothing else, you need a good hot meal after the ordeal you've been through."

"I'm feeling pretty hot." His deep baritone voice penetrated her defenses, offering protection and silky seduction. Warmed by the fire, his chest pressed against her back. "How about you?"

Sizzling, as in having one of those hot flashes her mother always talked about. But it had nothing to do with the fire, and all to do with the Greek god warming her backside.

He stroked Tessa's hair with tender caresses, and she suddenly wasn't hungry. Instead, she wanted to turn around and kiss him. She was pretty sure his kisses could melt the polar ice caps the way he looked at her and touched her, heating her from the top of her damp head to her boot-covered toes. The way his first kiss had done.

Despite the circumstances that brought them together, she felt a sense of relief that he was here. Well, more than a sense of relief. Here, she could have been sitting in the chilly house alone, without any electricity, still trying to get a fire going, worried that whoever broke into the house was lurking outside. She would never have imagined cooking a meal over the fire either, even though Michael had done so outside a number of times while she'd watched. If she'd been on her own, she probably would have fixed a tuna fish sandwich and sat in the cold, eating it while a flashlight illuminated the place, poking into the dark with a faint light, the rest in shadows. Worrying that the intruder would return.

Hunter stroked her hair some more with the towel, then leaned over and kissed the back of her head, his groin pressed hard against her backside. He was totally aroused and she was getting herself into hot water. What if the guy was married? He didn't remember anything about his past. He wasn't wearing a ring, but maybe in his occupation, he couldn't. Or maybe he was the kind of man who refused to wear a ring, because it stifled his sex life. Like her father.

"Thanks so much for drying my hair." Her tone was formal, an attempt at keeping her distance.

"A natural redhead." He combed his fingers through the strands, inspecting it as if he had never seen anything quite like it, caressing, awed.

And for a minute in time, she felt adored, when no one had ever treated her that way. But then she shuttered her heart, reminding herself it could all be a show. He might be a womanizer extraordinaire and it was his nature to beguile women with his irresistible magnetism.

He moved his long legs and rose.

Instantly, the heat his body had generated faded from hers and the loss of their touching affected her profoundly, when her mind told her she shouldn't feel a thing. But with her brother gone, the house so empty—hell, what was she telling herself? Hunter was the first man who'd made her feel like a real woman ever. It had nothing to do with her brother or an empty house and all to do with an empty life. The only thing that kept her busy was taking care of her brother, and photographing anything and everything for a living.

One look at Hunter and the lustful expression in his gaze, and she knew he wanted her. Or at least he was fully aroused and needed release. She figured any woman who was readily available would do.

He lifted a brow and she wondered what he was reading in her expression. Skepticism? Interest? He would be right on both accounts.

He gave her a small smile, then grabbed his plate and sat next to her in front of the fire, his knee touching hers. Did he practice seduction? Or did it just come naturally?

"You could hire a detective to look into your brother's situation."

"I have. He charged me lots and didn't find anything."

Hunter nodded.

"Michael's innocent," she said, her voice harsher than she intended.

He didn't respond one way or another, and she knew there was no sense in trying to convince another disbeliever. He devoured his steak as if he hadn't eaten in ages, but worked slower on the rolls and asparagus, and then gulped down two glasses of milk. When he snagged another roll, she studied his face again. She swore when she first saw them, the bruises were dark purple and cuts were deep and bloody in places. But now they looked like they were fading.

"Does your head hurt? Or anywhere else? I don't have anything really strong but I've got headache and backache medicines."

"No, I'm feeling better already."

Now it was her turn to look at him unbelievingly. "Why would you have been swimming in the ocean? You must have some idea."

"Two possibilities. I was pushed or I jumped off one of the cliffs up the coast. Probably drifted to your beach."

Pushed? She couldn't imagine him being the type to jump.

First, she'd put out the word she was going to locate Bethany's killer, now an intended murder victim was staying with her? Bad things come in threes, her grandmother had always said. Michael was found guilty, the electricity was off during an ice storm, and she found a near dead guy on the beach. Oh, and a guy had broken into her home and stolen her gun. That was four in her book. Now was past time for something good to happen.

"You don't remember anything? Except that you like your steak rare?"

He smiled a hair. "I guess that's instinctual."

"Well, it's a good thing you didn't lose all your memory, including how to walk or talk like some do in really bad amnesia cases. Do you at least remember where you live?"

"No." He finished another roll and sat back against the leather footstool, his knees bent, his legs spread, his posture openly sexual, stating he was available if she was, while he studied her with that intense way of his as though he could look into her soul. "So what were you and your brother doing living way out here?"

"Our grandparents gifted us the house when they died. I'm a professional photographer." She motioned to the wall opposite the fireplace where around thirty framed photos picturing wildlife, both flora and fauna hung. "And my brother is an artist. He loves to paint the Oregon Coast in all its moods. His work is now in several galleries across the country. You might have seen a couple of his paintings in the hallway and in the dining room."

"Both of you are very talented. I love the way you capture nature in all its beauty." He observed her photos from where he sat, but the light was fading too much for him to see them well.

Maybe he had gotten a closer look at them earlier when she was changing.

"The way the light plays off the storm-driven waves. The deer eating undisturbed in the sun-mottled forest. Even the seals basking on the rocks near the caves below the cliffs. As if you were an unobtrusive observer preserving nature at its best with one click of the camera," Hunter said, motioning to them.

She could tell he wasn't just making small talk, that their work really touched him, which confirmed what she had assumed about him—he was a rugged outdoorsman. Probably a hunter. She didn't see him as the fisherman type.

Yet something else flickered in his expression. A darkness, or concern. She wasn't sure what.

"What are you going to do now that your brother is gone?"

"Find a way to get him out of prison. I have to discover who Bethany Wade was seeing behind Michael's back. I really believe he's the clue to this."

"If you're right in thinking someone had anything to do with her death, it's too dangerous for you to look into."

What other choice did she have? Not that she would personally chase after a killer. That would be way too risky. She'd hire a good detective who could discover the truth.

"I'm not giving up."

Hunter folded his arms across his chest and speared her a look that said he would have his way or else. "Here's the deal. I need to find out what happened to me. If someone pushed me off a cliff, I don't want whoever did it to know I'm still alive, *yet*. So I need a nice out-of-the-way place to stay. You require some protection. Michael's window is broken and needs to be repaired. And if you think you locked the back door, then someone used a key to get in. You'll need your locks changed, and I can assist you. In the meantime, I'll snoop into Bethany Wade's death."

Tessa's mouth gaped.

He added, "For room and board."

"But if you can't be seen, how can you investigate?"

"I'll manage."

Again, she had the feeling he knew more about himself than he was letting on. He sounded like he was an undercover operative used to slipping in and out of dangerous situations, unseen and unheard. He certainly was built like a man who physically trained all the time. Plus, he exhibited an unswerving confidence, bordering on out-and-out male arrogance, as she assumed someone in the Special Forces or Rangers would act.

"All right. You can sleep in the spare bedroom."

"I'll sleep wherever you bed down for the night."

That left unbidden thoughts of rugged sex with a mountain man blazing across her brain. She clamped her mouth shut, blinked, and managed to reopen her mouth and say, "Pardon me?"

Chapter 3

If every muscle hadn't ached so much—the pain slicing all the way through to the marrow of his bones—the incredulous expression on Miss Tessa Anderson's face would have made him smile. But the situation was too dire to make light of it. He might not remember his whole name or what had happened to him, but one thing the concussion had not robbed him of—his wolf instincts.

They warned him whoever had broken into the house and stolen Tessa's gun had also lain in her bed—on the side of the mattress where she always slept—rolled in her scent and carried it with him. Which meant only one thing. The perpetrator wanted her for his own—and since he was a *lupus garou,* that was bad news.

Worse than that, she triggered a craving in him to such an extent, he was having a hell of a time tamping down the feelings, and remembering *why* he had to keep his interest to himself.

Her hair cascaded over her shoulder blades, thick, soft red curls he longed to plunge his fingers in again. Her clear green eyes were tinged blue, not a speck of amber: bright, expressive, not wary as he expected, being that he was a stranger without any memories and here most likely due to foul play.

And the frumpy emerald sweats she wore, although designed to hide a woman's sensuous shape, did nothing of the sort. The swell of her generous breasts, the curve of her thighs, her rounded ass, all were perfectly outlined by the soft attire. No belts or buttons to hinder their removal either.

He took a ragged breath and sat taller, absorbed the heat from the fire, which helped to ease the ache in his bones, and raised his brows. "I'll stay with you wherever you make your bed. The house isn't secure. Either we sleep here by the fire, or if you have enough blankets for your bed, we stay in your room."

If it was up to him, he would have opted for the comfort of the mattress, but most of all snuggling with the woman. But her scent, her pheromones, the feel of her silky hair, the way her soft body had pressed against him—and the *kiss*—had aroused him to such a degree, everything about her was throwing him off kilter. A one-night stand with a human female was one thing. But he was certain one tumble with her wouldn't satisfy the carnal urge. And since he needed to stay longer to protect her, it was better to keep their relationship as platonic as possible. Yet, the wolf part of him was already heading down a dangerous, forbidden path.

She licked her lips and turned her gaze to the fire. His groin tightened. The light sparkled off her eyes and her moistened lips glistened. He'd been in a half-aroused state ever since the woman had manhandled him on the beach in her tight black denims and breast-hugging turtleneck, dampened by the sleet, her hardened nipples teasing his chest when she had tried to revive him. Even half-conscious, the wolf side of him had been aware of her special scent, sensed her fear—not of him, but for him. If she learned what he was, what he was capable of, she would fear him.

"I guess we could sleep here. By the fire. It would probably be warmer." Her gaze shifted from the flames to him.

The look in her eyes said she'd be safer curling up next to the fire. Less intimate than sleeping with him in her bed. Yet there was a hint of something else. Desire to be with him? But she seemed to be waiting for him to make a decision. Which couldn't help but please him. His sister was so testy of late, seeing a female bow to his leadership was much appreciated.

Sister? Where the hell had that memory come from? He tried to dredge up more, but came up blank.

"Don't you think?" Tessa asked, when he didn't respond.

Jarring him back to the situation at hand, he rubbed his right arm, the muscle caught in a spasm. He should have said she was right, sleeping by the fire was a good choice. Safer for both of them. But his animal needs were getting the best of him. He took another deep breath of her scent, sweet and musky. He wanted her, no matter how much he tried to persuade himself it would be a mistake.

"That would be fine," he said slowly, his gaze never leaving hers, all the while judging her reaction. "But already I'm stiffening up pretty badly. Maybe I will take something for the aches and pains."

He wasn't lying, but normally he would suffer rather than let a woman know how he felt.

Tessa's face grew shadowed, and she hurried to take the plates. "Oh, oh, of course. You must be feeling awful."

She rushed into the kitchen, and he *almost* felt guilty. But he liked her maternal instincts, and no matter how much he knew he should shove his baser needs aside, he wanted to share the bed with Tessa. She was a grown woman after all, and he, a grown… well, man of sorts.

He glanced at the living room window, the curtains drawn.

Had the gray been watching them when they climbed to the house from the beach? The sleet was coming down hard, cleansing the air. He couldn't have smelled him if the *lupus garou* was being careful. Not a true alpha male then. If he had been one, the wolf would have made his presence known, indicated up front that he had laid claim to the woman. As a beta, the wolf would have rolled in her sheets *before* he saw Tessa hauling an injured gray up the hill. The *lupus garou* must have observed them, hiding in the trees, loathing him.

If the thief got anywhere near the house, he would regret it. But even a beta *lupus garou* could be a dangerous proposition for a lone human female.

Tessa returned with a glass of water and a couple of white pills. "This should help. I'll be right back." She whipped around and headed for the kitchen, then banged inside the cabinets.

He took the medicine, finished off the water, and rose from the floor. Not meaning to, he groaned, and she caught him in the act.

Her brows furrowed deeper as she tightened her hold on a stainless steel saucepan. "You're really hurting, aren't you? Why don't you lie down on the floor next to the fire, and I'll rub some liniment into your muscles. I'll warm this water over the fire, and you can wash the saltwater off your skin. When the electricity's back on, you can shower properly."

He meant to conceal his satisfied expression, for her sake, but he couldn't help it. She was eating right out of his hands.

She twisted her mouth and set the pot on the fire. "I'll be back."

After watching her walk down the hall to the bathroom, and seeing nothing amiss, he returned to the living room, stripped out of her brother's sweats and reclined on his stomach on the carpeting next to the fire. He rested his head on his arms, but even that movement sent a streak of screaming pain from his arms to his back.

Tessa stepped into the room and he heard her intake of breath. Her eyes grew big and her lips parted, but she had already seen him nude.

"I hope that stuff works." He attempted looking as innocent as an alpha gray pack leader could manage who was already fully aroused, his voice way too husky.

"Uhm, you're awfully cut up. Let me get some antibacterial cream, too." She set the tube of liniment next to the fire and left. Down the hall, she rummaged around in some drawers.

She returned posthaste, carrying a handful of creams, his salvation. In anticipation, he relaxed his stiff muscles.

After leaving the creams on the coffee table, she knelt beside him and dipped a washcloth in the water. She slid the hot wet cloth over his shoulders, her touch gentle, and he gave a raspy sigh. "Got hot fast."

"Too warm?"

"No, feels just right."

"The faucet still had some hot water. The pipes would be cold and it takes forever for the bathroom water to heat even on a warm day, but you might be able to take a fast lukewarm shower."

He needed a cold one to keep his libido in check with the woman touching him so tenderly. "This is fine." *Better than fine.*

She washed his right shoulder and arm and before he could grow chilled, she patted the skin dry with a towel. He closed his eyes and enjoyed her ministrations. No one had ever treated him with so much kindness that he could recall. Hell, his sister would have shoved him in a tub of cold water, not wanting him to soil the sheets with the odor from the sea.

Again, an elusive memory of his sister. But he couldn't dredge up anything further.

Tessa probably couldn't smell the fishy odor on his skin like his kind could, but the scent was pretty pungent. He felt like he had been dropped in a vat of freshly caught fish off the coast. Not that it bothered him. Getting skunked was about the worst odor any wolf would have to contend with. Although he had been a pup when it happened, too curious for his own good, his parents wouldn't let him inside the house for days. Thankfully, the weather had been mild and the moon out so he remained a wolf the whole time, foraging in the forest, no chores to do.

Again, a memory. But even so, he couldn't recall what had happened to his parents or anything else about the incident.

After Tessa washed his neck, she left. Hating to admit it, he wanted in the worst way to drag her back, beg her to finish, then make love to her. He opened a sleepy eye, wondering what she was up to.

With a slight blush to her cheeks, she stood over him holding the afghan. "You must be cold." Before he could tell her she was heating him up just fine, she covered the lower part of his body with the soft blanket, and then started to wash his back, her touch methodical and soothing. "You sure took a beating."

She might have talked further, but he couldn't be sure. His thoughts had drifted to his current predicament and how he'd gotten here. If he had a sister, were they in a pack? He had to be the leader. He couldn't imagine serving in any other role. But what of his people? Were they from this area?

The *lupus garou* skulking around Tessa's place didn't remind him of anyone he knew. And then another concern: if his pack thought he was dead, one of the emergent alphas—if there were any—would try to take over. Well, he would remedy that when he got back.

"I had a premonition something bad was going to happen," Tessa was saying.

He opened his eyes, turned his head, and stared at her.

"Oh, I'm not psychic or anything. I just have these—bad impressions sometimes. Anyway," she said, scooting the afghan down to the tip of his spine, "sometimes I feel like something is wrong. When my parents died, I felt that way. Before they arrested Michael, it hit me again. Now tonight. I just couldn't pinpoint the feeling, but I couldn't squash the sensation of being watched."

Yeah, by the gray. He assumed the man had been stalking her for some time before he finally made a move.

She finished washing his back, slipped the afghan higher, covering his back and shoulders, and began washing his lower extremities. "Are you all right? Not getting too chilled?"

More than all right. In heaven, as much as he could be, the way he was so bruised and every muscle ached. "It feels good to have the salt washed off my skin," he said, his voice muffled in relaxation.

"Tell me if I hurt you and I'll quit."

He would suffer anything as long as she kept touching him.

When she began to work the liniment into his shoulders, the way her fingers massaged the muscles sent a sizzling heat through every fiber. He groaned with pure pleasure.

She stopped. "Am I hurting you?"

"Only if you quit."

She chuckled.

Despite how good she was making him feel, he couldn't prevent his mind from working over the problem with the gray wolf intruder. "Who would have a key to your house?"

She hesitated and then began to rub his lower back. "Michael, of course. Bethany had a key." Her fingers rested on the tip of his spine.

Move lower, he silently pleaded.

"Ohmigod, what if the killer had taken it off Bethany? What if he was looking for evidence Michael might have against him, except my brother was unaware of it?"

What if the whole scenario was a setup to get rid of Michael so the *lupus garou* could have a free shot at Tessa? What if it had nothing to do with Bethany Wade?

It would make sense that a sneaky beta was seeing Bethany behind Michael's back, cagey enough not to get caught, but giving Michael an alibi he couldn't prove. Oh, hell, if a *lupus garou* killed Bethany, no way could he expose him for the crime. If the killer went to prison, the moon's appearance would eventually force the man to turn wolf. But to get Michael off, they needed to catch the murderer and have him convicted.

Hunter let out his breath in exasperation.

"Did you want to turn over, and I'll wash the rest of your skin?" she asked.

He didn't think she could handle what she had done to him with her sweet touch, but he was more than ready and rolled over. He groaned with the effort and any fear she might have had that he would want to take their relationship too far seemed to fade as her eyes widened and her mouth opened slightly. Not that he couldn't make love to her despite the way he ached. Dealing with that torture would only help alleviate other discomforts she was now making worse.

She covered him quickly, although the afghan couldn't hide his full-blown erection, and her cheeks blushed anew. "I don't believe anyone else had a key to our place."

He studied her face as she washed his chest, her lashes hiding her eyes as she concentrated on her work. He wanted to ask her if she was seeing anyone regularly. The scent of several different males filled the house, but they might have been her brother's friends. He hoped they were her brother's friends. But if he asked if she was seeing anyone special, she might make more of an issue of his question than he intended. Still, being an alpha he couldn't skirt around the situation. What if a suitor turned up and found Tessa and him sleeping together?

He didn't want to ruin her relationship with a guy if it was important to her. He couldn't claim her for his own. He didn't believe in changing humans, and he hadn't known anyone personally who had ever done so. At least that he could remember.

Certainly, he couldn't imagine anyone doing it in this day and age. Although he supposed if the two were mutually agreeable… he mentally shook his head. It wasn't possible without the wolf telling the human what they were, which wasn't allowed. And even if a *lupus garou* did explain the situation, how could a human truly understand the ramifications of the change? He or she couldn't.

Tessa lowered the afghan and then worked on his stomach, her hair caressing his belly. Tickling, tantalizing. He itched to take handfuls of her hair and lower her fascinating mouth to his and kiss her again. Only this time with a lot more stamina.

When she began washing his legs, she avoided looking in the direction of his erection staking the cover in the form of a mountain peak.

"Tessa," he said, raising up on an elbow, "are you seeing anyone regularly?"

Wide-eyed, she looked at him.

He sure as hell didn't mean it like it sounded. "I don't want to ruin your relationship with a man if you're serious about one while I'm staying with you, and he was to drop by unexpectedly."

"We could say you're gay."

He raised his brows. Not only did he *not* care for the idea, he didn't like that she had a boyfriend. "Then you're seeing someone?" He hated how gruff his voice sounded. He meant to ask casually, not like he was ready to rip the guy's head from his shoulders.

She shrugged, but avoided looking at him. He smiled. She wasn't seeing anyone, but was afraid to admit it—maybe embarrassed that she didn't have a guy, or maybe she thought she could prevent her houseguest from getting too frisky with her in the event he wanted something more.

He leaned back again, his head resting on the crook of his arms while she washed his feet. From the moment he'd found himself half frozen and hurting beyond belief on the beach, he'd never thought an angel would be the one to save him, or tempt him like she did.

"What about you? Do you have anyone?" She set aside the wet washcloth and applied ointment to a cut on his shin.

Hell, he'd never considered that. What if he did have a mate waiting at home for him? There were too few to leave widowed, before another male would jump to claim an unattached female.

Tessa rubbed more antibacterial ointment on a deep scrape on his inner thigh, stirring his erection. But he couldn't quit worrying if he had a mate. Surely if he did have one, she'd wait for some time before giving up hope on him.

When he didn't respond, Tessa looked up at him. "Do you?"

Tessa felt Hunter's pain, the poor man. He couldn't even remember if he had someone special in his life. But it was probably good she brought it up, to put a halt to whatever he was thinking might go on between them. He was way too aroused for her to believe he was interested in only protecting her. And she couldn't help but notice his irritation when he thought she might be attached to a man.

She glanced at the dwindling fire. They would need the dry firewood for tomorrow's heat and breakfast if the electricity didn't come on during the night. She wasn't sure if taking Hunter to bed with her was a sound idea, but it would be warmer under the covers if they couldn't have a fire all night long. And the mattress was definitely preferable to the carpeted floor.

"I'll get some fresh sweats for you to wear. You look worn out. Maybe we should go to bed now."

He attempted to look serious, but his eyes and mouth hinted at humor. Yeah, he had suckered her right in. He might have been dead tired, but the way he regarded her with such fascination—her hair, her clothes as if he could see right through them, the way he captured her gaze, holding her captive—he was way too interested in her.

"But remember," she said, grabbing a camp lantern, "you're gay, so no funny stuff or you'll be sleeping on the floor."

This time he gave her a smug smile and a little chuckle. "As you wish. Thanks, Tessa, for taking me in."

"I'd say we both benefited." She tried to sound businesslike, as though she ran a first-rate hotel for half-drowned victims who earned their keep, and hurried down the now dark hall. But then she thought she heard someone in Michael's bedroom. She had closed the door to keep the freezing wind blowing through his window from chilling the rest of the house, but she was sure a drawer opened and shut.

Maybe the wind had made the noise. Still, she listened and couldn't force herself to reach for the doorknob.

"Tessa?" Hunter walked up behind her, this time wearing the afghan slung low over his hips.

The effect was nearly as erotic as when he wasn't wearing anything. She would never look at the blanket her grandmother had made the same way again either.

He seized the doorknob and jerked the door open.

She held her breath.

He stalked into the frigid room, and she hurried to give him the lantern. He peered into the closet, and then walked inside. She half-expected him to bring the intruder out, with an arm locked around the culprit's neck. But instead, Hunter carried a bundle of sweats. Then he went to the window and looked out.

"See anyone?"

"No one's there." He turned to face her, the breeze blowing his hair across his cheeks, softening his dark expression. "What do you think you heard?"

"Someone opening a drawer."

Hunter dumped the sweats on the mattress and peered under the bed. He set the lantern down, and then crossed the floor to the dresser. When she saw what he was about to do, she hurried to help him move the furniture. His muscles strained as he did the majority of the work, and she cringed to think he might injure himself further.

After they had blocked the window with the heavy mahogany dresser, he grabbed the sweats and lantern.

"He won't be getting in that way again."

"Do you think I really heard him? Or do you think

I imagined it?" she asked, hoping the intruder hadn't slipped back in as she led Hunter into her bedroom.

"Could have been the wind. I'll board up the window in the morning and replace it once we pick up a new one."

Brother, here she worried about him getting too amorous with her in bed, and he was saving her butt again. The long-standing distrust of men she had didn't help. Not after her father had been one of the worst womanizers in the small community. How her mother had put up with him and his philandering ways she could never fathom.

"I'll leave this lantern on in the bathroom in case you need something in the middle of the night." She noted he had put on a pair of pale gray sweatpants, but not the sweatshirt. "Aren't you going to be cold?"

He cast her a small smile and her cheeks heated. Since he was so comfortable showing off his nudity, he probably usually slept in the raw.

"I'll leave a spare toothbrush on the bathroom counter for you. Be right out."

"Thanks, Tessa. I'll lie down until you're through."

But he glanced at her bedroom window, and she bet he wanted to check outside for the intruder. "You've got to be exhausted, Hunter. Don't worry about him. I'll be quick."

As much raw sexual energy as he exuded, she wasn't sure sleeping with him was such a good idea after all.

But when she exited the bathroom, expecting to find him lying on the bed, half-asleep, she found the room empty. Sitting by the remnants of the fire then?

Cinching up her velour robe, she hurried down the hall with lantern in hand to let him know the bathroom was free, but there was no sign of him in the living room. She rushed to the picture window and peered out. He couldn't be out in this awful weather.

Not anywhere in sight. Hurrying to the back door, she halfway expected him to trudge up the hill with another enormous load of firewood.

"Looking for someone?" he asked behind her, his voice dark and husky.

She squeaked and whirled around. "My god, Hunter. Where were you?"

He held up a shaving kit. "I found it in the guest bathroom. I hope your brother won't mind if I shaved."

His skin was smooth as satin and she wanted to run her hands over his face, feel the velvety skin, smell the citrus spice aftershave, but more than that, she wanted another of his soul-piercing kisses. She chastised herself. He probably had a wife.

"He won't mind that you've used his things while he's… away. He'll be glad you were here to watch over me. And that you've offered to help me find Bethany's killer so we can free him."

A subtle shadow fell over his face, and she wondered if he'd changed his mind. Well, *she* hadn't. "If you don't need anything else…"

He moved out of her path and bowed his head slightly.

The frigid air wasn't the only thing that chilled her to the bone. She had quickly become used to the idea she'd have a real man on her side to help her locate Bethany's murderer.

She shouldn't have gotten her hopes up.

❖❖❖

Tessa grabbed the tie to her robe, then apparently thinking better of it, she climbed into bed dressed in fluffy pink socks, polka-dot pink and green pajamas, and the emerald robe. He had never seen a woman so clothed in bed. He stifled a chuckle. The big bad wolf would not eat her all up, unless she chose it and he was free to do so.

She kept her distance, staying near the opposite edge of the soft queen-sized mattress, which was understandable since he was a stranger. But she needed someone to hold her tight after her harrowing day—the trial, the intruder, finding a near dead man on the beach. She cast wistful looks at him when she didn't think he could see her in the dark.

He took a long-suffering breath. Patience was definitely not one of his virtues, but he needed a place to stay until he could sort out his situation. The best thing he could do was ignore his cravings when it came to the woman who stirred his desire with a smile, a touch, and the scent of her subtle aroused state.

Forget patience or the right or wrong of it. "Join me, Tessa. The room's too cold. I promise I'll behave." At least that was the plan.

"You're injured."

He'd suffer anything to have her in his arms. "I'll let you know if I'm hurting."

Silence. He smiled. She was thinking on it. He waited, anticipating enveloping her soft body in his. She shook her head. He groaned inwardly.

"I'm fine. If you get too cold, throw on Michael's sweatshirt. You can get some of his sweaters, socks, whatever else you need to stay toasty."

"If you change your mind and want me to warm you up, just slide over here."

Forever, he waited for her to come to him. The wind whipped around the house in a howling frenzy while the rain continued to pelt the roof and windows. Every bit of the cold seemed to have made it inside her home and the bedroom was icier than her freezer. But still, he would not bundle up in tons of clothes when he had a perfectly good woman to snuggle with.

Then her leg jerked. Her arm twitched. She was asleep. She rolled over. Was she joining him?

Her foot shot out and connected with his knee. Pain flared through the tendons and surrounding tissue. Hell, he already had a bruise the size of a melon there. Before he could pull her into his arms, she rolled over again. Night terrors? Nightmares? He reached over to rub her back, to comfort her, when her elbow jabbed him in the chest.

Not what he had in mind after frolicking in the ocean, battered against the rocks in the icy water. Then the sound of distant gunfire caught his attention. As a *lupus garou*, shouldn't the shots grip him with terror? Adrenaline flooded his system, but he wasn't afraid. In fact, for whatever reason, he felt the oddest urge to take up a gun and retaliate.

If the shooter was nearby, Hunter would make him move so he wouldn't wake Tessa. Time to see if the gray who broke into her home was wandering around outside at this hour also.

Careful not to wake Tessa, Hunter climbed out of bed, covered her up, observed her hair splayed across the pillow, her lashes twitching, her alluring lips parted slightly, inviting another kiss. He took a deep, settling breath. A mermaid from the sea, and just as alluring. He groaned to himself, seized Michael's shoes and sweatshirt, and hurried from the bedroom.

He thought of changing by the shed, but he couldn't risk Tessa catching him shapeshifting. With Michael's field jacket and gloves tucked under his arm, he found a plastic garbage bag to stick them in to keep them dry while he searched for the gray in his wolf form.

At least it seemed like a good strategy. But the way things were going for him lately…

He'd had enough bad luck to last him at least one human's lifetime.

In the middle of the night, the sound of gunfire in the distance woke Tessa. She jerked her head around and stared at the empty bed. *No Hunter.* Her heart raced and she practically flew off the mattress. Grabbing the lantern from the bathroom, she hurried down the hall. "Hunter?"

No answer.

She half-expected him to be asleep on the couch because she'd been tossing and turning so much, her usual mode of sleep since her brother had been incarcerated.

"Hunter?" She peered into the living room.

No sign of him. She headed back down the hall to the guest bedroom. He wasn't there either. Michael's bedroom would be way too cold.

Where was he?

Another shot rang out.

It was January and no one should be hunting big game along the coast, and not this early in the morning for game bird hunting either. Two more shots were fired. Then silence. She barely breathed.

Michael's field jacket was gone, so were his gloves and her ski hat.

"Hunter," she said under her breath.

The back door jerked open, and she squealed. Hunter frowned at her as he stalked inside with an armload of wood. "You should be sleeping."

"It's the middle of the night. Didn't you hear that maniac shooting out there? He shouldn't be hunting, but what if you'd gotten in his line of sight? What if he was a poacher?"

Hunter dumped the firewood on the dwindling stack, yanked off the gloves, and her hat. "Four more hours until it's daylight. Electricity is still off."

She relocked the back door. "Hope that idiot hunter doesn't shoot anymore. I hate it when they come into the area."

He looked in the direction the gunshots had been coming from and shrugged. "He probably ran out of bullets."

"Like they ever do."

"Miss me?"

She rolled her eyes as they returned to the bedroom. "The gunshots woke me."

He reached up and massaged the tension from her shoulders. Man, did his fingers work magic on her tension-filled muscles—she felt like dissolving into the carpet.

"Then after you woke, you missed me. Admit it.

Having me warm your bed hasn't been so bad after all, has it?"

She *hmpf*ed. "Now you're icy and will make the bed cold." She climbed under the covers while he slipped the field jacket off his shoulders, and then stripped out of the sweatshirt.

He reached for the sweatpants, then seeing her mouth drop and probably thinking better of it, he joined her in bed still wearing them. "You're right. I'm cold. I promise I won't do anything you don't want. I'm… *gay*, remember?" He gave her a devious smirk. "Just come over here and warm me. I gathered enough firewood to keep us toasty for most of the day, didn't I?"

Although a hint of pleading was evident in his tone of voice, his words were still more of a command.

She knew this was a very bad idea. But she always seemed to be helping others. Why not get something good out of the experience, even if it didn't last? He was the kind of guy that wouldn't stay in a long-term relationship, she would bet. One minute, he would be there for her, and the next, gone. Especially once he learned who he was and where he belonged. Probably had a good paying job, certainly a family, and a home somewhere. But heck, as long as she didn't get stuck on the guy, what did it matter if they warmed each other for the rest of the morning?

As macho as he was, she expected him to join her, but maybe he was too honorable, waiting to make sure it was okay with her. She sighed and moved close to him. His cold feet left an icy imprint on the back of her legs where her pajamas had drawn up, and she swore under her breath. "Damn, Hunter, your feet are ice cold, and now I'll never get warm."

He chuckled low and pulled her into his heated embrace. And she did warm up, way too much, but he seemed honor-bound. Maybe because he was concerned he still had a wife or fiancée or special woman in his life. Too bad. She sure could get used to a guy like this. Once she'd returned home after college, pickings had been slim. Rourke, the reporter, wanted to renew old acquaintances, but he was the last one she'd want to be stuck with on a desert island. The sheriff's son, one of Michael's best friends, was another, but those were the only two single men she knew still living in town after finishing high school who were close to her age. Everyone was eons older, younger, or married. But, Hunter, although she wasn't sure about his age, seemed perfect.

His warm breath teased the back of her head and his arms wrapped around her in a loving embrace. His erection stiffened against her back, and she sighed. Too bad he didn't know who he was. If he wasn't hooked up with anyone, they could have had a nice fling not that she was into that sort of thing, but with someone as hot as him—why not? It was about time she let loose, had some fun, and did something for herself for a change.

Hunter kept Tessa still. He had never known a woman who tossed and turned so much in bed. At least, he didn't remember anyone like that. What night terrors was she dealing with? After she had beat on him, the only way he was returning to bed with her was to hold her tight, give her solace, and keep her from kicking and hitting him any further.

At least the hunter wouldn't be shooting any more for a while. Not until he purchased a new rifle and found another location to hunt in. If Hunter hadn't needed to remain in hiding for the time being, he would have turned the bastard in for attempted murder. He hoped Tessa wouldn't see the hole in her ski cap and question him about it.

How would he explain how he could run faster than a normal human being? He was just fortunate the second bullet had only grazed his upper arm. He'd even forgotten about it when he pulled the sweatshirt off, but thankfully, she didn't see the wound the way he was turned slightly away from her toward the dark. With any luck, she wouldn't see the bloody mess before it healed.

The man swore he thought Hunter was a black bear attacking him. As if Hunter looked anything like a bear. At least, the maniac's rifle wouldn't do him any good, even if it survived striking the rocks below and landing in the ocean. The only thing Hunter regretted was the fact he had littered.

He took a deep breath of Tessa's scent, knowing he shouldn't. When he shared one-night stands with lonely human females, that he recalled, he kept it strictly business, pleasuring them, and experiencing the joy it brought him. But he never attempted to memorize their scents, or make anything of the relationships, like two clouds passing each other in the night, barely touching, and then disappearing.

He was already too wrapped up in worrying about Tessa, her brother, and the gray *lupus garou* who had set his sights on her.

He brushed one of Tessa's curls tickling his cheek away and grunted when the bullet wound sent a shard of pain through his arm.

Tessa stirred. "Are you hurting a lot?" She reached over and touched his arm and felt the moisture. "My god, Hunter. What..." She stared at the blood tingeing her fingertips in the lantern's soft glow from the bathroom. "You've been shot."

"It's not anything," he said, frowning. Leave it to a human female to make a big deal out of nothing.

"You're bleeding." Her face contorted with worry. She pulled out of his grasp, climbed out of bed, and rushed to the bathroom. After opening and shutting several drawers, she returned with gauze and tape. "Is the bullet embedded?"

Ah hell, he hadn't wanted her to see the evidence, or worry her. "Just grazed the skin, really, Tessa. No big deal."

"You need to charge him with attempted murder. He shouldn't be allowed to get away with this. Why didn't you tell me you were hurt? No, I'll tell you. You're too macho to let me know, damn it."

He hid a grin. Her alpha posturing triggered his primal craving for her all over again.

She wiped away the blood, but it pooled up more. She clamped the gauze on it and the frown returned to her brow. "Hold this while I cut the tape. So what happened exactly?"

"I was gathering firewood. I guess he thought I was a new species of game bird."

"He wasn't supposed to be shooting in the middle of the night." She finished taping the gauze to the wound. "Are you really all right? Have you had a recent tetanus shot?"

"Yes, to both."

She stared at him for a second, her look concerned again, and touched his arm, a jolt of electricity heating his blood. "I can't afford to lose you before you help me find Bethany's killer."

He raised a brow. "And here I thought you had a hankering for me."

"*Humpf.*" She jerked Michael's sweatshirt off the floor and waved it at Hunter, her face stern, but he could see she was half-teasing. "You're only borrowing my brother's clothes. I expected you'd give them back in the same shape you received them."

"I'll try to run faster next time."

She shook her head. "I can't imagine you running from anyone."

She had that right.

She returned to the bathroom and rinsed the blood out in the sink, and then the shower curtain rings slid across the rod. A dripping sound in the bathtub followed that.

When she climbed back into bed, Hunter leaned down, kissed the top of her head, breathed in her heady sweet scent, and pulled her into his arms. And wished he could have her, that she was one of his kind, and she'd want him in return.

"I'll try not to get any more of his things shot up. And when I'm able, I'll buy him replacements. Sleep, Tessa. Or we'll have to take a nap in the middle of the day to make up for not sleeping half the night."

"You have to report this to the sheriff's office."

"The shooter said he would."

She turned and stared at Hunter. "You talked to him?"

He tightened his hold on her, keeping her soft body pressed against his chest, her bottom seated provocatively against his arousal. "Don't worry about it," he said, his voice growing ragged with need. "It has nothing to do with you."

"He shot you on my property so it has everything to do with me. What did he say? That he was going to report how he'd shot you?"

"More like that he was going to tell the sheriff how I destroyed his brand-new rifle."

Her eyes grew even bigger, the blue specks highlighting the green gems. "What… what did he look like?"

"He said I stole Michael's clothes. He had shoulder-length blond hair, stood a little shorter than me, talked big, but was shaking in his boots."

"Ashton Wellington."

"Who?"

"The sheriff's son and Michael's best friend. *Great.* His father can be a real pain in the butt when it comes to protecting his son."

"I wouldn't worry about it too much." He wrapped a curl of hair around his finger and examined the color and texture. "After all, the guy shot me, not the other way around."

"Yeah, but you destroyed his gun." She frowned at Hunter. "How?"

"I tossed it in the ocean. Figured he'd wake you up, and he shouldn't have been shooting that close to your house anyway."

She groaned and hugged his arms wrapped around

her chest, drawing him into her silky embrace, making his blood sizzle—*siren.*

"Expect the sheriff's visit early in the morning," she warned.

He nuzzled his face in her hair, smelled the fragrant peach scent, wanted to lick every inch of her skin to see if she tasted just as sweet. "What role do you want me to play?"

"Cousin from back east. You're staying with me until we clear Michael of his crime."

His hand stilled on her hair. "Gay cousin?"

She snorted. "Like anyone would believe that."

He smiled and rubbed her arm with a slow, stroking caress. "Good. Not that I care much for being a cousin either, too easy to get caught up in a lie."

"What then? My lover?"

He chuckled darkly. "Works for me."

Chapter 4

Early the next morning before Tessa woke, Hunter searched through her house for any reason a *lupus garou* would have specifically targeted her other than the fact her pheromones undoubtedly had something do with attracting him and soon found something he couldn't comprehend. Wolf pictures filled three desk drawers in the guest bedroom. Since *lupus garou* wolves looked just like regular wolves, he couldn't tell if they were real wild wolves, or his kind. Not unless he could smell them. Against a wall, shelves housed several books on wolf behavior also.

But why she'd have tons of photos and books on them, and why her scent attracted him to such an arousing degree—

A sepia photo half-hidden by the wolf pictures caught his attention, and he pulled it out. "*Seth.*"

Sitting next to a woman with a baby on her lap, Seth appeared more youthful than Hunter remembered him, his handlebar mustache curled high, his pale eyes as serious as the rest of the expression on his face. Hunter recalled seeing him in a photo panning for gold in California with his great-grandfather and great uncle, the three of them the best of friends. But he didn't remember Seth having a mate before a rockslide had taken his life.

Hunter glanced at the back of the photo. No identification. Why would Tessa have a photo of him? And how come Hunter remembered who Seth was, when nothing else was clear?

In the closet, Hunter found a bunch of half-finished paintings, the focal point of the pictures, wolves—gray, red, Arctic.

He frowned. Maybe Tessa's brother used the wolf photos to create the paintings. But why not finish them? Why hide them away?

Tessa stirred in her bed in the master bedroom. Hunter shut the closet door and left the guest bedroom to make the fire and start breakfast, but he had a lot of questions to ask the little lady.

When Hunter's arms had been wrapped tightly around her, Tessa felt warmer and more secure than she had in months—since the time the sheriff told her that her brother was suspected of murder.

Except for Hunter nuzzling his face in her hair in the middle of the night, and rubbing his cheek on her shoulder another time, he hadn't made any overtures that amounted to wanting something further. Probably because he didn't know if he had a significant other, which made her appreciate him even more.

After finding her father making out with different women on three occasions at home when her mother was gone, Tessa didn't think any man could be faithful. Well, maybe she did. For a while. Until she began dating and then she knew the truth. Most men she'd known didn't care who they were with as long as the woman agreed to have sex.

Hunter's warm embrace had been comforting, and

Tessa wanted to bask in the feel of him, the masculine smell of him, the heat of his body all night long, but she finally had fallen into a deep slumber.

When she fully awoke, she wasn't surprised to find Hunter making eggs, sausages, biscuits, and coffee over the fire. Another load of wood was stacked neatly on the log rack. He seemed at home under the circumstances, which again made her wonder if he was an undercover operative or a Navy SEAL or something.

Navy SEAL. She snorted. Yeah, that nearly drowned in the Pacific.

Part of her hoped he'd remembered something about his former life, mainly that he wasn't attached to anyone. But part of her was afraid he would recall too much, and he would leave her for his old life pronto. Right now, she needed him, if nothing more than for moral support, well, and protection.

If someone had tried to kill him, she had no doubt he would want to square things with the person also. She still couldn't believe Ashton Wellington had shot him.

"Morning. I'll get dressed and be right back," Tessa said.

"Morning." Hunter's masculine voice heated her through and through, his eyes capturing hers.

She smiled. "You're a sight for sore eyes." Cliché, right. But god, he was—crouching before the fire, an elusive smile on his lips, his windswept hair curled about his shoulders, a shadow of a beard darkening his square jaw, a look of seduction as the fire flickered in his eyes.

"Ditto, Tessa."

She waved in the direction of the bedroom. "I'll be right back." Yet she didn't want to leave. Never before had she wanted to be with a man 24/7. It wasn't that she felt like moss that clung to a stone, rather, she just enjoyed his company—a little too much.

In the bedroom, she slipped into a pair of jeans and a red turtleneck and sweater, then threw on a pair of warm knee-high socks and suede slipper boots. After washing her face in the icy water in the bathroom, she applied foundation, darkened her red lashes, and brushed her hair. She stared at the sink. Hopefully, the pipes wouldn't freeze.

She glanced at her brother's sweatshirt hanging in the shower, the hole visible.

Ashton was the reason her brother had gotten into so much trouble over the years. The sheriff always said Michael was the instigator. But he wasn't. Michael was a born follower, Ashton, always the leader. So it didn't surprise her he would pull something like this. Well, maybe a little. She didn't think he'd do something so dangerous. What in the world had gotten into him? Drinking. Maybe. He could get crazy then—as she well knew.

She padded down the hall into the living room where Hunter still hovered over the fireplace. He seemed so contemplative as he flipped the eggs and sausages, she didn't want to disturb him, but he turned and smiled. The look was more smug than sweet, almost as if he had known she'd been quietly observing him.

"I hope you don't mind." He served up the eggs.

She laughed a little under her breath. "What woman would complain? If Michael had ever made breakfast before I got my lazy bones out of bed, I would have been elated. And in shock."

Hunter would make some woman a darned good husband. But he seemed more like a mountain man, rugged, capable of living alone in the wilderness, yet he had a wonderful tender touch, too. He was perfect. If he wasn't already attached.

He handed her a plate. "I found some planks to board up the window, but wanted to wait until you were awake before I began banging around."

"Oh. Great. Thanks. I'll help you."

His expression said he didn't need assistance, but she owed him and she wasn't about to let him do all that work himself.

They took their meals to the dining table and sat down.

"It's still sleeting, a stalled storm front. I can manage without your help."

She raised her brows. "I bet you tell all your girlfriends that."

The forkful of eggs stopped midway to his mouth and his lips turned up a little, his amber eyes reflecting amusement.

"We're playing the part of lovers, remember?"

"Ah. I wasn't sure we'd agreed on that. I imagine people in this community might find that hard to believe."

She took a sip of her coffee. "You're right. They would, so when the sheriff comes, he'll be our first test subject."

"Not sure he'll make it in this weather. I'm surprised his son was able to get here."

"Or the intruder." Tessa set her mug down, a lump lodged in her throat. "I never considered it before, but what if Ashton was the person who broke in? He was in the area, could have gotten a key from Michael—he'd been at the house plenty of times—and it would explain why he was still out here."

"What is Ashton's relationship with you?" Hunter asked, super casual-like, but the undercurrent of edginess to his voice couldn't be missed.

And why not? The bastard had shot him. "I'm Michael's *annoying* sister."

He looked skeptical. "Ashton appeared to be close to your age. Are you sure there's not something more to it than that?"

"We're both twenty-three. Went to high school together. Michael met Ashton at a town fireworks display. My brother is two years younger and always looked up to Ashton. So no, Ashton has never shown any interest in me. He's been in all kinds of trouble ever since we were kids. Senior high pranks, junior high pranks. You name it, he was always the ringleader. His dad was a police officer, then deputy sheriff until he was elected sheriff. He always covered for Ashton and blamed Michael for leading his son astray."

"Hmm, so then I must have led him astray last night when he shot at me."

"Shot you," she corrected, her voice bitter. "Even if the bullet only grazed you, he still shot you." That's when she caught a glimpse of her ski cap… and the hole. "What… what happened to my hat?"

Hunter shrugged and finished his eggs.

Her heart raced lickety-split. "He didn't shoot at you twice, did he?"

"He missed me the one time, Tessa. Don't worry about it. I'm sure we have an understanding now."

"Ohmigod, he could have killed you! You *have* to tell the sheriff."

The expression on Hunter's face indicated it was no big deal, and he wasn't mentioning it.

"All right, fine. I'll tell him." She jerked their dirty plates off the table. "The sheriff won't be able to use my brother as a scapegoat for his son's actions any longer."

"Let me handle this, Tessa." He leaned back in the chair, his expression serious. "Not to change the subject, but I was looking for a phone book, to see if I recognized any names or addresses. Didn't find one, although I came across a bunch of wolf photos in the desk drawer in your guest room."

Tessa's heart hitched. How could she explain how she and her brother were incurably obsessed with wolves? She shrugged, then rinsed the plates.

He took a deep breath, studying her, as if he was trying to catch her in a lie. Of course, she only felt that way because she was trying to hide her reaction.

"I saw the paintings Michael did, too. Wonderful job. So where were the pictures taken?"

"At wolf reserves or zoos. Michael and I do a fair amount of traveling so we can paint or photograph what we need to." She stuck the dishes into the dishwasher.

"Ah. And the books on wolf behavior?"

She hesitated, and cleared her throat, hating the way her hands had grown clammy. Hunter probably had some hang-ups, too, so what was the big deal? "Some good wolf photos in them."

"For Michael's paintings."

"Yes." She wanted to see Hunter's expression, but she busied herself with scrubbing the cooking pan. Did he believe her? She didn't think she sounded believable. And she didn't think he sounded like he was convinced.

"What about the old-photo with the guy and the woman and baby?"

She glanced back at him. "What?"

He was so coolly noncommittal, it was almost as though he was hiding his own emotions. Which didn't make any sense. "It was with the wolf pictures. Caught my eye because it was sepia, and I wondered if it was an old-time photo of a wolf. So it seemed out of place with the others. Who's the family pictured?"

Why would he ask? She didn't know any guy who was interested in genealogy. "My great-grandfather, great-grandmother, and grandmother."

Unblinking, he stared at her.

"You seem a little surprised."

Hunter joined her at the sink and massaged her shoulders with deep, comforting strokes and she relaxed.

"I thought he looked like someone my great-grandfather panned for gold with. But I must be mistaken."

"Do you have a photo of them?"

"Only of Seth Greystoke and my great-grandfather, but the photo's gone—lost in a fire. But he couldn't have been your relation." Hunter straightened. "About this situation with the sheriff, *I'll* take care of this, man to man." The dark threat to his voice indicated he meant it.

She wouldn't want to be on the receiving end of Hunter and the sheriff's confrontation. She relaxed a little. "My great-grandfather's name was Jeremiah Cramer. So you're right about them not being the same man. As far as the sheriff goes, if you don't tell him everything, *I will.* Had Ashton been drinking?"

"No." Hunter gave her shoulders a warm squeeze and headed for the living room.

"Wait! Where are you going?"

"To board up the window." He tossed on Michael's field jacket, the ski cap, and gloves and was gone.

The frying pan could wait. She rushed to get her snow boots, parka, and gloves on. Why in the world would Ashton have shot at Hunter *twice* if he'd been sober? Was he the one who was seeing Bethany behind Michael's back? He had plenty of opportunities and motive, jealous that he couldn't get a girl like Michael could and that her brother had become so popular because of his artwork.

Tessa hurried outside to help Hunter, when she saw a figure dressed in a gray parka trudging and slipping along the winding road headed in their direction. She stared at him, trying to make out who the familiar figure was.

Hunter cast a glance in the man's direction. "You sure have a lot of visitors way out here as isolated as it is and as bad as the weather has gotten."

He began pounding a plank over the broken window.

"It's not—oh, hell, it's Rourke."

Hunter paused and looked at her. "Rourke?"

"The newspaper reporter."

Hunter raised a brow.

"An old boyfriend from high school."

"From high school." He pounded another piece of wood in place.

Tessa grabbed the next board for him. "He's looking

into Michael's claim someone else was seeing Bethany. At least if he wants dinner with me, he will."

"A date." He took the plank from her and nailed it up.

"I told him to use his investigative skills and find out something useful concerning Michael's innocence."

He stopped and studied her. "So he believes Michael's innocent?"

"No. He just wants dinner."

Hunter smiled, but quickly masked the expression and took the next board from her.

She frowned at him. "I'm not interested in Rourke."

"He's simply a means to an end."

"Right."

"Ho!" Rourke hollered from a distance after picking himself up from the roadway a second time.

"Hey, Rourke! What brings you way out here?" Not wanting to get her hopes up too much, she prayed he'd found something that would help her brother's case.

His cheeks red, Rourke drew closer and wiped his runny nose on a handkerchief. He gave Hunter a long, hard look, although Hunter continued nailing up boards and didn't spare Rourke another glance.

"I worried about you being alone in this ice storm. An eighteen-wheeler plowed into an electric transformer. I tried calling, but ice storms brought the phone lines down. I see you had some storm damage." He looked around. "Good thing you were able to hire a handyman to board up the window this quickly. Guess someone dropped him off."

"Where's your pickup?" Tessa asked, not wanting to explain who Hunter was when she wasn't even sure herself.

Besides, if Rourke knew the story, he would propose taking Hunter into town to see the doctor and get him away from her, then where would she be? Probably Rourke would offer to stay with her in Hunter's place, as if he could be the kind of help Hunter was. She imagined Rourke had never cooked anything over an open fire for one. And replace a window? Never. He'd offer to keep her warm during the night, but she wasn't interested in him like that.

"My truck's up that way." Rourke waved in the direction, and then looked Hunter over really good. "Slid off the road and couldn't get any traction. Figured since you were alone, I'd stay with you until the ice melted."

How could she say no, if he was stuck? But she still didn't want to explain Hunter.

"*I'll* help you get on your way." Hunter's voice was low and gruff.

Rourke was sure to not like Hunter's suggestion. He raised his brows, and then turned to Tessa. "Let's go inside. I'm chilled to the bone. I see you have a fire going."

Tessa looked back at Hunter. He still needed to nail up three more boards.

"I'll manage," he said to her.

She waffled. She'd promised to help, but she didn't want reporter Rourke snooping through her things if she told him to go inside and get warmed by the fire while she helped Hunter.

He cast her a glance. "I'm nearly done. Go, Tessa. I'll be inside in a minute for another cup of hot coffee. If you wouldn't mind making us some more."

Rourke glowered at Hunter.

"All right," she said to Lord Hunter. She felt she

should be curtseying to him. Handyman, hell. He was the rooster that ruled the henhouse. *Her* henhouse.

"You know, Tessa," Rourke said, as he escorted her to the front door, his hand on the small of her back, "you let people walk all over you too much. Take the hired hand, for instance, he should be doing the job you're paying him, and *you* shouldn't be in this awful weather helping him."

She thought she heard Hunter growl when Rourke touched her, and she could have strangled Rourke for speaking loudly enough for Hunter to hear.

"I don't like it," Rourke continued, as he walked inside with Tessa and shut the door. "You're by yourself and the company this guy works for just let him off at your place? What if he's some kind of criminal? You never know who these companies hire. He could be on a prison work release program."

Tessa swore Hunter was pounding the nails into the boards twice as fast as before while she warmed up by the fire and peeled off her gloves. "Did you find anything concerning Michael's case that will help?"

Rourke removed his gloves and shoved them in his coat pockets, and then pulled off his wet parka in front of the fireplace. "Yeah, but it doesn't go any further than this room."

Her heart skipped to overdrive to hear Rourke's news.

He handed her his coat and rubbed his hands over the fire. Even in this weather, he was dressed in one of his impeccable gray suits. At least he was wearing sensible snow boots for the icy conditions. "Bethany was seeing some other guy."

Her heart nearly stopped. Maybe finally the break they needed. "I knew it. Who was he?"

"You won't tell anyone else, right?"

Hunter opened the door and looked from Rourke to Tessa. "Coffee ready?"

Jeez, Hunter, not now!

"Who was Bethany seeing, Rourke?" She hoped he wouldn't clam up with Hunter listening in.

Rourke's expression turned blank, and he shifted his attention to the fire. He shrugged. "The DA's office proved no one was seeing her."

Tessa could have shaken him and screamed bloody murder.

"Nice suit," Hunter said to Rourke, and then gave Tessa a knowing look. "On second thought, I'll check on your truck and see if I can move it." He headed back outside.

She hung up Rourke's coat and her own, and then set the pot of water on the fire, anything to busy herself so she wouldn't hurt Rourke. "Who was it?"

"Who is that guy? He doesn't act like a handyman."

"Rourke, who was seeing Bethany besides Michael?"

"I said too much already. It doesn't matter. What's done is done. You'll never be able to prove Michael didn't murder her."

"Who… was… seeing… her?"

"The sheriff's son. But it can't leave this room, Tessa. I swear it."

Ohmigod, she knew it. Her bones dissolving, she collapsed on the couch.

"Are you okay, Tessa? I probably shouldn't have mentioned it to you."

"No, no, I'm all right." As right as could be expected to know her brother's best friend could be the murderer. *Bastard.* And how would they prove it when his father was the sheriff?

"You promise you won't confront Ashton about this, right?"

"I'll hire someone really discreet to investigate it further."

Rourke sat next to her on the couch and patted her hand. "We can have dinner together now, right?"

Dinner? Sheesh, one track mind. But she promised. She pulled her hand away from him.

"Sure, but there's no electricity so it would have to be some other evening."

Like a couple of months from now. Her mind flipped through different scenarios, remembering all the times Ashton had been to the house, smiling and joking with Bethany and Michael. Why hadn't Tessa noticed what was really going on between Ashton and Bethany? Maybe she had, but she hadn't wanted to admit it to herself.

Rourke waved at the fireplace. "It sounds like the water's ready for the coffee."

Still in disbelief about Ashton, she gathered her composure and rose from the couch. But then again, Ashton could have murdered Hunter last night. And he had been hunting with a rifle since he was too young to do so. Not that Bethany was killed that way, but it could prove Ashton was capable of committing murder, couldn't it?

"So who's this guy really who was fixing your window?" Rourke asked.

Hunter stalked back inside, catching Rourke's question. "Tessa's lover," he said, with a smirk and the look of the devil sparkling in his eyes, his cheeks slightly red from the chill.

She could have socked him. Rourke's jaw couldn't have dropped any lower.

"Handyman, cook, personal masseur, whatever she needs me to be. So who else was Bethany seeing?"

Rourke turned slightly green.

"Who?" Hunter asked again, his voice threatening as he helped Tessa with the coffee mugs.

Rourke swallowed hard. "Ashton Wellington."

"Good. I drove your truck into the driveway. But why don't you stay with Tessa for an hour or so while I take a walk in the woods."

To investigate? Please, God, don't let Ashton be wandering in the woods armed again.

Rourke frowned and she knew it was because he didn't like Hunter ordering him about.

"As a favor to Tessa. I'll be searching for the stalker who's been breaking into her house."

"Stalker?" Rourke looked at Tessa.

"He stole my gun last night."

Rourke ran his hand through his wind-ruffled hair. "Sure, right."

Hunter quickly drank a cup of coffee, kissed Tessa on the cheek, and gave her a sexy smile. If Rourke hadn't been here, she would have snagged Hunter's arm and made him kiss her on the lips like he really meant it—like he had on the beach—only this time proving for real she hadn't dreamed it. As if he read her innermost thoughts, he raised his brows slightly, dimples appearing in his cheeks as his smile broadened, and her cheeks blossomed with heat. Not just her face though as the heat soon spread all the way to her toes.

He winked, *the cad*. "Be right back." Then he gave Rourke a quelling look as though he'd better behave where Tessa was concerned, and stalked outside. She prayed he wouldn't run into Ashton again.

Rourke looked from Hunter to Tessa and frowned. "Who the hell did you say he was?"

"Loser beta male," Hunter grumbled under his breath as he headed deeper into the woods, the branches dipping under the weight of the icicles clinging to the pine needles.

At least he didn't have to worry about Tessa's interest in the man. He could tell she could barely stomach the guy as a lover.

So maybe Hunter had it all wrong. If the intruder—the gray—was only after Tessa, maybe the sheriff's son did the killing. That would solve everything. All Hunter had to do was prove it. But at least once he did, Ashton would go to prison for the murder, Michael could go free, end of Tessa's problem. As for the gray—that's who he was hunting now.

He wondered too about the sepia picture of Seth and the woman and baby. Maybe it wasn't Seth. A werewolf couldn't have children with a human, and Tessa definitely wasn't a *lupus garou*. Or maybe the picture wasn't of her family like she thought. But why she would have it then—

Gunshots rang out across the woods. Crazy hunters. Hunters. *Hunter*. He paused, trying to recall the rest of his name. Nothing. *Damn it*. His borrowed snow boots crunched on the frozen ground as the coastal pines shielded him some from the sleet. If he had been in his wolf coat, no one would hear his approach. But for now, he wanted them to see him coming so they didn't shoot him by accident.

He narrowed the distance between him and the two shooters. The shorter, bearded one lowered his gun. "Hell, man, wearing a green field jacket makes you blend right in with the woods. You're supposed to be wearing orange so we don't shoot you."

"I'm not a hunter." At least not the kind that used bullets, and normally he preferred blending in with his surroundings no matter the form he took. He guessed it was natural, instinctive.

"Well, hell, if you don't watch out, you'll be one of the hunted."

"Why don't you move farther north?" The way Hunter proposed the question, there would be no doubt he'd issued an order.

"Why don't you mind your own business?" the taller of the two men said, sizing Hunter up.

Don't go there. Cool macho hunters. Tough guys. But neither was a match for him. Which made him wonder if a gang of thugs had gotten the better of him. Had to have—or else he wouldn't have taken a dip in the Pacific.

"Private property," Hunter said.

"Yeah, owned mostly by the timber companies," the bearded of the two men said.

"This land is privately owned. And you don't have permission."

The two men cast each other looks.

"We'll get permission and be back." The bearded man spit on the ground. "If you're still wandering through the woods, blending in like you do now..." He shrugged. "Wouldn't be our fault."

"Happen to be a good friend of the local sheriff's." Hunter gave him a steely-eyed glower—the same kind he would use during a wolf-to-wolf confrontation when he needed to make another back down, tuck tail, and leave. If that didn't work, he added, "Don't think you want to go there."

The two men seemed a little ruffled at the revelation, or maybe it was the look he gave them that changed their minds as the one stamped ice off his boot, and the other fidgeted with his rifle. They finally cursed under their breaths, but headed north.

"Find a place a good five miles—*at least*—from here to hunt," Hunter added.

They both glared at him and continued walking.

Hunter searched for clues to where the gray wolf had been, the trails he had taken, any evidence he had gotten into a vehicle that left tire tracks behind. Although as a wolf, the *lupus garou* could travel a great distance, his thick coat protecting him from the cold. Hunter located several paths the gray had walked, found where the agitated hunter had paced, snagged strands of gray fur on a couple of branches, rubbed his scent on several trees.

Was he a rogue or did he live with a pack? The fact he had a key to Tessa's place didn't fit. Was he someone she knew? Another one of Michael's friends? Or one of hers?

Not locating the intruder, Hunter assumed he was sleeping off his nighttime activities, and he would be back again tonight. What if Hunter moved Tessa somewhere else? Somewhere safe? But where? If he had a place, he could relocate her there. He didn't have a clue where it could be though.

"Hunter?" Tessa hollered from deep in the woods.

Hell. Didn't he tell her to stay with Rourke at the house? He hurried toward her voice.

"Hunter?"

"Coming!" Then he heard them. Two sets of footfalls. They had better be Rourke's and Tessa's.

When he saw them, the adrenaline rush began to drain off.

Rourke looked annoyed and out of breath.

Her frown fading, Tessa seemed guardedly relieved, her hair blowing in the breeze, her skin glowing with the cold, her full red lips pouting, begging to be kissed. "I was so worried about you. We heard the gunfire and I told Rourke how Ashton had shot you. We thought maybe he'd killed you this time."

"Take more than that to get rid of me. We couldn't have that now, could we? Not until I can at least locate Bethany's real murderer and put him behind bars." Hunter managed a smile as he wrapped his arm around Tessa and walked her back home.

She felt warm and soft and his thoughts shifted to dangerous notions of getting naked in bed with her. He attributed some of his feelings to wanting to claim her in front of her old high-school boyfriend. Some of his problem was just being attracted to the minx—more than he thought he'd ever been toward any woman, either human or *lupus garou*. He kept telling himself it was just because she'd rescued him from the beach, and it was nothing more than appreciating the tender care she'd given him. On the other hand, he might have often felt this way toward women. Hell, maybe he was a real Casanova.

"*He's* the guy you're hiring to look into this?" Rourke asked, his voice incredulous.

"Yeah. He's an *ex*–Navy SEAL." She looked up at Hunter with adoring eyes.

He thought she was playing her role a little too obviously.

"A Navy SEAL?" Rourke looked sick again.

"Yep." She patted Hunter's arm. "Can't you tell by the great shape he's in?"

"Why is he an *ex*–Navy SEAL?"

"He got tired of being away from home, the secret missions, unable to settle down and start a family, right, Hunter?"

Rourke watched them like an investigative reporter looking for another juicy story.

Hunter sighed deep inside. He didn't like making up tales that were too far from the truth, but then again, what if his cover of being an ex–Navy SEAL put the fear of God in the sheriff and his bad seed? It didn't hurt for Rourke to think so either. Hunter imagined the word would soon get out about his "former occupation" since Rourke was a reporter. Hmm, then he would probably investigate him. One good thing about being an undercover operative—Rourke couldn't learn anything.

"Hunter..." Rourke waited for a last name.

Hunter knew only that he was a gray *lupus garou*. Wolf? Grey?

Grey. That rang a bell. Not quite right, but it would do. "Grey. And we haven't been properly introduced."

Tessa's eyes widened as she stared at Hunter and she missed a step. He tightened his hold on her. Wishing he had better news, he gave her a subtle shake of his head, warning her he didn't know for sure.

"Rourke Thornburg," the reporter offered and stuck his hand out.

Hunter gave his hand a firm shake, firm enough to let him know the power behind the man.

Rourke's eyes watered and he quickly pulled his hand away. *Message received.*

Tessa pursed her lips. "Did you see the man who was shooting in the woods?"

"There were two of them. I told them to find game somewhere else, farther north."

"They must have loved you," Rourke said, chuckling.

"They didn't argue and moved along."

"Thanks," Tessa said. "But I don't expect you to chase off all the idiot hunters in the area and risk them shooting you accidentally."

"They're too close to your—" As soon as they came into view of the house, Hunter saw the back door standing wide open. He felt Tessa crumple slightly against him. Tightening his hold on her, he knew she wouldn't have left the house unlocked. The intruder was once again warning them he could come and go as he pleased. Maybe not such a beta after all.

Rourke's chill-bitten cheeks instantly lost their red color. "I saw you lock the door."

"Someone's got a key." Tessa's voice shook.

Hunter gave her a reassuring squeeze, but until he could eliminate the threat, nothing he did would alleviate her concern and for good reason. The stalker was a real danger.

Rourke rubbed his gloved hands. "Who?"

"We don't know. Ashton maybe. But whoever it was got in last night when I went to get firewood from the beach," she said.

"Ashton?" Rourke asked.

"No," Hunter said, not wanting Tessa to fear the wrong man. "Someone else. Wait here with Tessa. I'll check out the place first."

Tessa looked like she had a million questions to ask Hunter, but with Rourke here, the inquisition would have to wait. Hunter stalked inside, monitoring Rourke and Tessa's conversation as he checked the rooms.

"Why didn't you tell me about this?" Rourke asked Tessa on the porch, sheltered from the sleet and wind.

"Hunter was here. He can take care of it."

"Hunter was here all night?" Rourke asked, his tone not hiding his surprise or irritation.

Hunter couldn't help smiling, figuring Tessa hadn't meant to let it slip. Good to let Rourke know he had no chance with her.

"Good thing that he *was*."

Glad she felt he was an asset despite the fact he hadn't gotten rid of the stalker, Hunter smelled the bastard's scent where he had rolled on Tessa's sheets again. Hunter growled low.

"And the window he was boarding up?" Rourke asked Tessa.

"The intruder broke it."

"Hell, Tessa, you should never have said you were going to locate the killer and clear Michael's name."

Headed back down the hall, Hunter stopped in his footsteps, not believing Tessa would say that to a reporter. Then again, he could, as angry as he imagined she'd been.

"Did you print the interview?" she asked, her voice accusing.

"Damn right I did. Best news I've had in a long time. But I didn't think anyone else was guilty of the crime except your brother so I didn't believe there was anything to worry about. If I had thought differently, I would never have printed that story."

Hunter wanted to kill the reporter.

"All clear," Hunter said, rejoining them on the back patio. He gave both Tessa and Rourke a hard look. "Looks like nothing's been disturbed." At least as far as he would let Tessa know for now. The gray had returned to find out where Hunter had slept for the night and returned to mark his claim to Tessa. Sorry to disappoint him. "What's this about an interview?"

Tessa swore Hunter had the hearing of a cat, although she had hoped he hadn't heard what Rourke revealed about the interview. "I was angry." Not that she felt she had any need to explain the way she felt to Hunter.

Did he remember anything more about his past? She knew Grey wasn't his real name. Not if the way he had shaken his head at her earlier was any indication of the truth of the matter. She only wished Rourke would go away soon so she could ask Hunter what else he had recalled and why he was so certain the intruder wasn't Ashton.

A shiver crawled up her spine. She felt she could deal with knowing it was Ashton, but if it was a total stranger... No, it had to be someone she knew because he had a key. But still, not knowing who made it more frightening.

Rourke pulled off his wet coat and handed it to Tessa. "I'm staying for dinner."

Her mouth dropped. Now, she remembered why the guy had been an on-again/off-again boyfriend in her youth. He decided things for her, which were not in her best interests. She meant to remind him the electricity was off, but Hunter cut in.

"Sounds good. Why don't you stay the night, too?"

Tessa glared at Hunter. *Of all the damned nerve!*

Ignoring her threatening look, Hunter continued, "The roads are too slick. You might not get very much farther down the road and be in the same predicament. If you got injured, we wouldn't be able to forgive ourselves."

Her mouth gaped open. The thing was, Hunter was right. But whose house was it anyway? Shouldn't *she* have a say?

For the first time since the two men had met, Rourke seemed to change his attitude about Hunter. He gave him a serious nod. She could tell he was damned thrilled to get Lord Hunter's invitation for the slumber party.

She hung up Rourke's coat on a wooden peg near the back door. "You know, guys, it would be nice to ask the hostess her opinion. The electricity's still not on and—"

"I'll fix the food," Hunter said, and before she could object further, he added, "Rourke won't mind cleaning the dishes afterwards." He gave Rourke a conspirator's wink.

"Not at all," Rourke said, jumping in, ensuring he got a bed for the night.

"I might not have enough food to eat for the three of us, especially since we have to cook so primitively."

"I saw a tenderloin roast in the freezer. Looked to be big enough for the three of us."

She scowled at Hunter. "What if I was saving that for—"

"I'll buy you another. A couple more."

Hell, he didn't even have the clothes on his back. How was he going to replenish her fridge?

"I'll buy you another, too," Rourke said, cheerfully.

She groaned inwardly. She wasn't winning this battle. But she realized Hunter wasn't worried about Rourke's welfare, so much as he was about hers. Her irritation melted some.

"So," Rourke said, taking a seat on the couch, "I'm an only child, Tessa has a brother. What about you, Hunter? Have any siblings?"

Hunter cast Tessa a look, and then started working on building up the dwindling fire. "A sister."

Ohmigod, he remembered who he was? Maybe he did have enough money to buy her another roast. But did he have a girlfriend or wife?

"I've never seen you around town before. Where did the two of you hook up?"

"The beach," both Hunter and Tessa said at the same time.

Rourke laughed. "Figures, being he's a Navy SEAL. *Ex*–Navy SEAL, rather."

"That's what I thought," Tessa said, under her breath. Having Rourke stay the evening when it was barely afternoon was going to make for an incredibly long day and night. "I suppose I have to feed everyone lunch also."

"How about tuna fish sandwiches?" Hunter suggested.

Jeez, when did he take an inventory of her food?

"Then you can make a list of all the men who have been in the house over the last few months."

"You mean Michael's friends," she said, spearing Hunter a dark look.

"Any male, Tessa, who has been in the house for the last few months. Deliverymen, repairmen, anyone."

"Old boyfriends," she said, sarcastically as she proceeded to the kitchen.

"Yeah, all of those, too."

"None of them should have had a key to the place." She yanked two cans of tuna fish out of the cabinet.

The doorbell rang and her heart hitched. Rourke announced, "Sheriff's here."

Tessa accidentally dropped the can opener on the kitchen floor and swore under her breath. She'd hoped the bad weather would keep him at bay a while longer.

She hurried into the living room, but Hunter was already nose to nose with the sheriff at the front door.

Chapter 5

HUNTER GLOWERED EVERY BIT AS FEROCIOUSLY AT THE sheriff as he did back, but he couldn't quit thinking about Tessa and her interview with that jackass reporter. How could Rourke have printed her threat? What an imbecile.

Rourke was pretty rattled—he'd used her interview and now someone had broken into her house. Too late for regrets. The damage was done.

"I'm Sheriff Wellington," the man said, who looked like an older version of Ashton, same blond hair, only his was graying at the temples, and the same blue eyes. "You're the one who destroyed my son's rifle?"

"Ashton must have been mistaken, Sheriff. After he shot me, he was so shaken that he might have killed me, he dropped the rifle over the cliff side. It's probably still there, if anyone wants to chance climbing down to get it." Although Hunter had thrown it far enough, the rifle butt cracked on the rocks, and then the weapon flipped into the briny sea.

The sheriff glanced at Tessa with murder in his eyes. Hunter steeled his back, fighting the urge to show the sheriff how much he didn't like his posturing. But then the sheriff caught sight of Rourke. His gaze quickly shifted to the truck parked out front. Recognition dawning? Yep, reporter here looking for another story.

"He didn't shoot you." The sheriff's voice was so harsh, he sounded like a *lupus garou* trying to persuade another of his mistake.

Hunter couldn't help but admire that aspect of him. Definitely alpha material. Hunter reached for his sweatshirt sleeve and intended to yank it up, but the sheriff raised his hand and stopped him.

"All right, let's say it happened like you said. What were you doing wandering around in the dark?"

Like that was a crime? He wanted to tell the sheriff it was none of his business and would have if he'd been on his own property. But since he didn't know where his own property was located, he acquiesced.

"Gathering firewood." Hunter motioned to the fireplace. "That's our only source of heat for the moment. Hadn't planned on letting us freeze to death. And I didn't expect to get shot in Tessa's backyard." He raised a brow.

"Ashton said you charged him."

Hunter smiled inwardly. Yeah, he had. Like a wolf with a mission. Hunter lifted a shoulder. "He shot at me twice. I got closer so he could see I wasn't game."

Tessa raised her ski cap off the coffee table and poked her finger in the hole. Seeing the way she did it, made him think of things he shouldn't be thinking.

"I'd say Hunter could press charges against Ashton for attempted murder," Tessa said, her expression indignant. "If he'd managed to hit Hunter in the head, it would have been murder. With the lines down and my Escort unable to navigate in the icy conditions, we would never have been able to get help for him."

The sheriff's eyes bulged. He rubbed his chin and looked like he'd finally been put in his place. "Who the hell *are* you?"

"Hunter Grey, Tessa's boyfriend. Tell Ashton to hunt somewhere else from now on."

The sheriff narrowed his eyes and looked like he could shoot Hunter himself for telling him what to do, especially concerning his son. "If you're Tessa's boyfriend, why weren't you at the trial, giving her moral support?"

"He's been away," Tessa said. "Just got in late yesterday afternoon."

He glanced back at Rourke, then warned Hunter, "Watch yourself. The community's had enough bad publicity over Michael's criminal activities. Don't let me hear that you're causing any more trouble."

Hunter wanted to retort that as long as he didn't keep Ashton's company, he would be fine, but he kept his mouth shut.

"Hunter's a celebrity," Rourke proudly exclaimed, his chest puffed up twice its size.

All eyes turned toward him.

He raised his brows and smiled like he had the greatest news of the century. "He's an ex–Navy SEAL. You probably noticed the great shape he's in."

The sheriff's narrowed eyes grew rounder.

Rourke nodded. "Yep, a real celebrity in our sleepy little community."

Her expression still fierce, Tessa motioned to the sheriff. "Tell him about the intruder."

Hunter hadn't planned to mention the gray. *He* would take care of the *lupus garou*. But he didn't have much choice now. "The guy broke into Tessa's place twice and knocked out Michael's window the one time."

"You're not suggesting—"

Hunter shook his head. "No, Sheriff. A man broke in, but it wasn't Ashton."

Tessa folded her arms. "The guy stole my gun."

"File a report at the office when you have time." The sheriff gave Hunter a warning look. "Heed what I say, Mr. Grey. Watch your step. I keep a safe district."

Right. That's why Michael is in jail, the killer is on the loose, your son is shooting innocent people in the middle of the night, and someone's stalking Tessa.

"Did you know Bethany Wade was your son's lover behind Michael's back?" Hunter asked casually, watching to see the effect the news had on him. Did the sheriff already know? Or was he as clueless as everyone else?

Rourke's skin turned colorless. Tessa appeared just as pale. The sheriff's expression grew crimson, and he looked like his head was ready to explode. Hunter wasn't sure if that meant the sheriff knew or not. To his credit, the sheriff didn't say anything, whipped around, stalked off down the walk toward the patrol car, slipped on the ice, landed spread eagle, and swore a few choice words. Hunter smiled and closed the door only to face Rourke and Tessa's angry expressions.

"What? It's true, isn't it? He needs to be aware his son isn't the angel he appears to be. *If* he even appears to be that."

Tessa groaned. "You just made an enemy of the only man in the county who can make your stay—and mine—a living hell."

Rourke ran his hands through his hair and collapsed on the sofa. "You've really done it now."

"Good thing you were here, Rourke. I'm sure the sheriff would have made more of a scene otherwise," Tessa said.

"Thanks. I think. You should've told the sheriff you were a Navy SEAL, Hunter." Rourke gave him a devious smile. "He listens to that kind of talk. Set him back a peg or two. If he thought he could bully you, he lost his nerve."

"Yeah, but according to the rumor mill, the sheriff's known to hire ex-cons to get his point across," Tessa warned.

"Maybe we should hang a sign out that says ex–Navy SEAL lives here." Hunter feigned annoyance as he headed into the kitchen.

"Hey, I imagine you're used to keeping your former occupation secret, but for now, I'd say it could save your ass." Rourke followed him into the kitchen and cast him a warm grin, as if he was honored to be on Hunter's good side.

"Can't hurt. The sheriff will tell Ashton for sure. He won't want his only son getting hurt if Ashton thought to mess with you again," Tessa agreed.

Hunter opened one of the cans of tuna fish on the kitchen counter.

"Oh, for heaven's sakes, let me do that. I can at least make lunch." She pulled a jar of mayonnaise out of the fridge.

"At least if he calls in heavy muscle, they won't want to mess with an ex–Navy SEAL either." Rourke grabbed the jug of milk from the fridge.

"Unless they have something to prove. Badge of honor, best one of the government's finest," Tessa warned.

Hunter leaned against the counter and watched Tessa poke a butter knife into the mayonnaise jar. Her hips wiggled slightly as she worked on the sandwiches, which made his body tighten with need.

Attempting to get his mind off her sweet ass, he thought about his supposed Navy SEAL training. He had learned a few maneuvers over the centuries that could help him deal with just about any scenario, which he could pass off as Navy SEAL expertise. Some martial arts training, taught by some of the best, too. At least he thought that's where he learned all his lethal moves as a human. And why he remembered that but not his last name, he hadn't a clue.

Tessa finished making sandwiches and they sat down to eat, but all Hunter could think of was retiring to bed with her. The way she pushed her hair out of her face, licked her lips, smiled, raised her brows at him in question, made him want her all the more. Not that his wanting to go to bed with her only had to do with the craving he had for her—to get along in a human's world, *lupus garous* adjusted to daytime activities and slept part of the night, since they still participated in nighttime activities. Which meant naps during the day were often a necessity. But napping with her was even a greater necessity.

After they ate lunch, Hunter snagged Tessa's hand, the heat from her touch making him wish he knew whether he had a mate or not all over again. "Why don't you clean up, Rourke, while Tessa and I take a nap? We didn't sleep very well last evening. You can pull guard duty for now. I'll be staying up some of the night to watch for this guy's return. I figure he'll be lurking in the woods nearby."

Initially, Rourke looked annoyed that Hunter was taking Tessa to bed. But when Hunter mentioned guard duty, recognition reflected in Rourke's gray eyes and his expression turned to concern.

"All right?"

"Yeah, of course. I don't have all the training you do, but I'll think of something."

Hunter was pretty sure no one would mess with them during the day. "Just holler if anyone intrudes. I'll come running."

"Sure. I can do that."

Hunter stalked toward Tessa's bedroom, hauling her with him. Her hand tightened on his as she rushed to keep up with him.

"Are you in a hurry?" she asked, her words laced with amusement.

"I feel like a tired old dog. Don't you?"

"Speak for yourself. A sleepy cat maybe, but a tired old dog?" She smiled up at him, her sparkling green eyes and shiny red hair a tantalizing combination. "Never."

"A cat?" He chuckled, slipping his fingers through her silky strands. "Sounds like we could get into quite a tangle."

"Yeah, and I'd come out on top."

"On top? Not underneath?"

She rolled her eyes, but her cheeks turned crimson. "I meant as in winning."

When they walked into the bedroom, she stared at her floral sheets thrown in a bundle on the floor. "He did this?" she whispered.

Hunter had forgotten he had removed the sheets. "No. I did. I'm sorry, Tessa. I didn't want to mention it, but the bed smells like him."

Her eyes grew huge. "He got into my bed?"

"Do you have any other sheets?"

"Yeah. But he really got into my bed?"

"Yep, he did." *The bastard.*

She pulled out a fresh set of blue and white striped sheets from the linen cabinet, and Hunter helped her remake the bed. "Why would he do that?" she asked, her voice threaded with worry.

"He's a sick bastard."

She paused as they were pulling the blue velvet comforter back in place. "It's someone I know, isn't it?"

"Probably. But maybe not anyone you know well. He might be someone you met just once, but I believe he's fixated on you."

"A stalker?"

Worse. "Something like that."

"Great."

"I'll take care of him tonight." He yanked off the sweatshirt, and Tessa's eyes shifted to his bandaged arm. The wound felt like it had nearly healed, but the bandage sported dried blood so it looked worse than it was.

"I'd better change that bandage." She reached out to touch his arm.

He wrapped his hand around hers. "Come, sleep. I can't function properly tonight without getting more rest."

"How much do you remember about yourself?"

She looked so hopeful, he hated to disappoint her. "Just bits and pieces."

"You don't really remember your last name, do you?"

He shook his head and began pulling her turtleneck up, his desire to see more of her wreaking havoc with his need to keep his distance. Her smile was contagious and although he thought she might try to stop him, considering the way she'd been dressed the night before, she didn't.

"You don't remember if you're married or have a significant other?"

"No, sorry, Tessa. I wish I did, but those memories still elude me." However, he hoped that the fact he couldn't recall, meant he didn't have a mate.

Tessa's brows raised. Yeah, she was wondering where he was going with this. Not that he didn't wonder himself enough for the both of them. He stared at her white lace bra, her nipples darkened against the fabric, mesmerizing him.

She unbuckled her belt and slid her jeans down. Teasingly tiny, white lace bikini panties showed off a wealth of silky skin. Every inch kissable.

He wanted to take her right then and there. But he couldn't. Not until he knew for certain whether he was mated. Until that time, he was free to pleasure human women. But once he was mated with a *lupus garou*, the bond was for a lifetime. No divorce. No ending the mating unless one of them died.

He pulled Tessa into bed, determined to bury his lustful intentions until he knew for certain whether he was attached or not. Covering them with her comforter, he held Tessa tight, her back against his chest, breathed in the smell of the wind in her hair, the fragrant scent of her skin, her soft heat captivating him. Although he only planned to sleep, her titillating touch aroused a throbbing need he couldn't fulfill.

Tessa saw the longing in Hunter's gaze, knew he wanted her. And she wanted him also. But she loved the way he was reluctant to take the relationship further until he knew for sure if he had someone. Maybe he wasn't attached, and with the way his memory was returning, it might not be long before he knew the truth.

She melted in his heated embrace, snuggling closer. She swore he let out a muffled groan against the back of her head as he tightened his hold on her, his hard and aroused body fitting snuggly against hers. She had never felt so protected in her life, and she didn't want the sensation to stop.

"Rourke really respects you," she said under her breath. "He doesn't have many friends, mostly because he always sees a story in anything anyone does and it either irritates people or makes them nervous, which causes them to shy away from him. But he really likes you."

"He's all right."

"Hmm, well, I can tell you like him, too. He might not be of the same caliber as your rough and tumble Navy SEAL friends but he's not so bad."

"Oh?"

"Not for me—as a boyfriend. But as a friend for you. That's why you invited him to stay."

Hunter grunted. "To watch over you while I look for the intruder. I couldn't leave you alone unprotected, worried he'd sneak into the house while I was searching for him outside."

That's what she thought, but she wanted to hear him say it. She kissed his arm. "Night." Even if it was midday.

"I wasn't a Navy SEAL."

"Maybe not, but you are now. And the way you react to situations, cook like you're used to living out of doors, have such an uncanny awareness of danger and how to deal with it, you must have trained in military or police operations. So you might as well be a Navy SEAL. It fits with the beach scene anyway. Maybe you're really an Army Ranger or Special Forces or a member of a specialized SWAT Team." She shrugged. "Doesn't matter."

"Would to me if I were trained in one of the other fields."

She turned her head, his lips curved, and she gave him a small smile. "But it doesn't suit our first meeting half as well."

He ran his hand over her hair, then combed the strands with a silky touch. "Do you think a Navy SEAL would have ended up where I did? Flat on my back, half dead?"

"You were flat on your *stomach*, half dead." She sighed, loving the feel of his fingers sweeping through her hair and wished they could take the relationship further. "Only a Navy SEAL or some other highly trained professional in survival tactics would probably have endured the ordeal."

His hand drifted to her breast, his touch blazing a trail of heat across her skin.

Her nipple tightened, begging for release from the lacy bra. She'd never known anyone as sexy as Hunter, so sure of himself, but sensitive, too.

"I wish I knew for certain if I had a significant other, Tessa." He wrapped his arms around her and growled. "You're way too intriguing."

"Hmm, I hope you're unattached, Hunter." She closed

her eyes and breathed in his masculine scent, coveting his heated embrace. *And I hope you plan to stick around for a long, long time.* But she feared the way her luck was going lately, there wasn't much chance at that. Even now she envisioned a wife and a couple of small kids sitting by a fire, waiting for Hunter to return home. She groaned inwardly.

No way did she ever want to be a home breaker like her father had been.

After he'd been sleeping for a couple of hours, Hunter's fingers swept across Tessa's breast. Just a whisper of the most tantalizing touch. Was he asleep? Oblivious to the way he was sending her heart into overdrive? Making her wet in anticipation? Her nipple tingled, but she didn't move a muscle, listening, trying to discern if he was awake and had felt her up on purpose, or was asleep and it was just an accident.

His hand rested on her breast this time, the palm in contact with her taut nipple, his caress tormenting her. He was awake, *the cad*. Then he moved his hand lower, rubbing his thumb across the sensitive nub in a slow, sensual caress.

Lulled into sweet ecstasy, she didn't respond, afraid he'd stop if he knew she was awake. He stroked her breast, and then as if the sensation couldn't have been more erotic, he slid the lacy cup down, exposing her. She took in a sharp breath. His hand molded to her breast, and she wanted to scream, "Take me, oh godly one!" She didn't even know him! He didn't even know himself, for heaven's sakes.

Did he remember he wasn't attached to another woman? Please, make it so. She took his roaming hand and kissed it.

"I knew you were pretending to be asleep," he said, the timbre of his voice dark and seductive.

Her body heated with chagrin. *Caught in the act.* She smiled to herself. "I thought *you* were asleep, at first."

She was dying to ask if there was someone special in his life, but was afraid to learn the truth—that maybe he still didn't know, but he was too horny to care, or he did have someone, but he was still too horny to care.

"I can't promise anything," Hunter warned, pressing a kiss against her hair with a feather-light touch.

His action sent a shiver of expectation down her spine. "Are you free?"

"There's no one."

She let out a heavy sigh.

"I still can't promise you anything long term."

"I'll take whatever I can get," she teased, but she was afraid he might have heard the regret in her voice. She tried again. "Really slim pickings around here."

"You haven't been with a man in a long time," Hunter said, as if he knew her whole blamed, pathetic lifestyle.

But she couldn't lie to him. She figured he would see right through her.

"I'll try to be gentle. It's been a good long while for me, too," he admitted, his voice already husky, his fingers encircling her breast in a slow caress.

As much of a hunk as he was, she didn't believe it for a minute. But forget gentle. She wanted him to devour her whole.

His hand shifted to her shoulder, and he rubbed her

with a tender motion, as if he was waiting for her to make up her mind.

"I'll try to be gentle, too," she said.

His lusty chuckle heated her blood. Boy, had she found a pile of treasure when she went to gather wood on the beach yesterday afternoon.

Hunter unfastened her bra, and then slid the straps down her arms, every move he made deliciously sensual. No man had ever undressed her before, and the sensation sent a delectable heat skittering through her. He brushed aside her hair, exposing her neck, then licked the super-sensitive skin, his warm breath fanning her. He turned her around, his gaze hot with wanting. And then he bent his head, pressed his mouth lightly against hers, his fingers tracing her arms downward, the skin tingling with his action.

She placed her hands against his naked chest, noting the tension in his hard, lean muscles, his skin tan, no longer bruised or cut, the smattering of dark, curly hair trailing to the waistband of the sweats—enticingly provocative.

Although the room was icy cold, his touch heated an internal flame so white hot, she wanted to ditch the covers and expose every delectable inch of him for her viewing pleasure. But he made no move to pull the covers aside, instead dipping his fingers underneath the top edge of her panties, teasing her skin, back and forth.

He brushed his lips against her mouth, making her want more, and drew his fingers upward across her stomach, blazing a trail to her breast. All her bones dissolved as she melted to his touch, his fingers kneading her swollen breast. A wet ache between her legs commenced, and she tugged at the drawstrings on his sweats. Not waiting for his reaction, she jerked the pants down to his thighs.

His arousal sprang free and he half-groaned or growled. And lost control of his slow and measured seduction, as if she'd finally given her mountain man permission to ravish her like a woman in need and not treat her like she was a delicate flower.

He kicked off the sweats and slid her panties down her hips and lower, his tongue penetrating her mouth, conquering, decisive, as if the invisible bars of the cage holding him back had vanished. Pressing his knee between her thighs, he opened her to him, his fingers slipping downward through her short curly hairs, all the way to her womanly folds. His smoldering expression changed subtly, a hint of a smile tugging at his lips.

Yeah, she was ready for him. Had been ever since he'd pinned her to the beach.

His mouth moved to her throat, and he licked a trail to her breast. Then his warm lips latched onto her nipple, suckling, his fingers dipping deep inside her folds. A shiver of need streaked through her, and she arched her pelvis against him, never having wanted sex this bad, or for it to feel so damned good.

His wet fingers stroked her swollen nub, and she grabbed handfuls of his dark hair, his heated breath on her neck as he kissed her there. Every touch felt more erotic than the last and her nerve endings drew in the sensations.

She wanted him inside her, stoking her needs while fulfilling his own, but she didn't want him to stop what he was doing either. Oh, what the hell. If he didn't like that she wanted more, that was his problem. "I want you inside of me, now."

He pressed his leg between hers again, raising up until he connected with her mound and rubbed. She was ready to burst into flames. She groaned, well, kind of whimpered.

Which seemed to spur him on. His fingers worked faster, stroking her, drawing her to the peak, while his mouth did sweet things to one breast and then the other, her fingers digging into his shoulders, then releasing and sweeping down his firm sides. His hot tongue tasted, teased, his teeth grazed her reverently, sending delicious chills exploding across her skin.

"You smell of peaches and cream, and an enticing scent that's all you," he murmured heavily against her cheek.

Before she could respond, his fingers brought her to the edge of the world and she came, shattered into a million sparks of wonderment, the first time she had ever felt such a sensation, her insides quaking with ripples of orgasm.

Her heart thumped rapidly, her breath shallow as he took her in his arms, his eyes smoldering with hunger.

"You still want me?" he asked, his voice raspy and tight.

"Hmm," was all she could manage. If he quit now, she'd strangle him.

He laughed under his breath and pulled her onto her back. "I don't mean to brag, but you're pretty small, and I'm pretty—"

"Huge," she finished for him.

His amber eyes and delicious mouth smiled. "Just thought I'd warn you."

"Appreciate the warning, but you're wasting time." She still couldn't shake the feeling that any second now, he would just vanish in a puff of mist, like a genie recalled to his bottle.

He captured her mouth with his, not slowly, or sweetly, but like he hadn't had a woman in a very long time, and he couldn't wait a second longer. He smelled of the wind in the pines, and hot-blooded male, his gaze clouded with lust. His hands captured her hair and squeezed.

Her heart couldn't beat any faster as he centered himself between her legs. She might have found her treasure on the beach in the form of the hunky naked guy, but Hunter was about to plunder his own treasure as he eased inside of her.

No matter how much Hunter had tried to deny his craving for the woman, he knew it would come to this. Thankfully, he had been able to control his wolf's desires long enough to remember he didn't have a mate. Still, hooking up with Tessa was *not* a good idea. She was too damned needy and should have had a decent guy who would care for her, one who wanted to stick it out for the long run. Someone who wouldn't hunt on moon-filled nights in a wolf's coat.

He eased deeper into her tight sheath and began massaging her breasts to loosen her up. He could tell she hadn't been with a man in a very long time and the notion pleased him. He was even more convinced than before—if she had been a gray *lupus garou*, he would never let her go.

Her sweet, musky scent had all but undone him when he first stroked her breast, triggering her arousal. And thinking of the way she had touched him—rubbed his muscles with such finesse, cleaned the salt from his skin with tenderness, covered his injuries with the faintest of touches—every sensation was permanently etched into his brain.

He embedded himself inside her to the hilt and slowly began to withdraw. She smiled in a way that would heat any man's blood. What was worse, he already wanted her to smile at only him like that. The problem? Not enough *lupus garou* females to satisfy the male population.

He meant to draw out the lovemaking, take it slow and easy the first time with her. But she combed her fingers through his hair in such a sensual way, and then her fingers drew higher and began to massage his scalp, he felt he would lose his seed before he could make it very much farther.

He plunged in deeper, harder, fulfilling his raw need to conquer, to possess her. And she was worthy of being his, but he would *not* go there.

He watched her expression as he pumped deep inside of her, her sparkling eyes observing him, challenging him to give her everything he had. He felt the end coming and with one last hard thrust, he filled her with his seed. Sweet heaven, she was a gift from the gods.

Sexually satiated, he kissed her upturned lips, and then rolled onto his back, pulling her into his arms, loving the way her soft body molded against his hardness. "I wasn't too rough, was I?" he asked, his voice raspy against her ear, although it was a little too late for asking.

She shivered and touched his extended nipple. "Just perfect. I've never taken a nap that's been so—stimulatingly satisfying."

He chuckled. "Health experts say a nap a day can add years to your life."

"I believe it. Well, especially while napping with you."

He could have snuggled with her until nightfall, although they managed to sleep for an hour, but Rourke began stirring in the living room. More than stirring. He was banging around, probably tired of Tessa and Hunter "sleeping" together.

Hunter gave a ragged sigh and kissed the top of Tessa's head. "Let's get up. I need to gather more firewood and start that roast if it's going to be ready by dinnertime."

"You'll be careful tonight when you go looking for the thief, won't you?"

"Yeah, but you and Rourke stay together and *don't* leave the house this time."

"Do you remember everything about your life? Where you're from, where you were born?"

"No. It's coming back in annoying fragments." But he hoped he would soon remember what had happened to him before he ended up in the Pacific. Then he would take care of that little matter, too.

The tension ran high the rest of the evening. Rourke seemed perturbed Hunter had slept with Tessa earlier in the day and would again for part of the night. And she couldn't quit worrying about Hunter's safety tonight. Something seemed to be bothering him also. Another recollection? Maybe concern that they shouldn't have made love this afternoon. If he left tomorrow, she would have no regrets about what they had done. Well, no. She wasn't being honest with herself. She doubted she would ever find a man who was quite like Hunter. No one would ever measure up to him.

But something was going on with him. He kept watching her, his look so dark she couldn't fathom what was the matter. If Rourke hadn't been there, she would have asked. But she didn't want to in front of him.

Rourke noticed Hunter's ominous mood, too. Even though he was pissed about her and Hunter's relationship, he wasn't saying a word about it. But she bet he would if Hunter hadn't looked so lethal.

"You didn't make that list of names for me," Hunter finally said to Tessa, fixing her with a piercing gaze as he shoved his empty plate at Rourke.

Although Rourke was supposed to do the dishes, he wasn't finished eating, and he cast Hunter an irritated look.

Tessa had forgotten all about the list of suspects. "I'll do it after I finish dinner."

She realized then, the change had come over Hunter after he'd left to gather firewood earlier. She frowned. Although she knew she shouldn't bring it up, she wasn't used to burying problems. "Did you discover anything when you went down to the beach to get firewood?"

Rourke glanced up from his roast.

"You said Ashton wasn't anything to you. You said he only saw you as Michael's annoying sister. What the hell's going on between the two of you? Is he your lover? Former lover? Is that why he shot me?"

A sickening flood of fear washed over her. He watched the emotions playing across her face, his hard look instantly changing to a hint of compassion. How did he come up with the conclusion that she and Ashton were lovers?

The… the incident in the shed out back? How could he know about that?

"Don't lie to me, Tessa."

His voice was so stern she might have cowered if she had done something wrong.

But she hadn't, *damn it*. She hadn't even known Hunter back then. What right did he have bullying her?

No longer hungry, she rose from the table. "You want a list of possible suspects, I'll give you a list. But beyond that, go to hell."

She swore his lips turned up a fraction before he stood like one pissed-off giant grizzly.

He tossed a pair of her shredded silk panties on the table. "Want to talk about it?"

"Where… where did you get those?"

"In the shed."

Rourke looked anxious, like he wished he hadn't agreed to stay the night. Some hero he would make. On the other hand, he looked like he wanted to know what the panties had to do with Ashton Wellington. Good news for the morning paper?

"It was my fault," she said, gathering her composure. Once she told Hunter the truth, she figured he would want to kill Ashton, so somehow, she had to minimize the seriousness of what had happened.

"So tell me. Did you seduce him in the shed, Tessa?" He advanced on her. "Did you? Or did something else go down?"

She fought fleeing to her bedroom to avoid the topic. She had never told anyone about it. How could she? No one would ever have believed her. But Hunter had instincts that were more attuned than anyone she had ever met. She didn't think she could get away with outright lying.

"What business did *you* have in the shed?" She tilted her chin up and glowered right back at him, but wondered again where the panties had been that *she* hadn't found them.

"The intruder had been there. I was looking for clues when I found those." Hunter motioned to the incriminating evidence.

Oh, hell, the stalker.

"Ashton had been drinking, okay?"

Hunter's face turned even more hot-tempered. "He forced you? Damn it, he raped you?"

"No! He tried to get me to do it with him, but I… I knocked him out with a shovel and when he came to, we never discussed the incident. All right?"

"Why didn't you tell me?"

"Why? No one would ever have believed me! Ashton can do no wrong! I tried to tell my brother, but he wouldn't hear of it. I'd seen Ashton smoking out by the shed. Michael was still at the art gallery at one of his special exhibits. I thought it was a good opportunity to tell Ashton to go to hell."

"Like you did me?"

"Yeah, well, you deserved it. I told Ashton I didn't want him seeing my brother any longer. He was a bad influence, but it was my fault for confronting him. I shouldn't have interfered. Not when I saw that Ashton was drunk. He left before Michael came home, and we didn't see him for a couple of weeks. He wasn't pleasant to me after that, but he kept his distance."

Rourke whistled. "Hell, a shovel, eh? Good thing you didn't crack that worthless skull of his in half. Not that he wouldn't deserve it, but you wouldn't have deserved the consequences either."

Hunter took Tessa's hand, but she jerked free and folded her arms. "Next time you want to ask me a question, do it in a nicer way, and *not* with a reporter in audience, all right?"

Rourke shook his head. "I swear, Tessa, on my mother's grave, I wouldn't breathe a word of this to anyone. I swear it. Although that worthless piece of shit deserves the bad publicity."

Hunter took Tessa's arms and unfolded them. Holding onto her hands, he scowled, "I don't often apologize for my actions, but finding the evidence in the shed made me a little crazy."

She wanted to say for someone who didn't want to make a commitment, what was the big deal? But she bit her tongue, because somewhere deep in this mountain man's psyche, he seemed to be fighting with himself over wanting to be with her longer.

She gave him a wry smile. "Apology accepted. But don't you dare kill that tapeworm."

"I can't make any promises." He cast Rourke a look like he better not print a word of any of this.

Rourke threw his hands up in capitulation. "Secret's safe with me. But you can't bind me to any oath either if that bastard gets in my way after what he's pulled."

She wanted to laugh. As if Rourke would ever get more violent with a body than shoving a recorder in his face to do an interview. Hunter smiled, as if he were thinking along the same line.

"You're making up to me tonight for this," Tessa warned Hunter, poking her finger against his solid chest.

He learned over and cupped her face, gliding his lips over hers, then captured her mouth and gave her a searing kiss that promised much more. He bowed his head slightly, touching his forehead against hers. "I'll do my best to apologize more, later."

Her lips tingled with heat and pleasure, and she wished Rourke hadn't been here. "Hmm, you'd better."

He grabbed her hat and Michael's jacket and gloves. "Got to take a look around now that it's getting dark. Keep her inside the house no matter what, Rourke. Even if you hear gunfire, don't let her out of your sight."

"Be careful," she said, her heart in her throat, because no matter how capable he seemed, someone had already nearly killed Hunter, and she was having awful feelings about this. Just like before.

Chapter 6

WHY HUNTER HAD JUMPED TO THE CONCLUSION HE had concerning Tessa, he didn't know. Well, yeah, he did. She had really gotten under his skin and one thing he didn't like was being lied to. When he had found her panties on top of a shelf of some old paint cans, an unreasonable rage had filled him. But seeing her expression made him realize he had gotten the scenario all wrong, and he wished to hell his wolf instincts had played more of a role in his handling of the situation.

He meant what he said. He would make it up to her. Hopefully, she was being honest when she seemed to understand his anger and didn't hold a grudge against him for it. But maybe if she stewed about it for a while, she would be mad at him all over again. He wouldn't blame her. Why he had brought up the matter in front of Rourke was another thing.

What had gotten into him? *Damn it.*

He'd fallen hard for the woman—that's why. For some inexplicable reason, he wanted her for his own, despite the fact she was human, which went against all that he stood for. He took a deep ragged breath, trying to focus on the business at hand. He had every intention of locating the gray tonight, assuming he would be in his wolf form. Hunter figured that as badly as the gray had the hots for Tessa, there was no persuading him to cease his stalking. The *lupus garou* wanted her for a mate, and if Hunter didn't kill him, he was sure the gray would try to change her. If she didn't go with him willingly, he would murder her.

Hunter's blood heated even more. The gray wouldn't get the chance.

Movement in the woods caught his attention. He peered into the dark and saw a rifle poised in his direction and the bastard holding it. But as soon as Ashton Wellington realized Hunter had spied him, he raised the gun in surrender. Hunter charged toward him, his temper red hot.

He reminded himself the reason he had to get rid of Ashton was to ensure he could tangle with the gray, wolf to wolf, without witnesses. But as angry as he was with Ashton concerning Tessa, he couldn't control the urge to put the sheriff's son out of his misery, quickly.

Ashton stood his ground, although his face had turned as pale as the snow now falling.

"Didn't I tell you to stay away from here?" Hunter growled, using his most lethal voice and glower.

Ashton shivered, and Hunter figured it was due in part to the cold, in part because of his threatening posture.

"I promised Michael I would watch out for his sister, damn it. I already told you that."

Hunter balled up his fist and punched Ashton in the jaw. Pain streaked through his knuckles. Ashton fell back against a pine tree with a grunt.

"That's for attempting to rape Tessa." Hunter readied his fist again.

Ashton dropped his rifle in the accumulating snow and held up his hands in submission. "I didn't mean it. I'm sorry. I was drunk. Angry. I know it doesn't excuse my behavior. Michael has been the only friend I've ever had and when his sister told me to get lost and leave her brother alone because I was a bad influence, something inside me snapped."

Hunter grabbed the rifle, intending to send it over the cliff, but Ashton yelled, "Wait! Hear me out. You wouldn't listen to me last night you were so riled, but someone's stalking Tessa. I thought it was you. Dad gave me hell about being here late last night, but I told him Michael wanted me to promise I would look after Tessa. And I'm going to do it, damn it. I owe her for the way I behaved, and I owe Michael."

He sounded sincere enough, but the guy was always in trouble, according to Tessa. Why couldn't he be lying?

"What about your seeing Michael's girlfriend, Bethany Wade? If you're such a good friend of Michael's, why would you do that?"

Ashton's face darkened. "You don't know the half of it, Hunter. Why did you have to bring that up to my dad? He gave me hell for that, too."

"Maybe you ought to come clean with me, before I throw your worthless carcass off this cliff."

Ashton looked like he was ready to pee his pants. Despite trying to put on a tough guy act, the smell of fear cloaked him. "I didn't kill Bethany. I went to see her that night. The one when I was so drunk. I'd been feeling sorry for myself because Michael had a talent I didn't have, and he was so successful. His painting had nothing to do with me, and I felt left out. While he was getting all his accolades during the showing, I drank too much. After Tessa beaned me with the shovel, I finally came to my senses, somewhat."

He took a deep breath. "I went to see Bethany, although I halfway suspected she would be at the art gallery with Michael. Hell, Tessa was supposed to be, too, but she had stayed home because she had a bout of the flu. Which she gave me also! Anyway, Bethany had been drinking, too. She felt like I did. Michael had a new circle of friends, and we didn't fit into his new lifestyle. She hated all the women who threw themselves at the great artist. His works were beginning to appear all over the states at museums and in books. We knew before long, he wouldn't have time for either of us."

"So you screwed his girlfriend and—"

Ashton's shoulders slumped. "At first, it was because we were mad at Michael. A sneaky form of revenge, I'll admit. But we became really fond of each other. I think we were falling in love. Michael was spending more time with his artwork and exhibits and less time with us, so what difference did it make?"

Hunter growled, "He was your best friend! You could have had the balls to square it with him first."

"Yeah, and lose his friendship?" Ashton shoved his gloved hands in his pockets. "After Bethany died—"

"You're trying to tell me you didn't kill her over a lover's spat and frame Michael for it?"

"Shit, Hunter. I didn't kill Bethany. I figured Michael had done it. Sure, I had been seeing Bethany behind his back just like he said, only he didn't know who it was. We'd been supercautious so no one could ever prove it. I figured he murdered her because he knew she was seeing someone else. Who else would have killed Bethany?"

Hunter shoved the rifle into Ashton's chest. "I don't want you coming around here any longer. I told you that last night. I won't warn you again."

Ashton rubbed his jaw, his blue eyes piercing Hunter with a frigid glower. "I promised Michael. Someone's stalking Tessa. I'm not breaking my promise."

"*I'm* looking out for her."

"As much as I hate to admit it, I'm glad. But you'd better let me in on this. My dad's contacted two ex-cons, extortionists, murderers, although they weren't convicted on the last count since the DA's office couldn't locate enough evidence. Believe me, they wouldn't hesitate to eliminate you. I told my dad you're good for Tessa's protection. But he was so mad about the rifle and everything else, he wouldn't listen. I'll help you."

"If you didn't kill Bethany, I'd say you don't really have it in you."

"Maybe, maybe not. You've solicited that idiot Rourke's help, and he definitely won't be able to protect her."

Hunter glanced back in the direction of the house. "All right, but make sure your dad is agreeable. Let him know we're in on this together. You get yourself killed, I don't want your dad thinking I'm the one who did it."

Ashton bobbed his head up and down. "Okay. You got it. Are you sure you don't want me to stick around a little longer? What if the guy's out here?"

"He probably is. But I don't want your ass out here until your dad agrees. All right?" Hell, when had Hunter become such a damned softy? He ought to have thrown the rotten cuss over the cliff with his new rifle.

"Yeah, agreed." But Ashton looked like he wanted to stay.

"*Now*, Ashton. You don't want to see me when I'm really pissed. Your dad might have mentioned I'm an ex–Navy SEAL."

"Yeah, yeah, he did."

"Well, we're trained to eliminate any threat no matter how small, so just remember that. Got it?"

"Yes, sir. I'll be back."

"Not before tomorrow. And come to the front door of the house, *only* if you get your dad's okay."

Ashton vigorously nodded and waited for Hunter to move out of his way since he had his back wedged up against the pine tree.

"Be back tomorrow," Ashton promised.

Hunter shook his head and stalked off in the direction he smelled the gray's scent. The stalker was back and had probably listened to their whole blasted conversation. Hunter should have thrown Ashton over the cliff, if for nothing better than to prove to the gray he wasn't a damn pushover.

The doorbell rang and Tessa looked at Rourke, both of them standing in front of the fire, rubbing their hands, trying to stay warm. Tessa didn't think the stalker would come to the front door. Maybe the sheriff had returned? Or perhaps he had sent some of his minions to rough Hunter up a little. But in front of witnesses? Probably not.

She headed for the front door, but Rourke bolted in front of her and grabbed her arms, his gray eyes wild. "What if it's *him*—the *stalker*?"

"What if it isn't?"

"I'll check." Rourke released her, hurried to the door, and peeked out through the peephole. "No one there."

Before she could tell him not to open the door, he unlocked it and swung it wide. "Holy crap!"

Rourke jumped away and tried to shut the door, but something knocked him flat on his back. Tessa stared at the large, pale gray wolf as he stood next to Rourke lying unresponsive on the floor. The wolf turned his attention from Rourke to Tessa, his amber eyes feral. In disbelief, she stood frozen in place. He... he was the same one who lunged for her in California?

Couldn't be.

Heart racing, she dashed for the fireplace and grabbed the cast-iron tongs. The wolf leapt halfway across the living room, barely missing the coffee table, and landed only feet from her. She swung the tongs at the animal's head, connecting with his nose in a loud whap, and the tongs flew from her grasp. He yelped and shook his muzzle.

She dove down the hall and reached her brother's room, the blood pounding so hard in her ears she couldn't hear the wolf following. But as soon as she grabbed the door and tried to slam it shut, the wolf lunged. Like a replay from the incident in the woods in California, the animal snarled and snapped, only this time he blocked her from shutting the door.

"Tessa!" Hunter yelled from the living room.

"I'm in here, Hunter! Watch out for the wolf!" Except she was the one still fighting with the wild beast, his paws against the door, his teeth snapping at her.

"I'll take care of it."

The wolf turned its head and she knew he would attack Hunter next.

"Stay there. Don't come out until I holler it's all clear," he shouted.

She slammed the door closed. "Hunter, be careful! The wolf's probably rabid."

What if it bit Hunter? And what about poor Rourke?

Furniture crashed. Her heart jumped. Growls sounded. She raced through Michael's room, searching for a weapon.

More crashing noises. More growling.

"Hunter?"

Hunter tore off the field jacket and then kicked off the sneakers as the wolf slinked around the sofa, snarling at him. Thinking to kill Hunter as a human? It *would* be easier for him. Hunter jerked off the sweats and hurried to shapeshift. The gray was dead meat. Rourke was out cold, thankfully, and Tessa couldn't see Hunter's new look, standing as a wolf, waiting for the stalker's approach. He just hoped to god she stayed put, but he didn't trust her one bit.

The *lupus garou* skirted around the overturned table, the brass lamp on the floor, the bulb shattered. He inched forward, slowly, cautiously, his tail straightened, his eyes focused on every movement Hunter made, from the twitch in Hunter's ears to the tautness of his tail. The gray's nose was bleeding and Hunter made the connection with the bloodied fireplace tongs. *Tessa.* He was certain Rourke hadn't used the tongs on the gray and then fallen by the door.

Had the stalker listened to Hunter's conversation with Ashton before he approached the house? Attempting to judge Hunter's strengths and weaknesses? Hunter hadn't thought he'd had much in the line of weaknesses when it came to human dealings. Then again, maybe he didn't usually come into contact with them. He couldn't recall.

Hunter surveyed the furniture in the way, hampering their ability to fight well. He needed to get the wolf out of doors, away from the humans.

The wolf snarled and then charged. Hunter swiftly retaliated. Both growled fiercely and struck with such force, neither made any headway. They dropped back to their pads and separated.

Hunter hoped Tessa didn't hear all the noise they were making, or she would be trying to figure out why there were now two wolves, but the instinct was so inborn, he couldn't stop it. Growling was like a war yell for a fighter in battle—a need to frighten the enemy into submission or inaction, and he would use every means necessary to eliminate the threat.

The gray was an equal match in size and agility. In his wolf way of thinking, Hunter was glad he had a worthy advisory, which would make it that much sweeter when he destroyed him. The two clashed again, their powerful jaws snapping, their teeth connecting. Hunter tasted both his blood and the gray's.

They landed on their paws, their chests heaving. They truly were matched. But Hunter couldn't work him toward the door. The *lupus garou* probably wanted to stay near the woman he intended to claim.

The gray dove in again, biting at Hunter's neck. Hunter tore the gray's cheek, exposing the muscle. He yelped, retreated, waited. Hunter charged him, grabbed for his throat, but the *lupus garou* turned, and Hunter bit him in the flank instead. Another yelp.

Rourke groaned.

The distraction caught Hunter off guard, and the wolf went for Hunter's throat again. Hunter shifted the weight of his body to avoid the wolf's bite and ran into the damned leather footstool. The stalker's teeth sank into his shoulder. Pain radiated through the wound. Hunter growled.

Rourke moaned.

The wolf glanced at him as he began to stir, and then the stalker leapt toward the door. With another bound, he was outside.

His shoulder bleeding and hurting like hell, Hunter bolted after him. This ended, *tonight*.

Rourke weakly hollered, "Tessa? Tessa?"

Her nerves wired, she opened Michael's bedroom door and peeked out. No more growling. "Hunter?"

No reply.

Irritated she couldn't find a weapon in Michael's bedroom for protection, she called out, "Rourke, are you all right?"

No answer.

Her spine tingling with apprehension and feeling vulnerable without a weapon in hand, she crept down the hall toward the living room.

The place was deadly quiet except for the wind blowing through the open door. She feared the worst—Hunter was dead or unconscious and the wolf was waiting for her. The adrenaline in her system was running high, her heart pounding hard. If she could get to the fireplace tongs or the poker…

She peered into the living room. No sign of the wolf. Both brass lamps had crashed to the floor. Blood was spattered throughout. Tan, pale, and darker gray fur clung to the edges of the couches and love seat. Rourke had again passed out by the front door. The clothes Hunter had been wearing were strewn all over the place.

She gasped, her hand to her mouth, her eyes tearing up. The wolf must have killed Hunter and dragged his body off. But what if he hadn't? Then again, what if the wolf came back? She grabbed the fireplace poker and rushed to the door. Except for drops of fresh blood on the porch, she didn't see anything in the blowing snow.

"Hunter!" she screamed. If she'd had a gun, she would have gone after the wolf and shot it.

Rourke groaned, and she quickly closed and locked the front door. "Rourke, Rourke, wake up. I… I think the wolf killed Hunter. But if it didn't…" She wiped tears from her cheeks. "Rourke! Wake up! We need to save Hunter."

The gray was racing through the woods as fast as he could while Hunter kept track of him in the blowing snow. Where the hell was he fleeing to? Maybe a getaway vehicle. He had the tenacity of an alpha. Yet some of his posturing, like escaping through the forest, indicated he was more of a beta. It didn't matter what he was because the gray served as a threat to Tessa either way.

For three miles, Hunter chased the *lupus garou*, the icy air whipping across his open wound, making it burn like the devil. *Stop and fight like a wolf, damn you!*

Another two miles after that. At least Tessa and Rourke were safe now that Hunter had the gray on the run. Hopefully, Rourke had only suffered a bump on the head and nothing more serious.

The wolf suddenly slowed. Tiring? Weak? He was bleeding, too, leaving a trail of blood in the fresh snow. But he didn't smell like he was afraid, which confused the issue. Maybe he was mad. Some *lupus garou* were crazy, just like their human counterparts.

Another smell—another wolf. No two. Damn it, Hunter was in a pack's territory. Something seemed familiar. He glanced at the cliffs. One blackened pine stood naked in the snow at the edge of the outcropping of rocks. Oh hell. Here's where he was thrown from the cliff.

He smelled the air. *They* were the three who'd fought him. That's how they had gotten the best of him the last time. But why had they attacked him?

Which made him wonder if he had tried to take over the pack, or had targeted one of their females as his own. Yet since this one wanted Tessa, had they thought Hunter would discover her and want her also? No matter how he tried, he couldn't remember.

One of the males moved around to his right flank, the other behind him, while the one he had already fought stayed where he was, panting, dog tired. Hunter almost felt the same way, but fresh adrenaline surged through his veins again, preparing him for the fight. He imagined the injured wolf was feeling complacent now that his buddies were here to bail him out.

He had a whiter mask on the underside, except for the blood caked on his nose and cheek. The one to Hunter's right was a darker gray. The one behind him was a little heavier, but they all had a similar scent, way of moving, overall look. He guessed they were brothers, triplets. Packs protected their members, but family could be even more ferocious in taking care of their own.

His tail stiff like a flag of warning, Hunter kept his eye on the stalker, but listened with regard to the other two. This time someone else, preferably three someone elses if he could manage, would be taking a dive into the ocean, over the cliff side. And then he would make sure Tessa didn't return to her beach for a good while afterward. No sense in her dragging home any more wounded, naked *lupus garou* males. Or finding their remains if they didn't survive.

The wolf behind him moved forward, his pads crunching on the upper crust of snow. The one on the right stepped toward Hunter, trying to box him in. Hunter didn't budge. He might as well put some of that supposed Navy SEAL training to use. At least if nothing else, he wouldn't be pushed toward the edge of the rocks. And he knew just who to target this time. The weakest link. He dove after the stalker.

For an instant, the wolf's ears flattened. Hunter smiled inwardly. The stalker was afraid of him. That's why he brought Hunter here. To get his brothers to back him up. He probably thought he could take Hunter down initially because of the way he was so "humanized."

The wolf fled. Hunter whipped around so suddenly, he caught the wolf chasing him off-guard. Hunter immediately lunged at him and bit the gray's snout. He yelped and dove away. The remaining wolf attacked. Hunter aimed low at his front right leg. With a snap, he brought the wolf down. The wolf howled. Hunter again turned, prepared to take on the other, but he and the stalker had disappeared into the blinding snow like a couple of gray wraiths. Calling for reinforcements? Hunter knew his limits. He couldn't fight a whole pack of grays.

The wolf with the broken leg lay panting on his side. Hunter knew he should kill him. But he still couldn't remember why they had thrown him from the cliff. Maybe *he* had been the one in the wrong. Not concerning Tessa though. No matter what, the stalker had no right to claim a human, and Hunter wasn't going to allow it.

He growled at the injured wolf. The gray closed his eyes in submission. Probably readying himself for the killing blow. Hunter glanced back in the direction of Tessa's house. What if the other two wolves went back for her?

Hell. He dashed back the way he had come, mile after mile. A quarter of a mile from the house, he heard Tessa calling, "Hunter!" Her voice was filled with tears.

Crap. Was Rourke with her? She *wasn't* supposed to leave the house. Somehow, he had to return to the place, get dressed, and… No, he couldn't risk her being out here in the event the other *lupus garous* were coming for her.

With the pine trees still shielding him, Hunter shape-shifted into his human form. He'd suffer frostbite for sure. If Tessa and Rourke had just stayed in the house, he could have gotten much closer before he'd had to change.

Racing into their line of view, he found Rourke wielding the fireplace poker and Tessa ready to swing the bloody fireplace tongs.

"Ohmigod, Hunter." Tessa's gaze shifted from his face to his bloody shoulder as she rushed forward. "*Ohmigod.*"

He dashed toward her and grabbed her hand, pulling her back toward the house. "You shouldn't be out here. I told you to keep her in the house, Rourke. Didn't I?" The threat in his voice was real, but Rourke was smiling. Probably because of Hunter's state of undress.

So much for his ferocious image.

"I kept telling Tessa we would find you in pretty good shape." Rourke threw his parka over Hunter's shoulders. "I told you he'd have wrung the wolves' necks and would bring their tails home as souvenirs."

Now that was a barbaric notion. Tessa wrapped her arm around Hunter's waist as they hurried to the back porch. Tears streamed down her cheeks, and she didn't say anything more.

Rourke wouldn't shut up and handed Hunter Tessa's ski cap. "Sorry. We didn't think of bringing any of your clothes. We should have thought of it, but all we had in mind was attacking the wolves that had dragged you off, and the best weapons for the job. But I kept telling Tessa you would be all right. That we'd find you alive."

"None of this is to be reported to the newspaper," Hunter warned.

"We have an obligation to warn folks that wild wolves have taken up residence in the woods here. We can't allow them to kill people."

Tessa was shaking so hard when they reached the back porch, she dropped the keys. Rourke retrieved them and unlocked the door.

"No reporting any of this." Hunter used his most threatening voice as they walked into the living room, his arm tight around Tessa.

Rourke stared at him. Tessa finally pulled away from Hunter and hurried down the hall.

He handed Rourke his parka and slipped the sweatpants back on.

"You can't mean it, Hunter. What if one attacked Tessa? It would have, too, if you hadn't come and saved us."

"It wasn't a wolf. All right, Rourke? Just drop it."

Tessa returned to the living room with rubbing alcohol and bandages. "It was *too* a wolf." Her voice was shaky and her body slightly trembled.

When she applied the alcohol to the wound, Hunter clenched his teeth. Hell, he hadn't hurt this much since the time he was wounded in the Mekong Delta. Again, a distant memory, but nothing else came to mind except the excruciating agony he was in.

Her gaze caught his. "I'm sorry." Her skin was as white as the gauze in her hands and her eyes glistened with tears.

"It's no big deal," he said between gritted teeth. He sure as hell didn't want her to worry that he was dying when he would heal within a few days and be as good as new.

She set the bottle of alcohol down and applied the gauze to his shoulder. "I saw it, Hunter. If it wasn't a wolf, what was it?"

"A wild dog that looked like a wolf."

"We still have to report it. A wild animal that attacks humans has to be destroyed," Rourke said.

Tessa taped the gauze to Hunter's shoulder and shook her head. "It was a *wolf.* I have a photo of one that looks exactly like him. And not only that, but he had almond-shaped eyes. Dogs have rounded eyes."

He stared at her for a minute, then recalled all the books she had on wolves. *Hell, now what?* Hunter collapsed on the sofa, the adrenaline fading and weariness settling in. He wanted to tell them he had destroyed the animal, but he couldn't because the stalker would undoubtedly return, maybe this time with his two buddies once everyone had healed sufficiently. Hunter didn't want Tessa and Rourke believing they were perfectly safe. But he didn't want to create a mad scene of hunters shooting every wolf throughout Oregon either. And they probably would, even though wolves were a protected species. They couldn't kill the *lupus garou* that way, but they could kill the real wolves, and for wolves and *lupus garous* it would be one long nightmare.

"Can I see the picture?"

She nodded and headed back down the hall.

Hunter ran his hand through his damp hair. "Listen, Rourke, I'm going to ask you for a big favor on this. I know what I'm doing. Believe me. I'll destroy the wolf—"

"I thought I heard two of them fighting in the house," Tessa said, returning with the printout of the photo.

"*Two* fought one another. So you see if we announce this, hunters from every crack and crevice in the state will be here shooting everything that moves. *Everything.* You know how it goes. Then even Tessa wouldn't be safe getting a load of firewood from the beach."

"She's got you and me for that now," Rourke said, as if he were staying for the long haul.

Actually, it probably was a good idea—for the time being.

Hunter considered the photo while Tessa hurried back down the hall. It *was* the gray all right. But the trees weren't correct. A hint of memory eluded him. He recognized the forest. Not here, but where?

Rourke whispered, "Did you kill it already? I could see you didn't want to say in front of Tessa."

Before Hunter could reply, she returned and frowned at them. He figured she heard Rourke's loud whisper.

She carried a man's flannel shirt and a pair of big fuzzy sock slippers. Kneeling at Hunter's feet, she pulled on one of the slippers, and then the other. He hadn't realized how icy his feet were until she warmed them. But what heated him even more were her tender ministrations and thoughts of returning to bed with her and snuggling.

He considered the picture of the *lupus garou* again. "Where did you get this photo?"

"I took it in California. Right before he lunged at me."

"When you were on that photo shoot for the magazine?" Rourke asked. "Hell, Tessa, I told you not to take the job, but—"

"He looks just like the one that knocked Rourke out," Tessa continued, ignoring Rourke's scolding. "But he couldn't be."

Hunter lied, "They can all look the same." Well, to an untrained eye, they could. He and his kind easily distinguished the differences. A change in the colors of the masks, or the patterns of coloration on the body and head. Sometimes subtle between wolf siblings, but still anyone who observed them closely enough could see the difference. Personality-wise, they'd be totally dissimilar.

"That's what I thought." Yet something in the way

Tessa looked at him and her tone of voice, indicated she wasn't being totally honest with him either.

He wanted to know what made her suspect he wasn't speaking the truth, or that he at least didn't understand the truth. She couldn't know this wolf was the same as the one she'd seen in California.

But that he had followed her from California showed how determined he was to have her.

"Have you seen the wolf that attacked us here before?" he asked.

"In La Grande. I'm pretty sure. I took a photo of him, but he was turned sideways, and I didn't get a good shot of his face."

"Has to be another wolf," Rourke said. "Don't you think, Hunter? That's a long ways for one to travel."

"Yeah." Hunter knew better. When looking for mates, they'd travel for miles. "Do you have the photo?"

She sighed. "Sure, but we need to take you to the doctor to see about your wound. The animal was probably rabid." She looked up at him, her eyes shimmering like emeralds awash in tears.

Her upset cut straight into his soul. He didn't think a human had ever touched him the way she did. Although if he had much to do with them, he probably wasn't usually this beat up around them. He touched her face and would have leaned down to kiss her as she crouched in front of him, but his shoulder hurt so much, he couldn't bend if his life depended on it. She stood and helped him into the flannel shirt.

Then she kissed his lips, her touch velvety soft, heating his chilled blood. "I'll find some blankets for you, but we need to make plans to get you to the clinic."

He grasped her hand and squeezed tight. "I won't deny I'm bone weary, Tessa, but the animal didn't have a case of rabies. I'll be fine in a day or two."

She glanced at Rourke as if looking for his support.

"She's right, Hunter. That wound's pretty nasty. It's going to need some sutures."

Hunter released Tessa's hand. "No." He closed his eyes and groaned as he tried to get comfortable. She hurried to help him stretch out on the sofa in front of the blazing fire. "Just make sure everything's locked up," he said. "If we drove in this icy snowstorm, we could run off a cliff."

"We have to get to a doctor," Tessa whispered to Rourke.

Hunter opened his eyes and scowled. Since when did his word not mean the law? "*No!* I'll be fine. I heal fast. Just let me sleep."

Tessa brushed away tears and then rushed back down the hallway. He only realized then she had been fighting them all along. He hadn't meant to sound so harsh, but he didn't need doctors messing with him. Not that they would discover what he was. Thank heavens the *lupus garou* genetics precluded that. As a wolf, they had only wolf genes and as a human, human genetics. But he still didn't want anyone seeing how fast he healed. Although as bad as the bite was, it would be a couple of days, maybe more, before it healed properly.

Rourke tried his phone, but shook his head. "Still no reception."

Tessa returned with an armload of blankets, a pillow, and the other wolf photo.

Hunter studied the two photos. Hell, it *was* the same *lupus garou*. "How long ago was this taken?"

"A month ago."

"Have you seen any wolves around here since then?"

"I thought I'd… I've heard howling up north."

"When?"

"About a month ago. Well, the first time. I've heard it on and off since then."

The bastard must have seen her at La Grande and tracked her here. Had he caught a whiff of her? Her special scent that ignited his own cravings?

Or had he taken objection to her photographing him? The fact he was rolling in her sheets meant he wanted her. He was taking her scent back to his wolf mates, declaring she was his and no one else's.

"I thought maybe he'd been owned before." She pulled the soft blue blanket up to Hunter's chin.

"Owned before?"

"Yeah. He doesn't act like a normal wolf. Well, I mean he does, with the snarling and chasing and all. But—he stares me down like he's trying to remember a past life, like maybe he was once someone's pet and I look like the owner, or something." She gave Hunter a couple of pills.

Rourke shook his head. "No way was that wild animal someone's pet, unless he already ate his owners."

Hunter gave him an annoyed look. He wasn't helping his cause. His shoulder feeling like it was on fire, Hunter offered Tessa a pained smile. "Why would I need a doctor when I've got Miss Nightingale?"

Her lips lifted a little, but he could tell her heart wasn't in it.

He closed his eyes and listened to Rourke and Tessa move to the kitchen where they discussed him and how they would get him to the clinic in town despite what he wanted. He let out an exasperated sigh.

Tessa was not normally a wimp, but she'd fought collapsing when she first saw Hunter's muscle torn to the bone. He had to have medical attention and soon. But he was right about the driving conditions. She would never normally chance driving in this kind of weather. Anyone with an ounce of sense wouldn't either. But infection could set in and he couldn't heal properly without getting some stitches no matter what Hunter said about it. Yet she wondered if he practiced some kind of mind-over-body meditation that helped him heal faster because all the injuries he'd suffered from his swim in the Pacific had healed.

How he could have survived the cold for so long before they reached him, she couldn't imagine. It was almost as if he'd holed up in a nice warm cabin for a while. Except there were none close by, and he had been too injured to have gone very far.

Rourke let out his breath. "I don't know what to do, Tessa. He needs a doctor for sure. My phone still isn't getting a signal or I'd call for an emergency crew to come get us."

Tessa looked out at the accumulating snow—already drifts had piled up half a foot around the back of the house. "I'm afraid we wouldn't make the six-mile trip into town. If we ran the truck off into the woods down one of those steep embankments—if we survived—we could all be injured so badly we might not be able to crawl back to the road. Then what? And if we just got stuck, we'd have to walk in these freezing conditions the rest of the way into town. I don't think Hunter can take any more of the cold as badly injured as he is. But I'm also worried about infection and continued bleeding. And although he says the wolf wasn't rabid, how does he know? What if it was? The way the animal came into the house and headed for me, he acted more like a rabid wolf than not."

"Agreed." Rourke glanced at his watch. "It's already midnight. One of us will need to keep a vigil on him all night. If he begins to run a fever or gets violently ill, either we can attempt a run into town, or we can wait out the storm and try then. The alternative is I can go by myself and try to get help."

Tessa shook her head. "I'd worry about your safety. What if you didn't make it? And then, too, the stalker could still be out there. Oh, hell, I hadn't thought about it since it happened, but remember, someone rang the doorbell and then disappeared? Do you think the wolf killed the person and dragged him away?"

Rourke collapsed on the dining chair. "Hell. We've got to report this as soon as we can. It's our civic duty, despite what Hunter says."

Rourke was right, but what kept running through her mind was the strange way Hunter had considered the photographs. The concern etched in his face and actions, the questions he'd asked—all led her to believe he thought the same as her, despite his words to the contrary and how insane the notion could be. The wolf was the same one she'd seen on the three separate occasions, and he was stalking her.

Chapter 7

For two hours, Tessa sat with Hunter, his head resting in her lap as he slept fitfully on the couch. Her nerves raw, she wanted to take him to the hospital in the worst way, to have medical personnel—who knew what they were doing—care for him.

Rourke had finally fallen asleep on the other sofa, snoring softly. The fire crackled and cast a soft glow into the room, but the lamps remained on the floor where they had fallen. Not wanting to disturb Hunter's rest, she'd clean up later. Battling to stay awake, she kept vigilant, watching for any sign Hunter's condition was worsening.

"Meara," Hunter mumbled and groaned. "Meara."

Tessa's soggy eyes widened, and she strained to hear him speak again. Was he remembering something more? Of course he was. But about a girlfriend or his sister? Her heart skittered with the thought.

She brushed the hair away from his forehead, the shadow of a beard giving him a rugged, sexy appearance, but his cheeks seemed flushed. She touched his cheek, her fingers recoiling at the feel of his skin. *No, no.* He was burning up.

She hurried to move out from under him, removed his blankets, and went to the kitchen. Pouring water into a glass, she glanced out the window to see how bad the storm was. Maybe they could chance taking him into town.

Half-hidden in the shadows of the shed, the security light revealed a wolf sitting, watching the house.

A shiver stole up her spine. Was it the one that had knocked Rourke out and come after her? No, this one didn't have any blood on his nose. She squinted her eyes, trying to get a better look. Its darker gray fur blended with beige and its snout had the same pretty beige on top, white underneath. Was he the one that Hunter said attacked the other then?

Maybe Hunter was right. She wouldn't want anyone to shoot a good animal.

She opened the window and tried to get a closer look. The animal's ears twitched and his eyes focused on her. He didn't seem vicious, but he was still feral.

She closed the window and returned to the living room with the medicine.

"Hunter," she said, trying to wake him.

He looked up at her, his eyes glassy. He closed his eyes and moaned.

"No, Hunter, take this medicine. We need to bring down the fever. Hunter!"

Rourke touched her arm and she nearly dropped the glass.

"What's wrong?" he asked, his voice ragged with sleep.

"He's burning up and I can't get him to take anything for it."

"Here, let me." Rourke helped Hunter sit up and forced the pill down his throat, but Hunter growled and bit him. Rourke jerked his finger free. "Hell, Hunter, I'm only trying to help."

"Let me get some antibiotics for that. *Jeez.* What next?" Tessa asked.

"I just hope to hell the wolf that bit him didn't have rabies." Rourke helped Hunter lie back down and joined Tessa in the kitchen. "He seems to be sleeping all right."

"Restlessly." She washed Rourke's finger in the sink and glanced out the window. No sign of the wolf. "Hunter broke the skin."

"I noticed. Here I get off pretty easily by surviving the wolf attack, resulting in only a lump as big as a melon on the back of my head and one hell of a headache, and the ex–Navy SEAL bites me instead."

"You can write it in your memoirs some day." She coated his finger in antibacterial ointment and then wrapped a bandage around it. "At this rate, I'm going to have to buy a whole lot more medical supplies. By the way, I saw one of those wolves out back." She got Rourke a couple of pills for his headache.

He leaned against the sink and peered out the window. "I don't see anything but snow."

"He's gone now, but it's not the one who attacked us. He had a bloody nose. This one didn't have a mark on it."

"If they were fighting, how did he get away without a scratch?"

"Maybe it was hurt somewhere I couldn't see. I just know it wasn't the one that came after us. Can you get back to sleep?"

Rourke took the pills, drowned them with a glass of water, and followed Tessa into the living room. "Why don't you try sleeping for a while? I'll watch Hunter and the house for a couple of hours."

She ran her hand over Hunter's temple, his face

flushed and sweaty. "I hope the roads are clear enough in the morning. No matter what condition they're in, we're going to have to chance taking Hunter to the clinic."

Everyone was fast asleep when the doorbell rang at six in the morning. *Déjà vu.* Immediately, Tessa bolted upright from the sofa opposite the one Hunter slept on. Rourke opened a sleepy eye as he lay back on the recliner. Hunter continued to sleep, his face still red.

She studied the door. "If there's no one there, I'm not opening the door."

"I'll get it," Rourke offered, pulling the blanket off his lap.

"No. Last time you did, it was a disaster. Are… are you okay? You look a little feverish."

The doorbell rang again.

Tessa rushed to peek through the peephole. "Oh, hell," she whispered. "It's Ashton and he's got a rifle."

Rourke hurried to join her. "Since Ashton got here safe and sound, maybe we can take his truck and get Hunter to the hospital."

"He's got a gun!"

"He won't know what hit him." Rourke bolted across the living room, grabbed the fireplace poker, and then rejoined Tessa at the front door. "Okay, open it."

"You're not going to hit him with that, are you?"

"I'm just going to persuade him to let us use his truck so we can take Hunter in for heavy-duty antibiotics and sutures."

Ashton rang the doorbell again.

"Hide the poker behind your back and don't hit him. I'll try to convince him to agree to help us."

"Hey! Hunter! It's me, Ashton! I got my dad's permission to be here."

Tessa glanced at Rourke. He shrugged. "Let him in."

Her heart pounding hard, she unlocked the door and opened it. Ashton was more cheerful than she had seen him in months. His blue eyes sparkled with humor and his grin couldn't have been any more friendly, but his jaw was slightly bruised.

"Where's Hunter? I told him I'd help him locate the stalker. He made me get my dad's approval first. Dad and I went around and around about it late into the night, but I finally wore him down. Hey, you look a little ill, Rourke."

Tessa looked at him. "Oh, Rourke, your face *is* as red as Hunter's." She clapped a hand on his forehead. "You're burning up, too."

Ashton peered around them at the mess in the living room, and his mouth gaped. "What the hell happened? Did the stalker break in? I knew I should have stayed."

"A wolf attacked Hunter. We've got to get him to the clinic. Can you get us there?" She closed the door.

Ashton swore under his breath. "He's got a fever."

"The animal might have been rabid," Tessa warned.

"I sure hope the hell he wasn't. Hunter bit me!" Rourke raised his bandaged finger to show Ashton.

"I'm not sure I want to know how that happened." Ashton set his rifle down. "Let's get Hunter to the truck. We'll go to the hospital emergency room. I have chains on my tires, so we should be able to make it."

"Thanks, Ashton," Tessa said, relieved that he would help without resorting to Rourke's tactics. She wondered if Rourke had wanted to clobber Ashton though, for what he'd pulled with her out by the shed.

"It's nothing. Rourke, can you help me? Or are you too sick?"

"I'll help."

Tessa got the front door and then the truck door while Ashton and Rourke carried Hunter to the extended cab. As strong as Hunter seemed, she couldn't believe how sick he was. Which was ridiculous. As torn up as he was, infection had to have set in. He was only human after all.

She threw on her parka and grabbed blankets, a pillow, and her purse. Rourke yanked on his parka and gloves, and they climbed into the truck.

"So what the hell happened?" Ashton pulled out of the frozen driveway.

Tessa knew her vehicle would never have made it. Rourke's either, since his had slipped into a ditch even before the storm had worsened.

"A wolf knocked Rourke unconscious and came after me. Hunter was searching for the stalker."

"Oh."

Ashton sounded so guilty, she immediately became suspicious. "What?"

"He found me looking for the stalker instead." Ashton rubbed his jaw. "I guess I distracted him from his mission for a time. Sorry, Tessa. I had to tell him I was there to protect you. I'd promised Michael."

"You did? Thanks, Ashton." Maybe the jerk was salvageable after all. She hadn't thought he could ever be.

"I shot Hunter because I thought he was the stalker."

She barely breathed. "Have you seen the guy then?"

"Yeah. He's tall like Hunter. Dark-haired, too. It really was an honest mistake. I have to tell you, I couldn't go to the trial, Tessa. I thought Michael was guilty of murdering Bethany. I thought he did it because she was seeing some other guy, and he found out."

"*You* were the other guy," Tessa said, her voice bitter.

"Yeah. But he'd asked me, begged me to watch out for you. I promised him I would. Believe me, I really didn't think there was anything to worry about concerning your safety. That first night I was out there, I saw someone peeking in the windows. I think Michael already knew there was someone, but like with me seeing Bethany, he couldn't catch the guy in the act. Anyway, I hollered at the Peeping Tom. Asked him what the hell he was doing. He took off running. Really fast dude. Just like Hunter when he charged up the hill toward me the other night."

"He was getting firewood. He was wearing Michael's clothes."

"He wasn't getting firewood when I saw him. He was naked."

Tessa closed her gaping mouth and stared at Ashton in disbelief.

"He began yanking Michael's clothes out of a plastic sack and jerked them on. I didn't recognize the sweats. But I did see the familiar eagle on the back of the field jacket and knew it was Michael's. So I thought maybe he'd gotten into the house and stolen some of Michael's things."

She cast a glance over the seat. Hunter was sound asleep, the blankets tucked under his chin. What in the world had Hunter been doing undressing and dressing in the bitter cold? Unless Ashton had been drunk, like she'd suspected, despite what Hunter had said.

"So I didn't know what to think. After Rourke said Hunter was an ex–Navy SEAL, I realized what he was doing. Hardening himself for the worst conditions he would have to face. That way he could survive anything. If I'd done what he had, I would have double pneumonia."

But Hunter wasn't an ex–Navy SEAL. If he hadn't been gathering firewood, she figured he would have been searching for the intruder. He *wouldn't* have been naked.

"Okay, I give, Rourke. How'd Hunter bite you?" Ashton asked.

He didn't respond. Tessa looked at him. He was sleeping, his head propped against the cold window. She wished she had brought some more pillows. At least they had plenty of blankets if they got stuck. Although she hadn't considered taking them for that reason.

"Long night for all of us," Tessa said. "I was trying to get Hunter to take some fever-reducing medicine, but couldn't wake him enough. Rourke finally got the pill down him, but Hunter clamped his teeth on Rourke's finger. Broke the skin even. I'm really worried that wolf was rabid. What if Hunter and Rourke have rabies now?"

"Hunter's bite was pretty bad, huh?"

"Tore the muscle all the way to the bone." Tessa shuddered.

"They'll get the shots and be fine. But if they don't, rabies in humans is fatal. The doctor will have to decide. But if we can kill the animal and bring him in, the medical personnel can check out his brain and know for sure. No sense in Hunter and Rourke having to go through the painful ordeal if it's not needed."

"Hunter doesn't want the wolf shot. He said it didn't have rabies, and he'd take care of it himself."

Ashton smirked. "I love his style. Get rid of the offender personally. Of course, when I was on the receiving end of his drive to right the wrong, I felt a little differently. But Hunter's all right. I mean, if the roles were reversed and some dude shot me, I probably would have killed him. On the other hand, I doubt I would have had the balls to charge up the hill after a guy who had his rifle sights on me. That took a hell of a lot of guts. It was as if he knew he'd shake me up so much, I wouldn't be able to get off another round. And he was right. I couldn't twitch a muscle, shoot, run, nothing. Must be his training."

Ashton shook his head. "I talked to my dad about going into the Navy SEALs. He's all against it, said I couldn't live with having my hair cut. But after we get rid of this stalker and Hunter reassures me he's sticking around to keep you safe... oh, hell, I promised Michael. Okay, here's the deal. I'll help Hunter find whoever murdered Bethany, and then once Michael's set free, I'm checking into the Navy."

Rourke lifted his head from the window. "I'm helping also. Maybe between the three of us, we'll discover something."

"Four of us," Tessa corrected him.

"I thought you believed Michael was guilty, Rourke," Ashton said.

"I did. I changed my mind. Since we now know he wasn't lying about someone seeing his girlfriend behind his back, what else was he being truthful about?"

"You think it was me?" Ashton asked, his voice growing hard.

"No. Someone else who knew all of you."

"The list. I've got to write that list of possible suspects," Tessa said.

"Of possible murderers?" Ashton asked.

"No, of stalkers. Hunter thinks it's someone who was in the house before he broke in that one night. Someone we knew."

"A gray," Rourke muttered under his breath as he rested his head against the window again and closed his eyes.

"A what?" Tessa asked.

But Rourke had fallen back to sleep.

"Why don't you get some sleep?" Ashton said. "You look pretty worn out."

"Who's going to watch your driving?"

Ashton gave her a small smile. "It's going to be slow going. This two-hour-long trip will probably be more like four."

The blowing snow made for whiteout conditions and the windshield wipers swept away the building snow, but it continued to shower down on them—huge white flakes. Thank God the truck's heater was working fine, and the cab was toasty warm.

Tessa closed her eyes and slept for a while. Until the truck jerked to a stop. Her eyes popped open. Ashton swore under his breath, yanked the door open, jumped out, and slammed the door shut. They were in the middle of nowhere still, surrounded by forest, no traffic, nothing but cold, wet snow and a gray bleakness. So what was the problem?

The truck was leaning at an odd angle. In the ditch? Great. Tessa pulled on her gloves to investigate.

Ashton threw open the door and jumped back into the

cab, shoving the door closed, his face ashen despite the chill in the air.

"How bad is it?" Tessa asked, afraid to know the answer.

"I left my rifle at your place, *damn it*."

"What?"

"My rifle! I left it at your place."

"What has that got to do with getting stuck in a snowdrift?"

"Rourke and I probably could get the truck out, but three gray wolves were watching me from the woods. They looked hungry. Maybe the one that attacked you was one of these?"

A shiver sped down her spine as she peered into the blowing snow, but saw nothing.

"They're wild dogs," Rourke said softly, peering out the window.

"I don't see them," Tessa said.

"Those are wolves," Ashton reiterated. "Wild dogs, my ass."

"We can't just stay here. What if the snow piles up behind the muffler?" Tessa glanced behind them.

"It will," Ashton warned.

"Okay, well, then we'd have to stop the engine, and we'd freeze."

Ashton rubbed his gloved hands together. "After what happened to Hunter, I'm not sure trying to move the truck while those animals are out there is a good idea."

"I'll move it." Hunter pushed the blankets aside and groaned.

"Oh, no, you don't." Tessa gave him a look like he had better not even think of it.

His brow furrowed. "I told you not to take me anywhere. I would have been fine in a day or two."

"Hunter, you're sick. We're taking you to the hospital and that's that."

"We're stuck in the middle of nowhere and not going anywhere fast."

"How are you feeling?"

Hunter glared at her. "Fine."

"Right. You look like you're still burning up with fever."

"The dogs won't attack us, will they, Hunter?" Rourke asked.

"They shouldn't."

"*Shouldn't* is the key word," Ashton said. "The wolf *shouldn't* have entered Tessa's home and bitten you either. Which means it has to be rabid."

"I'll try to move the truck," Rourke said, albeit reluctantly. He cast Hunter a dirty look over the backseat. "You stay here. You have a hell of a lot of explaining to do."

"Wait! Let me try my phone." Ashton pulled out his cell phone. "Maybe we'll have a signal here."

Everyone watched as Ashton punched in a number. He shook his head. "Nothing."

"I'll help." Tessa buttoned her parka.

"No, you stay and try to drive us out of the mess. Rourke and I'll stack up some wood under the tires, and then we'll push while you drive," Ashton said.

"I'll help," Hunter growled.

"No," Tessa said. "That shoulder of yours is too badly damaged. You're not going anywhere."

"We can't stay here, Tessa. I'll help. Then you can take me to the hospital and get me patched up. All right? But without my assistance, we may not be going anywhere." Before she could object, he added, "Three hulking men should be enough of a deterrent for the dogs. I don't want anyone else bitten."

"But your shoulder. You shouldn't do anything physical. And the fever. You shouldn't be out in this cold. What if you drove the vehicle, and I helped the guys?"

"No," all three men said at once.

Hunter pulled on the ski cap. But she hadn't brought Michael's field jacket for him because she didn't figure he could get into it with as bad as his shoulder was, and she hadn't thought he would be leaving the truck except to be wheeled into the hospital.

Ashton tossed his parka back to Hunter. "You owe me."

"Hell, he *really* owes me," Rourke grouched.

Rourke didn't elaborate, but she figured he was still pissed off at Hunter for biting his finger and worried he had rabies. He was sick with a fever, too. Working in these winter conditions couldn't be good for any of them.

Tessa started to remove her parka. "Here, Ashton, take mine."

"Size petite? Wouldn't fit over my broad shoulders." He rolled them back to make them appear larger. He wasn't half as broad as Hunter.

The men headed outside while Tessa moved into the driver's seat, wishing she could do more. The dogs must have been hiding or had run off. She didn't see any sign of them, although the guys kept casting glances at the woods while they were working. As soon as the men had piled up enough branches under the tires, Ashton motioned for Tessa to drive out. With them pushing and the truck tires finally getting some traction, she managed to pull back onto the road.

Ashton and Rourke whooped and hollered and she was glad, too, but afraid Hunter might have done more damage to his shoulder as quiet as he was.

With snow covering his long hair and sweater, Ashton helped Hunter into the truck while Hunter groaned. She knew he shouldn't have helped with the truck. Probably did most of the work, too, knowing him. Rourke climbed in and Tessa moved over to the center of the front seat. Once everyone was settled, Ashton put the vehicle in drive and began the remainder of the slow trek toward the hospital.

Tessa peered over the seat. "Are you okay, Hunter?"

He buried himself in the blankets and mumbled, "I'm fine."

She shook her head, imagining he could have broken every bone in his body and his response would be the same—I'm fine. "How about you, Rourke?"

"I'm fine."

She raised her brows. "Good. Then the hospital staff won't have much work to do when they check the two of you over. How about you, Ashton?"

He smiled broadly. "I'm frozen to the bone, I skinned my knuckle, and I pulled my calf muscle."

"An honest answer for once. What about the dogs? Did you see any sign of them?"

"Wolves." Ashton tightened his grip on the steering wheel as they plowed through another snowdrift. "They were watching. But like Hunter said, they didn't seem interested in attacking. Just curious, maybe. Pray we don't end up in the ditch again before we reach our destination."

When they reached the hospital later that afternoon, barely any of the staff had made it to work and unless patients had an emergency—like a couple of car accident victims, a baby delivery, and an elderly man who'd had a heart attack—most people stayed away. Woe to the patients stuck in the hospital whose families couldn't venture out in the storm to visit them.

Although Hunter hadn't wanted to be taken in on a stretcher, the hospital staff felt otherwise as soon as they saw his condition. Poor Rourke had to wait longer to be seen, but once they thought a rabid wolf might have bitten Hunter, they took Rourke right in.

As soon as Hunter was resting comfortably in a room after surgery, Tessa, Rourke, and Ashton went in to see him.

"Only family can see Mr. Grey," an officious nurse said, who had hovered over him ever since they had arrived. A striking brunette, tall, even more beautiful if she could manage half a smile.

Something about the woman irked Tessa. Maybe it was the way she cast Tessa condescending looks like she was beneath her, or maybe the way she'd taken charge of Hunter and dismissed them. Worse, a hint of recognition seemed to pass between Hunter and the nurse, and Tessa wondered if they had been lovers before. At once, she felt like an outsider.

"I'm his fiancée," Tessa said, her chin up, her eyes glowering.

The woman tucked a curl of hair behind her ear that had loosened from her bun. "I don't believe it."

How the hell would she know?

The nurse pointed at Tessa's unadorned fingers. "No engagement ring."

Tessa offered a fake smile. "Left it at home. But I don't really give a damn what you believe. The wedding's scheduled for the spring."

The woman laughed. "Right. And I'm the queen of England." She looked at Rourke.

"I'm his brother." He folded his arms. "Need any proof?"

"No. I believe you." She considered Ashton.

"Another brother."

Again, she laughed. "This is just too damned unreal. You've got fifteen minutes, and then visiting hours are over." She squeezed Hunter's hand like a lover would and brushed back a lock of hair from his forehead. Then she sneered at Tessa and left the room.

Hunter was sound asleep, and to Tessa's relief, the doctor said Hunter would have the full range of motion in his shoulder once he had gone through months of therapy after it healed.

Rourke pulled a chair over to the bed for Tessa and then turned to Ashton. "Can you get Tessa a cup of coffee? She looks a little peaked."

"Then I'll miss my fifteen minutes with Hunter."

Rourke raised a brow. "You don't really think we're going to allow that nurse to boss us around, do you?"

Ashton shrugged. "The thought had crossed my mind." He left the room.

"He'll be all right, Tessa," Rourke said. "He's a fast healer. And the rabies shots will ensure if the animal was rabid, Hunter will be fine."

"What about you? How are you feeling? You still look feverish."

"I received rabies shots and antibiotics, too. I'll be good as new soon."

"He didn't mean it, Rourke. He didn't bite you on purpose."

"Yeah, but you never know when one little bite can change your whole life."

She nodded and reached out to take Hunter's hand. "He's still awfully hot."

"The antibiotics and fluids they're giving him will make him feel like his old self before long. You were right to bring him here."

"Do you think that nurse knew him?"

"I got that impression. How did you and Hunter really meet? I never saw him before."

"The beach. We told you."

Rourke stared at him for sometime and then looked back at Tessa. "Naked? Injured? Tell me the whole story."

She hadn't wanted to say anything about how they had really met, not when they'd had such a good cover—at least up until now. But Rourke seemed to suspect the truth, and she really was a lousy liar.

Chapter 8

HUNTER WOKE TO THE CLOYING ODOR OF HOSPITAL antiseptics with a roaring headache and his shoulder feeling like it was on fire. But Tessa had been right to bring him here. He would heal much more quickly after the surgery, enabling him to fight the grays again. The room was dark and quiet, and Tessa was sleeping in the chair, a blanket from the car wrapped around her. She looked like an angel. Not the kind of woman he thought he would want to have for his own.

He wanted to pull her into bed and hold her close.

He closed his eyes. Hell, he had bitten Rourke. It wasn't the human bite that did it either. Already Rourke was aware of the change, although they hadn't been able to talk about it, and he wouldn't realize exactly what he was. His senses would be on higher alert. The urge to shapeshift hopefully would come on more gradually. But Hunter's gut clenched as he thought of how he'd changed Rourke. *Damn it.*

The nurse walked into the room, a gray *lupus garou* itching to make trouble where Tessa was concerned. The woman's eyes rounded when she saw Tessa sleeping there. When she reached out to wake her, Hunter growled low, "You touch her and you'll regret it."

The nurse folded her arms, her dark hair coiled into a bun, her amber eyes challenging him as she gave him a wicked look. "How did an alpha like you become so badly injured?"

"Don't you have *nursing* duties to perform?"

"You can't have her. So what's the deal? Got anyone else lined up that you're interested in? I need a mate."

"What are you doing working in this place?"

"I wouldn't put up with my pack's politics. What are you doing with the woman and that other man?"

"Don't mess with them."

Her eyes sparkling with deviousness, she bowed her head slightly and then left the room. He didn't trust her. But he knew if he breathed one word of leaving to Tessa, she would have a conniption. Rourke would understand. Somehow he had to solicit his help. Ashton would agree because of the perceived thrill of adventure. Rourke was bound to him as a newly appointed member of his pack. Of course, Rourke wasn't exactly aware of pack traditions yet, but he was instantly gifted with a wolf's wariness. The part about self-preservation of their species and keeping their secret was tantamount.

Hunter let out his breath in exasperation. Damn Rourke for poking that pill down his throat. Chomping down on the intrusive finger had been instinctual, but what a mess. Thank God he hadn't bitten Tessa. Teaching Rourke was going to be enough of a pain. *This* was why wolves didn't change humans. At least with *lupus garous* who were born that way, all the rules were known from day one, while their *lupus garou* parents reinforced the lessons from the beginning.

"Hunter?" Tessa whispered, her eyes trying to study him in the dark.

"Tessa, why don't you get a hotel room and get some sleep?"

In fact, that was the solution. Ashton could take her there and stay with her. Then Rourke could sneak Hunter out of the hospital in the morning, and they could say the hospital had released him.

"Would the stalker have followed us?" she asked.

"In this storm? I doubt it."

But then again, what if he and his brothers had? The three who had watched them from the woods when they were trying to get the truck unstuck from the snowdrift were different. Yet… familiar, somehow. He thought he recognized their scent, but not their appearance.

Hunter took a steadying breath. If the brothers had managed to follow them here, Ashton wouldn't be any match for them. Although the one wolf's leg shouldn't have healed this quickly either. Hunter ground his teeth. Maybe staying put for a while longer was for the best.

With the blanket wrapped around her shoulders, Tessa drew the chair over to the bed. "Rourke's upset with you for biting him. I told him you didn't mean it."

Hunter grunted. "He shouldn't have had his finger in my mouth."

"He was trying to help you. Would you have bitten me?"

"If I had, you'd have given me hell for it."

Looking wiped out, but as beautiful as ever with her long red hair in tangles around her face, she sat in the chair. "Do you know that nurse?"

"No."

"But you both seemed to recognize each other."

He noted a hint of jealousy, but he didn't want her believing he knew the woman when he didn't—just that she was a *lupus garou*. "I thought she seemed familiar, but I've never met her before."

"What about Meara? Who's she?"

"Meara?" He frowned. The name sounded familiar, but he couldn't recall.

"You said her name when you were delirious with fever. Is she your sister maybe?"

"Maybe, I can't remember."

Tessa reached her hand out to him. "Hunter, don't get mad at me, but Rourke realized our cover story wasn't true. I don't know what made him suspicious, but now he knows about your amnesia and how I found you on the beach. About the fact someone may have tried to murder you, too. He won't tell anyone. He's promised."

Rourke would know a hell of a lot more in a little while. "I figured he'd learn of it before long."

Her posture relaxed a little. "What about Ashton?"

"Not a word to him. I don't want to shatter his image of me."

Tessa smiled and rested her head on Hunter's lap, pressing against his groin and instantly he hardened. Despite the way his shoulder felt, she stirred his loins. Not only that, but her scent and the feel of her set his blood on fire.

"I wish we could snuggle together."

Just what the doctor ordered. Hunter patted the mattress. "It's small, but if we get really close, we should be able to manage."

She raised her head and looked at him. "But I don't want to hurt you."

"I'm feeling much better."

"If we get caught—"

"They can throw us out of here." He gave her a devilish smile.

"Yeah, but you need their help."

"I need you—more."

The smile on her lips said he won. She climbed onto the bed, one knee posed on the right side of him before she raised her other leg to cross over his waist. "Are you sure?"

"The anticipation is killing me, Tessa." With his good arm, he helped her get settled, groaning when her sweet body sank on top of his rigid erection.

"Oh, oh, I'm sorry. Did I hurt you?"

Hunter wrapped his arm securely around her, holding her hot little body tightly against his before she bolted from the bed. "Pure torture, but not in the way you mean."

She chuckled softly against his chest and relaxed.

Feeling Tessa's heated body against his, he had the overwhelming desire to screw convention and turn her, claim her. Had he ever felt this way toward a woman? He couldn't remember.

But he wondered how he could ever give up the minx. And yet he knew he had to. No woman in her right mind would willingly become a *lupus garou.* He wasn't sure how he was going to cope with Rourke's change, let alone a female he'd make his mate. It wouldn't be fair to her, any more than it was to Rourke. But the deed was done and there was no going back.

She took in a deep breath and kissed his chest covered in the thin hospital gown. Her lithe body pressed against his heavy groin. He moaned inwardly. Already, he wanted her again, when he had no business coveting her. But everything about her made him desire her, the way her soft body felt against him, her fragrance, the way she cared so about his welfare.

Her breathing soon grew shallow, and he sensed she had fallen asleep.

Maybe he could take her to Rourke's place for a while. At least until he healed up sufficiently. The stalker's wound wasn't as severe, and he would be back to Tessa's house soon, probably with the brother who wasn't injured badly either.

Knowing sleep would help his body to heal more than anything else, Hunter willed himself to shut down his concerns.

But he didn't realize he had even fallen asleep until sometime later the sound of footsteps entered the room, waking him. Hunter opened his eyes and stared at the man dressed in scrubs, his dark hair curling down to his shoulders, his face covered in a shadow of a beard. He looked way too scruffy to be a male nurse. Hunter expected him to come closer, to make a comment about the sleepy redheaded goddess in Hunter's arms, to check his vital signs. But this wasn't a medical call.

Hunter got a whiff of the man's scent. One of the stalker's brothers. The one who hadn't been injured too badly, probably now completely healed. If he'd thought to slip in and steal Tessa away while Hunter was drugged and asleep, he was going to have a fight on his hands.

"Why does your brother want her so bad?" Hunter hoped to learn more about these men before he had to eliminate them. Maybe he could still convince the brothers to give up the deadly quest.

"You have to ask?" The man snorted. "She's as close to one of us as we can find, and my brother, Yoloff, *will* have her. If I'd seen her first, she would've been mine."

"Had he followed her to California?"

The man's grim face brightened a little. "He almost had her there. Several times he's nearly taken her. The hunt is as appealing as the mating. Then you came along and he had to solicit our help."

Hunter could envision how frustrated the *lupus garou* was, but the previous comment stuck in his craw. "What do you mean by she's nearly one of us?"

"Hell, you can smell her pheromones."

Which didn't make sense, but there wasn't any way she was one of them. "She's not a *lupus garou*."

"Say what you will, but she's garnering a lot of *lupus garous*' attention in any event. Only she'll be my brother's mate. You can either give her up nice and easy or we'll take her the hard way. You don't want her in any event or you would have already turned her, so you might as well just let us have her."

"Then there's only one way this is going down." Hunter reached for the nurse's call button.

Before he pressed the button, a female nurse suddenly entered the room. "Who are you?" she asked the faux male nurse.

"I work on another floor." He gave Hunter a sinister smirk. "Just checking on my buddy here."

She glanced at Hunter, her eyes rounding when she saw Tessa asleep with Hunter. "What... you can't—"

The stalker's brother gave Tessa another long look. "Just remember what I said." Then he left.

"She can't sleep with you in the bed. I can get another bed for her."

"The man who just left has been stalking Tessa. He'd planned on grabbing her while I was knocked out on pain medication. She's not moving from here."

The woman's face paled. "I'll call security and report him." She whipped out of the room and shut the door.

Hunter must have fallen asleep after that because the next thing he heard was Ashton's chuckle near the doorway. Hunter opened his eyes, his arm still wrapped securely around a sleeping Tessa. His shoulder was stiff, but not half as painful. Although the medication dripping into his veins could have had something to do with that.

"You have style, Hunter. Real style."

"Where's Rourke?"

"He's still sleeping at his apartment down the road. He was pretty wiped out, but before I left, I checked and his fever was gone. We were going to take Tessa with us, but found the two of you like this before we left. Guess Nurse Godzilla didn't bother you any longer. I asked about her schedule and she's gone home, but she comes back on duty tonight."

Tessa stirred. Her eyes opened and she would have jumped from the bed if Hunter hadn't held on tight. He kissed her good morning on the lips and wanted more, but she was squirming in an attempt to bolt, stirring him to high heaven, and he released her.

He gave her a smile, then said to Ashton, "I'm starving. When do they serve food around here?"

Tessa climbed off the bed, her cheeks blushing beautifully.

Ashton cast her a conceited smirk. "Never knew you had it in you to break the rules, Tessa."

She glowered at him and headed for the bathroom.

"My breakfast?" Hunter asked Ashton, before he ripped off the I.V. and wiped the smirk off his face.

"Food's on its way."

"I want sausage, bacon, and a mess of scrambled eggs. Biscuits, too. And three pints of milk."

"I'm not sure what they ordered for you last night," Ashton said.

"Tessa told me you were a real prankster in school. I'm starving. I need solid food to build up my strength. Go get me—"

Rourke poked his head in the door, his eyes blurry, his hair mussed up, dark whiskers covering his chin, not the look of a reporter on his way to work. "You could have woken me, Ashton."

"You needed your sleep."

"I'll get your breakfast," Rourke said to Hunter, and he headed down the hall.

"Wait up, Rourke! I've got to see this." Ashton rushed after him.

Tessa stepped out of the bathroom. "I'm taking a hot shower. Don't let anyone in the bathroom."

"I'll join you."

"Ha! You can't get those bandages wet."

"We could manage." He started to climb out of bed.

"Don't you dare or I'll call a nurse." Tessa ducked back into the bathroom, shut the door, and started the water.

Hell, wet bandages wouldn't bother him. He was about to remove the I.V. when Rourke and Ashton walked back in the room, each carrying a covered dish.

"Ashton said you wanted both sausages and bacon. They came with one or the other. So we had to procure a couple of dishes to accommodate you." Rourke glanced at the bathroom and sniffed. He smiled and then frowned. "Surprised you're not in there with her."

"I would have been if the two of you hadn't returned with the food."

"You shouldn't get those bandages wet anyway," Ashton said.

Rourke gave him a get-real look. "You think that would have stopped Hunter?"

"Probably not." Ashton uncovered the dish of eggs and sausage. "Two poor patients will be without breakfast."

"The kitchen staff can make them more," Rourke said. "Come on, Ashton. Let's go to the cafeteria."

"What about Tessa?"

"She probably won't leave Hunter's side." Rourke gave him a pointed look.

Enough with the innuendos. Hunter knew she was becoming way too attached to him. But what could he do about it? He had to stay with her until he got rid of the gray threat and helped free her brother. Of course, his human side said to cool it with her. His wolf instincts told him she was the one for him. But those were deeper, more primal needs. They didn't take in account the horror she would most likely feel if he changed her. She could hate him. Probably would. She was close to her brother. How could she not tell him what had happened to her? Why she had to become a wolf for a jaunt in the woods sometimes during the moon's appearance, how she aged so slowly? Yet, if she were changed, she couldn't tell a human soul.

The shower shut off and Rourke grabbed Ashton's arm. "Let's get something to eat before anyone catches us in here with the stolen food and blames us for it."

Ashton laughed. "Hell, I thought you were as straight-laced as Tessa."

The two hurried back down the hall.

Tessa came out of the bathroom, wearing a towel on her head.

"Come," Hunter said, patting the bed. "Share breakfast with me."

"How'd you get two breakfasts?"

"Courtesy of Rourke and Ashton."

"Oh, brother." She peered down the hall. "Here come the food trays. Now you're in for it."

"It's your show." He grinned at her.

"Oh, great, so I have to explain this? The two Stooges left me with the evidence? I should leave you alone here to explain it yourself."

"I'm the innocent patient. I couldn't have left the bed." He shook his I.V.

She whipped the towel off her head, tossed it on the bathroom floor, and then stepped into the hall. "Here, I'll take Mr. Grey's breakfast for him."

Hunter smiled with satisfaction. If the circumstances had been different, they would all have made pretty decent pack members.

Tessa closed the door and carried the tray in to Hunter. He sniffed the air. "Do you like pancakes?"

"Sure."

"Why don't you eat them then."

She opened the lid. "How did you know?"

"Excellent sense of smell. Did the doctor talk to you about my condition last night?"

"Yes, he said it might take months of therapy to recover the full use of your shoulder."

"Won't take that long. What did he say about my release?"

"You just got here."

"I'm ready to leave."

She poured syrup on her pancakes. "You're *not* going anywhere, Hunter. You were in terrible shape when we brought you in. Even the doctor said so."

"All I need is you to take care of me. I'll heal ten times faster. Fever's all gone even."

She looked up from her pancakes and frowned. "Your face is still flushed."

"Nearly all gone then. I was thinking we ought to go to Rourke's place until I'm healed."

"He's got a studio apartment. No bedroom, couch makes into a bed. Kind of cramped."

"Oh. What about Ashton's place?"

Tessa licked the syrup off her lips and laughed. "He lives with his dad. Big house, but somehow I don't believe he'd appreciate it if we moved in with him."

"Still lives at home?" Hunter shook his head. "He *does* need to join the Navy."

"He's never held a job long enough that he could afford to live on his own."

"I wish I could remember where I live. That would solve the problem." Footsteps sounded down the hall headed in their direction. "Someone's coming. Probably the nurse."

Tessa flew into action. He hadn't planned on hiding the evidence, but Tessa took his empty dishes and stuffed them in the clothes cabinet. She sat back down on the chair, her face crimson.

"Good morning, Mr. Grey. I'm here to take your vital signs," the nurse said, smiling broadly at him, her long, dark curls bouncing as she walked with a spring to her step.

"I'm ready to leave."

She gave a breathy little laugh. "We try to get patients out of the hospital as quickly as we can, but—"

"Good. I'm ready. Just sign the papers."

"I'm sure you'll be here a couple of more days at least."

Hunter wasn't waiting that long. Not with the *lupus garou* nurse itching to destroy his relationship with Tessa and the rest of the grays still a real problem.

"The fever's come down quite a bit. The doctor will be here after a while to check on you. Do you need anything?"

"Just the release papers."

She chuckled. "We need more male patients like you. Just push the button if you need me." She wiggled her butt a little too much as she left the room.

"You can't leave until the doctor says so. Enjoy all the pampering. You deserve it," Tessa said.

Hunter was surprised she wouldn't be upset with the way the nurses were making fools of themselves over him. "Food's not as good as yours."

"Yeah, but you get three times as many dishes here." She motioned to the leftover pancakes.

Ashton and Rourke returned looking well fed. Rourke sniffed the air. "When did you get pancakes?"

Ashton laughed.

"Yeah, very funny, guys. I had to hide the other dishes," Tessa said.

Hunter pointed to the clothes cabinet. "I'm ready to go. I was trying to come up with a safe place to stay, but…"

"Snow's melting off the roadway," Rourke said. "Temperature rose to forty-five degrees."

Tessa shook her head. "He has to stay here until the doctor says."

Ashton folded his arms. "Yeah, I agree."

"My place is kind of small." Rourke rubbed the back of his head. "But you and Tessa could stay there for the time being. Place is well stocked. The electricity's back on all over the county. And phone service has been restored."

"What about the stalker?" Ashton sounded disappointed.

"Hunter can't mess with him for a while," Tessa said.

Hunter considered his options. But only one seemed viable. "All right. We return to Tessa's house. We need new locks, a window, and lots of food."

"And medical supplies. Bandages, tape, gauze, antibiotics. But you're not leaving here until the doctor releases you." Tessa gave Hunter a hard look.

"You've got your mission," Hunter said to Rourke.

Ashton's face brightened. "You've got it!"

The two vacated the premises pronto. Hunter took Tessa's hand and kissed it. "Want to snuggle some more? All that food made me sleepy."

She rolled her eyes. "I can just see the doctor catching us."

"Now there's an idea. Then he would release me, figuring I was well enough after all." But when she didn't make a move to join him, Hunter smiled and let go of her hand. "Wake me when he comes, if I don't get up before then."

Although it didn't matter if he got the doctor's permission or not. He couldn't stay much longer before someone discovered he was healing too fast for it to be normal and wonder why.

❖❖❖

Wake Hunter when the doctor came? No way. Tessa was determined to keep him right where he was. Rourke should have had better sense. Ashton was being Ashton, impulsive, devious, loving to go against the rules whenever he could.

The time dragged on and she knew if the doctor didn't hurry, Hunter would wake. She didn't want Rourke or Ashton returning either and trying to convince the doctor to let Hunter go. Then again, she figured at least someone on the medical staff would say no.

When the doctor arrived, she wanted to shove him into the hall and talk to him privately. The blond-haired man looked like he had barely finished high school.

"Hi, I'm Tessa Anderson," she whispered. "Hunter wants to leave, but he needs to stay for a couple of more days, don't you think?"

"After being torn up by that Rottweiler? I'd say so."

"Rottweiler?"

"Yeah. His friend said the dog had attacked Mr. Grey, but that they were so close to the edge of the cliff, the dog fell to its death. Tide washed him out or we would have been able to run tests on him to see if he had rabies. But Mr. Grey and Mr. Thornburg are receiving the rabies shots anyway as a precaution."

"The dog looked more like a—"

"Rottweiler," Hunter said. "Ready to release me, Doc?"

"Where's the man who was bitten by a wild dog?" Sheriff Wellington asked down the hall.

Hunter's expression darkened. Tessa took a deep breath. Now what story would Hunter tell?

The sheriff stalked into the room like he owned it,

glanced at the doctor, and then at Tessa. His eyes widened. He whipped his head around and stared at Hunter.

Hunter gave him an arrogant smirk.

"*You* were the one bitten?"

"It's me."

"Where's my son? He said he was coming to see you. If anything happened to him—"

"He went into town to get some supplies for Tessa's house. Doc's releasing me and we're returning to her place."

The doctor cleared his throat. Good, he would set Hunter straight. Even if he did look like he'd just graduated high school. The doctor took a look at Hunter's injury. "Hmm, looking better, Mr. Grey, but you'll be here for a couple of more days as bad as the wound is."

Tessa smiled at Hunter. She was glad at least the doctor had enough sense.

He wrote something in his chart. "I'll be back later to check on you."

The doctor walked out and the sheriff folded his arms. "I don't want you filling my son's head with glorified stories of how wonderful serving in the Navy SEALs is."

"Wouldn't think of it. The notion of joining them is all his idea, not mine."

"You could have told him why you quit. The downside of being in the Navy." The sheriff shook his head. "So what's the story about this wild dog? Are you sure it's dead?"

Hunter repeated the farfetched tale that Rourke had made up. Tessa couldn't believe it. Was he trying to protect the vicious animal? Or was it like

Ashton had said? Hunter wanted to take care of the menace personally?

She watched his facial expression—the amusement in his lips and eyes—even though he was trying to keep a straight face while he told the story. What did she really know about him? *Nothing*. Except that he was super-protective of her, dependable when it came to survival instincts, a great handyman, a born leader, a damned good cook, and the greatest lover she'd ever had. But she still didn't know who he was, where he had come from, or how he had gotten there. What if he was a bad guy, but didn't remember being one? Could a person forget a past life of crime and become someone new? But when the memories returned, then what?

"Is that what happened?" the sheriff asked Tessa.

"What?"

He frowned at her. "Did it happen like Mr. Grey said?"

"Sure." She gave Hunter a scathing look. She didn't lie, normally, and she didn't appreciate being forced into one when she didn't have a clue as to the reason.

"We got the…" Ashton said, walking into the room, but quit speaking and stopped dead when he saw his father. "Hey, Dad."

"What did you see concerning this dog incident?"

"Nothing. When I arrived, the damage was already done. I just drove Hunter and the others here so he and Rourke could get medical treatment."

"When are you coming home?"

"We've got a job to do. Rourke and I are replacing Tessa's broken window and door locks. Then we'll scout around for that thief."

The sheriff grunted. But Tessa could see a hint of admiration in his face. He cast Hunter an ill-boding look, but again, it was more like it was to cover his true feelings. "You keep my son safe. He's a good shot with a rifle, but he's no ex–Navy SEAL."

"We picked up enough provisions to last a week," Rourke said. "When are we leaving? Some of the stuff needs refrigeration, although for now it's in cold storage in the truck."

"The doctor said a couple of days at least," Tessa said with great satisfaction.

"Call me and let me know what's going on with this intruder," the sheriff said to Ashton. "With car accidents and cases of asphyxiation due to the misuse of generators during the power outage, my investigators are spread pretty thin. But if you need anything, call me." He looked at Tessa. "And file the report on the gun as soon as you can."

"How about now, Tessa?" Hunter asked. "We're here, I'm stuck at the hospital for now. Ashton can run you in and bring you back. By then, we could share lunch." He smiled. The look was totally faked.

"I will, only because I'm afraid the thief might use my gun to commit a crime, and I don't want to be in trouble for it."

"What about the food?" Ashton asked.

"You can pick up Rourke in a little while and take it to—"

"Drop by my place after Tessa files the complaint. We can store the food there. No sense in driving the two hours to her place and back here again." Rourke looked at Hunter for approval.

He nodded.

"Good, let's get this done." Tessa figured when they were at Rourke's place, she would question him about this new dog story. Hell, the animal had knocked him unconscious. How would he have known what it was?

When she started to leave with the sheriff and Ashton, Hunter smiled. "No good-bye kiss?"

She gave him an annoyed look. He grinned. Stalking across the floor, she meant to give him a peck on the cheek—show him. He grabbed her with his good arm, kissed her thoroughly—mouth to mouth, tongue to tongue—which melted her insides, and she wanted a hell of a lot more. Her face suffused with heat, she pulled away.

He gave her a sly smile. He knew what he did to her, damn it! "Don't be gone too long."

"I won't be," she whispered, "because I don't trust you."

He laughed. "Good. Best to be alert always."

Ashton grinned, but Rourke looked annoyed. The sheriff had already left.

"Watch him," she said to Rourke. "Don't let him sneak out of the hospital." Then she thought about the food incident and added, "And don't *you* help him do that either."

Then she left, but she had a very bad feeling about the situation.

For a human, Tessa had pretty good wolf instincts. As soon as she was a little way down the hall with Ashton, Rourke got Hunter's clothes for him. Hunter pulled out the I.V. and then hurried to dress. "I take it you have a way to get us to your place until we rendezvous with Ashton and Tessa and head to her house."

"Taxi." Rourke got on the phone and called for one. He took the knife from one of the breakfast dishes and sawed through the hospital tag around Hunter's wrist.

"Can you occupy the nurse while I go to the lobby and wait for the taxi?"

"Got it." Rourke left the room.

Hunter waited until Rourke asked the nurse when the doctor was releasing Mr. Grey. Then Hunter stalked down the hall, found the stairs, and bolted down them. When he reached the lobby, he paced. Rourke soon joined him.

"It won't take long for them to realize you're gone."

"They can't hold patients against their will." Hunter glanced out the window. "Taxi's here."

"That was sure quick." Rourke raced after Hunter.

"Mr. Holloway?" the driver said.

"Yes." Hunter climbed in and Rourke shut his door and then ran around to the other side.

"Five-twenty-two Sycamore, right?" the taxi driver asked.

Rourke smiled as he entered the cab. "Take us to 1032 Redwood."

"You got it."

"I hadn't thought of giving an alias," Hunter said to Rourke.

Rourke motioned to an old guy standing in front of the hospital, leaning on a cane. "I told you I thought it was awfully quick for the cab's arrival. I think we took his."

Another cab pulled up.

Hunter watched out the back window. "Good. He took ours then."

"Hope he tells him a different address than my place."

When they arrived at the brick apartment complex, Rourke paid the driver and Hunter headed toward the front door.

"You've got a hell of a lot of explaining to do." Rourke fumbled for his keys as he joined Hunter. "Like why I can see in the damned dark? And why I can see things in the distance when I used to have to wear glasses. And hell, why that nurse smelled like a gray wolf—you, too. But also why I knew what a wolf smells like in the first place."

"Yeah, well, you shouldn't have stuck your finger down my throat."

"You tried to spit the pills out. I was trying to push them down farther so you'd swallow them. Wish I hadn't. Well in a way. I mean, I like some of these abilities, but I want to know what I've gotten myself into." Rourke shut the door behind them and turned on the heat. "Here, I'll make the couch into a bed, and you can lie down before Ashton and Tessa show up."

"The couch is fine. I'm feeling better already."

Rourke removed the bandage from his finger. No sign of a bite. "Okay, start talking."

Hunter meant to sit on the couch, but he was wearier than he thought. He reclined instead.

Rourke frowned. "Hell, I thought you were nearly healed."

"Not for a few more days. But I'm healing too fast to stay at a hospital any longer."

Rourke got him a pillow and blanket. “Need any pain medication?”

“Yeah, but this time, keep your fingers to yourself.”

“Deed’s already done, but believe me, I’ll be careful when I’m around you from now on.” He left and then returned with a glass of water and two white pills. “Start talking.”

“We’re *lupus garou.* Werewolves.”

Rourke collapsed on the leather chair in front of the coffee table. “Holy crap. You can’t be serious. But damn, you can’t be making it up either.”

“It’s true. When we shapeshift we’re like real wolves, except we still have our human reasoning. When we’re humans—”

“We have the increased senses of the wolf. I already got that part since I smelled women’s scents, pine needles, the shift in the weather from snow to drier conditions.” Rourke rubbed the newly sprouted whiskers on his chin. “The antiseptics in the hospital were nearly killing me, they were so strong. And I heard people talking way down the hall—not just talking, but heard what they were saying when I shouldn’t have been able to discern a thing. Then my finger began tingling like crazy, and it felt like it was healing at the speed of light. But I couldn’t figure out what had happened to me—only that it had to do with you. You really don’t remember who you are?”

“No. Only that I have a sister. I’m sure I lead a pack. And three grays pushed me off a cliff north of Tessa’s place.”

“Because?”

Hunter shrugged. “I might have deserved it. I don’t know.”

"So," Rourke said, easing back in the chair, "if we bite someone, we turn them?"

"Not always. And we can't when we're human. It would put a damper on our sexual relations with human women if we had to worry about changing them by accident."

"But you bit me! And gave me your condition."

"I bit you, yes. But I'd tangled with the stalker before that. Our mouths clashed a couple of times and I tore his ear. I bit the other two wolves also. Either it was their blood or the stalker's blood or saliva that transferred the genes. We'll never know."

"So you're saying, technically, one of *them* changed me."

"Technically yes. Because as a human, I couldn't bite you and transfer the condition, but since my teeth opened your skin, it helped the transmission."

Rourke relaxed. "Good, because I thought… well, I worried about Tessa."

"I won't turn her."

"But the stalker—he's a gray and he plans to, don't you think?"

"That's what Yoloff plans. I'm not giving him the chance."

"Yoloff?"

"Yeah, and he has two brothers. The one paid me a visit in the middle of the night, figuring he could slip Tessa out from under my nose. I broke the one's leg. He'll probably heal in about the same amount of time it takes me to get back to normal."

"Shit. They're not going to give up." Rourke combed his fingers through his hair. "So what are the negative aspects of being a *lupus garou*?"

"Having the uncontrollable urge to become a wolf when the moon is out, particularly strongest when it's the full moon, although it's not a constant craving. Once we fulfill the urge to hunt, we can manage several weeks without changing again. On the other hand, I've never personally known anyone who was changed by a bite, so it might be a little different for you."

"What do you mean?"

"Most of us were born *lupus garou*."

Rourke's eyes widened. "How many of you are there? I had the impression that a wild wolf had some kind of a weird virus and infected a few people."

"We have no idea how many there truly are of us. Since we live in secret, most of us only know about our local packs. Sometimes we learn of others while we're searching for a mate."

"A mate." Rourke perked up.

"Yeah, and that's one of the more important rules we have to live by. We don't turn humans."

Rourke made a disagreeable face. "Right. Very important to remember that."

"Yeah, otherwise we have to deal with the consequences." Hunter raised a brow.

"Like me."

"Exactly. That's another thing. You're part of my pack now."

"Just curious, but why wouldn't I be part of the pack of the ones who actually turned me?"

"Just a gut feeling, Rourke, but I don't think they're soliciting newly changed *lupus garou* pack members. I doubt another male would be accepted."

"Okay, not that I was interested since they'd tried to murder you, but I just wondered."

"Another thing—when we take a female for our mate, it's for life. We don't have marriage rituals, wear wedding rings—or any other jewelry for that matter—too hard to change into our wolf form quickly. We don't believe in divorce. It's for life. And we live very long lives."

Rourke's expression brightened. "For how long?"

"After we reach eighteen, our aging metabolism slows down. We age one year for every thirty we live."

Rourke whistled. "Man, oh man, what a deal."

"We *can* die early."

"Silver bullets?"

"Supposedly, if they're in the heart or brain and not extracted quickly enough. But we can drown, die in a fire, a snapped spinal cord at the base of the neck will do it. Probably other ways. Old age eventually, too. Although our bodies have an unusual capability to heal quickly, as we grow old, the ability wanes. So we're not completely invincible."

"Good enough for me. So what are you going to do about Tessa?"

Chapter 9

ASHTON RANG THE DOORBELL AT ROURKE'S APARTMENT and although Tessa worried Hunter would try to steal away earlier than the hospital staff recommended, she *never* expected him to leave this soon or be resting on Rourke's couch.

"I can't believe this! What did the doctor say, Hunter? That you needed to be at the hospital for at least a couple of more days. At least! Didn't he? What happened to sharing lunch with you? What happened to..." She growled, whipped around, and stalked out of the apartment.

Outside, she shivered and rubbed her arms, her frosty breath filling the air. How could Hunter be so damned stubborn and illogical about this? What if he got sick again?

Rourke joined her outside. "He's got a horrible phobia about hospitals, Tessa."

In disbelief, she stared at him. Was he telling the truth or making up another Rottweiler tale? "Why?"

Rourke shoved his hands in his pants pockets. "I don't know. Maybe somebody special died in one. I don't think he remembers. He's doing really well physically. Psychologically, he couldn't handle the hospital stay any longer. If he starts running a fever, we can bring him back here. All right?"

"No, it's not all right. You didn't get the doctor's permission, did you?"

"I talked to the nurse."

"*She* doesn't sign the release forms."

"He can't go back, Tessa. Trust me on this."

"If he gets worse…"

"If he gets worse, I promise we'll return him to the hospital and chain him there."

"I don't like it."

"I think he's afraid of Nurse Godzilla's return also." Rourke winked.

Tessa frowned. "Not Hunter. I don't see him being afraid of anyone or anything."

"Maybe not, but that woman was scary. She'd definitely wear the pants in the family."

"Is Hunter well enough to travel?"

"Yes, Hunter is well enough to travel!" he roared from the couch. "And I want to arrive at your place before lunch."

Despite how annoyed she was with him, she smiled to hear his gruff voice. "Hmm, he's sounding better already. Grouchy and hungry." She returned to the apartment and glowered at him. "If you get sick again, we're bringing you back and chaining you to the hospital bed. Phobia or no phobia."

"Hell, Rourke, you didn't tell her about my phobia, did you?"

The devil shined in Hunter's amber eyes, and Tessa had the feeling he and Rourke were bamboozling her.

When they arrived at Tessa's house, she wanted Hunter to return to the couch, but he organized a search of the place to ensure the stalker wasn't there first. Always business first, although she felt Rourke and Ashton could have done the deed so Hunter could rest.

After Rourke and Hunter checked the rooms while Ashton stayed with Tessa, she made Hunter lie down on the couch and covered him with blankets. Rourke and Ashton hauled in the groceries and Rourke's bags. Ashton had brought his own. One big happy family. If only her brother were here. And here she thought she would be alone until she could obtain her brother's release.

What else could go wrong? If it hadn't been for her stalker and the wolf attack, Hunter might have made some headway into investigating Bethany's murder.

Disheartened at the turn of events, Tessa started putting away the groceries: meat, and lots of it.

"Rourke and I are going to replace the window now," Ashton said. "If you need anything, just holler."

"Thanks. I should have gone grocery shopping with you. Don't you guys believe in eating vegetables?"

They laughed and headed outside. When they began pulling the boards off the house over Michael's broken window, it sounded like a tornado was ripping the place apart. She hoped they didn't do more damage than the thief had done.

"I'll fix lunch if you don't need anything else," Tessa said to Hunter.

"I'm fine."

"Good. Just yell if you need anything."

She started preparing ham sandwiches for lunch and was glad that Rourke had helped foot the bill. When Ashton and Michael ate her out of house and home, it was bad enough, but at least Michael always brought in an income, too.

Hunter's shoulder seemed okay, but he appeared disquieted about something else. He and Rourke had shared a look between them after checking out the house, although it was fleeting enough it had been barely noticeable, but she suspected something was wrong. Had the intruder been here again? She suspected so.

Ashton was oblivious, happy to be one of the "gang." She guessed maybe one of his problems was he had never fit in with most anyone, and for whatever reason, he had latched onto her brother. Hunter was more of a leader figure, and Ashton seemed to need his kind of guidance.

"Tessa," Hunter called out.

She set the bread on the kitchen counter and hurried into the living room. "Are you feeling badly?"

Still looking weary, Hunter was sitting up on the couch.

"Why don't you lie back down?" she asked, touching his good shoulder.

His expression uncomfortably serious, he motioned to the couch. "We need to talk."

She didn't like those words. They were the same the sheriff spoke when he informed her he had arrested her brother for murder. She stood rigid.

Hunter took her hand and eased her onto the couch next to him. He draped his arm around her shoulders and his free hand held one of hers in her lap. "I've been so wrapped up in this business with the stalker, I haven't talked to you about some things I need to."

She barely breathed. Did he remember who he was?

"When I went after the wolf—"

"The Rottweiler?" she asked, her voice and brows arched.

"The wolf. I discovered the place where I was pushed

off the cliffs. I need to return there, to discover clues of why I was thrown from there."

Her heart raced. "Do you know who did it?"

"I remember there were three men, but I didn't know them, and I don't know why they did it. I might have deserved it. I don't have any clue. I just wanted you to be aware of the fact I need to return there. Maybe seeing the place will help the rest of my memories return. I'll take Rourke with me, but I want you and Ashton to stay here."

"Not right now. You can't leave until you're perfectly healed." She hated how desperate she sounded. "You haven't seen these men again, have you? Is that why you need Rourke? Why don't you call the sheriff? Even if these men were mad at you, they had no right pushing you off a cliff. That's attempted murder."

"I'll deal with it, Tessa."

"You're *not* invincible, Hunter. When will you get that through your thick head?"

He smiled and melted some of the icy worry collected in the pit of her stomach, but she still couldn't shake loose of all her concerns.

"Listen, there's another matter Rourke and I were anxious about," Tessa said.

Ashton opened the front door and he and Rourke walked inside.

"Window's done," Rourke announced. "We're not interrupting anything, are we?" He almost looked like he hoped they had.

"I was just about to tell Hunter another of our concerns. About the guy who disappeared after he rang the doorbell. We opened the door and the wolf jumped on you. Had he killed the man first and dragged his body off?"

"The guy got away," Hunter said. "When I was fighting with the wolf, I saw the man looking scared to death in the cab of his truck. Then he drove off."

"And he didn't offer to help you?" Tessa asked, frowning, not believing someone could be that horrible.

"Some people are afraid of dogs," Hunter said.

Especially when it was a wolf. But still, couldn't he have done *something* to help Hunter? "So what did his truck look like? Who was he?"

Hunter shrugged his good shoulder. "I didn't get much of a chance to look. Phone lines were down or I'm sure he would have called for help."

"I saw another wolf on the back patio last night when I was getting a glass of water for your fever. He wasn't the one I'd hit with the fireplace tongs though."

Hunter frowned. "Can you describe him?"

"Darker gray and beige, white mask, no blood on nose. He was sitting, watching me as I looked out the window. That's it. I didn't see any wounds on him, but he might have had some somewhere. Where he was sitting was dark. Oh, and he was a little smaller than the one who bit you. Was that what the wolf looked like that fought the other?"

Hunter nodded. "Yeah."

But she could tell by the way he seemed to puzzle over the matter that he didn't think so.

"Lunch ready soon?" Ashton asked. "We're going to install the new doorknobs next."

"As soon as you're finished, the sandwiches will be ready," Tessa said.

"I'll help you in a minute, Ashton. Be right back."

Rourke went out back and Ashton hurried to join him.

Hunter ran his fingers over Tessa's hand with a reassuring touch. "So where and how did Bethany die?"

"Oh, I guess you wouldn't know. Like you, she was pushed off a cliff. Right beside a burned-up pine tree, about six or seven miles north of here. But of course, she didn't survive the fall."

Hell. The same place the grays had thrown Hunter off the cliff?

They would probably come in a pack the next time. He didn't want Tessa out of the house, ever, until he took care of the menace. Now with this newest revelation about Bethany, he again wondered if the stalker, Yoloff, had something to do with her death to get Michael out of the way so he could go after Tessa.

"You look pale. Are you all right?" Tessa touched Hunter's forehead. "No fever, thank goodness."

"That's the same place where I was shoved from the cliff."

Her eyes grew big and her lower lip quivered. "No," she whispered. "Do… do you think the same guys who pushed you could have killed Bethany? We've got to tell the sheriff."

"No, we can't."

"But we have to so we can free Michael."

"They may not have been the ones who'd thrown her from there. Besides what would I tell the sheriff? That everything I've said is a lie?" Hunter ran his thumb over her hand, trying to pacify her, wishing he could reassure her. "Then what would he believe? Maybe I did it."

"But Bethany's murder happened months ago."

"Yes, and then here I was at the same crime scene months later. Who's to say I wasn't the one who did it, and then like murderers will often do, I came back to investigate the area where I'd committed the crime?"

"You couldn't have done it. You didn't." Her eyes filled with tears and his stomach clenched.

"You're right, I didn't. Three men pushed me off that same cliff. But I don't know who they were, where I'm really from, or what my last name is even. How will the sheriff believe any of it?"

She stiffened her back and folded her arms. "Why did you and Rourke lie about the wolf?"

Hell, what was he to say now?

"I'm an advocate for wolf rights. They cull out the weak and old, unlike human hunters who target the biggest and healthiest elk or deer. Humans kill the prime stock that would provide for more offspring. Wolves go after the easier prey."

"Like me? You?"

"That's different."

"But this one's so dangerous."

"Tessa, hunters won't discriminate. Believe me in this. They'd come here in droves, killing anything that moved, hoping to get a chance to take down the devil wolf. I'll take care of it."

"A Rottweiler." Tessa shook her head. "Dumbest story Rourke could have made up. He should have at least thought of a dog that looked more like a wolf—that had fur even! Let me finish making lunch, but we've got to figure out what we're going to do about clearing Michael so we can get him released from prison."

"Did Bethany have a cabin near that burned-up pine tree?"

"About a mile north of there."

"Rourke and I'll check it out. But I mean it, Tessa. You and Ashton have to stay here in the house at all times when we go."

"All right." As long as the two of them were together, Tessa figured they would be okay once Hunter had healed up.

She returned to the kitchen and finished the sandwiches. Looking out the window, she saw Rourke and Ashton talking and examining the ground. So much for replacing the back doorknob.

"After we eat, I'll look at your injury and see if the bandages need changing yet," she called out to Hunter.

He didn't answer. She peeked into the living room. The front door was wide open, letting in the frigid air. He was gone. Her heart in her throat, she rushed to the door and looked outside. Hunter was examining the work Ashton and Rourke had done on Michael's window.

"Jeez, Hunter, you about gave me a heart attack."

He smiled. "They did a super job."

"Come in here before you get sick again."

He saluted her.

"Wrong hand," she grumbled.

"Can't use the other. Shoulder's too stiff."

"Oh. I was afraid you'd forgotten how a Navy SEAL salutes."

"Navy SEALs don't salute. Not while they're on a mission and undercover."

"Ha! Like you'd know. So what are you, really?"

❖❖❖

When Rourke and Ashton came back inside to eat lunch, Hunter could tell Rourke had some news for him. Somehow he had to slip away to speak to him in private without Tessa fussing about his injury. But after a nap. He was feeling weary again. Another nap with Tessa would definitely help.

"Find anything?" Tessa asked as she set out the sandwiches.

"Gray fur," Ashton said. "Rourke's got great eyesight. *He* ought to go into the Navy SEALs."

"Where had they been?" She sat down and everyone followed her lead.

"Everywhere. He found fur down on the beach clinging to driftwood, on the back porch, front porch, by the shed. Just everywhere," Ashton said.

Hunter finished off his food in record time and scooted his plate toward Tessa. "Got any more?"

"Why don't you let her at least eat her food first?" Rourke asked.

She smiled. "While Hunter's incapacitated, I don't mind babying him. But after that..."

Hunter gave Rourke a satisfied smirk.

Tessa glanced at Rourke's hand. "Your bite. It's all healed up."

"Guess it wasn't as bad as it appeared. The antibiotics helped, too."

She stared at his hand and then got up from the chair. "It looked terrible before." Taking Hunter's plate, she made him another sandwich and returned to the table.

Hunter gave Rourke an irritated look. Keeping a new *lupus garou* in line was a chore. He would have to tell him everything he could and couldn't do. Like remove a bandage only after a sufficient amount of time had passed to give the illusion the injury was still healing when around humans. Of course, the bandage scenario was sure to come up with Tessa again where Hunter's shoulder was concerned, but he would handle it with a lot more finesse.

Rourke looked a little sheepish and continued to eat in silence.

Ashton said, "We went to the cliff where you pushed the wolf off, but didn't see any sign of it."

"Tide had to have washed it out," Hunter said. "We'll take a look north of here and see what we can find."

"You're not thinking of exploring with Rourke this afternoon, are you?"

"Another storm's coming in," Rourke warned. "We've got to look around before that happens."

"When did you watch the weather report? I haven't heard a thing about it." Tessa finished her sandwich and sat back against the chair.

"At my place. Anyway, you can feel the air growing colder again and smell the wintry moisture in the air."

Hunter gave Rourke a warning look, but he wasn't paying any attention to him.

"I'd say we were going to get sleet and snow before nightfall."

"Now you're guessing?" Tessa began clearing away the dirty dishes. "I thought you got this from the weather report."

Hunter finished his lunch. "Why don't you show me what you found, Rourke? Ashton can stay with Tessa and change the door locks."

"I want to go, too." She shoved the plates in the dishwasher.

"Later, Tessa." Hunter left the table and grabbed Michael's field jacket. But when he couldn't put it on by himself, Rourke helped.

Tessa watched, her arms folded, her mouth a thin grim line. "You shouldn't be going out there."

"Come on, Tessa. You can help me with the doorknobs." Ashton grabbed a paper sack and headed for the front door.

"You got one for both the front door and back? He only seems to have a key to the back door."

"Just to be safe. And we bought security glass for the window in Michael's room. The guy won't be able to break it again. We can replace all of them with that glass if Hunter thinks it's a good idea, and you want to foot the bill."

Hunter figured once he got rid of the stalker menace, she wouldn't have any more trouble. He went outside with Rourke while Ashton occupied Tessa.

"What did you find?"

"Hell if I know. You're the expert *lupus garou*. I discovered dozens of wolves' scents, tons of wolves' prints, thousands of wolf fur fibers, and a smattering of wolves' urine in various places. So you tell me what it all means."

Hunter hadn't realized the smells would probably overload Rourke's new abilities. From birth, *lupus garou* filtered out the smells and sounds, but he guessed the sudden onslaught would confuse someone who had just been turned and at the same time, the enhanced abilities could be a distraction.

Hunter led Rourke down to the beach. "If you get injured, from now on, hide the fact you are, or keep the injury bandaged for longer than necessary. And don't show off your abilities to humans."

He thought that went without saying, but apparently not.

Rourke scowled. "I can't help it. I kept seeing fur everywhere. I forgot Ashton couldn't, and I didn't even realize how it might sound to him."

"You always have to remember what we are. When we're in a wolf pack, no problem. But around humans, watch yourself, always."

"I was just turned, remember? I haven't had much time to get used to this." Rourke looked up at the clouds. "I can't see it for the gray skies, but I can feel the moon's strong pull. I keep wanting to strip off my clothes and run naked through the woods. It's driving me crazy."

Hunter bent down to check out a piece of fur caught on driftwood. "*Later tonight.* You and I will take a run, and I'll show you what it's all about. That should break you of the urge for a while."

"What about your shoulder?"

"It won't be properly healed for a couple of more days, but the exercise will do it good, give it a stretch. Getting out of Tessa's sight for a couple of hours is the problem. I'll take a nap when we get back. We'll have supper, and then after she's gone to bed, we'll take a run."

Rourke motioned to the area. "So what do you make of all this?"

"I've counted six different gray wolves that have left their mark. The three I fought and three others who seem familiar, but I can't recall why."

"Great. Can we fight them all off?"

Two shots rang out from the front porch of the house.

"Tessa!" Hunter's heart pounded against his ribs as he bolted up the rocky path with Rourke hot on his heels.

Three more shots were fired and a wolf yelped twice before Hunter barreled through the living room, concerned Ashton might shoot them if they came around the side of the house.

Tessa was holding the rifle, getting ready to fire again, the weapon propped against her shoulder, when Hunter saw Ashton sprawled out on the front porch, his hand bloodied, his face pallid.

"Hell," Hunter said under his breath. If the damned wolf had turned Ashton… Hunter took the rifle from Tessa.

She was shaking so hard, he thought she might collapse, her own face flushed, but tears filled her eyes. She dropped to her knees and held Ashton's uninjured hand. "Ashton, can you hear me?"

Rourke took the rifle inside, and Hunter crouched beside Tessa. "He'll be all right."

She started to cry and her tears undid him. He wrapped his arms around her, her body still trembling.

"I… I think I hit the wolf twice. At least he yelped twice. But… oh, Hunter, he's got to be rabid."

"What are we going to do?" Rourke asked.

"Let's get Ashton inside."

"We have to take him to the clinic in town, or to the hospital in the city. He's got to be treated for rabies," Tessa insisted.

Hunter crouched to lift Ashton, but Rourke grabbed his arm and stopped him. "You can't reinjure that shoulder. I'll lift him."

"I'll help," Tessa said.

"You get the door, Tessa. I'll just use my good

shoulder." Hunter hated playing the part of a damned invalid even if Rourke was right. He needed to heal so he could be prepared to fight again, as bold and rash as the *lupus garous* were getting.

Rourke lifted Ashton's torso, his gaze shooting up to meet Hunter's while Hunter carried Ashton's feet. Yeah, another ability. More strength. Rourke smiled. At least he seemed pleased with the change. Now Hunter had to deal with Ashton, damn it. What the hell was wrong with the *lupus garou*? Every time they changed a human who had family, it could cause problems. Although there was a slight chance the wolf hadn't turned Ashton.

"We've got to take him to the clinic at least." Tessa locked the front door after them.

"We've got the rabies vaccine and antibiotics with us." Hunter helped carry Ashton into Michael's room. "Rourke will give him a shot. If you'll get some soap and water for the bite, we'll take care of it."

Tessa hurried out of the room and down the hall.

Hunter rushed to wrap Ashton's hand in a towel to hide the bite from Tessa, although he was sure she had seen enough of the damage. When she returned, Hunter took the washcloth and water from her, then handed it to Rourke.

Ashton was scowling and alert. "Bloody damn wolf. Didn't even see him coming as I finished changing out the doorknob. Thank god he didn't get Tessa."

But most likely he was trying to. Hunter was sure they had frustrated the bastard because they had left the house the night before and were gone for so long, and now had another "guard" to keep Tessa safe.

"Come on." Hunter took hold of Tessa's hand. "You

can't have slept well last night, and I'm feeling dog tired again. What about you?"

She looked back at Ashton as Hunter led her out of the room. "We've had this discussion before." Her gaze shifted to Hunter. "You're right, I didn't sleep well in that hard chair at the hospital, and when I rested with you, I kept feeling like the nurses would catch us. I must have dropped off right before Ashton walked in on us though. Wouldn't you know."

Hunter smiled at her. Even when she was tired, she was agreeable. Even when she was mad at him, especially when she was mad at him. She reminded him of an alpha then.

Mentally, he shook his head at himself. He had to quit thinking of her in those terms before he went down the path he knew he shouldn't.

"You locked the back door, didn't you?" Hunter asked, helping Tessa out of her sweater.

"Yes. You guys left it wide open. I'm going to have to start charging you for the high electric bill I'm bound to get." She helped Hunter ease out of the field jacket. "You seem really stiff."

"I need to work the shoulder out."

"You need to let it heal first."

He swept his hands down her arms and kissed her forehead. "You'll help to make it happen."

"No, Ashton!" Rourke shouted down the hall. The back door slammed shut.

Now what the hell?

Footsteps ran toward the bedroom, but Hunter jerked the door open and met Rourke midway down the hall. "What's happened?"

"Ashton said he had to take a… walk."

"Damn it." Hunter turned to see Tessa standing in the hallway, her eyes wide. "Why don't you take a nap? I'll join you in a few minutes. Rourke will stay here with you."

"But your shoulder."

Hunter didn't reply, just headed for the back door. No time to waste. "Did he take the rifle?" he hollered back to Rourke.

"Yeah, he did."

Good. Maybe Ashton hadn't been turned after all. Maybe he intended to shoot the wolf that bit him. Not good, but better than if he'd been turned.

Hunter hurried outside, sniffed the air, then saw the rifle next to a patio chair. *Damn it.* He grabbed the rifle and handed it to Rourke. "I'll be back shortly."

Then he tore across the patio and headed for the woods. "Ashton, come back here this instant!" Hunter hollered in his most threatening alpha voice.

The wind howled back and he knew the storm would begin soon. But worse, Ashton was bound to get himself into a hell of a lot of trouble without a guide his first time as a wolf.

Tessa pulled her sweater back on, figuring she couldn't take a nap now. Not with worrying about Hunter and Ashton's safety. But she wondered now if Ashton had been infected and could carry rabies, which might account for his strange behavior. Yet she thought it would take longer for a person infected to react. She just hoped to God he didn't have rabies.

Trying to settle her upset, she meant to fix a cup of cocoa for her and Rourke and then replace the back doorknob. But when she walked down the hall, she felt the cold wind blowing into the house through the back door.

A chill sliced through her, and she ran toward the kitchen. "Rourke?" she yelled.

He didn't answer and Tessa felt as afraid as the day she came home from the trial and suspected someone was watching the house. She stepped onto the back patio and stared at where she thought the guys might have gone—north. She hollered again.

No reply.

With apprehension, she closed the door and locked it. She'd manage if she didn't let her fear run amok. Grabbing the new doorknob for the back door, she hoped to replace it before the stalker realized she was home alone, and tried to squash the nerves wreaking havoc with her stomach. She opened the door, her heart gave a jolt, and she squeaked out a scream.

Nurse Godzilla. Wearing her long dark hair down, she had on a jeans jacket, turtleneck, jeans, and snow boots, the only part of her outfit that looked warm enough for the weather.

The attractive woman smiled at her in a fake way. "Mr. Grey took a powder. The doctor reported his 'escape' to the police. The sheriff should be coming here soon."

"So why are you here? To warn him?" Tessa assumed the woman wanted to see him instead, try to ignite a flame between them, maybe outside the hospital setting.

"Sure, to warn him." She looked around the place. "Cozy, pretty forest green color scheme. Soft, like you." She took a deep breath. "Hmm, your other male friend's changed. Mr. Grey bite him, too?"

"No. Thank you for the news, if that's all...? "

"I'm Cara Woodson, by the way. Can I help you with that?" She pointed at the doorknob in Tessa's hand.

"No, thanks. I can manage. Hunter won't be back for a long while. Maybe you could return some other time." How was she going to get rid of the pesky woman without just shoving her out the door?

"He won't stay with you, you know." Cara grabbed the Phillips-head screwdriver resting on the countertop. She began removing the old doorknob. "Why are we doing this?"

Barely hearing the question, Tessa was too wrapped up in the woman's comment about Hunter. "Why do you think he won't stay with me? Are you his former lover?"

Cara laughed. "Hardly. Although I'd like the chance to be his new lover."

"He's not interested." Tessa had no doubt he wasn't interested in her. But what if the woman plied her sexual charms on him? Any man would succumb eventually to a seductress.

"He's not interested in me yet because of you. But you're a temporary fling."

"If you don't know him, how could you think you know so much about him?"

"I just do. So, has someone been getting into your place without permission?"

"Yeah." Why Tessa said so, she didn't know. And afterward she wished she hadn't.

"He has a key? Someone you've known? An old lover?"

"I don't know who it might be."

Tessa began installing the new lock while Cara examined the old one.

"What if he didn't have a key to your place?"

Tessa glanced at her. "How could he not have?"

"What if he had a skeleton key? A lock-picking toolkit so he can get in anywhere he wants?"

Tessa felt sick to her stomach. If the guy could get in no matter the kind of lock they installed, she would never be safe until he was caught. Then what? He would get a slap on the hands? A restraining order? Then he would most likely be back to stalking her again.

"Is Hunter trying to locate the intruder?"

"Yes. But then he got bitten and…" Tessa shrugged.

They finished replacing the doorknob, and Tessa glanced back at the woods. A couple of inches of snow had already fallen. She turned around and found Cara watching her. "Since you came all the way out here, did you want some cocoa before you return to the city?"

"Sure. That would be grand." Cara pulled off her jeans jacket and slipped an envelope out of her pocket. "Thought maybe you'd like these since your insurance was paying for Hunter's accident on your property, and he left the hospital's care early."

Tessa glanced at them.

"The release forms. That way you weren't charged for Hunter's stay when he'd already left because he hadn't officially signed out."

"Thanks. I appreciate it." Truly she did, but Tessa was torn between being glad the woman was here so she wasn't alone while the men were gallivanting in the woods, and not liking that Cara would undoubtedly try her womanly charms on Hunter again as soon as he returned.

"So what does your intruder look like?"

"I haven't seen him, but Ashton says he's tall, dark-haired like Hunter, and runs pretty fast."

"Uh-huh. So what's Hunter going to do about it?" Cara grabbed up a couple of napkins like she was used to playing hostess, and when the cocoa was ready she took the mugs to the table.

Tessa grabbed a package of chocolate wafers and joined her. "He's going to turn him over to the sheriff when he catches him. He broke one of my windows and stole my gun."

"Gun. Oh. So you couldn't shoot him."

"Or so he can commit a crime. Listen, I don't want to keep you long in case the weather gets too bad. Aren't you working tonight at the hospital?"

"I called in sick." Cara smiled. "How did you know I was working tonight?"

"Ashton checked."

Cara's smiled broadened. "My, my. He's the cute guy with the long, blond hair? Sharp blue eyes? Muscular build, but not quite as much as Hunter? So he wanted to know when I was coming back on duty?"

Tessa laughed inwardly. Wouldn't the woman like to know the real reason Ashton wanted to know and what he really thought of her? On the other hand, it wouldn't hurt for Tessa to spark the woman's interest in Ashton if it meant she would leave Hunter alone. Ashton definitely deserved some payback after what he had pulled with her.

"Maybe you could take a look at his wound. Hunter and Rourke took care of it, but since you're a nurse, I'd feel better if you made sure it was really all right."

"I'd be happy to." Cara frowned. "Why did they leave you alone? Are they in pursuit of this guy?"

"No. Not exactly. Ashton took off for whatever reason. Hunter told Rourke to stay with me, but the next thing I knew, he'd taken off after them. At least I presume he had." Tessa pointed at the rifle. "They left that for me."

"You know how to shoot?"

"Sure. Why would I own a gun if I didn't? I got off a couple of rounds into the wolf that bit Ashton, I think."

Cara's eyes widened. "Oh, well, good shooting."

Tessa raised the mug to her lips to take another sip when the doorbell rang. Her heart skipped a beat, and she nearly dropped her mug.

"Shall we see who it is? Maybe it's the sheriff." Cara sounded perfectly fearless.

Tessa wished she felt as sure of herself. But the wolf attack that had followed the ringing of the doorbell earlier still had her spooked.

Tessa set her mug down and grabbed the rifle, just in case it wasn't the sheriff. Or maybe it was Hunter or one of the others. She *had* locked them out of the house.

But when she looked through the peephole, she saw a striking brunette, her amber eyes peering back at her. Uncle Basil's niece?

Figuring as irritated as the woman looked, she'd give Tessa some more guff, she opened the door. "Yes?"

Her eyes narrowing, the woman growled, "Where the hell is Hunter?"

Chapter 10

Hunter found Ashton's clothes ditched about a mile north of Tessa's house and swore under his breath. He removed his clothes, shuddered in the frigid air, ripped off his bandages, and changed into the wolf. But it wasn't painless this time. Sharp streaks stabbed through his injured shoulder, hurting more than he thought it would. All he wanted was to return to Tessa, nap, snuggle, and a hell of a lot more if she was receptive. He would kill Ashton.

For three miles he trotted after him, stopping to sniff at the scents in the air, checking the direction Ashton went. Ashton had marked "his" territory four times already. *Idiot.* If he came across the brothers Grimm, he would never be able to handle a wolf-to-wolf fight. Not as a newly turned *lupus garou*, Hunter didn't think.

Although if Tessa did manage to shoot one of them twice, he probably wouldn't be messing with anyone for a while. The one with the broken leg would be pretty incapacitated still. Hunter relaxed a little.

Until he heard a wolf howl somewhere in the distance farther north. *Ashton. Maybe.*

Hunter headed in the wolf's direction. The snow was falling heavier, the air colder, the flakes burying the evergreens, making them droop like white-bearded old men. The place was already looking like a winter wonderland again.

The pain in Hunter's shoulder seemed to grow incrementally every step he took. Going for a run with Rourke later was now out of the question. He hoped Rourke could hold off a while longer.

Something moved to the west, catching his eye. He whipped around. A cougar stood still, holding a rabbit between his teeth, his eyes wary as he watched Hunter.

His heart thundering, Hunter waited, twitching his ears back and forth, listening to the rapid beat of the cougar's heart. With any luck, the cougar would take his meal and go, but he stared Hunter down like any feral predator would. Messing with a wild cat when they were protecting their meal could be a dangerous proposition. One of his *lupus garou* pack had perished when fighting a cougar this big, and Hunter had no intention of tangling with him when he needed to protect that idiot Ashton.

A twig snapped west of them. The cougar bolted through the woods and the reason came into view. Ashton—his fur more of a beige, his snout a little darker, a dead duck in his mouth. If Hunter could laugh in his wolf form at the ridiculousness of it, he would.

Movement in the woods behind Hunter made him twist around. Pain sliced through his shoulder. Fury slid through his veins, setting his blood on fire as he found Rourke facing him. His fur a dark brown, he bowed his head slightly to Hunter.

Holy crap! He would kill the two of them. Hunter raced in the direction where he'd left his clothes, but even so it would take valuable time to get there, dress, and run home. If anything happened to Tessa, he would never forgive himself.

Even though he kept telling himself he should have left Ashton and Rourke to fend for themselves after what they'd pulled, he couldn't. Not by *lupus garou* laws. Once they were turned, they had to be somebody's responsibility and no one else was stepping up for the job.

Technically, Tessa wasn't his responsibility. So why was his human side casting away all his inborn rules? *Damn it to hell.* If anything happened to her… there would be hell to pay.

When he finally reached his clothes, he shoved them on, no longer feeling the pain in his shoulder because of the adrenaline spiking through his system. Ashton ran up beside him, the stupid dead mallard still in his mouth. Rourke ran ahead toward the house. No sign of his clothes, so he must have changed sooner after he left the house. Hell, hopefully, not in front of Tessa.

His heart hammering, Hunter sprinted for the house. A couple of hours had already passed since he had left Tessa, and he still had another damn mile left to go in the snowdrifts.

The brunette's amber eyes speared Tessa, then she turned her attention to Cara. "Where the hell is Hunter?" she repeated.

"Is he your brother? Uncle Basil's nephew?" Tessa asked, hoping the woman could trigger the rest of Hunter's memories and he would recall his past, praying the woman wasn't his girlfriend.

Cara raised a brow. "I thought you said his last name was Grey. It isn't?"

Oh hell. Tessa hadn't meant to tell the world, but if this woman knew Hunter… "Come inside. Hunter had a terrible accident, and he's lost his memory, but he's been regaining it in bits and pieces."

The woman's eyes widened. "Where is he?"

"He's… he's okay. Just taking a walk with a couple of other guys in the woods. But how do you know him? Please," Tessa said, motioning to the living room. "Come in and get warm by the fire. Would you like some cocoa?"

The woman pointed at Cara and growled, "Who's she to Hunter?"

Cara smiled in an evil way. "His personal nurse." She tilted her nose up and took in a deep breath. "And you're his sister?"

Having had the sinking feeling the woman might be his girlfriend, Tessa could now see the resemblance, the same dark hair, the same colored eyes, the well-defined cheekbones and aristocratic noses, and relief washed over her. "Meara?"

The woman frowned. "How did you know my name if he lost his memory?"

"He called it out when he was delirious the one night. He remembered having a sister, but not his full name or where he was from."

"How was he injured?"

The women followed Tessa into the kitchen where she refilled mugs with fresh cocoa. "He said three men pushed him off a cliff."

Her face colorless, Meara gripped the back of one of the kitchen chairs. "Uncle Basil said you were trouble."

Tessa didn't fully believe it when he'd been so kind

to her, yet an inkling of self-doubt wormed its way into her system.

"Oh boy," Cara said, casting Meara a look. "Not good. A guy's been breaking into Tessa's house also."

"Figures." Meara shook her head. "Greymere's our name."

At least Hunter had half of his name right.

"So if you work at the hospital in the city, what are you doing way out here?" Meara asked in the same manner she spoke to Tessa, and she figured it was just her way. Or she didn't like women much.

Cara didn't seem to be bothered by the sarcasm in Meara's voice and shrugged. "Hunter left the hospital without being released first."

"Oh," Meara said, her brows knitting together. "He was in the hospital because of the fall?"

"A wolf bit him." Tessa served up the cocoa. "He said he had a phobia about hospitals. That he couldn't stand being in a hospital longer than necessary."

Meara cast Cara a look.

Cara smiled. The look was a bit devious, which made Tessa wonder what was up between them. Even though Meara didn't seem to care for Cara, a mutual connection seemed to exist, like between Cara and Hunter. Tessa shook her head, annoyed at herself for overanalyzing people's darker motives when there was probably nothing to them, as usual.

"Can you tell me why he has such a phobia?" Tessa ushered them into the living room.

"No."

No, as in she didn't know? Or she did and wouldn't tell Tessa?

Meara sat down on the couch, her eyes taking in every detail in the place from the fire in the brick fireplace, to the photos of wildlife on the wall. Tessa wondered what she was thinking, but the woman's face remained impassive. "How long has Hunter been here?"

"A couple of days."

"An overnight stay at the hospital also," Cara added.

"I'll take him off your hands," Meara said softly, changing her whole demeanor. "Where did you say he went?"

Tessa didn't want Hunter taken off her hands. She wanted to wrap him in her arms and stay there until spring. Already lack of sleep was giving her a major headache.

Cara gave Meara a small smile. "I think Hunter's *way* over his head on this one."

Both women looked in the direction of the kitchen seconds before someone banged on the door like he intended to break it in. Tessa grabbed the rifle and headed for the kitchen, but when she saw Hunter and Rourke at the door, she quickly set the gun down and unlocked it.

Hunter took Tessa into his arms and squeezed the breath out of her. "Thank god, you're all right."

And at once she sensed he really did feel something for her deep down, while she felt the same kind of incomprehensible bond between them.

He separated from her a little and gazed down at her. A hint of tears filled his eyes, and the sight of them touched her soul. He hugged her again. Wrapping her arms around him, she basked in his heated embrace, forgetting for the moment his sister was behind her, or that Nurse Godzilla would make a move on Ashton next. At least Tessa assumed she would.

Ashton entered the kitchen and set a dead duck on her counter. *What…?*

Rourke came up behind Hunter. "What the hell is the nurse from the hospital doing here? And who is she?"

That was when Hunter saw his sister and dropped Tessa like she was a burning ember. Not expecting to be coldly thrust aside, she felt a heartbeat of rejection, but then quickly reminded herself his seeing his sister had to be quite a shock. But would he remember her? And everything about his past life?

"Meara." He stared at her for a long moment and then hurried to hug her. "Meara."

Thank god, he remembered her.

"Dear brother. I thought I'd lost you. I've been looking for you for three days. Then I tracked you here. Tessa said you'd lost your memory."

"Hell, Meara, you'd taken off with…" He glanced back at Tessa, his eyes and face hard. "We'll be right back." He pulled Meara outside. "Who the hell were they and where the hell did you go?" He slammed the door closed.

So he did remember more.

Figuring the family reunion would go a lot better than that if her own brother had been returned to her, Tessa's mouth gaped in surprise. Apparently Hunter's seeing his sister did bring back memories, but that didn't seem to be a good thing.

Hunter escorted his sister far enough away from the house that no one could hear them. He glowered at her, waiting for Meara to tell him what had happened, the notion of her disappearing from the house in the company of the three gray males hitting him like an icy avalanche of bad memories.

"Quit looking at me like the devil's possessed me, Hunter!" She looked out to the ocean.

She was beautiful and any one of a number of males would want her, but her reluctance to choose a mate from the alphas she'd seen fit to date was one thing—running off with a bunch of horny betas quite another.

"I'm sorry," she finally said under her breath. "I… I came right home after the idiots talked me into running with them for a while. It didn't take much time for me to appreciate none of them would interest me for very long. I… I didn't realize someone would have tried to kill you in the meantime." She glanced up at him, her body shuddering in the cold wind.

He took her arm and pulled her into his embrace. "We've got to stick together, Meara. No matter what else happens with the pack, we're family."

"I looked everywhere for you, and then thought about this Tessa Anderson woman and how she'd intrigued you. I thought maybe you'd come here to be with her. I smelled your scent here, and sat on the back patio, hoping you'd look out and see me. But Tessa peered out the window instead. I figured you'd succumbed to her charms. I'd considered howling to let you know I was out back, but I was afraid the men I'd run off from might locate me. So I returned home. The next morning I drove here, but no one was here. I had no way of knowing you had been injured so badly." Tears glistened in Meara's eyes, and as much as she tried to hide her feelings, he knew she felt badly that her irresponsibility could have gotten him killed. But worse, she would have been left alone to fend for herself, and that made his stomach clench even tighter.

"Tell me what happened," she said.

He explained about the three brothers, the mess Tessa was in, and the problem with the two newly turned *lupus garous*. Meara had been quiet, taking everything in, until he came to Rourke's story. And then she laughed out loud.

"I never expected to find you—the great Hunter—in such a quandary."

"Yeah, well, hell, if you hadn't run off..." He said the harsh words before he could stop himself.

She focused on his chest, and he was afraid she was going to dissolve into tears. But then she raised her gaze, cast him an irritated look, and tried to put the blame on him again. Knowing her, she couldn't deal with the guilt.

"You know how important it is to keep our situation secret from humans. Isn't that what's drummed into us? Kill them if they get wind of the truth. Or change them only if the situation truly warrants it. What a mess. How are you going to fix all this, Hunter?"

"I should have been getting the cabins ready to rent out, waiting on the pack to tire of the city and join us." But even thinking of that, he couldn't believe how all the memories flooded back to him so quickly. The fire, losing their home, Uncle Basil's warning him to take "care" of Tessa Anderson, and the subsequent fight he'd had with the gray wolves when he'd gone in search of his wayward sister. He was certain his uncle hadn't quite had this scenario in mind when he gifted the properties to Hunter though.

"None of our people have returned yet." Meara pushed her windswept hair out of her eyes.

"I'm surprised Leidolf, the red pack leader in Portland, hasn't chased them off yet. Maybe our pack members are behaving themselves for a change." He shook his head. "I don't believe it for a second." He took a deep breath. "As soon as I resolve this situation with the gray who's stalking Tessa, I'll make the trip to Portland and force the pack to return."

"You can't stay here. You can't get involved with her."

"I *am* involved." He wondered if other pack leaders had this much trouble. "No more running after men I don't approve of." He tilted her chin up with the tip of his finger and looked directly into her eyes, warning her to mind him this time.

She nodded, her look angry, but then it softened a hair with a hint of a smile. "Can't afford to. You'll change half the population of Oregon if I leave you alone again."

He grunted and moved her toward the house. "You're staying with me until I take care of the gray."

She growled, and he knew the fight had only just begun.

"Family feud," Cara said, motioning to Hunter and Meara outside, then turned her attention to Ashton. "Went hunting, I see. I like duck, too."

Rourke rolled his eyes. "I'm getting a shower before supper." He looked at the clean kitchen. "You *are* fixing it soon, aren't you?"

"We just ate a little over three hours ago!" Tessa declared.

"That's long enough. I'm starving. So is Ashton." Rourke waved at the dead duck.

"Hunter, too, after all the exercise we had." He stalked down the hall.

"I didn't have a chance to have lunch," Cara said.

Well, Tessa *wasn't* hungry. She glanced out the kitchen window. "Looks like we're going to get snowed in. You might want to leave before that happens," she said to Cara. Tessa had no idea why she would want to save Ashton's butt. Although he cast her a grateful look.

"I'll hang around. I haven't been with… a lot of people… on a more social basis for a number of years. This is the most fun I've had in eons," Cara said.

Tessa couldn't understand what the woman was talking about. No one seemed enthusiastic about seeing her even. Why would she think anyone wanted to be around her?

"Did you lose your bandages, Ashton?" Cara asked, her voice sultry and sexy as she took hold of his injured hand. "Tessa, do you have some new ones? I'll fix him right up."

"Sure, I'll get them and the antibiotics." Tessa glanced at Ashton's hand, but Cara was holding it so that she couldn't see the bite wound.

When Tessa returned to the kitchen, Hunter and Meara had come back inside. For being reunited after losing her brother, and considering the ordeal he had been through, they scowled at each other and didn't appear grateful in the least. But worse, gone was Hunter's lustful interest in Tessa. At once she felt *she* was the center of the controversy and wasn't good enough for the family.

Well, he *had* said he couldn't promise her anything. Just that he would help her find Bethany's murderer and set her brother free. Tessa should have known when his memory came back, she would be history. But no matter how she tried to reconcile herself with the notion, she couldn't squash the dismal feeling he would soon abandon her.

"Here, Cara." Tessa handed her the bandages. "I guess everyone's staying for dinner?" She cast Hunter a questioning glance. She halfway expected him to say he was leaving with his sister for good now.

His brows still furrowed, his lips grim, he nodded. He gave Meara a hard look. She folded her arms and looked doubly cross at Tessa. So much for a lovely dinner when she wasn't even hungry. Cara was the only one who seemed to be pleased to be here, and the one Tessa really wanted to see leave.

Tessa pulled out a package of hot links. "Can everyone manage spaghetti with hot sausage, bell peppers, and onions?"

"Hmm, sounds good to me," Cara said, licking her lips while she bandaged Ashton's hand with tender loving care. He tried to jerk his hand away, but she held on tight and *tsk*ed.

"Anything you fix is fine with us." Hunter's tone of voice was terse.

Meara didn't have a choice?

Wearing a towel, Rourke came out of the bathroom and hollered from the hallway, "Fine with me."

How had he heard what she'd asked? She stared after him as he slipped into Michael's room to grab some clothes. What had gotten into him? She'd never thought he'd dress so scantily in front of a bunch of women.

"The snow's bound to make the road impassable again. Is anyone leaving soon?" She directed the question at Cara and Meara. "The food won't take long to fix so we can eat and let you get on your way."

"No work for me tonight," Cara said cheerfully.

Hunter grunted. "Meara's staying here with me for as long as I need to be here."

For as long as he needed to be here. Well, that said it all. Once he was done helping her, Hunter was out of here.

Fine with Tessa. "I guess you'll want to sleep with your sister then, and—"

Cara laughed. "A macho male like Hunter sleeping with his sister? That would be the day."

Tessa sure wasn't sleeping with Hunter under the current circumstances. "Okay, well, you and Meara can sleep together and—"

"I'll stay with Ashton," Cara announced, her eyes flashing with humor. "He might need medical attention during the night. Look at how pale the poor man is."

He had been, but now his face flushed crimson. Tessa had never seen him blush. She expected some objection from Lord Hunter, but he didn't say anything. She was really surprised Ashton wouldn't have nixed Cara's suggestion himself.

Tessa threw the fajita bell pepper and onion mix into the saucepan, added the sausage links, and then the tomato sauce. "Okay, then Hunter and Rourke can take the spare bedroom and Meara and I—"

"I sleep alone," Meara said, fire burning in her eyes.

Wearing a clean pair of jeans and a sweatshirt, Rourke walked into the room. More casual than she had ever seen him. In fact, the sweatshirt belonged to her brother.

"I don't mind sleeping by the fire. I can watch the rest of the house that way in the event anyone plans to break in," he said.

Tessa considered Hunter's expression, but it was still dark as ever. About the sleeping arrangements? Or something else?

She coyly smiled. "Hunter, you can sleep with Rourke by the fire and keep him company."

Meara laughed, a catty, annoyed kind of laugh. She stalked into the kitchen and began opening drawers. When she found the silverware, she set it on the table.

Guess she could be a little bit of help. Maybe Meara was mad at Hunter and not at her. Still, Tessa had every intention of cooling her relationship with Hunter because when he left, she didn't want to be upset over it for days, weeks, months afterward. Best to end this insane infatuation now.

Life had been so simple for Hunter after Tessa had found him on the beach: discover his identity, learn what had happened to him, deal with Tessa's stalker, and find Bethany's murderer so Michael could be released from prison.

Now he had to deal with two freshly turned *lupus garous*. And Meara. Unfortunately, she had been right concerning everything they had fought about.. All that mattered was the *lupus garous'* safety and secrecy. He knew that. As pack leader, he sure as hell didn't want his sister reminding him of the fact. He should have taken Meara, Rourke, and Ashton back to his cabin resort up north once he learned that's where he lived and pretended Tessa and her problems didn't exist.

Any other alpha leader would not have allow himself to be dragged into human affairs.

But he couldn't and wouldn't abandon her. *Not yet.* Tessa had taken him in and cared for him when she didn't have a clue as to who he was. If he left her alone, the stalker would change her against her will. Hunter wouldn't let him. Another alpha leader, given the same scenario, would take the gray to task also, if he had been in his territory, but beyond that, she would be on her own. For now, Tessa's property was in Hunter's territory—newly franchised.

He couldn't let her brother stay in prison for a crime he didn't commit. No other wolf would feel obligated to help out in a case like this—except in the event one of their kind did the killing. Dealing with the *lupus garou* would be the end of it though. No *lupus garou* would try to release an innocent human. In fact, he would serve to keep the *lupus garous* out of the limelight. But Hunter couldn't allow it, although how he was going to get Michael out of his incarceration eluded him. First of course, he had to prove the grays had committed the crime.

To complicate matters, Hunter had to force Meara to stay with him and keep her out of trouble. Her first wolf heat was making her crotchety and difficult to handle. Thank heavens he didn't have any more sisters and that none of the three wolves she had taken off with had forced a mating. She needed an alpha to spar with and keep her in line.

Tessa placed the spaghetti in the pan of boiling water, her back rigid. He took a ragged breath. His shoulder was killing him after running in the woods for so many miles as a wolf today, and all he could think about was making love to the woman who heated his blood as hot as the raging fires they'd left behind in California.

Sleep with his sister? That would be the day. And have Rourke sleep with Meara? She would bite him for sure and *not* in a playful way. Hunter was glad Cara was targeting Ashton as her love interest. He needed to remind him, though, if he mated her, it was a one-time deal. No fooling around a few nights, and then parting ways, although if she did mate him, that might be the solution to one of his problems. She would teach Ashton the ways of being a *lupus garou* and take him off Hunter's hands.

If Tessa thought Hunter was sleeping with Rourke in the living room, she could think again. For one, he didn't trust that the gray might not attempt to break her window and get in while she was alone. All he would do was bite her, and then come back to claim her later once she was a *lupus garou*. Hunter assumed the gray had intended to kill Ashton, and then bite Tessa, but when she brought out the rifle and started shooting, he gave that notion up in a hurry.

"Hunter," Meara said. "Gathering wool? We're all sitting down to eat."

Tessa had moved her plate to the foot of the table and had seated Meara next to him in her place. He smiled at Tessa's tenacity. Still, he was angry with himself for feeling more than he should toward Tessa and that Meara had to remind him of his duty to their pack, but most of all to their kind. Yet, he couldn't help but admire the spunky human female.

"They're getting married in the spring," Cara said, as the tension escalated in the dining room as thick as the snow was getting outside. "Won't they make a cute couple?"

Meara choked on her water. Tessa avoided looking at Hunter and cut up her sausage.

"She just said that so she could get in to see Hunter at the hospital." Rourke glowered at Cara. "Why are you here anyway?"

"To bring the hospital release forms for Hunter. So what do we do after dinner? Do you have any board games? Cards? Anyone want to play strip poker?"

"After we finish here, I need a word with Ashton, and then we're all going to bed. We've had quite a day of it. And we've got a lot of work to do tomorrow," Hunter said.

"Can I be in on this little adventure?" Cara asked.

"You can keep Tessa company. Both you and Meara. Rourke and I have some hunting to do."

"Can I go, too?" Ashton asked, looking chagrined.

Cara patted his arm. "We need you to protect us."

"Are you going to Bethany's place? They've removed the police locks, and I have a key if you need one," Tessa said.

"Yeah, we'll need a key."

Tessa's eyes filled with tears and Hunter couldn't tell if she was happy he was still looking into this situation for her brother, or was worried they wouldn't discover who really murdered Bethany.

Meara cleared her throat and patted Hunter's hand. "And if you see those three guys I was with while you're at it, don't kill them, okay, Hunter? We were just having some fun. Nothing more."

Hunter gave her a dark look. He wanted to bang those guys' heads together for stealing an alpha leader's sister right out from under his nose. They had to be some of the dumbest betas around. He thought his sister would have had better sense. He was surprised neither Ashton nor Rourke showed any interest in her. But maybe they were afraid of how Hunter might react—and for good reason.

After dinner, Cara and Meara helped Tessa with the dishes. Rourke and Ashton went with Hunter to get another load of firewood in case the electricity went out again. The wind was gusting higher and the waves were growing more violent. If the weather got much worse, the increasing storm would flood the beach, and they wouldn't be able to forage for firewood.

"Remember how I told the two of you that mating is for life? That's something that can't be broken except by death. It might be a hard concept for you to understand since you've always been human, but it's the wolf way and the *lupus garou* way."

Rourke grabbed an armload of wood. "What about Tessa?"

"She's different." Hunter didn't want to have to defend his actions to a subordinate wolf and wouldn't have if it hadn't been that Rourke was Tessa's friend and was sincerely concerned about her well-being.

"You mean, she's human so her feelings don't count." Rourke headed back up the hill.

"Damn it, Rourke, of course her feelings matter. We're both adults. We had consensual sex and that's all there is to it. As a *lupus garou* we can't have sex with another *lupus garou* unless we accept the female as a permanent mate. Humans don't live by the same rules, as well you know. And I've already explained to her our relationship can't be permanent."

"So if we want to party with a woman, she has to be a human." Ashton trudged up the slope with an armload of timber behind Hunter.

"Yeah, so that means you can sleep with Cara, but no sex. If you go all the way with her, you're mated—for life."

Rourke chuckled. "What if she forces herself on him?"

"In the case of a forced mating, the punishment for the perpetrator is death. Unless the victim chooses to accept the perpetrator as his or her mate. We don't tolerate the abuse of our *lupus garous* or laws."

Wide-eyed, both Rourke and Ashton stared at him.

"Hell, I knew it would be a lot of trouble teaching the two of you all the rules." Hunter gave Ashton a sympathetic look. "If you don't want Cara for a mate, just say no. *Firmly!* Don't waffle."

Rourke laughed out loud. "She doesn't look like she readily accepts taking no for an answer. Thank god she latched onto Ashton and not me."

When Hunter opened the back door, he heard Cara say, "If you want him—" She abruptly quit speaking, but he wished he knew who she had been talking to and who "he" referred to.

"Ashton, do something with that dead duck." Hunter motioned to the kitchen on his way to the living room. "Stick it in the fridge or something."

Then he walked into the living room and found the three women watching him. "Early morning, ladies. Let's get some sleep."

"Is he always this bossy?" Tessa rose from the couch, scarcely giving him a look.

"Always," Meara said.

"I'll get you some sheets and blankets, Rourke." Brushing past Hunter, Tessa headed down the hall.

Cara hopped up from recliner. "Need some bandaging, Hunter?"

Hell, he forgot he'd removed his bandages on the run, and Tessa was sure to wonder how come he was healing so fast as soon as she saw his naked torso when they went to bed. "Yeah, let's go to the bathroom."

In the hall, they passed Tessa carrying an armful of bedding, and she gave Hunter a scornful look. He was definitely in the doghouse, but he didn't know why. He closed the bathroom door behind him.

Cara located the bandages in a drawer. "You're going to have to turn her."

"No."

"The way you look at her, you could melt her heart. She'll accept our ways before long." Cara taped up his shoulder.

"She has a brother. Even in the distant past, *lupus garous* targeted those who had no families so they wouldn't be missed."

"All right, so change her brother, too."

"I've already got enough trouble on my hands in the form of two new *lupus garous*."

"Your wound is looking much better, but I bet it hurts after that run you took for as long as you were gone."

She found some medicine and handed him a glass of water. "I want to join your pack."

He choked on the pills. "I thought you didn't like pack politics." All he needed was another female alpha upstart in the pack. Although they were always short on females, and she might entice some of the rest of his pack to return.

She smiled and wound a dark curl around her finger. "I didn't like *my* pack's politics. But I'm intrigued with yours. Besides, you need some help with these new guys. I don't think your sister is interested in showing them the ropes."

"Don't push Ashton too hard."

"Hmm, he's an awfully interesting candidate. The vote is still out on him. But I'll let you know one way or another what I decide."

"I mean it. He doesn't understand our rules, even though I've explained them to him. Don't force him on this."

"As in seduce him? I'll try not to."

Someone banged on the bathroom door. "Are you going to hog the bathroom all night, Hunter?" Meara scolded. "Why don't you use the master bathroom since you'll be sleeping in the *master's* bedroom anyway?"

Cara patted Hunter on the chest. "Yep, you could use my help."

Hunter opened the bathroom door, brushed past his sister, and stalked into the living room. Time to settle matters between him and Tessa and get a good night's sleep.

Tessa was speaking low to Rourke while she helped him make a bed on the couch. Hell, couldn't Rourke make his own damned bed?

She gave Hunter a cursory glance and then ignored

him. He shared a look with Rourke that meant he had better not be getting any ideas about Tessa either.

Rourke quickly caught the message. "I can do the rest of this. Thanks, Tessa."

Hunter seized Tessa's hand. "We'll be leaving early in the morning, Rourke, so get a good night's sleep."

Before Tessa could object, Hunter hauled her down the hall.

Cara winked at her from the entrance to Michael's bedroom. "Sleep tight."

Meara was already running the shower in the guest bathroom, and Ashton had gone to bed. Hunter hoped Ashton could resist Cara's charms if he didn't truly want her in the event the woman decided to seduce him after all.

In Tessa's bedroom, Hunter released her hand and shut the door.

She folded her arms and glowered at him. "What, Hunter? What do you want from me? I'm not in the habit of having flings with guys I've just met. And since you've made it abundantly clear you're leaving as soon as you fulfill your promise, I don't want you staying in here with me any longer."

Hunter motioned to the window. "If I leave you alone, the stalker could try to break in. So I'm staying with you, end of discussion."

"That's it? That's all the reason you're giving for wanting to sleep with me?" Her eyes flamed hotter than a fire's blue flame.

"That's a pretty damned good reason."

She whirled around and headed for the master bathroom, walked inside, and slammed the door.

He raised his brows. If he didn't know better, he

would think Tessa was going through her first wolf's heat. *Women.*

He yanked off his shoes, sweatshirt, *and* pants and climbed into bed. Why couldn't women be more like men? More… logical? Surely, she could see how he needed to be here for her protection after all that had happened. He pulled the covers to his waist.

She took forever in the shower and even longer drying her hair. The mattress in Michael's bedroom began to squeak, the bed frame banging lightly against the opposite wall. Hunter shook his head.

Tessa came out of the bathroom wearing a pair of pink flannel pajamas covered in red lips and pink hearts and a pair of fuzzy pink, red and white striped socks. She again folded her arms and gave him an icy look, although her bedroom attire ruined her angry effect. Not only that, but if she thought wearing pj's hid that sexy body of hers, she was mistaken.

Even now her nipples stood out against the soft fabric, and he was ready to tackle her, drag her to bed, and ravish her.

She opened her mouth to speak, but Michael's bed banged violently against the wall, making her hesitate and glance in that direction. Hunter smiled.

She snorted. "Great. I hope *that* doesn't go on all night. Why don't you just move the dresser in front of the window like we did in Michael's room? Then you can stay with Rourke and you won't have to baby-sit me."

"Come on, Tessa. Get in bed. Heater's off. The room's cold. Join me under the covers and get warm."

"I'm warm enough." She jerked her covers aside and climbed into bed.

"Do you always wear such sexy nightclothes?"

She gave him a derisive *hmpf* back. He chuckled. "I thought all women wore T-shirts to bed."

"Have you been with a lot?"

As many years as he had lived, yes. But in the scheme of things, no. And certainly not recently. The worst was during the Victorian era. Although some of the ladies were daring enough to strip down to bare skin, some insisted they remain fully dressed in their long nightgowns while he satisfied them. Pj's were certainly no obstacle. "There's been no one for a long time, Tessa."

And never anyone as special as her.

"I wear pajamas in the winter because I don't like to waste electricity heating the place at night."

"Hmm-hmm."

"What? You think I'm just wearing these because you're here? I usually sleep alone and *that's* why I wear warm pj's."

"Snuggle with me, Tessa. Then we'll both be warm."

She didn't say anything. He waited for her to come to him like she had done before, but she didn't.

"I don't wear T-shirts in the summer either," she finally remarked.

Nude, that's the way he liked his women, but he didn't figure Tessa ever went to bed like that. "So if you don't wear pajamas in the summertime, do you slide naked into a bed of satin sheets?"

She offered a derisive chuckle. "Right."

"I'll have to visit you in the summer then."

She remained silent.

"Come on, Tessa. I'm getting cold."

"Put Michael's sweatshirt on then."

Fine. He took the initiative. He knew he shouldn't. She was right in trying to keep the distance between them. But he also recognized she wanted him as much as he wanted her.

He moved closer to her and pulled her into his arms, but she remained rigid. He tried to caress her hair, but a twinge of pain streaked through his shoulder, and he groaned.

The tension seemed to drain from her spine, and she melted in his embrace. "You shouldn't have carried that load of firewood up to the house. What were you trying to prove? How macho you are to the other guys? They weren't injured as badly as you. You could use some common sense."

He smiled and kissed the top of her head.

She turned slightly toward him, her brows pinched, her eyes narrowed. "Are you hurting really badly?"

"Some," he admitted, since she seemed to like him better when he was in pain or he would never have said.

"Well, lie on your back and I'll…" She took a deep breath. "I'll snuggle with you so you don't have to hurt your shoulder."

He was about to say something, but decided he would be better off not in case he ruined her generous offer. Instead, he rolled onto his back. He wanted to feel her against him, skin to skin, even though her flannel pajamas were soft and cuddly. At this point, he didn't figure he could push her to remove her clothes. She reached over to join him, brushing her fingers over his naked thigh.

She recoiled. "Where are your sweatpants?"

"You know, in situations where a person is

hypothermic, naked bodies pressed together provide more heat than if they're clothed."

Her mouth gaped and her gaze narrowed again. "Well, I'm not hypothermic. Are you?"

Luckily, because of the dark, she couldn't see the way he was grinning at her. "I'm feeling chilled to the bone after chasing down Ashton and then getting a load of firewood."

"We *could* turn on the heat."

"Nah, waste of electricity." He reached over and unbuttoned her top button. "Come warm me, Tessa."

"Like Cara's warming Ashton?"

He was pretty sure Tessa's voice held a hint of sarcasm not hope.

Hunter didn't answer and when she didn't stop him, he finished unfastening her buttons and removed her top, taking a deep breath to see her breasts heavy and her nipples already hard.

Despite wanting to make love to her, he knew he had to leave the decision up to her. They both recognized it couldn't last.

At first, he took it slow and easy, sliding her pajama bottoms down her silky thighs. He forgot how much his shoulder hurt or how he shouldn't be making love with the woman again. All because she licked his lips, hummed her pleasure, and combed her fingers through his hair with tenderness. His arousal jumped, and she chuckled deep and sexylike. Again, he found himself wishing she were a *lupus garou*.

She leaned her supple nude body against his, heating his skin to the nth degree. "Cara said I should try to keep you for my own," she whispered against his lips, then licked them again. She slid over his erection and he moaned.

"Oh, sorry about your shoulder." She started to slip off him, and he grabbed hold of her lissome body, his hands cupping her buttocks, keeping her tight against him.

"Not my shoulder." But he couldn't conceal his annoyance with Cara that she would interfere in his affairs. She knew better than to encourage Tessa's further interest in him.

"Hmm," Tessa murmured, nuzzling her face against his cheek, "she said you're a real alpha male." Tessa slid her body lower and kissed his nipple.

The sensation sent a jolt straight to his rigid erection. He grabbed fistfuls of her hair and became mesmerized in the peach-scented, soft red curls.

"But of course, I already knew that." She swirled her tongue around his nipple and then teased the stiff peak.

Hunter groaned. She was killing him. A shiver stole through every nerve ending. No one had ever brought him so close to climaxing with such a simple, sweet touch.

"So then, how do I keep someone as wild as you, Hunter? How would I entice you to want me for longer than a fling?" She folded her arms across his chest and rested her chin on them.

Although he knew she couldn't see his face for the dark, she looked straight at him, her eyes challenging.

"I know for whatever reason, you don't want me," she said, her expression dead serious.

His hands stilled on her bare arms. Hell, where did she get the idea he didn't want her?

"So that's fine. We do it, and both satisfy some primal

urge and that's it. No strings attached. I've never had it so good as with you. And so…" She shrugged. "I might as well enjoy it until the next guy comes along. Maybe I'll get lucky and he'll be just as good as you. Or, heck, maybe even better."

Hunter didn't say anything for a moment. Despite her goading him, she wouldn't get him to say that which was on the tip of his tongue—that he wouldn't let her be with *anyone* else. That he would be the only one for her. But he couldn't. "There *won't* be anyone better."

She smiled in the most devilish way. "Never know, Hunter. You just never know."

Forget the damned shoulder. He would show her how good it got. He pushed her onto her back, and she laughed.

"Vixen." Now it was his turn to tease her enticing nipples, his tongue laving over one while his thumb stroked the other, preparing it for its due.

"Hmm, what about your shoulder?"

"I'll survive."

She smiled as she ran her fingers over his whiskered cheek. "I could ride you."

"Too late for that. You had your chance." *Ride him?* Yeah, some other time, but for now he wanted to be on top, controlling, possessing her. No one could replace him. "I should give you one of those sexy rubs you gave me."

"When your shoulder's better."

He'd take her up on it. Massage everywhere, too.

He slipped his hand between her legs and pushed them apart. "Hmm, warm, wet, and willing." Hot, she was hotter than any woman he'd ever been with.

He wanted to take it nice and slow, but his shoulder was acting up too much. He gritted his teeth, centered himself between her legs, and plunged his erection deep inside her.

"You might be right," she whispered against his mouth.

"I'm always right."

She laughed and pinched his butt. "Always so modest and not in the least bit arrogant."

He growled, "No one will be better."

Hunter was sooo good, Tessa thought as he sank into her again and again, stretching her, rubbing against her sweetest spot, making her yearn for more. He lowered his mouth to hers as her insides burned a thousand fires, the hair on his chest caressing her nipples, sensitizing them even more, his body sliding against hers, intoxicating her.

She savored every bit of his hot-blooded nature, his wanting his way with her, his possessiveness, his protectiveness. She never wanted the lovemaking to stop because with it she felt complete, whole, satisfied, and a part of his life that she didn't care to end.

"Hmm, Hunter," she mewed, loving every bit of him, and he recaptured her lips as if to say he knew he did wicked things to her body no man had ever done—carried her to the heavens and back in a million shattered, ecstatic pieces. And here she thought the reason for her inability to feel anything for another man had all to do with her. That she couldn't inspire such passion.

Hunter rubbed her most sensitive spot at the juncture of her thighs, making her beg for more—for faster, harder, fulfilling completion. And then she reached the point of no return, a blast of heat washing through her, mind-numbing satisfaction as ripples of orgasm gripped her in the final throes of passion. He joined her, milky heat filling her womb, warming her like a hot bath, and he groaned with deep satisfaction.

He pulled away, but not separating from her, just rolling backward, keeping her close as he settled on his back, her leg resting between his, her arms wrapped around him and his around her tightly. To sleep with her in his cocoon of an embrace, his rapid heart thumping out a comforting rhythm in her ear, to keep the connection.

She wanted to say how much she loved him, not in a marriage kind of way, but because of all he already meant to her. No one had ever been so shielding, or considerate of her feelings, or so determined to take care of her in her time of need, without wishing anything in return. And the sex? Oh, yes, no man had ever made her feel so sexy and wanted her like she was an aphrodisiac he couldn't get enough of, or made her nearly climax with a seductive glance, touch, whispered word. And no man had ever wanted to keep her close after the love-making was done, showing her he wanted more than just the sex, but also the intimacy of sharing the same space, of maintaining the connection.

From his muscular arms that held her tight to his sculpted abs and the firmest butt she had ever seen on a guy this close up, Hunter was physically as beautiful as one of the Greek statues of gods. Deep down, he was all she'd ever hoped for in a man. And for the moment, he was all hers, although it wouldn't last.

But the tender memories would be hers forever.

Chapter 11

Someone pounded on the master bedroom door the next morning, jump-starting Hunter's heart. Tessa cuddled against him, her voice whisper soft as she nuzzled his chest. "Tell whoever it is to go away."

"Hunter! We need to talk!" Meara said. "Now!"

Hell, what now? Leave it to Meara to ruin a perfectly good morning wake-up.

He kissed Tessa's lips, gently at first, then building up steam as she wrapped her arms around him, leaning into his arousal. Instantly, he hardened.

"Hunter!"

Hunter growled under his breath. "Time for Rourke and me to check out Bethany's place anyway." With reluctance, he kissed Tessa's cheek, then left her warm embrace, dressing as she watched every move he made, licking her lips, purring, a slight smile curving her lips. *Vixen.*

"More, later."

"Promises, promises."

He gave the siren one last look, then took a deep breath and joined Meara in the hall and scowled at her. Giving him an equally disgruntled look, she motioned to the guest bedroom as he shut Tessa's door. He knew then what this was all about. Meara entered the room and waved at a stack of wolf photos spread out on the desk, the sepia picture of the man he'd thought was Seth taking center stage.

"What's all this?" She put her hands on her hips.

"Her brother paints wolves. Did you see his oils in the closet?"

"This!" she said, lifting Seth's photo. "Explain what an old-time photograph of Seth is doing here."

But it wasn't *that* photograph that interested him now, or the concern that she also thought the man pictured was Seth, but another photo lying underneath that caught his eye. Sepia like the other, but this one was of a group of gold miners—their great-grandfather included, and a great uncle, Seth, and some others Hunter didn't know. Although one seemed familiar.

"Where did you find it?" He studied it more closely, his heartbeat ratcheting up several notches.

"Buried at the bottom of the drawer underneath all these wolf pictures. So, what's going on? We both know Seth had a mate who died in Colorado and then he left his small son to live with his pack while he went to California because of the Gold Rush. But *this* woman isn't his mate, and he didn't have another when he died. So who is the woman and infant in the photo? And why does Tessa Anderson have the two photos?"

Hunter rubbed his chin in thought. "Hell, Tessa thought Seth, by another name—Jeremiah Cramer—was her great-grandfather and the woman, his wife and child."

Meara's eyes widened and she looked at the photo again and at the one with their great-grandfather in it. "I would say she's mistaken, or that this wasn't Seth, but the one with our great-grandfather proves he was." She stared at Hunter. "She's not a *lupus garou* and our kind can't produce offspring with a human."

"My thoughts exactly."

"So, what if he was fooling around with the human woman after his mate died, and this woman already had a baby?"

"Possibly, except for the fact that Tessa's as much of a magnet for male *lupus garous* as you are. Why? There's got to be a reasonable explanation."

Meara touched the baby in the photo. "She's not one of us."

"What if for the sake of argument, her grandmother had mixed parents. What if through some freak mistake of nature, her human great-grandmother conceived Seth's child?"

Meara shook her head as she studied the photo again. "We've never known a case like that in all the years we've lived. Never."

"So explain the photos, Tessa's fascination with wolves, and their interest in her."

"What about her brother?"

"The females have enough males to choose from. If they weren't so picky," he amended, giving his sister a pointed look. "Most *lupus garou* females wouldn't be interested in a male who had only a small percentage of *lupus garou* genetics running through his veins, I suspect. But Michael seems to be as drawn to our kind—well, wolves—as Tessa is."

"She doesn't have any of our senses. I know because she can't tell what we are."

"It's just a thought. I don't know how else to explain this."

Meara's stubborn streak was shining through. "She's *not* a *lupus garou.*"

But if Tessa was in part, it would make it a hell of a lot harder for Hunter to leave her as she was. Word would undoubtedly spread about a mixed *lupus garou* female who didn't have a pack to protect her.

The back of his neck prickled, and Hunter rubbed it.

"Okay, Hunter, so if Tessa's grandmother was half *lupus garou, who* protected her from *lupus garou* suitors during her lifetime?"

"Probably none in the area so no one learned about her. Which makes me wonder if the woman was Tessa's maternal or paternal grandmother."

"Had to be paternal," Meara said. "Otherwise they'd have had another generation of females with the *lupus garou* pheromones."

Hell, did Uncle Basil know about this all along? "Do you have your cell phone?"

"Why?"

"I'm wondering why Uncle Basil befriended her, then implied I had to take drastic measures to eliminate her."

"Did he mean as in mating the woman? Making her one of our own?"

Hunter swore under his breath. It was one thing for it to be his own idea, but he sure as hell didn't appreciate his uncle setting him up.

Meara handed him her phone and folded her arms. "I knew he was up to something and that his sudden desire to retire was due to something lots more devious."

Yeah, Hunter should have known the way his uncle was so eager to leave, something was up.

When his uncle's answering machine came on, Hunter let out his breath and left a terse message. "What's the true story behind Tessa Anderson? What's her relationship to Seth? Call me soonest."

Meara raised her brows. "He's not answering?"

"I got his machine." He handed her the phone.

She snorted. "You should have been more cryptic. Said you'd run into troubles. Call back. ASAP. *Better yet,* get your butt back here and explain yourself. Once he sees what you're calling about, he'll undoubtedly let it slide until you resolve it one way or another on your own."

As if Hunter had any intention of worrying his uncle when there wasn't any need.

"You can't turn her," Meara finally said, her voice softened.

"I don't plan to." Yet the more things got out of control with Yoloff and his brothers, the more he was considering just that option.

The doorbell rang and the master bedroom door opened. *Tessa.*

Hell, she'd better not go near the door without his protection. His heart pounding, Hunter bolted out of the guest bedroom and gave her a warning look as she was going in the direction of the door. "I'll get it." He was certain his sister was shaking her head at his overreaction, but he knew it was only a matter of time before the grays tried for Tessa again.

The doorbell rang once more, and he heard Cara and Ashton stirring in Michael's bedroom.

Hunter opened the door to find the red *lupus garou* pack leader of Portland standing on the front porch.

Meara said under her breath, "Uh-oh."

His expression dark and menacing, Leidolf barged into the house. "Your people are causing trouble in my city. When I attempted to contact you at home where your pack members said you were living, I got your sister. She gave me this address. I want them out in three days, or I'll take care of the situation myself. And you *don't* want that to happen if you care anything about them."

Hunter slanted his sister an irritated look that she would give the red Tessa's address. Meara gave him a half smile.

Leidolf was bigger than most reds Hunter had seen. Although that amounted to only a couple of dozen over the years. But the man was as tall as Hunter, his chestnut hair tinged red, his eyes a slightly more olive color than Tessa's. But it was the dark brooding look that really defined Leidolf.

He glanced at Tessa, his eyes widening when he saw her. Surprised to see a human in a house full of *lupus garous*? Or was he interested in the redhead?

Irritated that Leidolf had seen Tessa, Hunter moved across the floor to block Leidolf's view of her. "I've got a situation here I need to resolve before I can go to Portland."

"With the woman?" Leidolf asked, his voice and brows raised.

"I'm Tessa Anderson, and you are?" She moved around Hunter to shake Leidolf's hand. She didn't look pleased Leidolf would treat her as *some* woman when the house was hers, or that Hunter would stand between them.

But Hunter didn't like that she would get near another alpha male. Where Rourke and Ashton were concerned, they seemed to know their place. Leidolf was an unknown quantity—*and* an alpha leader.

"Leidolf Wildhaven." He tilted his nose up and took a deep breath, his eyes darkening as he took her hand and held on longer than necessary, not shaking it, but restraining her.

For long enough that Hunter's blood heated.

Hell, if her pheromones were triggering Leidolf's interest—and worse, she seemed intrigued by him also and didn't pull away…

"Fascinating." Then Leidolf released her hand and saw the wolf photos on the coffee table. He motioned to them. "Who took these?"

"I did." Tessa sounded as ready to defend herself as Leidolf's tone was accusing.

"Let's go outside, Leidolf." Hunter motioned for him to take the lead and shut the door behind them before he gave in to his wolf nature and fought him over Tessa. "Like I said, I have a situation here, and I need to resolve it before I can leave."

"Concerning the woman? She knows what we are?"

"No."

"I smelled at least six different *lupus garous* in the house, and she doesn't have a clue what's going on?"

"None. A gray is trying to change her. I need to stop him before it gets that far."

"The one who's been in the house? The one in the photos? Hell, he's Yoloff and he and his brothers and three more of their pack members are from La Grande. All males. All looking for mates. They came sniffing around Portland, but we don't have any unattached red females, so the grays moved farther west. You're bound to have more trouble with them. I take it you want the woman for yourself?"

"I don't believe in changing humans."

"At least that's something we agree on." Leidolf offered an arrogant smile. "Yet two are newly turned, am I right?"

"Yoloff changed the one and the other was an accident."

"Ah. I don't blame you about the woman. I'm a royal and mixing our kind with a newly turned *lupus garou* doesn't appeal."

A royal? But Leidolf's attentions toward Tessa hinted at more than a little intrigue. Mixing his purer *lupus garou* line with a human just turned might become an option if the red got desperate enough for a mate.

"I'd guess she has a red in her family tree because of her hair color and as petite as she is."

Hunter snorted. "A *lupus garou* can't impregnate a human."

"In all of the years I've lived, I've learned one important thing: there are exceptions to nearly every rule."

Hunter snapped his gaping jaw shut, glanced back at the house, saw Tessa watching him through the picture window, and turned his attention back to Leidolf. In all the years *Hunter* had lived, he'd never seen a case like that. "You know someone like that?"

Leidolf motioned to the house. "Right inside. Maybe a couple of generations back. Maybe more. But she's got a *lupus garou* in her genes somewhere along the line. Got to have if she's chasing down *lupus garous* like Yoloff, drawn to us, curious, and we're just as attracted to her."

Hunter glanced back at the house. Tessa's brows lifted.

"She may not smell like us or have our enhanced wolf abilities, but she triggers your craving, doesn't she? I can see in your expression you don't believe me, but I met one other nearly a hundred years ago. A human female. She moved close to where my father's pack lived in Wildhaven. Several of our unmated males fought over her. Finally, a red won her over and that was that. But she had *lupus garou* pheromones that triggered quite a bit of testosterone between our males before the situation was resolved. A grandfather was the culprit."

"But the woman didn't interest you."

Leidolf shrugged. "I told you. I want a *lupus garou* who's close to being a royal. Why don't you bring the woman to Portland where you can keep an eye on her, and then you can force your pack to return to the coast?"

Bring her to Portland to watch over her? Or give Leidolf another opportunity to check her out? Only this time in *his* territory.

"If I don't resolve this by week's end, I might do that."

"Good." Leidolf looked back at the house and bowed his head to Tessa. "Too bad she isn't a red *lupus garou*. I imagine though, you wish she were a gray."

So Leidolf *was* interested in her. "She's human, and I intend for her to stay that way. But if she *were* part *lupus garou,* she would have *gray* lineage." Hunter made the comment as pointed as he could. He didn't want one horny red thinking *he* might claim her.

Leidolf perked up. "How so?"

"If it's true she has distant *lupus garou* lineage, her great-grandfather was probably Seth Greystoke."

Leidolf's eyes rounded. "The devil gray who beat Alfred's great-grandfather?"

Hunter frowned. "Who?"

"Alfred was the previous red pack leader in the Portland area. His great-grandfather was as much of a terror when he was the pack leader in the Oregon territory. Seth had come here with the gold fever. Made a mint. Then after he took down Alfred's great-grandfather, he returned to his home in Colorado. Seth's great-grandson, Devlyn, came here looking for a female red, Bella, and destroyed Alfred three months ago, after Alfred and some of the males in his pack had killed young women in the area."

"Seth." Hunter shook his head. "We'd heard he had a son."

"Yes, whose own son fathered three boys. But everyone died in a house fire set by vigilante humans, except for Devlyn. Being punished for disobedience, he was sleeping in a shed that night."

Hell, if Tessa and her brother were truly Seth's descendants, they were Devlyn's distant cousins. Which could be more of a problem, *or* Hunter's solution, depending on the way he looked at it. "Never would have figured Seth to oust a leader. He was in California when my great-grandfather met him."

"Earlier gold fever?"

"Yeah, guess he never did get over it."

Leidolf glanced back at Tessa. "I'll get word to Devlyn that he's possibly got a couple of distant relations still living. Never know. He might want to take her back to his pack—for safekeeping. Once others discover she's available, the stream of lusty suitors will never end. You know as well as I, a vulnerable human will soon succumb. As for your people, don't wait too long to get them." Leidolf climbed into his black Hummer, gave a wave, and drove off.

He'd had every intention of getting rid of Yoloff to protect Tessa, but if Leidolf was right and Seth truly had been her great-grandfather, the trouble would never end. So why not take the easy way out and hand her over to Devlyn? If he truly was family, he'd take care of her. Her brother, too. So why did that make Hunter want to fight to the death for her before anyone took her away?

His only other option as he could see it was to change her and claim her for his own. But not without her consent. So if he chose that path, how the hell was he going to get it if she knew what they were without using some damn caveman approach? And then there was one other nagging worry—that she might not be alpha enough to be his mate.

Hunter ground his teeth and headed back inside.

"What did he say, Hunter?" Meara's brows pinched together in worry.

"Nothing. Rourke, hurry up and finish eating so we can go."

Looking sour, Ashton shoved his hands in his pockets. "Can't *I* be the one to go with you?"

"*You* can shoot. *Rourke* can't. Stay here and protect the women."

Cara ran her hand over Ashton's arm. "Besides, we can take a nap later since we didn't get a lot of sleep last night. Wouldn't you like that?"

Ashton threw his coat on and stalked out back.

"Watch him, Cara. Make sure he stays here when we leave," Hunter warned.

She smiled. "That I will, Hunter. He's all mine."

He wasn't so sure. Ashton didn't seem to be taking the change well, unless something else was bothering him. Maybe he didn't like that Rourke seemed to be Hunter's favorite now. But it wasn't that. It really had all to do with who could use the rifle.

While Rourke was finishing off a banana, Hunter took Tessa aside, cupped her face in his hands and kissed her mouth, enjoying the warm, soft feel of her. Her tongue flicked against his lips, her arms reaching around his neck, her body screaming she wanted him to take her. And he sure as hell wanted to oblige. Some of it was the need to prove he was more to her liking than Leidolf was, damn him for interfering.

He took another deep breath of her uniquely heady scent and groaned inwardly. Afraid Leidolf was right in speculating Tessa was in part one of them and with him notifying Devlyn of the situation, Hunter knew he had to take drastic measures one way or another soon. "Don't take a nap without me."

"Wouldn't be half as satisfying."

He kissed her again and gave her another warm embrace, not wanting to let her go, but he had to take care of this matter with her brother. "Come on, Rourke. Let's get this done."

She gave Hunter a concerned smile. Afraid for his safety? Or that he wouldn't learn who Bethany's murderer was? She had a lot more than *that* to worry about.

He and Rourke headed outside and into the woods, wary of signs of danger in the form of three *lupus garous*. Although if Leidolf was right, there were six of them he'd eventually have to contend with.

Praying they wouldn't encounter any trouble, Tessa watched Hunter and Rourke until they disappeared into the woods. Cara coaxed Ashton inside. Tessa couldn't understand why he was behaving like a spoiled child.

Meara cleared her throat. "They'll be all right, Tessa. Let's go back in the house."

In one respect, Meara acted as though she wanted to keep Tessa safe. But on the other hand, she didn't seem to care for Tessa and Hunter's relationship. Although why it would matter to Meara was a puzzle.

Leidolf was another mystery, the way he tore into the house, roaring about like he was in charge, when if he'd known Lord Hunter at all he would have realized *Hunter* was always the one in charge.

Tessa turned to Meara. "What did Leidolf mean about Hunter's people being in Portland and that they had to leave? Was he talking about more of your relatives? Why does he act like he owns the place? Sounds like he's head of an organized crime ring in the city."

Her expression indifferent, Meara shrugged. "A couple of Hunter's friends must be causing trouble in Leidolf's business."

"What does he do?"

Meara paused too long before answering, which made Tessa suspicious.

"He has a… bar in town. You know, the guys probably have been drinking a little too much and stirring up trouble."

"So… why does Hunter have to take care of them?"

"They're friends from way back. You know."

Meara and Cara exchanged looks, and again Tessa felt like an outsider, while the women who'd never met each other before shared some dark secret. Fine. She'd ask Hunter when he returned.

Tessa unloaded the dishwasher while Meara and Cara put away leftovers from a hastily grabbed breakfast. Tessa thought she heard Ashton stacking more wood by the fireplace. But Cara suddenly dropped the napkins she'd gathered on the table and dashed through the house and out the front door.

"Damn, Ashton!" she yelled. "You come back here this instant!"

"We could go after him," Tessa offered, although why he was acting the way he was, she didn't have a clue. Unless he felt hurt that the "boys" were leaving him out. Probably didn't want to be tied down to babysitting the women.

With tears in her eyes, Cara closed the door and shook her head. "No, we can't leave. It wouldn't be safe for us."

Meara actually looked sympathetic.

"I can use the rifle, so don't worry." But of course Tessa *did* worry about Ashton. What if the wolf attacked him again? No. She had shot it and it was probably half-dead somewhere in a pile of snow.

Remembering she'd neglected to write the suspect list and glad for the diversion, she grabbed a piece of paper. Except for Michael, Ashton, Rourke, and half a dozen of her brother's artist friends, she couldn't think of anyone else that visited regularly. A man cleaned their chimney once. An electrician checked their heater when it kept flipping the circuit breaker. A plumber had to repair a frozen pipe. That was it.

"Hot cocoa, anyone?" Meara asked, while Cara watched out the front window.

"That would be great." Tessa considered her list. "The chimney sweep didn't look like the guy Ashton described—dark haired, same approximate build as Hunter. Michael had dealt with the electrician and plumber so I didn't get a chance to see either. I think I was selling photographs to shops in Portland at the time."

"Hell," Meara said in the kitchen.

Tessa dropped the list on the coffee table and hurried to join her. Ashton was pacing on the back patio. "What's wrong with him?" She had never seen him so agitated, except for maybe the time he was drunk and had attacked her.

"Uhm, Cara!" Meara said. "Ashton's back here. Why don't you take care of him?"

Cara raced from the front window to the back door. She bolted outside, slammed the door shut, and grabbed Ashton's arm, but he shook loose. Tessa couldn't hear their words, but his face was red, his brows furrowed, and he snarled back at Cara when she tried to calm him.

Then he started tugging off his clothes as if he had gone totally mad. Tessa's mouth gaped.

Meara seized Tessa's arm. "Come on, we don't want to watch this. Cocoa's ready."

But Tessa *did* want to watch. What if Ashton had rabies? What if Cara was in danger? "Wait, Meara. Cara could be at risk. We need to get her away from him."

"No, she'll be fine." Meara tried to yank Tessa toward the living room, but she was rooted to the floor. "Finish your list. I'll bring—"

Ashton stretched his arms upward toward the gray clouds, his face began to distort, elongate, and his naked lean body began to change, his back arching. Pale gray hair, no it was more like… fur, began to cover his body, the whole thing happening so quickly it was like watching a movie playing at triple speed or more in a blur. He dropped to his… his paws, no longer a man, but a gray wolf. A beautiful creature, wild and dangerous.

She barely breathed. If she hadn't seen the sudden transformation with her own eyes, she would never believe it. Even now, she had a hard time accepting it. Every inch of him looked like a real wolf.

Her heart pounding and her head swimming, Tessa's knees buckled. Meara was still holding her arm and when Tessa collapsed on her knees, Meara fell with her. "Ohmigod… did… did you see… what happened to Ashton?"

Meara watched Tessa with wide eyes.

"Cara! We've got to get her away from him." Tessa scrambled to her feet and peered out the window, clinging to the kitchen sink for support.

Shaking her finger at him, Cara scolded the wolf—Ashton. For a couple of seconds, he listened to her, but then bolted for the woods.

Turning, Cara saw Tessa watching. Her face turned pasty despite the fact her cheeks had been cherry colored from the cold. Tessa stepped away from the window, her heart thundering.

Cara was one, too. She had to be. Had she turned Ashton last night when she seduced him? *Turned* him? What was she saying? They were shapeshifters?

Tessa bolted for the door and locked it.

"Let me in, Tessa. I don't have my coat on and it's freezing out here." Cara half-coaxed, half-demanded, rubbing her arms with her bare hands.

Tessa couldn't find her voice. What if the wolf that had bitten Ashton was the culprit and not Cara? But then, why wasn't Cara surprised when Ashton shapeshifted?

Tessa didn't realize how much she was shaking until Meara touched her arm. "It's too cold out. We've got to let her in."

Tessa stared at Meara. She saw Ashton turn into a wolf. She observed the whole thing and wasn't surprised.

What if she was one? And what did Ashton say about Hunter? He saw him naked in the freezing weather before he dressed and charged up the hill after Ashton for shooting him. Why? Because Hunter had been shapeshifting beforehand? Ashton hadn't been drunk. She groaned.

"Tessa, we have to let Cara back in."

"You're one of them." Tessa's eyes misted. "You're one and Hunter is one and he bit Rourke. Leidolf is, too, isn't he? Everyone but me is." Her heart beating too rapidly, she backed up.

"Tessa, you're just imagining things." Meara took a step forward, cautious, concerned.

Where had Ashton left the rifle? In the living room?

Tessa dashed for it just as the back door squeaked open. Meara was letting Cara in.

The door shut and the lock clicked, but no one said a word. They didn't need to. They'd share one of those conspiratorial looks that said it all.

She grabbed the rifle and headed back into the kitchen where Meara was pouring Cara another mug of hot cocoa. "I want you both to leave, now. Get in your vehicles and drive away. I won't say anything to anyone. Hell, what could I say? Anyone would think I was nuts. But I want you out of here, *now*."

"We can't leave," Meara said, softly. "Hunter would kill us if we left you unprotected."

"He would kill his own sister?"

"In a manner of speaking. He'd be angry, and I don't want to go there. You know how upset he was with me for taking off with three other guys. Believe me, this would be worse."

"Do you want to know why, Tessa? Because that intruder who's after you is also one of our kind," Cara piped in. "We can't leave you to face him on your own. If he manages to get you alone now, he'll change you."

Tessa sat down hard on the dining chair. "The one who bit Ashton, was he the same man/wolf?"

Meara sighed. "I imagine he's the same one."

Everything that had happened in the last few days ran through Tessa's mind—Hunter being naked on the beach, the way he knew the man had been in her bed, and that it was him and not some other man. He knew things he shouldn't.

"Tell me what you are, exactly."

Meara shook her head. "You know too much already. In most cases, the pack leader would have two options. Kill you, or turn you. Hunter won't want to change you."

"Why not?" Not that Tessa wanted that option, *no way*, but death wasn't the greatest choice either. Not that she would go willingly either.

"He doesn't believe in it," Meara said. "We haven't known anyone personally changed by a bite. It's just something we prefer not to do."

Tessa gave a haughty laugh. "Yeah, right. He changed Rourke, didn't he?"

"By accident."

"So then he'll have to kill me. That's why he said the relationship would never work." Tessa swallowed a lump in her throat. "Will he at least get my brother free first?"

"I don't believe he'll want to eliminate you. But enough said. Like you mentioned, people will think you're certifiable if you breathe a word of this. So here's the deal. You don't ask questions or learn anything more about us, and when we free your brother, we all will..." Meara snapped her fingers. "... disappear. You'll never hear from us again."

"Unless Hunter wants to terminate me."

Meara took in a ragged breath. "We won't tell him." She cast Cara a warning look.

Cara bowed her head slightly.

In disbelief, Tessa stared at Meara. "Why?"

She shrugged. "He'd want to eliminate all of us for putting him in this bind. It'll be our little secret."

Keeping secrets from Hunter was like trying to drive a car across the ocean. Tessa knew she would sink and drown before she got anywhere.

"Want some cocoa?" Cara put on a fake smile and offered Tessa a mug.

Tessa had known something would go terribly wrong after she had come home from Michael's trial, but she never guessed the nightmare could get this bad.

Rourke looked over the edge of the cliff where the men had pushed Hunter. "I don't know how in the hell you managed to survive. The tide must have come in just at the right time."

Hunter examined the nearby trees, looking for signs of a struggle. Half a foot of snow had fallen, so the ground would yield no clues.

"Looks like you gave them a hell of a time." Rourke twisted a broken branch back and forth.

"I still can't figure out why they would have attacked me. If I came into a wolves' territory unannounced, the pack leader would either welcome me, or tell me to leave. The only way he would fight me with the intent to kill was if I had seriously violated pack laws, killed one of his wolves, tried to claim a female he had other plans for, or threatened to take over his pack. Maybe I was headed in the direction of Tessa's cabin and Yoloff, the one who wants her, got riled, thinking I was after her."

Hunter led the way to Bethany's log cabin. Like Tessa's place, the house sat cliffside with a view of a rocky beach, woods all around, and no sign of any other homes.

"Why she would live out here by herself is what puzzles me," Rourke said. "I can understand Tessa's situation. She and her brother lived together and had inherited the house. But Bethany?" He shook his head as Hunter unlocked the door. "She was kind of a loner, like... ." Rourke stopped dead inside the house. "It's him, isn't it? The smell of Tessa's stalker."

"Yoloff, yeah. He's been here. His brothers, too. And recently. Did they have a key to her place also? No broken windows." Hunter checked over the two-bedroom, one-bath house. "She wasn't killed here."

"No, the coroner said she'd died when she fell to her death on the rocks."

"But why not here? Why a mile away?" Hunter searched through her bedroom drawers.

"She loved to take walks in the woods. That's what Michael said at the trial. He didn't like it that she was taking them alone. Of course, it sounded like a perfect alibi since no one could confirm that she was seeing someone behind his back. Either this phantom guy did it, or some stranger. Neither the sheriff or his deputies bought Michael's story."

"Sheriff's been here. So has Ashton. And three of the wolves that had been around Tessa's place? They've been here, too. Which meant they were tied into her death, or curious possibly."

"And a ton of other humans. Coroner, deputies. But I wouldn't know whose scent I'm smelling unless I got a whiff of them now." Rourke motioned to the house. "What did you want me to look for?"

"Any sign of anything out of the ordinary."

"You won't find her diary. The D.A. kept it as evidence. But there was nothing incriminating in it about Ashton. Or anyone else for that matter. Just Michael. They fought concerning her seeing someone else, but she never confirmed it one way or another."

"Ashton said he kept a pretty low profile," Hunter said.

They moved back into the kitchen. Rourke pulled open a cabinet door. "Yeah, he didn't leave any clothes in the house. Nothing personal to tie himself to her."

Hunter paused. "Don't you think that's odd?"

"What? He didn't want Michael to learn that he was here with Bethany on the sly. Ashton still valued his friendship, even if he wasn't showing it in a very loyal way."

"Unless he had some things here and got rid of them after he'd murdered her." Hunter pulled open another drawer.

"I thought you believed the grays had killed her."

"I'd considered it. The one might have wanted Michael out of the way so he killed Bethany, and then Michael was blamed for it. Tessa would be left unprotected."

"But why not just kill Michael?"

"The wolf's a beta. If he'd been an alpha, he would have killed Michael and taken Tessa. But he didn't. He's stalked her, waited, watched, for what? He couldn't get up the nerve. Maybe he cared for her too much and was afraid if he turned her and things didn't work out, he'd have to destroy her. On the other hand, what if the guy couldn't even kill Bethany? What if Ashton did it? But now Bethany's murder played into the gray's hands, and he had a chance to make Tessa his. Only he still stalked her, worried about her acceptance of him."

"Then you appeared on the beach."

"Right. And he got anxious. Started playing games. Showing how he could get in, leaving his scent on her sheets, wanting to claim her, getting more and more rash."

"And then he bit Ashton to…?"

"I believe at that point he wanted to kill Ashton so he could get to Tessa since you and I were gone. Even more desperate, he took a bigger chance, but when Tessa got the gun and started shooting, he tucked tail and ran."

Rourke shoved his gloved hands under his arms. "What if the gray did it? Or Ashton for that matter? We can't prove either did because they can't go to prison. Not when they're werewolves."

"We just have to find the evidence, and I'll sort it out from there."

Rourke took a deep breath. "All the evidence points to Michael."

"He didn't have an alibi?"

"Nope. He was supposed to be home sick with the flu, but nobody was there to verify he'd stayed home in bed either. Tessa had run to the city to get supplies and sell some more of her photographs. When she arrived home, the sheriff had already arrested Michael and taken him in for questioning."

Not that Hunter wanted to believe anything bad about Tessa, but his wolf's wariness instantly made him suspect anyone and everyone. "How long was she in the city?"

"Four hours." Rourke's eyes widened. "Oh, no. Don't you go thinking Tessa had anything to do with it. Between receipts and store personnel and surveillance tapes at the stores where she sold her work, she had an airtight alibi."

"For all the time?"

Rourke looked out the living room window. "Yeah."

"Not for all the time. You'd make a lousy liar, Rourke. Don't try it with me."

"All right. So she had enough time. But she wouldn't have done it."

Hunter smelled the air. "She's been here before."

"Sure, Tessa has. She was friends with Bethany, too, damn it, but she didn't do it."

"Did the defense think she might have?"

Rourke looked at the floor.

"Did they, Rourke?"

"Yeah. Michael's defense attorney said she had motive because the attorney was trying to cast doubt on Michael's supposed guilt. Tessa suspected someone else was seeing Bethany, too. That's what the defense attorney said. That as loyal as Tessa was to her brother, she could have killed Bethany in a fit of rage. Two police officers had to restrain Michael to keep him from hitting his attorney, he was so pissed. His temper didn't help his case."

"Did Michael always have a temper?"

"Not that he showed publicly. I always thought he kept pretty quiet, except for getting in trouble for minor infractions of the law. Breaking and entering, joy riding in a car once, but I figured Ashton was the mastermind."

Hunter returned to the bathroom and sifted through the drawers.

"What are you looking for?"

"I can understand why Ashton wouldn't leave anything incriminating here in case Michael came across it, but why wouldn't Michael have left anything?"

"He didn't like coming here, so he said at the trial."

"Why not? Seems to me it would be a great place to have private time with his girl."

Rourke gave a derisive laugh. "He thought it was haunted."

"Haunted?" Hunter shook his head. "I need to pay Michael a little visit at the jailhouse."

Rourke peered out the bathroom window. "The wind is really picking up. *Holy shit!*"

"The grays?" Adrenaline instantly flooded Hunter's system, preparing him for another fight.

"No, that idiot Ashton."

Hunter's blood heated several degrees. "I'll kill him." Although Hunter's sister and Cara were still at Tessa's house to protect her, if the three male grays tried to take off with Tessa, his sister and Cara could be in a world of trouble.

As soon as Hunter headed outside with Rourke on his heels, a patrol car drove into the driveway. *Hell.* Ashton in his wolf form judiciously moved away from the house, slinked deeper into the woods, and slipped out of sight. But Hunter and Rourke had a lot of explaining to do.

"Have you got permission to be breaking into Bethany Wade's house, gentlemen?" the deputy asked, as he climbed out of the car, his hand on his holster. He was a scrawny, sawed-off little guy and Hunter could have eaten him for a midnight snack if he gave them any real trouble.

"This is Deputy William O'Neal," Rourke said. "And, William, I want you to meet my friend, Hunter Grey. He's an ex–navy SEAL. He's done quite a lot of investigative work for the navy, and he's trying to dig up more clues concerning Bethany's murder. I'm doing an investigative report for the newspaper."

"You didn't answer me, Rourke. Did you get permission from her family first, or not?"

"They want this resolved one way or another. Got the key right here." Rourke dangled it from a heart-shaped key chain.

With his head turned slightly south, Hunter listened for Ashton. He better be in a dead run, heading straight back to Tessa's place.

"That's good. Then I'll call the sheriff and have him verify with her family that you had permission and you can run along." The deputy glanced around. "Where's your vehicle?"

Rourke shoved the key in his pocket. "We walked from Tessa's house, looking for any clues on the way over and by the cliff where she fell."

"In this weather? It's only going to get worse. After I clear this matter up, I'll drop you off at Tessa's place."

"Why don't you take us back to Tessa's house while you're verifying this?" Hunter asked. "The winds are whipping up more, and we don't want to get stuck here in whiteout conditions."

The deputy held the phone to his ear and he nodded at Hunter, but then turned his attention to the phone. "Hello, Katie. Is the sheriff there? Where?" He laughed. "Tell him to call me when he has a chance." The deputy shook his head and pocketed his phone. "Sheriff's seeing some new woman. After all those years of pining over his two-timing ex-wife, it's about time, but he's trying unsuccessfully to keep it under wraps. Climb in. I'll get you back to Tessa's."

The road conditions worsened by the mile. A violent gust of wind blew the deputy's car to the other side of the road. Between the slick conditions and the increasing wind, Hunter was surprised they weren't blown off the cliff.

"The sheriff will probably issue an evacuation order soon. We've never had winds this high. And waves cresting forty-five feet? Unheard of. Some fool kids were even trying to surf. If you can imagine," the deputy said.

"William and I played soccer together on the high school team," Rourke explained to Hunter. "We always said we'd blow this town when we graduated."

The deputy chuckled. "Yeah, look at us now."

The two continued to talk about old school days while Hunter watched out the window, hoping Ashton would get to Tessa's place and that Hunter's worries about the grays were unfounded. But he could still thrash Ashton for leaving the women alone.

At one point, he had to fight the urge to take over the deputy's driving, they were inching along so slowly. Hell, at this rate, Hunter could jog faster.

As soon as the house came into view, Hunter grabbed hold of the door handle. Once the deputy stopped the vehicle, Hunter threw open the door and bolted for the house.

"He's worried about Tessa," Rourke explained to the deputy. "Sheriff probably mentioned to you that she's had a couple of break-ins. You drive safe."

"Will do. I'll let you know if the sheriff issues an evac order."

Rourke waved good-bye and the deputy drove off. Hunter tried the front door. Locked. He rang the doorbell. No answer. He and Rourke raced to the back of the house. Ashton's clothes were sitting half-buried in snow on the patio. Hunter stared at the kitchen window. If Tessa had been at the sink, she could have seen Ashton shapeshift.

Hunter bolted to the back door and tried the doorknob. Locked. He pounded hard enough he figured he'd break the door down.

"Coming!" Meara yelled.

He released the breath he had been holding. Everything sounded fine. But when Meara let him in, he sensed the tension in the air. Meara was the only one of the three women who hid her fear well. Cara reeked of it and he figured it had to do with the fact Ashton was still missing. Tessa stared at Hunter as if he had sprouted devil's horns, her back rigid against the dining room chair.

Ashton's disappearance was probably the reason why all of them were so fearful. Unless something else was wrong, like Tessa had seen Ashton change into the wolf.

"Have you seen Ashton?" Cara asked, her voice wobbly.

"He's coming." At least he hoped he was. Despite being angry over Ashton's actions, Hunter still felt responsible for him.

Rourke patted the snow off his gloves. "I'll take a look to see how far behind us he was."

Hunter nodded and Rourke exited the house, seized Ashton's clothes from the patio, and headed for the woods.

Cara grabbed her coat and gloves. "I'll go with him." She slammed the door shut behind her.

Meara looked like she wanted to search for Ashton also, but it wasn't in her nature. She was more the wait-and-see kind of woman. Except in Hunter's case when he disappeared. He figured she knew he would go after her "friends" when he discovered her missing and wanted to stop him from killing them. They were lucky Hunter didn't find them with her still.

Then he wondered if something else was going on with Tessa. "We didn't find anything incriminating, I'm sorry to say, that would automatically clear your brother of the crime, Tessa."

Her shoulders slumped and her jaw tightened.

He drew close and ran his hand over her arm, the muscle tensing. "We'll keep looking. I need to speak to Michael. When the weather clears up, I'll see him."

Her teeth were so tightly clenched, he assumed she was fighting tears. "Tessa, maybe we could—"

"No!" she snapped.

Meara grabbed her coat and gloves. "Maybe you could fix Hunter some cocoa? Warm him up a bit? I'll see what's happening with the others." She threw on her coat and hat and bolted outside.

Hunter stared after his sister. What the hell was up? Meara didn't want him to make anything of a relationship with Tessa, yet her actions were tantamount to proving otherwise. She wouldn't have cared about Ashton's welfare when the others were handling it.

Hunter crouched next to Tessa, lowered himself to her level so he wouldn't appear so imposing like a wolf who lay down before one who was standing—a non-threatening posture.

She wouldn't look at him, but toyed with the full mug of cocoa, cold now.

"Tessa, I know you're disappointed that we couldn't find evidence to support your brother's case of innocence, but I've only begun to look into Bethany's murder."

Still, she refused to look at him. He wouldn't press the issue.

"When Ashton returns, will you take a nap with me?"

Her gaze shot up and he sensed her fear—the look in her eyes, the smell of it on her skin, the hint of perspiration on her brow, the tension in every muscle returning. He reached for her hand, but she pulled away from him.

She remained seated as if the chair and table shielded her from his getting too close.

"What's wrong? Is it something other than Michael's situation that distresses you? My sister? Did she upset you in some way? She can be pretty unconventional at times."

Tessa choked on a laugh. "Unconventional." But the way she said the word was bitter, not with humor.

"Yes," Hunter said softly. He reached for her hand again and this time she didn't avoid him, but she didn't respond with tenderness either as if he had captured her, the reluctant victim, and held her hostage. "Tell me what's wrong. Did Cara upset you? Or did Ashton's actions worry you when he left the three of you alone?"

"I can shoot, Hunter. You know that already." Her eyes flashed annoyance.

Something else then. "Yes, you're a damned good shot."

"Yes." She looked like she wanted to say something more, but clammed up.

He rubbed his thumb over her hand, wanting to set her at ease, but she didn't relax. "So what's wrong? I promise I'm not going anywhere until I discover who murdered Michael's girlfriend."

The back door opened and Meara entered first. "You didn't say how bad the storm was getting. Jeesh, the winds must be topping one hundred miles per hour."

Cara and Ashton both entered after that, Ashton's arm around her shoulders, neither of them looking very happy. "Sorry," Ashton said to Hunter, slouching as if he thought he was about to be whipped.

"I'll have a word with you later." Hunter would not

accept this kind of insubordination, not when it endangered others' lives.

Rourke closed the door behind him. "That shed's about ready to—"

A grinding metal sound and then a scrunching noise and a bang followed. Everyone went to the window to see what happened.

"Hell, there goes the shed," Rourke said. "We saw several trees uprooted when we located Ashton and if this weather keeps up, we're bound to lose the—"

The kitchen light flickered and died.

"Electricity," Rourke finished.

"The beach will be flooded so we can't get any more firewood," Hunter said.

"Makes for good snuggling weather." Cara tugged at Ashton's arm. "Right?"

"We've got enough firewood for a couple of days, if we conserve," Ashton said.

Hunter turned to speak to Tessa about the candles and flashlights for when it got dark, but she had left the dining room.

"What happened while we were gone?" Hunter asked his sister.

She shrugged. "Ashton left. Tessa wrote a list of suspects. We had cocoa. That's about it."

He didn't think that was all of it. "Where's the list?"

"Living room. Coffee table, I think."

Hunter headed into the living room and grabbed up the piece of paper. "As soon as the weather clears, I want every one of these men checked out. In the meantime, Ashton, Rourke, see if you can salvage anything from the shed before everything blows away."

"Will do." They headed out the back door.

Meara looked guilty as hell. Cara did, too, although he didn't know her that well, but in the short time he had been with her, he hadn't seen her so nervous—the way she avoided looking at him and chewed her bottom lip instead of challenging him like she usually did. Ashton was back safe and sound. So what was the problem? The storm?

"What's the matter, Meara?"

"Nothing. I thought you were going to take a nap with Tessa." She motioned to the kitchen. "I'm going to clean the cocoa mugs."

"I'll help you." Cara vamoosed to the kitchen.

A strange noise sounded in Tessa's bedroom. He listened, trying to discern what it was. A grating sound? A window opening?

He raced down the hall and grabbed Tessa's doorknob. *Locked.*

His blood chilled. "Tessa! Open up!"

No response, but the wind was blowing into the room, papers fluttering, curtains flapping, the frigid air seeping under the bottom edge of the door. "Tessa!"

Turning, he saw Meara watching him, wringing her hands. He didn't even *want* to know why at this point. He made a dead run for the front door and threw it wide open.

Tessa struggled with the key in her car door lock. His heart beat out of bounds, the thrill of the chase deeply ingrained in him.

She wasn't leaving him. Not unless he chose for her to do so.

He glanced at the key. Not making any headway on the lock. Frozen?

He stalked toward her, his footfall crunching on the glazed snow. She glanced up at him, held herself rigid, testing him with an icy gaze, but she shivered and looked like a rabbit caught in a trap. He gave her credit for not running away.

"Let's go inside and discuss this, Tessa."

"Like two human beings?" she asked, her eyes narrowed.

He couldn't help the smile that tugged at his lips, but then he frowned at her. "If you stay out here, you're going to catch pneumonia."

"But *you* won't?"

"We can discuss this inside, *now*."

Her brows knit together, and she stormed past him. Meara and Cara watched from the front entrance, but quickly moved out of Tessa's path. Hunter gave Meara a look that meant he would have a word with her later. Cara closed and locked the door behind him. Ashton and Rourke came inside from the back way.

"Not much worth saving at this point." Ashton shook snow off his parka.

Everyone was glowering at Ashton, except for Tessa. Trembling, she knelt before the fire, her hands spread over the flames.

Hunter crouched beside her. "Ask me what you will."

She glanced at the others and then focused on Hunter. "You have two options as far as taking care of me. Make me one of you, or kill me."

Chapter 12

HUNTER SUSPECTED THE WORST—THAT ASHTON HAD shapeshifted in plain view of Tessa and now he was faced with a new dilemma.

Rourke swore under his breath.

Hunter clenched and unclenched his hands. *Damn Ashton.* "Ashton, the window's open in the master bedroom. The door is locked. Go around the front and climb in, shut the window, and unlock the door, why don't you?"

"I'll go with him," Rourke hastily said.

When the men left, Hunter pulled off one of Tessa's cold wet gloves and then the other.

Meara said, "I'll make lunch."

"I'll help her," Cara quickly added, and the two disappeared into the kitchen.

"Tessa, what did you see?" Hunter's gut clenched with concern for what she was feeling.

If he could undo the last few days in a heartbeat to save her from what now had to be done, he would. He couldn't believe Ashton had caused so much trouble. No wonder changing humans wasn't a good policy.

Tessa swallowed hard and stared at the fire while Hunter rubbed her cold fingers. "Ashton was acting crazy, pacing all over the place, and then he went outside and stripped off his clothes in the snow. I thought he was rabid, and I was afraid he would hurt Cara. Instead he… he changed. Transformed into a wolf. Cara wasn't surprised. Your sister told me nothing had happened. And if neither of them was shocked, it meant they were whatever he was also. And you, too."

Wanting her, despite everything—her cousin, his own feelings about changing a human, the fact she had a brother, which would cause even more problems—Hunter unbuttoned her coat, knowing now he had no choice but to explain his world. "I'm sorry."

"That you have to terminate me now? I won't tell anyone." Her eyes glistened with tears. "How could I? They'd lock me away."

He let out his breath, unsure how to approach the problem. He didn't want to upset her any further, but he couldn't be dishonest with her at this point. "Letting you go, isn't one of our options." Their laws had kept them alive and their secret intact for this long, he wasn't about to break one of the most important rules they lived by.

She blinked away tears and looked back at the fire. "Will you at least help my brother get his release?"

Her tearfulness cut straight through to his soul. "Changing you was the other choice." *Or giving her up to Devlyn Greystoke.*

"Your sister said it wasn't an option for you."

He shook his head. Leave it up to his sister to be truthful at the most inopportune times.

Tessa's bedroom door opened, and Rourke stomped back down the hall. "What else did you need done?"

Ashton slinked in behind him.

"Rourke, why don't you take a nap in the guest room? Ashton, you take one in Michael's room. We'll need some sleep so we can pull guard duty tonight."

Rourke cast a sympathetic look Tessa's way and gave Hunter a hard look. Then he and Ashton headed down the hall.

"If I turned you…" Hunter said.

"I don't want to be crazy like Ashton."

"You'll be the same person you are now even after the change. Maybe he was already a little crazy." Hunter stroked Tessa's hand. "There are benefits for being what we are."

"What exactly *are* you?"

"Shapeshifters. *Lupus garous*. Werewolves. We normally don't associate much with humans, and we don't normally change them."

Tessa's eyes were so big, Hunter knew telling her the facts of life wasn't going to be any easier than it had been when he told the guys.

"You can't have been born this way."

"Yes, we're born this way. Normally, it's much easier to stay with our kind since we've grown up this way. Teaching a newly turned human can be a real trial. Both Rourke and Ashton have already made innumerable mistakes. If I could, I'd take them to my home and keep them there, isolated from humans until they more thoroughly understood how dangerous it is for us to let down our guard."

"Dangerous?"

"Yes. Can you imagine if people knew of our existence, what would happen? DNA testing, for one, to learn why we heal so quickly, how we can shapeshift, what makes us age so slowly."

"You… you don't have the life span of a human?"

"No. Although we can die." He pulled off her coat. She looked so petite sitting there, he again wondered if she could handle being his mate. "Think on it, Tessa. I won't pressure you into making a decision."

She snorted. "Death or life as a werewolf. No pressure. Right." She took a ragged breath and stared at the floor. "You wanted to take a nap."

And the fact she wouldn't look at him made him worry she was intending on trying to slip out while everyone was napping. "With you."

She looked so damned vulnerable, he didn't want to push her into accepting any of this until she could handle it. What was he supposed to do? Letting her know their secrets, but allowing her to live on her own as a human was not an option. But killing her wasn't either.

He ran his hands through her silky hair, wanting to bury his face in the sweet peach-scented strands. "In part, you and your brother are already one of us, if it helps any. It seems Jeremiah Cramer, your great-grandfather, was Seth Greystoke, a friend of my great-grandfather's. One of his great grandsons still lives. Which creates another situation. Maybe the solution, or not. Once Devlyn Greystoke learns of your existence, I'd be willing to bet, he'll want you to join his pack."

Tessa looked so distraught, Hunter took her hand and kissed it, and he noted how small her fingers were compared to his, just like the rest of her—petite, delicate, not tall like his sister or Cara, which meant she'd be a small wolf when she shapeshifted, and most likely unable to deal with the heftier grays if one of them tried her. But touching her turned his body into a torrent of need—the desire to claim her overcoming any rational judgment.

Trying to get his mind off what Tessa's sweet body did to his, he considered the matter of turning her further. He didn't object to making her one of their own for the same reason Leidolf did because of his roots, even though he and Meara were of royal lineage also, but having offspring who were not, didn't matter to him. Turning a reluctant woman did. But if she had wolf roots already and she was willing...

"You have a choice, Tessa." As much as he hated to admit it.

"You mean to go with some stranger?" She sounded slightly hysterical, her eyes wide, scared. "I can't leave. My brother—"

"As the last of his kin, I'm certain Devlyn would want to do whatever he could to help free your brother."

Although Hunter had every intention of freeing her brother himself, somehow.

Tessa's expression changed subtly—almost as though she thought family might be more of a help than he would be. And the notion irked him. *He* was her savior, no one else.

But then she squeezed Hunter's hand and his groin tightened. "What about you?"

Hell, he wanted her, but in reality, since Devlyn was a pack leader and her kin, by their laws, he should decide her future. Hunter chided himself. That was one law he wasn't willing to abide by—not when it came to Tessa's fate.

She bit her lip, her hands nervously rubbing her jeans. "What, Hunter? If it pertains to me..."

"Hell, Tessa." He tugged her from the floor and pulled her toward her bedroom. "If I was being perfectly honest with you, I'd tell you it's out of my hands. That according to our laws, your cousin would decide what would happen to you and your brother."

She slumped a little. "But…? " She looked up at him with a mixture of emotions—hope, worry, insecurity.

"I don't want to give up control." Well, a hell lot more than that. He didn't want to give her up, period.

Her lips twitched up slightly.

"Yeah, well, it's a natural curse when you're an alpha pack leader. Give no quarter."

"But…? "

"If I make you mine to prevent the other grays from having you, Devlyn might choose to fight me because of it—if I didn't get his permission first. All packs have female shortages. He may want to give you to one of his own sub pack leaders."

Not that Hunter wanted that, but alpha leaders didn't mate betas. Both an alpha male and female ran the pack. If Tessa wasn't alpha enough, she would never survive as his mate. Devlyn could pair her off with a subleader or a beta. If Tessa stayed with Hunter, there wasn't any way he was giving her to anyone else and that could put her in harm's way. He couldn't do that. But he didn't have the heart to tell her she might not be able to be an alpha's mate.

He took her into the room and shut the door.

She folded her arms and glowered at him. "Right, damn it. Like some guy I don't even know can come here and tell me who I have to marry."

"Mate. We don't marry."

Her brows rose.

"I have a lot more to tell you about us before you really know what you're getting into." Although he wasn't sure how much to reveal all at once.

For a moment, she looked annoyed, and he figured it had to do with not saying he'd fight for her. He had no qualms about fighting Devlyn for her, but the fact of the matter still remained he had to do what was right for Tessa's safety.

But then Tessa began unbuttoning her blouse. He recognized that devious look in her eyes that meant she was up to something. Get him so worked up he didn't want to give her up, perhaps. He didn't want to give her to anyone, but if it meant keeping her safe, he'd... well, he'd have to do what was right for her.

Hesitating, he didn't want to give her the wrong message. She gave him a wickedly sinful smile in response and *that* decided it. Talk about having no willpower when it came to the red-haired goddess.

She ran her fingers down Hunter's chest with a provocative stroke of her long nails and reached for his waistband. "What happened to your pack? Are they the ones Leidolf said were in Portland?"

What pack? Hell, his other head was thinking for him now.

He yanked her shirt down to her elbows, leaned over, and kissed her soft throat, his voice husky when he replied, "They weren't happy about losing their homes in California to the forest fire. They thought living in a city would be a nice change. But we're not urban wolves. Leidolf's pack is established in Portland. He has every right to defend his territory against encroachers."

"Hmm," she murmured, lifting her chin as he ran his mouth lower, trailing kisses over her collarbone, down to the top edge of the lacy bra covering the swell of her breasts.

Despite not looking to see where her fingers roamed, she dipped them inside his sweatpants and a shiver of need stole through him.

Lower, he silently pleaded, wanting her to stroke the itch she'd created. And she touched him, smiling when his arousal jumped in her hand.

Unable to restrain the urge to rip off her clothes and have his way with her, he reached down and attempted to unbuckle her belt, vowing she'd wear sweats like him from now on, less to remove and lots quicker.

She chuckled as he fumbled with the belt, and he growled. Somehow, despite his lust-soaked brain, he was able to remove Tessa's clothes without destroying them, baring all that luscious skin, her pert breasts, the nipples already peaked, but screened by her silky mane of red hair. She trembled in the frigid room, and Hunter scooped her up in his arms and carried her to the bed.

"Then you'll have to go to Portland and bring them back."

Bring who back? Hell, all he cared about was Tessa at the moment. And he sure was rethinking the Devlyn situation, cousin or no, alpha leader problems notwithstanding. "I can't leave you behind while I deal with my pack."

He set her on the bed, then climbed onto the mattress and pulled the covers over them to keep the chill out. Trailing a finger around his nipples, she tortured his body, caressing with featherlight touches. "Why does the stalker want me for real?"

Jeez, she had to ask? Everything about her was sexier than sin—just to look at, to touch, to taste, to smell her special scent. But beyond that? She drugged him with her easygoing manner, her innocence, yet her strength to right wrong, to persist when everything told her the situation was futile, to risk her life to protect him. *What more could a* lupus garou *ask for in a mate?*

He gave a ragged sigh, hating that she'd garnered others' interest as well. "Your pheromones, looks, actions. You caught his attention, but he's cautious in taking you because he's a beta."

He kissed her lips, possessively, craving every inch of her, to hold, to protect, to keep her for his own forever.

"Ahh, betas, of course. Your sister and Cara are alphas, aren't they?"

He groaned inwardly. Some part of his brain realized it was important for her to talk about this, but he sure as hell wanted to get on with what his other brain felt was important. "Yeah."

"And Rourke and Ashton?" Her fingers slid over Hunter's arm, her gaze focused on the way his muscle tensed.

"Betas."

"What would I be?" Her eyes shifted to his, and he could see the concern there.

Hunter took a deep breath. "All that I want in a woman."

Her jaw tightened, her green eyes spearing him with a determined look. "I'm an alpha," she said, with great conviction. When he smiled, she pinched his pebbled nipple with a gentle squeeze. "You don't think so?"

He nuzzled her face, wanting to make love, but wanting to clear the air between them first. "Sometimes you're definitely an alpha." He couldn't lie to her and say she was always one, because he wasn't sure how she'd fare among the alpha of his kind, but he hated the way her brows pinched together, when he wanted to reassure her instead.

"A beta's not good, is it?"

He cleared his throat. Without betas, a *lupus garou* pack would constantly be in turmoil, alphas butting heads, what a mess. "Betas in a pack are fine. Alphas must lead the pack though."

"So if I were a beta and you turned me, I'd be stuck with someone like Rourke?"

Hunter tightened his hold on her. *Hell, no way.*

"*Or* someone of Devlyn's choosing," she whispered.

"We'll talk about it later." He ran his fingers over her smooth cheek and kissed her velvety lips, loving the way every bit of her felt to him, melding to him.

She parted her lips for him and touched her tongue to his, a sexy dominating caress, and then thrusting into his mouth, exploring, conquering, nearly undoing him.

He moaned and pushed her onto her back, her silky hair falling against the sheets, and he couldn't deny she was the most sensual and intriguing woman he'd ever met.

With a gentle push of his knee, he spread her thighs, opening her sweet body to him, her short red curls drenched, her swollen pink lips wanting. Her eyes half-lidded, she more than obliged, her hands tugging at his hips to join her.

Sliding his engorged arousal into her tight sheath, he savored the way her body stroked him as he thrust into her, clenching, tightening, wringing him to the nth degree, heightening the exquisite pleasure. He cupped her face and conquered her mouth with his, her lips and tongue fueling his desire. Tightening her hands on his back, she arched against him, deepening the bond, their hearts beating hard, their breathing heavy and ragged.

For the moment, she was all his, but it wasn't enough. It would never be enough unless he could have her for all eternity.

As if she felt it was her last chance at convincing him she wanted him to choose her for his mate, she wrapped her legs around his waist, her heels digging into his ass, pressuring him to deepen his thrusts. And he gladly did her bidding, diving deeper, craving completion, wanting to find release in the only woman he'd ever desired making his own.

She moaned, her orgasm gripping him with waves of pleasure, pulling him to the edge, and he quickly followed with a staggering climax that left him sated, but he knew it would never be enough.

Before he could roll off Tessa and pull her into his arms to enjoy the afterglow, someone pounded on the bedroom door as the wind roared over the house. Ignoring whoever it was, he shook his head and drew Tessa on top of him, wanting to snuggle and sleep, to recharge their batteries before they faced much more trouble.

"Hunter, I got through on the phone to the sheriff's office. Wind's are gusting up to one hundred miles per hour. Tessa's roof sounds like it's about to go. The sheriff's department wants everyone evacuated from the coastal areas," Rourke warned.

Tessa kissed Hunter's cheek, her hand caressing his chest. "Maybe it's time to go to Portland."

Hunter agreed. "Pack two vehicles, Ashton's pickup since it made it before, and Meara's SUV. We'll be out in a minute, Rourke."

He yanked the covers aside and grabbed Tessa's clothes and handed them to her, taking a long look at her tantalizing body, her breasts heavy, her nipples taut, a slight sheen of perspiration making her skin shimmer, and slightly red from all the hot friction they'd created. She gave him the same kind of salacious look, grinned at him when he caught her eye, and dressed.

When they entered the living room, something crashed outside and Tessa jumped. Ashton and Rourke ran to the front window and peered out.

"Ah, hell," Ashton said. "There goes my new truck."

Hunter shook his head, not happy about having to take Rourke's truck instead.

"We'd better hurry before another tree comes down." Rourke jerked on his parka. "Do we take my truck now?"

"Yeah. Ashton can drive if he's more used to the conditions." At least Hunter hoped so.

Rourke scowled as if Hunter had unmanned him. "No one can get 'used' to these conditions."

Tessa handed him an armful of blankets for the trip, and Rourke carried them out to his truck.

"Cara, you and Rourke ride with Ashton. He'll lead the way." Hunter turned to Meara. "You and Tessa will ride with me."

"Why two vehicles?" Cara asked. "Wouldn't it be better if we all stayed together in the SUV?"

"If one of us has trouble, the other can pick up the stranded passengers. Let's go." The way things had been going since they had arrived here, he had hopes for the best, but planned for the worst.

Shingles on the ridge of the roof flew off, and Tessa rushed to lock the front door. Then she and the others climbed into their respective vehicles.

Once they were on the road, Hunter hoped Rourke's truck would hug the road better with Ashton driving it.

"What are you going to do about our pack?" Meara stretched out on the middle seat, covered in blankets with a pillow underneath her head.

"Force them to leave the city. Either they'll return with us or they'll have to go elsewhere. Staying in Portland is not an alternative."

But only three miles from Tessa's house, Ashton slammed on the brakes, the tires screeching, the taillights coloring the snow cherry. The vehicle slid perpendicular to the road.

"Oh, oh," Tessa gasped.

His skin prickling, Hunter pumped the brakes and tried to avoid colliding with Rourke's truck. Tessa gripped her seat. The SUV slid to a halt. Rourke's pickup tore off the road, plowing into saplings down the steep incline.

"They'll be all right," Hunter said, his voice gruffer than he intended. At least he prayed they were all right. He cut the engine. "Stay here."

Tessa pulled on her parka. "You might need my help."

Not only did he not want her to see what had happened in case anyone had died, he didn't want her injured. Hunter grabbed her hand and shook his head, his look meant to make her obey. "Stay, Tessa. They'll be all right. We heal quickly, remember? If you become injured, we might not be able to get you any medical attention for some time. So stay." All he needed was for her to get hurt. No way was he going to permit it.

She pursed her lips, and then gave him a tight nod. He wanted to reassure her further, but time was of the essence and despite her noticeable reluctance, he was glad she'd listened to him.

Meara poked her head out from under the covers in the backseat. "What now?"

"Rourke's truck went off the road." The fact no one hollered up the hill to let them know everyone was all right furthered his disquiet.

"Oh, I'm coming with you." Meara jerked on her jacket, hat, and gloves. He could use his sister's help no doubt, although he hated to leave Tessa behind by herself.

She folded her arms and looked cross, her eyes narrowed, her brows pinched, a real hellion.

Hunter patted her leg, trying to reassure her. In a heartbeat, he would have taken her with him, except for the potential danger, and he really didn't want her to see the wreck if any of them hadn't survived. "We'll be right back."

He opened the driver's door and the frigid winds blasted him.

"Rockslide? What next. I told you we should have gone to the city to live or at least stayed in California where it's not so wet and cold," Meara grouched, then slammed the door behind her.

This was their home, for better or for worse. Hell, the forest fires were worse. Hunter closed his door, gave one last long look at Tessa, still feeling she was safer locked in the vehicle, and then at a rush, he and Meara headed across the road and down the hill.

Tessa rubbed her hands together. Now that the SUV's heater was off, the chilled wind quickly cooled the interior of the vehicle. She watched where Hunter and Meara vanished. *This is ridiculous.* She wasn't a fragile piece of glass that could break with the slightest motion. With her brother, she had hiked and climbed every trail into the wilderness and… well, this was just nonsense.

She buttoned her parka. Why should she stay in the car while everyone else was helping out?

She yanked on her ski cap.

Just because they could heal fast, Hunter thought she could never do anything, just to avoid being injured?

She jerked on one glove, then the other. As soon as she pushed the door open, she saw lights approaching from behind, glowing softly in the curtain of blowing snow. What if the driver didn't realize the danger ahead? Tessa dove back into the SUV and looked for the hazard lights button. *Where the hell is it? There!* She switched it on.

Glancing over the seat, she watched as the light blue pickup parked about twenty feet behind Hunter's vehicle. She shivered from the cold.

The truck's engine remained running. She waited, looking back in the direction Hunter and Meara had gone. Rubbing her gloved hands, she warmed her chilled fingers. *Come on, come on, Hunter.*

She sat on her hands and looked out the back window. The occupants of the truck didn't make a move. Did they think she was going somewhere, and they were waiting for her to do so? She climbed out of the SUV and shut the door. Stomping her boots to warm her feet, she shoved her hands in her pockets and stared at the tinted windows of the truck. *Come on. Get out of your vehicle and either ask to assist, or turn around and leave.*

The truck inched forward and slipped on the ice and snow. She waved her arms, trying to tell them to go back the way they came. All Hunter would need was to have this truck plow into his vehicle. Then where would they be?

The truck stopped again. Tessa glanced back at the trees Rourke's truck had plowed down. *Hell.* She had to help them. Hunter and Meara were taking too long. She turned around to look at the pickup. *Fine*. She would go to *them*.

She stalked toward them and slipped, nearly falling. Heat suffused every pore. She slowed her step to keep her footing, but halfway to the pickup, her spine tingled with apprehension. No matter that the air was frigid, her hands felt sweaty and her skin perspired.

Fearing the motorist was silly. After all that had happened to her concerning the stalker, she was becoming paranoid. But no matter how much she rationalized her fear, she still couldn't move. The driver could get out and ask her what the matter was. That's what froze her in place. If it was a woman, surely she wouldn't fear another woman. Which made Tessa worry the driver was someone more sinister.

The truck continued to idle, its exhaust leaving a wake of frosty smoke in its path. *Fine.*

"A rock slide's blocked the road," she hollered, motioning to the road ahead.

The driver didn't respond.

She whipped around, figuring she had done as much as she could to warn the idiot. Now it was high time she helped Hunter. She slipped on the ice-covered snow and nearly fell, her arms flailing to keep her balance. One of the pickup's doors opened. Another shiver stole up her spine. She didn't look back. Unable to shake free of the fear that gripped her, she walked as quickly as she could in the direction where Rourke's vehicle had disappeared, her heart racing faster than she could move.

Then running footfalls behind her, crunching on the crusted snow, warned her of the danger. Her heart in her throat, she tried to run, slipped, and landed on her butt. The person behind her was nearly at her back. Hoping her fear was unfounded, she turned. The man's ski-mask-covered face loomed in front of her before his fist slugged her in the forehead. She fell backward. Cried out. Knew at once this was the stalker. Had to be. And she was in a hell of a lot of trouble.

Amber eyes peered at her from the black knit mask. His lips turned up and she screamed, just before he clamped his gloved hand over her mouth and yanked her up from the road.

The truck inched closer. There were at least two of them. She tried to knee him in the groin, but he grabbed her around the waist and hoisted her over his shoulder.

She screamed, "Hunter! Help!"

"Tessa!" was the reply from down the hill.

He was too far away. Too deep in the ravine to come to her rescue. She struggled so hard against the man, squirming to get loose, he fell on his backside. Scrambling to her feet, she managed to jerk her arm free from his iron grip. The driver's door flew open and the one behind it, too.

Ohmigod, how many were there?

She dashed away from the truck and slipped on the ice, falling on her knees. Pain shrieked through her kneecaps.

"Get her, damn it," the man on the ground growled.

She jumped to her feet and took a step, but one of the men grabbed her arm, spun her around, and hit her in the cheek. Her vision blackened. She was doomed if she didn't do something—and quick.

Using her knee, she gave a hard, short jab to the man's groin. He dropped to his knees, clutching his crotch, swearing.

The first man seized her arm and dragged her toward the truck. She dug in her heels and tried to jerk free. With as quick a move as she could manage, she slipped her right leg in front of him, and he tripped and fell.

And pulled her down with him.

"Get in the damned truck!" the one yelled, who she had hopefully maimed for life.

She noticed then, the third man was standing next to the truck still, his leg in a cast. Thank god he couldn't help them.

A wolf howled, and then another. Her hope soared, Hunter would come to her rescue. The injured man ran with his hands clutching his crotch at a fast limp toward his truck, cursing violently. The other was behind him and jumped into the driver's seat. He shut the door as three wolves raced by Tessa and slammed their bodies into the truck, snarling and clawing. She was damned glad they were on her side.

Before she could react, the driver drove forward, ready to run over anyone in his path while he tried to turn the vehicle around. A new flood of adrenaline rushed through her.

With her heart in her throat, Tessa scrambled to her feet and dove off the road into the woods. Tumbling down the steep incline, she smashed into trees until she slammed into a giant fir. Upon impact with her right side, the breath whooshed out of her. Up above on the road, the truck roared off. Beyond the pain she was in, she prayed Hunter and the others hadn't been injured.

Her heart beating furiously, Tessa lay next to the tree, her face bruised, her ski hat snagged on a branch several feet up the hill. Icy snow filled her boots and gloves and clung to her hair. She couldn't stop shaking, wishing she'd had a fur coat and wicked teeth to deal with the brothers herself.

Three wolves peered down the hill at her from the roadway. "I'm all right," she hollered, feeling foolish to be talking to wolves, yet immensely relieved to see they were unharmed.

Two tore off down the incline toward Rourke's truck that was even deeper in the ravine than she had envisioned. Trees blocked her view of the truck. The biggest wolf of the three, a beautiful gray, his face masked in white, made his way slipping and sliding to her. And she wanted so to give him a big hug and kiss.

He nuzzled her hand and then her face where she hadn't been hurt. But she couldn't get over the fact that this big furry beast was a god in the flesh when he wasn't in his wolf suit.

"I'm… I'm all right. What about the others?" As if he could say anything more in response than woof. She sighed. Although she was damned glad he scared the men off, she was having a hard time believing Hunter and the wolf were one.

She tried to pull herself up, but as soon as she put weight on her right ankle, pain shot through it. She gritted her teeth and forced herself up. "Go. Help the others. I'll be fine." As long as she hadn't broken anything. But she wasn't going to be a burden to them. Not when two of them were still unaccounted for, and she imagined they had been badly hurt.

Hunter watched her struggle as she grasped at tree branches, trying not to put any weight on her ankle. She could crawl up the hill if Hunter wasn't observing her. He began to shapeshift, his gorgeous wolf form quickly shifting into the bronzed god she knew best. One minute, a feral wolf, and the next, a dangerously seductive semi-immortal.

"Jeez, Hunter, you're going to get frostbite."

Naked, he lifted her in his arms and hurried her up the hill to the SUV, his tight embrace heated, comforting, possessive, but still, she couldn't combat being annoyed with herself for her helpless condition when the others desperately needed Hunter.

As soon as he set her on the car seat, he commanded, "Stay. And lock the doors."

She didn't want to delay him, especially while he was standing naked in the frigid weather, but she had to know. "What happened to the others?"

"Rourke's unconscious. Cara's hurt. We can't get the doors unjammed. I'll be back soon." He kissed her forehead and locked the door, then shut it. Then he stretched, and began to shift, the transformation so fast, she couldn't get over how he could be a human in one moment and a wolf in the next. The change was fluid in its sensual elegance, powerful, seductive, and for a moment, she wanted to know what it felt like—exchanging skin for fur, brace-straightened small human's teeth for killer canines, having the speed and endurance and strength of a wolf instead of human frailties.

God, he was beautiful, no matter what form he took. Strong, gentle, protective.

A flash of a thought crossed her mind. What would *she* look like as a wolf if he changed her? Small, raggedy? Red?

Hunter loped off in his wolf coat and vanished down the hill.

Great. Just great. Here the others needed her and she was totally useless. Worse. *A handicap.*

She yanked down the visor to look in the mirror and see what a mess she really was. Cheek red and swollen. Matching knot on her forehead. Runny nose, red as Rudolph's. But her ankle throbbed worst of all. Although a pounding headache and aching hip came in for second place. *Damn the stalker and his brother.*

She peered out the window. How badly were Cara and Rourke hurt?

Headlights shone in the side mirror. She jerked her head around.

Ohmigod. It couldn't be.

The adrenaline in her system spiked again.

Had they been watching, waiting for Hunter and the others to leave her alone again? Or was it another truck that looked like the stalker's, pale blue, darkly tinted windows, slowly making its approach like before.

Chapter 13

Seeing the blue pickup approach, Tessa instantly forgot all her aches and pains. Her heart beat with renewed dread as she watched the truck's progress. The driver paused again some distance from the SUV. It had to be them. She looked in the backseat for a weapon. Ashton's rifle! Relief washed over her.

Her hands shaking, she grabbed the weapon and then unlocked the SUV's passenger door. With the greatest care, she managed to climb out without putting any weight on her ankle and leaned against the SUV's icy metal. Aiming the rifle at the pickup's windshield, she hoped they would get the message and back off, turn around, and leave for good, no matter who they were without having to fire a shot. No way did she want Hunter and the others to come running to protect her when they needed to rescue Rourke and Cara.

The driver didn't back off. In fact, the truck inched forward. She fired a warning round in between the driver and front seat passenger, blasting a hole in the glass, the gunfire reverberating in the woods. The rifle butt recoiled against her shoulder blade, bruising it, like the last time she'd shot at the stalker, only in wolf form that time. The truck spun around, slid, stopped, and retreated. She let out her breath, feeling she'd had a reprieve.

"What the hell's going on?" Ashton hollered, carrying Cara across the road. Her head was bleeding, and she looked dazed, her eyes focusing on nothing.

"Oh, Cara." Tessa nearly dropped the rifle when she got the door for Ashton and stepped with her full weight on her injured ankle. Pain shot all the way up through her thigh, and she gritted her teeth, stifling a pathetic whimper.

"I've got my hands full," Ashton grouched. "I can't be carrying both of you at the same time."

"Oh, shut up, Ashton," Cara mumbled. "Give the poor woman a break."

Despite his scowl and the hint of sarcasm in his voice, he sounded upset to see Cara hurt. "You're bleeding to death, and you think I'm not shook up about it?"

Cara cast him a sardonic smirk. "It's one way to get rid of your mate in case you're already dissatisfied."

"You'll live." Ashton helped her into the SUV. "At least Hunter warned me you would."

Cara puckered her lips and blew him a kiss. "Hmm, the honeymoon's already over."

But Tessa didn't think so. Rather, the way he acted so tenderly toward her, despite his disdain, he seemed to suit Cara perfectly. A match made in werewolf heaven.

Tessa hurried to sit with Cara and slipped her hat over the head wound, wishing she had a scarf instead. She applied pressure and hoped Cara would be all right.

"Go help Hunter. Tessa's taking good care of me," Cara ordered Ashton.

He grunted, considered her for a moment longer and then checked to make sure the truck hadn't returned. "Stay in the vehicle this time," he said to Tessa, then closed the door, and took off across the road, disappearing down the hill.

As if she planned on going anywhere now. “Are you really going to be all right?” As big a gash as Cara had, Tessa figured she might need a blood transfusion and stitches.

“Yes. Don’t look so worried. On second thought, continue to look worried. It’s nice having a friend who’s anxious over my welfare. It’s not really part of our lifestyle. We get hurt. We get better. Life goes on. Everyone knows that in a pack. No worry.”

“What about Rourke?”

“He’ll be fine.”

But the way Cara avoided looking at Tessa, she was pretty sure Cara didn’t know the truth.

“Did you kill any of them? The men in the truck?” Cara asked, her voice hopeful.

“I was afraid it wasn’t them. What if it was some other motorist with a pickup that looked like theirs?”

“It was them. The truck had the same engine rumble. Hunter couldn’t leave Rourke’s truck, as he was wedged in between the half-jammed door, trying to get it opened wide enough to get me out. Ashton was in the same predicament, and Hunter didn’t want Meara leaving, figuring you were safe inside the locked SUV. But when you fired the rifle, he swore you’d never mind him if you joined the pack. Meara said you nearly unmanned the one guy, and if she’d gotten a hold of him, she would have done the rest. You got her vote. Guess you’re an alpha after all.”

“Sure.” Like Tessa really believed that now, laid up with an injured ankle, unable to help anyone.

The sound of footfalls crunching on the frozen roadway caught their attention, and Tessa was relieved to see Hunter and the others, although seeing Rourke unconscious made her heart hitch.

"Here comes the rest of the crew. Help me into the very backseat, will you, Tessa? It's going to get a little crowded."

Tessa helped Cara into the backseat and was mad at herself for saying *ouch* when she pressed against her ankle. Cara and Rourke were the ones with the real injuries.

She smiled at Tessa. "Believe me, my head doesn't hurt a bit. I know what it's like to have torn ligaments or a broken ankle. *It hurts.* Nothing to be ashamed of. And if you hadn't dove over the cliff, that maniac might have injured you a hell of a lot worse."

Meara jerked the car door open, letting in a whirlwind of cold and snow. Hunter lay Rourke on the middle seat, his eyes shut, unresponsive.

Her heart hammering, Tessa leaned over the seat to touch Rourke's forehead. "Is he going to be all right?" He had to be. Didn't their kind have recuperative abilities? Yet, what if—

"He's got a concussion. We're returning to your place," Hunter said, his voice dark and strained.

"I'll sit with Rourke." Meara climbed in and lifted Rourke's head onto her lap.

Ashton got into the front seat with Hunter, then slammed the door shut.

"You didn't happen to get a license plate number off that truck, did you, Tessa?" Hunter backed away from where Rourke's vehicle had left the road and turned around.

"Before or after the one guy slugged me?" she asked. Hell, she was lucky to see that the truck was pale blue and had tinted windows in this snow. And now a bullet hole with a spider web of cracks trailing out from it in the center of the windshield. If they didn't replace it, she would recognize it anywhere.

Hunter chuckled darkly. "Yes or no would have sufficed."

"What are we going to do about them?"

"End their pathetic existence."

Rourke moaned.

"Can you hear me, Rourke?" Meara asked.

Tessa leaned over the seat again to get a look at him, keeping her hand still planted on the hat over Cara's wound to stem the bleeding. He focused his eyes on Meara and gave her a devilish smile.

Meara leaned away from him and folded her arms. "He's going to live."

Hunter looked in the rearview mirror and caught Tessa's eye. He hadn't thought Rourke would be all right. But now his shoulders relaxed, and he concentrated on the road again.

She took a deep breath of relief.

"Did you at least shoot one of them?" he asked.

"I shot the windshield. I wasn't sure the truck was theirs."

"It was them."

Rourke said, "I... got... a... call... just... before—"

"Shh, let Ashton tell the story," Meara said.

Ashton cleared his throat. "The Department of Transportation sent out the word that the coastal highway was closed because of downed electric lines, flooding, slides, and fallen trees and—"

Tessa looked up from pressing the cap on Cara's forehead to see why Ashton had quit talking.

Hunter pulled to a stop in front of a Douglas fir blocking the road. "Unless anyone thought to bring along a chainsaw, looks like this is the end of the road."

"How many miles left before we get to Tessa's place?" Meara asked.

"Two." Hunter shut off the engine. "Ashton and I can go back and grab your chainsaw, Tessa, and cut up the tree, then we'll drive home."

"No," Tessa said. Everyone waited for her to speak further on the matter. She had expected Hunter would just ignore her response. She straightened her shoulders. "We can't wait here like proverbial sitting ducks. Unless you think Cara and Rourke are too injured to move, and then we'll have to take our chances."

"Not me," Cara said.

"I'll be all right. Just someone help me up." Rourke tried to sit up with Meara's help.

"I'm thinking of you, Tessa," Hunter said.

"Well, *I'm* perfectly fine."

"We'll discuss this stubborn streak you have later. If everyone is agreeable, we'll all walk back to Tessa's place."

Both Rourke and Cara looked paler than normal, but they put on stoic faces and began the trek home. Tessa had planned to somehow walk on her own, but Hunter lifted her in his arms.

"You can't carry me all that way."

Everyone chuckled.

"If I didn't have a *lupus garou*'s strength, you'd probably be right."

"I don't think I've heard anyone question Hunter's strength before and get off that easily," Meara said, her voice amused. Rourke stumbled and she took hold of his arm and kept glancing at him as if to make sure he was okay.

Ashton had his arm around Cara's waist, and she snuggled under his arm.

"About the driver of the truck, I couldn't kill him. I was afraid he might not have been the same guy who was stalking me. And even if he was..." Tessa let her words trail off. She couldn't have murdered him in cold blood. If he had tried to run her over with the truck again, she wouldn't have hesitated then.

Hunter shook his head. "The bullets wouldn't have killed him."

"Unless they were silver?"

"So legend says. I don't know of anyone who shot a *lupus garou* with silver bullets. But it could have happened. That's often how legends get started."

They all grew quiet. The snow fell around them, the wind still blowing hard, and they slipped as they walked on the icy road. After a mile, Rourke had slowed his pace even more, and he seemed to be leaning on Meara's strength. Ashton finally lifted Cara and carried her. But before they reached the house, Tessa saw a black Hummer parked in the driveway. Her heart tripped.

"Leidolf," Hunter said, his voice couched in annoyance.

"The red *lupus garou* is back for the redhead," Meara said. "Don't you think?"

"Back for me?" Not that there were any other redheads in their little party. "Red *lupus garou*?"

"There are red and grays," Meara explained.

"Better not be the reason why he's returned," Hunter responded.

Tessa didn't see any sign of Leidolf in the Humvee, then observed him looking out the picture window.

"How'd he get in my house?" Her frigid skin turned icier.

Leidolf opened the front door and came outside. "Back door was unlocked. Road was blocked by downed wires the way I was headed. Looks like you ran into some trouble, too."

Tessa felt sick to her stomach. At least she was pretty sure she had locked the back door. Unless someone had gone out that way and hadn't relocked the door.

"Rockslide our way. Then on the return home, a tree had fallen across the road," Hunter said.

Leidolf dropped his gaze to Tessa as if he had only now noticed her in Hunter's arms. "Is she injured badly?"

"No, she is *not* injured badly." Tessa frowned at him. He didn't have to act like she was a child or didn't exist.

He smiled and then looked at Hunter. "We need to talk about the woman."

Woman, as in her? Hunter didn't respond, just carried Tessa into the house and headed for her bedroom. The red *lupus garou* was *so* intolerably arrogant.

"I guess I'll play nurse," Meara said. "Not my favorite role, but I can muddle through." She followed Hunter into the master bedroom.

"I'm fine, Meara. Go take care of Cara," Tessa said.

"I'm sure Ashton will want to look after her," Meara said.

Hunter lay Tessa on the bed, and then pulled off her gloves. "I need Ashton to play guard, and I'll take

Leidolf with me to cut up that tree so we can return with the SUV."

"What if they come after you?" Tessa asked, not liking this one bit.

"They won't mess with two alpha *lupus garou* males, guaranteed."

"Can you trust Ashton to stay put this time?" Meara asked.

"To protect his injured mate? I think so. Besides, I don't trust Leidolf to stay here with Tessa."

Meara laughed. "You know what, dear brother? I don't either." She headed down the hall and spoke in Michael's bedroom. "Here, Ashton, let me take care of Cara. Can you talk with Rourke for a minute? Make sure he's lying down in the guest bedroom? I'll see him after I bandage Cara's head."

"Did we really leave the back door unlocked?" Tessa asked Hunter. "I know for sure I locked the front door, but we were all busy getting stuff for the trip, I just don't know about the back door."

"Either we did, or we didn't. Don't worry about it, Tessa. They won't try to get in with as many of us as there are here now." He got her a glass of water and some medicine. "I'll be right back."

She leaned against the pillow and unbuttoned her parka, trying to ignore her throbbing ankle or the fact the house was frigid.

Hunter soon returned with an ice pack from the freezer. "Good thing you had this handy." He pulled the boot off her uninjured foot, and then carefully slipped the other off as she gritted her teeth in silent suffering.

"Broken or sprained?" she asked.

"Bruised and swollen. We won't know whether it's broken or sprained without an x-ray."

He placed the ice pack on her ankle, and then helped her out of her coat. Pulling the comforter off the bed, he moved it over her so that it didn't cover her foot. "Your socks are wet and cold. Let me get some dry ones for you."

As soon as he pulled open the top drawer, she opened her mouth to tell him where he should have gone. He held up a handful of colorful silk panties and smiled. "Wrong drawer."

She cleared her throat. "Try the one below that."

He pulled out a couple of pairs of pastel fuzzy socks and closed the drawer with his hip.

"They don't match."

He chuckled and pulled off her wet socks and then slipped on the dry ones. "The way to avoid spending hours looking for matching socks is to have all the same color."

"How dull."

"Works for me. It's either that or wear nothing at all."

She smiled. Yeah, she could see Hunter like that—in nothing at all.

"How's that feel?"

"Much better." Awful, really, but maybe the medicine would kick in soon.

"You're a terrible liar. Don't ever play poker."

"I play poker very well, thank you."

"Not with me. I'd insist on strip poker and I'd have you naked in record time."

She laughed.

"I'll be back after a little while."

She saluted him.

"Wrong hand. You'd never make it in the Navy SEALs."

"They don't salute when they're undercover. Remember?" She raised a brow.

"I'll take care of her," Meara said, walking into the room. "Cara's sleeping. Rourke is lying in bed. Ashton's working on a fire. Go talk to Leidolf."

"I'll be back." Hunter kissed Tessa on the lips, hot and wanting, pressing for more, until he pulled his mouth away with reservation, and she wanted to drag him back and devour him whole.

"Don't allow her to move from the bed, Meara."

"The one guy had a walking cast on," Tessa said, as Hunter was about to leave the room.

"Yeah, I saw. He had a broken leg."

"I thought you healed up quickly."

"Instead of six to eight weeks, it would be more like a week. Rest. I'll return soon." He winked and left.

Meara pulled a chair up to the bed and sat down. Tessa opened her mouth to speak, but Meara raised her finger to her own lips and raised her brows.

In the living room, Hunter said, "Come on, Leidolf. Let's get a workout on that downed tree. Watch the others, Ashton."

"Yeah, you can count on me."

The front door slammed closed.

Meara took a breath. "I hope Hunter doesn't get into a fight with Leidolf over you."

"You can't be serious." Unable to quit shivering, Tessa pulled the covers to her chin.

"Two alpha males interested in the same woman? Hell, you saw what happens when one beta wants you. You better believe now that you have to be turned;

Leidolf's interested, and there will be trouble between him and my brother. Not only that, but this business with Devlyn Greystoke is bound to cause problems. Hunter told me Devlyn lost all his family in a fire. Any family connection, no matter how slight, would most likely interest him. Which leads to the real problem."

Tessa tensed, not liking the warning in Meara's voice.

"Because of the shortage of females in a given pack, a leader who can entice a female to join his pack—particularly if it's his relation—can offer her to another member, strengthening his bonds with his pack."

Finally finding her voice, Tessa said, "That sounds like some medieval barbaric ruling. The king decides which of his wards weds and whom. Why didn't Hunter already tell me this?"

Meara shrugged, but Tessa could tell she wasn't saying all there was about the subject. "All right, so what about Leidolf? He doesn't know anything about me."

"Right. But for *lupus garou*, pheromones have a lot to do with the selection process. We're attracted to someone's looks, but also to the sexual scent each of us gives off. It's subtle, not noticeable to the human population. Since the *lupus garou* males outnumber the females, males are always on the lookout for a female. But what entices one male might not another. It's like having a craving for chocolate and entering a shop full of spicy pickles. Kills the desire. Walk into the store next door where a pot of hot chocolate is brewing, the male is in love."

"Pickles and hot chocolate?"

Meara chuckled. "Okay, maybe peppermint and hot chocolate?"

Ashton poked his head in. "Interesting discussion. Fire's going good. Did you want to move in there? This room is awfully cold."

"Sparks will fly if she's moved in there by the fire and Leidolf gets close to her when he and Hunter return," Meara warned.

Ashton gave her a devious smile. "No television, radio, nothing else better for entertainment. Besides, it's freezing in here and Tessa's shivering."

"Tessa?"

"It *is* awfully chilly in here. With the ice pack on my ankle, it's making me even colder."

Although she intended to walk with Ashton's help, he lifted her from the bed. "Can you bring the comforter, Meara?" Ashton asked. "Unfortunately, all the blankets are either in my truck or your SUV."

"Oh, well, hell, I never thought of it," Meara said. "At least when the guys come back, we'll have some of the blankets. Is Cara warm enough?"

"After we get Tessa situated on the couch, I'll check on Cara."

"You can stay with her. I'll be the guard for a while."

Ashton lay Tessa on the couch. "Hunter will be pissed if I'm not guarding."

"I'll take care of him." Meara waved her hand and then covered Tessa with the cover. "Go. Keep Cara warm."

When Ashton retired from the room, Tessa asked, "He really won't be mad at him, will he?"

"Probably. But, we can come up with a good story."

Right. As if Tessa could bluff her way through anything where Hunter was concerned.

With the incessant frigid wind blowing, Hunter trudged through the snow back to the SUV with Leidolf at his side, carrying the axe while Hunter held the chainsaw Ashton had rescued from the demolished shed.

"You haven't turned the woman. Yet, I imagine as cozy as you are with her, she knows what we are by now," Leidolf finally said.

Hunter knew the red was interested in Tessa, and he couldn't help but be irked by it. Hell, he had enough problems already. "It's my business to take care of. Where are my people, exactly?"

Leidolf ignored his question. "She's a petite redhead. If she's turned, she'll be more like a red wolf than a gray."

"She'll be a gray. But what's your point?" Hunter was trying to keep his temper, but he knew exactly where this line of reasoning was going.

"Two bachelors in my pack are seeking mates."

Well, *not exactly* what he expected Leidolf to say. "And you're not?"

"I'm a royal. I already told you that. The woman wouldn't interest me."

Hunter knew better, just the way Leidolf observed Tessa when he thought Hunter wasn't looking, the way he pretended disinterest when he looked at her and knew Hunter was watching.

Leidolf swung the ax as if fighting an unseen enemy. "But since you're not interested in changing her and two of my men are, it seems we could come to some kind of agreement."

"When the weather breaks, I'll go to Portland, strictly to take my rowdy pack members off your hands, and speak with Tessa's brother in prison at Salem on the way up there. Tessa will stay with me for her own protection."

"So you haven't eliminated the stalker yet."

"You noticed Tessa's injuries? The stalker did that. Or one of his brothers."

Leidolf's expression turned stormy. "And they still live?"

"For now. As soon as the storm quits pounding the coast, we'll be up to your place. You might have noticed Tessa lost her shed, part of the shingles on her roof, a couple of trees came down on her property, one on Ashton's truck, and she has no electricity."

"No electricity in parts of Portland either. Our winds haven't reached the levels yours have, but we've suffered a lot of devastation from this system."

"So where are my people?"

"I've isolated them in one of my barns."

Hunter stiffened his spine and glared at Leidolf.

He cast him a smirk. "Teach them to run out on their pack leader. Give them worse conditions than they're used to and they'll beg to return. Although I'll admit, two escaped to Washington State."

"Have you ever had problems with your pack of this sort—that you would admit to?"

Leidolf grinned. "No, I've never had your kind of trouble. But then again, I'd been a loner for a number of years before I came here. Some in my pack believe I have special powers."

Hunter bit back a laugh and with the most serious face he could muster, asked, "Do you?"

"Some say I do."

"Doesn't seem like it to me." Hunter hoisted the chainsaw over the other shoulder.

"Maybe it's because we're both alphas and the magic only works on betas."

"Or maybe because we're both royals."

Leidolf stared at Hunter for a minute. "*You're* a royal, but would take a human mate?"

"I wouldn't have, had the circumstances been different. But not because I'm a royal."

"Ahh, so keeping the lines pure doesn't mean anything to you."

Hunter shook his head. "No, changing a human is the only thing that makes the difference, only now it seems I have no choice."

"We always have choices. You can give her to me."

Hunter laughed. "You, or the two males who want a mate?"

"To me, my pack, for one of the males who wants her. Don't you think three newly turned *lupus garous* in one pack will be a little much to handle?" Leidolf asked, avoiding the issue.

"You live in the city. How could you manage?"

"I'd keep her at my ranch in the country."

"Why don't you take Rourke or Ashton off my hands?"

Leidolf laughed. "I need females, not more males." He shook his head. Then he tilted his chin up with a gleam in his green eyes. "I contacted Devlyn Greystoke in Colorado to let him know about his distant cousin, as a courtesy."

Courtesy, my ass.

"As soon as the weather clears, he's flying out here. He wanted me to give you a message since I didn't have your phone number. *Don't* touch her."

Hunter attempted to shrug off the annoyance that another leader was dictating to him, even if he was distantly related to her. “And you still want Tessa?”

“Let’s just say whatever happens before he arrives, happens. I wouldn’t have a problem dealing with him. Not after he slipped Bella out from under my nose when she was living secretly in *my* territory and she’s a *red*.”

So *that* was why Leidolf told Devlyn about Tessa? Not out of some admiration for the gray who’d fought the murdering red alpha leader, or because he felt it was his duty. *Hell no.* Leidolf wanted to get back at Devlyn for stealing Bella, in the event Hunter took Tessa for his own.

Leidolf stopped dead and stared at the tree blocking the roadway around the bend. “You didn’t tell me it was *that* big.”

Chapter 14

"Ouch," Tessa said as a stab of pain shot through her ankle while Meara helped her settle on the couch in front of the fire.

"If Hunter changes you, it won't take as long for you to heal." Meara sat down on the chair opposite her.

"I thought you didn't care for me much." Although if Cara had spoken the truth, Meara admired Tessa somewhat and had given her stamp of approval behind her back.

"I really have no choice, do I?" Meara offered her a wicked smile.

Tessa couldn't tell if she was teasing or being truthful. Maybe a little of both.

"Hunter will be changing you. Then you'll be our pack leader's mate. So..." Meara shrugged. "I'll have to live with it, or give you a hard time. And believe me, I'm very capable of it. Just ask Hunter. Are you alpha enough to take it?"

"I'll have to be, won't I?"

"So you're going to be one of us?"

"I don't see that I have much choice." Yet if Tessa could have had a semi-normal life with Hunter, she would have jumped at the chance. Marriage meant getting along with the relatives though, but mixing it up with the personalities of a werewolf pack?

The doorbell rang and Tessa glanced back at the door. *Please be Hunter and Leidolf.*

"I'll see who it is," Meara said.

Tessa's heart sped up. "Wait, let me come with you." She tried to stand.

"No, you can't walk on that foot."

"You stay put, Tessa," Ashton said, hurrying into the living room, zipping up his jeans, his chest bare.

Meara crossed the floor and peeked out the security hole. "Oh, hell."

"Who is it?" Ashton asked.

"Uhm, three guys I know. If Hunter catches them here, they'll be dead meat." Meara opened the door. "Go home before my brother finds you here."

"Come on, Meara. We're planning on heading up to Idaho for a change of scenery. Come with us."

"Leave," Ashton said, joining Meara at the door, his voice as threatening as Tessa had ever heard it. "Now."

He might be a pushover when it came to Cara, which made her wonder if Bethany had had the same effect on him. But when it came to most men, except for Hunter, he could get pretty physical.

Tessa couldn't see the other guys, but she was dying to get a look.

"Are you going to make us? One lone male?"

"Two," Rourke said, looking pale still as he made his way to the front door, a little unsteady on his feet. "Oh hell, they're three of the ones Hunter and I smelled down by the beach. Why don't you leave before the two alpha pack leaders return and rip you guys to shreds?"

One laughed. "Like there'd be two alpha leaders chumming together."

Her head bandaged, Cara walked into the room and grabbed the rifle. "Here, Ashton. Want to go hunting?"

"Hmm, maybe *you'd* like to go with us," another male said.

"I've got a mate. He's the one now holding the loaded rifle," Cara said. "So maybe you ought to run along like everyone says."

"Do they know anything about the gray Ashton saw? My stalker?" Tessa asked from the couch.

"A stalker, you say, little lady?" one of the men said. "We might know something about it. Got some beers?"

"Oh, no. You guys just get out of here," Meara warned. "If my brother catches you after you encouraged me to leave our cabin, no telling what he'll do to you."

"If any of them know about my stalker, I want to talk to them," Tessa said, trying to make it off the couch. "So let them in."

"No, we can't." Meara shook her head at Tessa. "Believe me, you don't want to see what Hunter will do if he finds them here."

Tessa sat on the arm of the couch and scowled. "Let them in now, or else."

"It is her house," Cara conceded.

"Then I'm leaving." Meara folded her arms. "I won't watch Hunter kill them."

"I'll go with them, we'll talk, and then return. All right with everyone?" Jeesh, Tessa couldn't believe she would have to leave her own house to interrogate possible witnesses.

"Then Hunter would *really* kill them," Meara said. "No way are *you* leaving with them."

"She's not one of us?" one of the men asked, trying to look around the wall of people at the door.

Tessa caught a glimpse of the man who appeared to be in his midtwenties, black beard and shoulder-length hair, dark brown eyes. Cute. No wonder he had enticed Meara to go with him.

He whistled. "I've never heard of a human in a *lupus garou* pack."

"Come in and tell me what you know about my stalker," Tessa commanded and would have dragged him into the house, if it hadn't been for her blamed ankle.

No one moved. Meara and the rest still blocked the three guys from entering. Ashton still held his rifle ready.

"Fine." Tessa hobbled to the front door. "Let me out and I'll speak with them on the front porch."

Rourke grabbed her arm so she could lean against him. "You don't even have your coat on."

"Well, someone get it for me."

"Oh hell, let them in." Meara raised her hands in resignation. "If they're too stupid to recognize the danger…" She shrugged and returned to the living room and collapsed on the recliner.

"Are you sure?" Ashton asked, still keeping the men at bay on the front porch.

"Let them in," Tessa said. "It's my house and my business. Besides, if Hunter learns you sent them away and they had information about the guy who's trying to turn me, he'd be even more furious."

The black-haired guy nodded. "I told my friends I thought that was what this was all about. Either that, or a pretty *lupus garou* female lived here on her own. Although we smelled a human female and suspected the gray got himself hooked on one of them instead."

Rourke lifted Tessa in his arms and carried her back to the couch. "Might as well let them in, Ashton. Tessa's right. If they know something about this gray and his brothers, and we chase these guys off, Hunter's bound to be furious with us." He cast Meara a sympathetic look. "Guess we'll just have to hope he doesn't kill them afterwards."

"Maybe we can get whatever information they have out of them quickly, and they can be on their way," Cara suggested, sitting beside Tessa on the couch.

Ashton motioned with the gun. "Get inside. You're letting all the cold air in."

"Like it's our fault," the black-haired guy said. "Jessup's the name. These are my friends, Redmond, on account he's got a red *lupus garou* in the mix way back when, otherwise he's all gray. We try not to hold the other against him." He gave Redmond a sly smile. "And Butch, cuz he chopped off all his hair, although we haven't figured out why he would do that now in the dead of winter."

Looking cross, Meara cleared her throat. "Now that you've made your introductions, tell us what you know about this guy and his brothers and then get your butts out of here."

Redmond stood next to the fire, warming his backside and grinned at Tessa. "I can see why he's got the hots for you. So, are *you* the one who's getting her?" he asked Rourke.

Meara gave a haughty laugh. "He might want her, but my brother is the one who's claimed her. Quit changing the subject and tell us what you know."

"Thought we might have a beer while we're talking." Butch's pale green eyes speared Tessa.

"No." Tessa wondered why the guy seemed so familiar. The courthouse! His hair was cropped short now, not long like when she had seen him at the trial, she was pretty sure. And he stood a little taller now, not as sloop-shouldered. But the eyes… she was sure they were the same eyes that had watched her so closely. "No alcohol in the house." Tequila, but not for the likes of them. "What do you know about my stalker?"

She noticed Rourke surreptitiously taking pictures of the three men using his phone. She knew if he put his heart into it he would make an excellent investigative reporter.

"He and his brothers aren't from around here," Jessup said. "Like most unmated males, they're looking for a female. He saw you sometime and decided you were the one for him."

"Have you met them? Talked to them? Know who they are?"

Jessup tipped his head to the side. "Yoloff is the one who wants you. The one with the broken leg, he's Andreas, and Ren is the other. They're from Arizona, not looking to settle down here. Too wet. I talked to Yoloff. He didn't say what he was doing here exactly, but I knew it had to be over a woman. They plan to return to Arizona once they've finished their business here."

Or Hunter finished with them. Tessa looked over at Butch. "How come you were at my brother's trial?"

He stared her down as if he was trying to intimidate her, then finally shrugged. "Why would I be at a human's trial?"

"I don't know. Why?"

Waiting for his response, everyone watched him. Either Redmond and Jessup didn't know their friend had been at Michael's trial, or they pretended innocence.

Butch gave her a smirk. "Don't know your brother, why he'd be on trial, or where it was held either. You must have mistaken me for someone else."

"You wouldn't have been at my house at some time or another, would you have? As an electrician? Plumber?"

He didn't say anything.

Then Rourke jumped into the fray. "The three of you were at Bethany's house. Why?"

Butch smiled in an evil way, turning his attention from Rourke to Tessa. "I thought we were discussing your stalker, Miss Anderson."

"Seems you might know something about Bethany's murder, too," Tessa said, her blood stirring. "Where do you live? Why have you been in the area? Seeking mates, too?"

"Always." Redmond winked at her. "Can't blame us. When the urge hits us... Human females are one thing, but they're not quite as feral as our own kind. No offense, miss."

She wanted to say that Hunter seemed to be attracted to her even if she was human. And so was this Yoloff. But maybe Hunter didn't really want her. Sure, he had said that all along. Not permanently. She would scratch an itch, but not in the long run. She could never be as wild as their kind. It wasn't in her nature. Look at her bedroom attire even—soft, cuddly pajamas, or slinky nightgowns in summer, but he was probably used to his women naked. Not that she was inhibited about sleeping nude, but it just seemed… weird. Especially since she was alone. Well, even with a guy unless they were making love.

Everyone was waiting for her response. She was sure her cheeks were rosy red as hot as they felt.

"Okay, so what about my other questions? Where do you live? Around here? I've never seen you in town before."

"Farther west," Jessup said.

"So what brought you here?"

"Looking for mates. Redmond already said so. But we couldn't find any. Not until we caught Meara's scent. We were curious about you, too, because Yoloff wanted you. So we've been hanging around, trying to catch sight of you."

But Tessa knew it wasn't true because Butch had been at the trial. "Did you see Hunter fighting the other gray?"

"No, but if we had, we would have come to his aid."

She didn't think Jessup or his friends would have helped Hunter. Why would they? When he was sure to keep them away from his sister.

Unless that's why Jessup and his buddies were hanging around here. To get rid of Hunter and it had nothing to do with Tessa. Sure, and then one of them could claim Meara. Or try to, if she was all alone.

Although he would probably have a fight on his hands. But if Hunter had died and she was so distraught over losing him, Jessup or one of the others would come to comfort her. He might have gotten his way with her then.

Jessup cast a glance at his buddies, looking a little uncomfortable when Tessa didn't respond to his remark about coming to Hunter's aid when he fought the gray.

"What about Bethany?"

"We were curious about what had happened to her. Sometimes the police can't pick up clues that we can," Jessup said.

Rourke stood taller. "Why would you care?"

Jessup raised a black bushy brow. "We wondered if they had the right murderer."

"Why?" Rourke asked again. "If you're not from this area, and the killer wasn't part of your pack, what difference would it make to you?"

He shrugged. "Just curious. Like I said."

Before Tessa could ask them another question, everyone but her turned their attention to the front of the house. She didn't hear anything, but she assumed they must have.

The door slammed open and Hunter stood in the entryway, his face dark as he considered the three new men standing in Tessa's living room. Leidolf stalked in beside him and his expression was just as lethal.

Jessup, Redmond, and Butch's posture changed from arrogantly sure of themselves to ready to run out the back door as they moved closer together and took a step backward.

"Meara?" Hunter roared, although he kept his eyes on the three men.

"Uhm, I told them they'd better hightail it out of here, but your future mate insisted they come in for a chat, since they know something of Tessa's stalker," Meara said, her voice a little shaky.

Tessa imagined not much shook her up.

Hunter's expression changed subtly as he looked at Tessa, not as angry, but she couldn't grasp what he was feeling. He jerked his attention back to the three grays. "Start talking."

His voice vibrated with raw anger and a shiver even streaked up Tessa's spine.

"We already told her who the stalker is. Yoloff."

"So which one of you killed Bethany?" Hunter asked, his voice still threatening.

"You got it wrong, mister," Jessup quickly said. "Sure, we went to her house and checked the place out. We were looking for valuables. She wasn't there any longer to care."

"Thieves? You three are thieves?" Tessa asked, her voice rife with disbelief.

"We had nothing to do with her death," Redmond said. "We were curious about who might have killed her though. So we looked around for any evidence the police might have missed. But we'd never met the lady."

Tessa pointed to Butch. "Why was he at my brother's trial then?"

Hunter focused on Butch, and he shrank under the harsh scrutiny. "The lady is mistaken," he quickly said. "I told her so already. I wasn't there. Don't know anything about it."

"Police car just drove up in the driveway," Leidolf warned.

Someone yelled from the driveway. "Hello!"

"Deputy William O'Neal," Ashton and Rourke said at the same time.

"I'll take care of him," Rourke said.

Before he made it to the door, the deputy poked his head inside. "Is everyone all right? Sheriff got a call that Rourke's truck careened down a hill. We didn't find anyone so assumed everyone made it out all right, but I had to make sure."

"We're a little battered," Rourke said, "but otherwise okay."

"Good, glad to hear everyone's all right. I'll let the sheriff know. Road's still blocked the way you were going, but north of here has been cleared."

"Thanks, Deputy." Jessup inched toward the front door, keeping his distance from Hunter. "We'll be running along then."

"You were going to stay awhile and explain some other matters to us," Hunter said, with a warning look.

"Later. Got to run." Jessup gave Meara a long look and then rushed out of the house.

Redmond and Butch followed him, although Butch glanced back at Tessa. She was sure he had been at the trial. But why?

Hunter took a step toward him, and he dodged outside.

"We've got road crews clearing the rock slide and the rest of that tree, but it'll probably be another day or so before it's cleaned up. Is your electricity still out?" the deputy asked.

"Yes, it is," Tessa said.

"We're going to Portland," Hunter announced. "At least some of us are. The rest are going to my cabins up north of here. They've got generators at least."

"Oh and by the way, Bethany Wade's parents confirmed they had asked you to check her house for any evidence that would lead to finding the right murderer. They never believed Michael had done it. So you're welcome to go there anytime," the deputy said.

Tessa closed her gaping mouth. Hunter and Rourke smiled.

The deputy looked at Ashton. "Your dad wants you to report in, let him know what's going on. See you all later." He returned to his vehicle and backed out of the drive.

Meara took a deep breath. "Who's going where?"

"Can you handle Ashton and Rourke?" Hunter asked.

"No moon for a few days," Meara said. "They should be fine."

"I promise I'll protect the women," Ashton said.

Rourke seconded his promise.

"Okay, then. I want the four of you to go to our place. Meara, we have a couple of rifles there, plenty of food, and the generator will keep you warm. Tessa and I are going with Leidolf. We'll drop by the prison to speak with Michael and then head to Portland."

"You trust me to not run off?" Meara gave her brother a wicked smile.

"Yeah, since you know what a problem this is if I can't rely on you."

"You can count on me. *So,* when are you going to change her?" Meara asked.

"When the time's right. I can't now until the moon reappears, for one."

Meara gave Hunter a get-real look.

Tessa wondered what that meant, although she again assumed Hunter wasn't interested in being saddled with her. Why didn't he just "give" her to Leidolf or Devlyn then? Not that she wanted to be handed off to another *lupus garou* pack either, and she wasn't sure she could handle becoming a werewolf in any event. She hadn't any family anywhere else that she could run to. Still, if she could get Hunter to help free her brother, she might be able to disappear and…

But she couldn't leave her brother. What a mess she was in.

Hunter carried Tessa out to the Humvee. When he had her settled on the seat, he propped her foot up to ease the swelling and covered her with a blanket. Watching him change from hostile when it came to dealing with Jessup and his friends to tenderness when handling her, she wished he could've been a regular guy. But then again, the fact he wasn't was probably why she loved him so much. *Love?*

"Let's go," Hunter said.

He and Meara moved some of the gear to Leidolf's vehicle and after Hunter locked Tessa's place, they all loaded into the two vehicles.

Hunter motioned to Ashton to take off. Meara waved as they headed out.

"Are you sure dividing our forces is such a good idea?" Tessa asked, as Leidolf drove out of her driveway.

Leidolf chuckled darkly. "A *lupus garou* would know *never* to question the alpha leader's decisions."

Talk about male chauvinists. Tessa folded her arms.

Hunter smiled at her over the seat. "She'll learn."

"You and your kind may live in the Dark Ages, Hunter, but I'm not going there."

"Are you *sure* you don't want me to take her off your hands?" Leidolf asked.

During most of the drive, Hunter had seemed to be brooding about something, but Tessa didn't want to ask what the matter was in front of Leidolf. When they arrived in Salem, the sun had already set and visiting hours at the prison were over. If it hadn't been for all the ice and snow, they might have made it in time. Tessa brushed away useless tears, hoping to hide her distress. Both Leidolf and Hunter caught her action though.

Leidolf drove them to a nearby hotel. "Two beds, one room for safety sake?" he asked.

"Two adjoining rooms will suffice," Hunter said. "But drop by the hospital first, will you?"

Leidolf cast a questioning glance Hunter's way.

"To get Tessa's ankle x-rayed."

Leidolf found the hospital and when he parked, Hunter skipped getting a wheelchair for her and carried her in. Once a technician had taken her in for an x-ray, Leidolf took a seat in the empty waiting room while Hunter stood nearby.

"So what was *that* all about?" Leidolf asked.

Hunter looked over at him. "What?"

"Not wanting to turn Tessa until the next moon appears. You're a royal. You can shapeshift anytime it suits you, moon or no."

"I want her to be ready for it."

Leidolf shook his head. "She'll never ask you to change her. The idea of confronting Devlyn bother you? If I were you, I'd have doubts."

"I'm not turning her over to you and your pack, Leidolf, so quit suggesting it."

Leidolf smiled and sat back in his chair. "She's too petite to be a gray. She couldn't handle your pack when you're away, could she?"

Hunter looked back at the hall where Tessa had disappeared.

"Three newly turned *lupus garous* all in one pack make for an awful lot of trouble. What are you going to do about her brother? Ashton's father, the sheriff? What about Rourke? Has he got any family?"

Hunter tried to ignore him, but the truth of the matter was he had no idea how he was going to handle any of it.

"Ashton might not be very close to his father, which will help some, although his father seems to keep tabs on him. But, Tessa, you can tell she's really close to her brother."

Hunter would deal with it, damn it. All of it, somehow.

The sound of a wheelchair rolling along the floor down the hall drew closer and Hunter's spine stiffened.

A nurse pushed Tessa into the waiting area, but all that Hunter focused on was Tessa's smiling face as she held onto a pair of crutches, her enticing lips beaming, her green eyes sparkling, the dimples in her cheeks endearing. His frown evaporated and he let out his breath as he hurried to join her.

"The ankle's not broken," she said. "Just a bad sprain."

"Good show. I'll take her," he said to the nurse and wheeled Tessa out of the hospital.

"Want to get something to eat?" Leidolf asked, walking them to the Humvee.

"It's late and it's hard for Tessa to get around. We'll get room service."

Leidolf opened the back door for Tessa. "Sounds good to me."

When they returned to the hotel and got the rooms, Leidolf dropped off their bags and leaned Tessa's crutches next to the bed while Hunter deposited her on the mattress.

Leidolf bowed his head slightly. "See you both in the morning."

Tessa frowned. "You don't want to have room service with us?"

"No," Hunter said, and then gave Tessa a half smile as soon as he realized how harsh he sounded. "Leidolf drove all that way. I offered to relieve him while you were sleeping, but he won't let anyone drive his Humvee. So he needs his rest."

"I'd take you up on sharing a… meal with you, Tessa, but I believe Hunter is feeling a bit possessive." Leidolf shrugged. "It happens to the best of us from time to time. If you have any trouble in the middle of the night, don't hesitate to holler for my help. Just keep the adjoining doors to our room unlocked, and I'll come running. Good night." He slipped into the hall and closed their door.

"You should have let him eat with us," Tessa chastised.

The lock to the adjoining door clicked open.

Wanting to be alone with Tessa and not about to change his mind, Hunter removed Tessa's parka and didn't comment.

"Aren't you going to unlock our door for Leidolf?" she asked, her voice annoyed.

"Later." Hunter lifted the phone off the hook and called room service. "Two steaks, one rare, one medium, baked potatoes, everything on them, blue cheese dressing on the salad, water. Thanks." He hung up the phone. For a moment, he stared at her.

She folded her arms. "What?"

"Pajamas?"

"Of course."

He turned the heat on in the room and then he came over to the bed and began unbuttoning her sweater. "I like summer best."

"Why's that?"

"Fewer clothes to remove." He grinned at her.

Her cheeks heated. She could just imagine he would be half-naked—no totally naked—all summer long. "As if it matters to you."

"What's *that* supposed to mean?"

She smiled. "I can imagine you don't wear much at all in the summer."

"You'd imagine right." He kissed her forehead and then unwrapped Tessa's injured foot. "I'll get some ice in the bucket for it."

He unlocked the adjoining door, then grabbed the bucket and headed for the door to the hallway. When he opened it, Leidolf had his hand raised, ready to knock. In the other hand, he was carrying a full ice bucket.

"For Tessa." He handed it to Hunter.

Feeling annoyingly humbled, Hunter gave him the empty one. "Order your meal yet?"

"Yeah, a rare steak. It's on it's way."

"Bring it over to our room when you get it." Hunter closed and locked the door, and then turned.

Tessa smiled at him.

"What?"

"Nothing, Hunter. Well, except you're a paragon of mixed messages. I can't understand why your people left you."

"They were mad about losing their homes in the forest. They have some notion that if they live in the city, or in the case of the others, down in the California vineyards, they'll avoid this tragedy again. It's understandable to an extent. But we've always lived on forested land. I can't imagine making do anywhere else. However, I don't begrudge them their choice. Pack members can leave any time they want."

"Except for Ashton, Rourke, or me."

"That's different. You're right. You'll need plenty of supervision for the first year at least."

"I don't like to be supervised, I can tell you that right now. I've always been responsible for my brother, the one in charge, the one who's had to deal with everything."

"Then it'll be a nice break for you." Hunter set the bucket of ice on the bedside table.

"I won't give up my independence, Hunter."

Someone knocked on the door. "Room service!"

Tessa folded her arms. "It's not something I do because I've had to. I'm wired that way. And not you or anyone else is going to take that away from me."

Hunter shook his head, grumbled something about another Meara under his breath, and opened the door. As soon as he did, he hesitated to let the man enter with the food. To Tessa's surprise, Hunter tried to shove the door closed in the man's face. But the metal cart blocked him and with a hard push, the server rammed it into Hunter's stomach.

He stumbled back, cursed, and tried to regain his footing.

But what happened next, chilled Tessa to the bone. Two wolves charged into the room, while the man with the cart brandished a large carving knife and taunted Hunter with it.

"Damn it to hell. They're royals," Hunter said.

The heavier-set wolf jumped onto the bed. Tessa grabbed one of her crutches. Swinging it at the wolf, she hit him in the side of the head with a whack. He yelped and jumped off the mattress and landed with a thud on the carpeted floor.

The other leapt up next, while Hunter seized hold of the food cart and rammed it into the knife-wielding menace. Tessa swung her crutch at the white-faced wolf, the one who had bitten Ashton, but he dodged her blow. And then he dove in again.

Unable to move the crutch fast enough, she dropped it and instinctively threw her hands to block him from ripping out her throat. She grabbed hold of his neck, his teeth snarling and snapping, but she was losing her grip.

Leidolf threw open the adjoining door when the wolf bit Tessa's arm. Hunter yanked the knife out of the gray's hand and plunged it into his neck.

For an instant, everyone seemed to stop in mid-motion. The man collapsed, holding his jugular, blood spilling all over the carpeted floor. The two wolves dashed out of the room. Hunter turned to Tessa.

Tears blurred her eyes and she held her bloodied arm.

He hurried to her and gave her good arm a squeeze. "I'll get a towel. Call 911, Leidolf."

"He's dead," Leidolf said, feeling the man's pulse.

Hunter let out his breath, grabbed a towel from the bathroom, and wrapped it around Tessa's arm. "Do you feel any differently?"

"Sick to my stomach." Tears trailed down her cheeks. "My arm hurts. And I twisted my ankle some more." But what distressed her the most was the sight of the dead man in their room. Why couldn't the men have left her alone?

Sirens sounded as emergency vehicles headed down the street toward the hotel.

"Guess someone else called the crisis in," Leidolf said. He pulled some yellowed newspaper clippings out of the man's pocket. "Are you sure you don't want to give her up to me?"

Chapter 15

As soon as Hunter smelled the gray who'd been wielding the dinner cart, he knew they were in for trouble. But he never expected the three brothers were royals.

"He might not have changed Tessa," Leidolf said, as Hunter paced in the jail cell across from him. "You can't worry about things you have no control over. Besides, she'll be all right anyway since there's no moon out tonight."

"What about the brothers of the gray I killed? What if they locate her?"

"The police said they'd watch her. So quit worrying."

Quit worrying. Like that was a possibility.

"When you called your lawyer, how long did he say it would take to get us out of here?" Hunter still couldn't believe the human police arrested them. It was clearly self-defense, but some witness, probably one of the brothers, had stated otherwise.

"Soon. Don't worry. My people will be at the hospital with Tessa and they'll take good care of her."

"Including the two bachelors who want her? Admit it, Leidolf. *You* want her. What were those newspaper clippings about? Anything important?"

"Yeah. One was a news story written in 1865 about a confrontation between Caleb McKnight and Seth Greystoke, stating Seth had stolen his gold."

"Caleb McKnight?" Hunter rubbed his chin, then swore. "Hell, that was the other man in the photo with

Seth, my great-grandfather, and great uncle when they were panning for gold in California."

Leidolf leaned against the wall and peered out the bars at Hunter. "The other news article was written twelve years ago about a John Anderson who had killed Caleb McKnight in self-defense over a gold dispute. Said John's grandfather had stolen the gold from Caleb's grandfather. But of course, it would have been Caleb himself. Guess who he left behind? Three sons by the name of Yoloff, Ren, and Andreas."

Hunter shook his head. "The three brothers who have been stalking Tessa. So there was more to it than Yoloff just wanting Tessa for a mate. The possibility he'd get her land and the gold supposedly hidden somewhere on the property. How much you want to bet the other three grays are all tied into this?"

"They're a pack from La Grande. If they could get rid of you so the one could have your sister and your property, possibly have killed Bethany to have hers, and now are trying to take Tessa and consolidate her lands—they'd have amassed quite a bit of expensive property. Not to mention the gold, wherever it is, and two females to add to their all-male pack."

The sound of footsteps distracted them, and Hunter let out his breath when he saw the guard walking toward them. It was about damned time. He didn't want Tessa alone without his protection for one more minute.

The guard unlocked Leidolf's cell. "You're free to go. The other one…" The hefty man shrugged. "Your lawyer said it'll take more time."

"Leidolf," Hunter roared. "What did you tell your lawyer?"

Leidolf waved at him as he headed down the hall with the guard. "We'll take good care of her until you're sprung."

Hell, Hunter should never have trusted a red pack leader. But he didn't have a gray lawyer in the area yet either. "I want to make a phone call!" he hollered to the guard as he led Leidolf out. "Now!"

Her skin frigid with fresh apprehension, Tessa sat in the waiting room of the hospital where she had gotten her ankle x-rayed earlier. After a couple of stitches, her arm was bandaged. She was beginning to look like Hunter after he fought his battles.

Supposedly, some of Leidolf's pack were coming to get her and watch over her until Leidolf and Hunter could come for her. Damned police! Why wouldn't they listen? Hunter killed the gray in self-defense!

But what if the people coming to get her were not Leidolf's people? What if it was her stalker pretending to be one of his pack members? She had no way of telling.

She closed her eyes as the pain in her ankle and arm intensified. Had she been turned? She didn't feel any differently. Wouldn't she feel like stripping off her clothes and turning into a wolf? But then again, Meara said there was no moon so they couldn't do that. Or maybe she wouldn't feel any different until then either. But her stalker and his one brother had turned into wolves. How?

The one whose leg had been broken was all healed up, too. Although she wasn't sure who was who.

"Miss?"

She opened her eyes and looked up at the fatherly looking cop, Allan Smith, his hair salt and pepper, his cheeks round and jovial, and his eyes the prettiest crystal green she had ever seen. Thankfully, he was guarding her until someone came for her. He handed her his cell phone.

"Hunter Greymere wants to talk to you."

She grabbed the phone and tried to steady her voice before she spoke. "Hunter, where are you?"

"Jail, still. I can only make a quick phone call. Leidolf's on his way there to pick you up. His people will be there soon also. I may be here for a while, unless I can get hold of someone on my own to get me out."

"You killed the man in self-defense."

"I know, but I'm not sure what Leidolf told his lawyer. In any event, I'm going to need help getting out. Meara's number is 431-110-5629. Don't go with Leidolf. Tessa, I've got to go."

"No, wait!"

The phone died. She felt like her lifeline had just been ripped away from her. "How can I get Hunter out of jail? He's innocent," she said to the cop.

"I've got a friend I can call." He winked, then punched in the number. Holding the phone to his ear, he waited for someone to answer and said to Tessa, "I don't think the wolf turned you."

Tessa closed her gaping mouth.

He smiled. "You didn't know I'm one, and if you'd been changed, you would."

"Are… are you a gray or a red?"

"Gray. I don't know Hunter or Leidolf either, but I wouldn't let a red have a gray's selected mate." He paused. "Hey, Charlie? It's Allan Smith. Got a problem. Need to get a gray out of jail who was defending his chosen mate. Another gray was killed in the fight. The name's Hunter Greymere. No, not from around here. Alpha leader from the coast." He chuckled. "It gets worse. A red alpha leader from Portland is trying to claim her for his own. You ever hear about the gray devil wolf, Seth Greystoke? Hell, his grandson claims the little lady is his distant cousin, and *he* wants her."

The cop looked at Tessa and smiled. "No, human still," he said into the phone, then laughed. "Yeah, I'd say she'd be worth it, *but* then you'd have three alpha leaders at your throat. Better leave her well enough alone. Hurry it up though. I'll conveniently tuck Miss Tessa Anderson away somewhere safe at the hospital. Call me when you have Hunter released. Well, you owe me for getting your brother off for drunk driving—how many times? And you know me—I'm a sucker for beautiful, redheaded damsels in distress." He chuckled. "Talk later."

He clicked off the phone, lifted his nose and sniffed the air. "Shit. They're coming." He lifted Tessa up and hurried down the hall.

"Who?" Tessa whispered. "The reds or the brothers of the gray Hunter had to kill?"

Hunter wasn't often impressed with bureaucracy when he had to deal with it, but whatever Tessa had done had worked. And he was damned proud of her.

He considered the cop as he drove him to the hospital, who looked like he was suffering from ulcers or a very bad day, older man, graying temples, sandy brows, very big scowl.

"When will we get there?"

"Ten minutes." The cop glanced at him with a frown splitting his forehead in two. "What? You want me to run the sirens, too? Who the hell are you? The judge rarely changes his mind on a case. But just like that, one call and you've got half the force hopping."

"I acted in self-defense when the man came at me with a knife. But I guess it pays to have friends in high places in any event. Been a cop long?"

The man smiled as if reminiscing about the good old days. "Texas Ranger when the first unit was formed. Worked my way west into this lawless territory in the early ages. Changed my name numerous times, retired several times, had to 'die' a number of times to keep up appearances. But yeah, I've been one of the good guys for a few years. What about you?"

"In the army for a number of years, different sides, different countries, different wars, time periods, trained in some of the more specialized forces later, Navy SEALs for one."

"No shit?" The cop shook his head. "I always wanted to be one of those." His face turned stern again. "So how come you have to change the woman? Judge says she's one of us, kind of."

"Long story, major nightmare."

"Too bad. It's better when you both are willing. Happened to me, too, though."

"What happened?"

"She's still giving me grief." The cop gave Hunter a

smirk. "As soon as they allowed women on the force, she became a cop also. Said she wanted to see what I did all day. But don't you believe it. She just wants to make sure I don't turn another woman."

"How long have you been together?"

"Ninety-eight years and counting." The cop pulled into the back of the hospital. "Let me call Allan Smith. He's a buddy of mine who's taking care of the little lady." He punched in some buttons on the phone and said, "Hey, Caruthers here. You got her?" He looked at Hunter. "The guy's here with me. He's a Navy SEAL. Yeah, that's why he got the jump on the gray with the knife. I'm sending him in the back way. The reds are there?" He smiled. "I'll tell him. Gotta go. See you this weekend to go fishing?" He laughed. "Okay, when it warms up a bit."

Caruthers shut off his phone. "Take the back stairs, third floor, Room 301. Let me tell you, pal, if I had it to do all over again, I'd turn my Greta in a heartbeat. There aren't enough females in the world to go around. Sometimes we've just got to take a chance and hope for the best."

Allan Smith tucked his phone into his belt. "I'll wait in the hall for your mate. All my best to you, young lady." The cop left Tessa alone and closed the door.

Sitting in a vinyl chair, she clenched and unclenched her hand. Now what would they do? She didn't think Hunter would want to return to the hotel. Not after the killing there. She sure didn't want to go there either. She shuddered. The look of death on the gray's face would haunt her forever.

"You must be Hunter Greymere," Allan said beyond the door.

Her heart gave a jump to hear that he'd arrived, and although she was relieved he found her before anyone else did, her stomach fluttered with apprehension.

"I'd claim her nice and official-like to set things straight with the red and before some distant relation tries to take her home with him, if I were you. The other gray didn't change her, by the way."

"Thanks, officer, for the advice, and the news," Hunter said, his voice gruff.

"Navy SEAL, eh? The guy must have been crazy to mess with you. I'll be right here, so take all the time you need."

Now that he had his memories back, had Hunter remembered truly being a Navy SEAL? It definitely suited his character. Or was he continuing the tale, enjoying it too much to give it up?

"Thanks." Hunter opened the door, closed it behind him, stalked across the floor to join her, looking like a warrior with a mission, his harsh expression a mixture of sternness and worry, and she had an inkling he intended to turn her. She definitely had mixed emotions about the whole thing.

"Navy SEAL? You really were one?" she whispered, raising her hands to offer herself to him, to take the plunge, to become something she couldn't begin to imagine being. Part of her welcomed the change, the chance to be with the man who heated her blood like no other had ever done, yet part of her wanted to remain as she was, still wanting Hunter for her own, but without the life-altering change.

"Yeah. You were right all along, Tessa honey. Meeting on the beach like we did was… karma. Although if I'd been more with it, I would have acted a lot more like one of the SEALs."

Her mouth slightly gaped. "How could you have been a SEAL as a werewolf?"

"We can be anything we want, if we're so inclined and have the aptitude." He winked at her and the sexy look slid a volley of heat through her.

And then she gave him a half smile. "Wonder what your SEAL friends would have thought if they'd known how we met."

"They would've been cursing my fortune that a beautiful woman had come to rescue me and not them." He lifted her from the chair, hugged her to his chest, tighter than need be as if he'd feared losing her and wanted to prove to himself she was all his—which suited her just fine—then carried her to the bed. "We've got to talk."

Talk? She felt the tension in his muscles, saw the way his eyes darkened with need, smelled the subtle change in him, indicating he was becoming aroused. She wanted him with all her heart. So why didn't his heated embrace make her melt against him? She stiffened instead, unable to hide a nagging concern. What if he changed her, then gave her to a beta wolf? "You don't think I'm enough of an alpha."

"You're an alpha all right. After you clobbered that gray with the fireplace tongs and tonight again with your crutch?" He gave her a small smile, set her on the bed, and tucked some of her hair behind her ear with a tender touch. "A beta female would have tucked tail and run. With your sprained ankle, if you'd been a beta, you would have easily given up. I saw you trying to keep Yoloff from biting you. If I could have, I would have ended his miserable life, too."

Hunter's fingers shifted to the buttons on her blouse, his urgent struggle making her smile.

But she still had to know—was he defying Devlyn? Taking her for his own? What were his intentions? Yet even so, she didn't stop him. She couldn't. Whenever he wanted her, she had no power to hinder him, just as she had no control over her own craving to have him. "I thought we were going to talk."

"I can't deny I'm uncomfortable doing this to you, Tessa. I don't want you to regret it. But I also don't want to bite you. Wolves do bite in playfulness, but as a wolf to human?" He shook his head and pulled her blouse off her shoulders.

So he was *changing* her. But that didn't mean he was taking her for his mate. Despite wanting to know the truth first, her body instantly responded to his touching her, flames stoking her insides, a wet readiness preparing her for sex—not change. Want and need replacing common sense. His gaze focused on her face—watching for any sign of hesitation?

The change. That's what he was concerned about. "I used to play tug-of-war with my Irish Setter when I had one. She'd sometimes go for my hand by accident." She hoped her lighthearted response would ease his concern.

Hunter smiled. "Want to play tug-of-war?" He pulled her blouse off the rest of the way. "I've got to do this. We don't have a choice."

She seized his hands and looked into his eyes. In

that instant, he looked even more concerned, his mouth tightening, jaw clenched, brow furrowing.

"I'm afraid, which isn't being alpha like, is it? But I worry I'll change too much. But more than that, what are you going to do with me afterwards?"

Still looking stern, a hint of relief flitted across his expression. "You're mine."

She should be ecstatic to have that question resolved, shouldn't she? But she couldn't quit worrying about the change. Instead of addressing his claim, she said, "I thought you couldn't shapeshift unless the moon was out." Yet she recalled the look Meara had given him.

His sensual lips curved upward just a little as he started pulling off his clothes, revealing his beautiful body, rough hewn, rugged, capable of enduring great hardships, or giving her carnal pleasure. "I'm a royal and can do anything I want." He gave an arrogant smile. "Almost anything."

"So as a royal, you can shapeshift anytime?"

"That's the beauty of it."

"That's why you could be a SEAL. No worry about shifting while under water."

He chuckled. "No. And the group I was with—all royals, just for that reason."

She sighed. No scars marked his smooth as silk skin, every bit of toned muscles from his wide shoulders to his well-developed chest, flexing in anticipation. She looked lower, from his narrow waist and hips down to his full blown erection standing at attention amidst dark curls.

"I have to shift, but if you keep looking at me like you want to eat me all up..."

Her eyes riveted back to his lusty gaze.

"You might want to look away when I begin to shift."

"I've seen you shapeshift. You're gorgeous. What if I'm motley?" Again, she tried to make light of the situation, although her stomach churned with renewed apprehension.

"You'll be beautiful. But Leidolf and Devlyn will want you unless we're mated. Ready?"

She nodded. He looked like he wanted to kiss her, his gaze lowering to her mouth again and lingering there… but then he took a deep breath and began to shift into his wolf form. She couldn't get over how fast the transformation was. Would she shift just as quickly? If Ashton was any indication of a newly turned *lupus garou*, then yes, she'd change just as swiftly. Probably of a necessity, to avoid humans catching sight of them between forms.

She watched in awe, how his body changed gracefully, effortlessly, painlessly, from the muscled hunk to the healthiest specimen of a wolf she'd ever seen. Beautiful almond eyes captured hers and then before she could say a word, the wolf that was Hunter jumped on the bed and nuzzled her cheek.

She stroked his head. "Hurry and do it before I change my mind." Her skin perspired lightly and in the cold hospital room, she shivered.

His amber eyes remained fixed on hers and then he dipped his head and nipped her uninjured arm.

"Ow," she said, frowning. "Jeez, Hunter. That hurt like a hard pinch and you didn't even break the skin. But I'll have a bruise for sure there now."

If a wolf could look contrite, he did and tried again. His second bite was as lame as his first.

"Ah for heaven's sakes, Hunter. Another bruise.

Hurry and do it right or I'm calling it quits." She hoped her words would make him stop worrying about hurting her. She'd heal quickly anyway, wouldn't she?

He bit again and broke the skin this time. Her eyes watered and she bit her lip. Blood trickled from the bite on her arm, and he licked it away. And waited.

Self-doubt filled her. Maybe he didn't turn her either, just like Yoloff hadn't. What if she was some strange anomaly and couldn't be turned? Maybe her great-grandmother couldn't be either and that's why she died of the fever? A sadness filled Tessa with the notion neither her ancestor or she could forever be with the one she loved.

But if the change had taken effect, what was she supposed to feel like? Except that her swollen ankle and arm where Yoloff had bitten her were tingling with the strangest sensations, nothing else was different.

Hunter continued to watch her, not shapeshifting. She hoped to hell he wouldn't have to bite her again.

"Too bad with all of your enhanced abilities, you can't talk when you're in your wolf form, too." She glanced at the door. "Someone's coming. You'd better hide under the bed."

Hunter didn't budge, just continued to observe her.

"I mean it. I… I hear several people." Her heart pumped harder.

"Howdy, folks," Allan said at the door.

"Did he do it yet?" Leidolf asked, his voice guardedly amused.

Leidolf. Her heart took a dive.

"It remains to be seen. I'm taking care of things here. Why don't you run along?"

"Tell Hunter four of his people want to return with him. The fifth wants to stay with one of my widowed males to be his mate. When Hunter's through here, he and Tessa can meet me at the hotel. Different set of rooms. Just check at the front desk. Dinner's on me."

Tessa relaxed. Leidolf didn't want her, thank God for small miracles.

"I'll let him know."

Tessa took a deep breath, smelled the air, and looked at Hunter in his feral wolf form, her eyes widening. "You're a gray. I mean, I smell a special scent that surrounds you. A wildness, like a fresh spring day, the woods, the great outdoors."

She swore his mouth curved up just a hair, before he began to shapeshift—his body straightening, his rich fur pelt vanishing, leaving behind bronzed skin over hard muscles. Until he stood before her, one gloriously built male stud.

He touched her face, his amber eyes gazing into hers, his expression concerned. "How do you feel, Tessa?"

She loved him for it, for being concerned about her welfare above all else. No one but her mother had ever treated her that way.

Tessa took his hand and kissed it. "Better. My ankle feels strange. Prickling and numb, but not sore any longer. And where you bit me, the skin's already sealed up. The bruise you gave me has gone away. Where Yoloff tore the skin feels ticklish, like when injured skin is scabbing over and new skin is created to take its place."

"How do you feel in here?" Hunter said, still frowning as he reached for her forehead with a whisper-soft touch.

"*Oh.* I don't think I'll know the answer to that question until I've experienced more of the changes."

He unbuckled her belt and then unzipped her jeans. "You're not upset?"

Her eyes grew big. "You're going to make love to me in a hospital bed?"

He leaned over and kissed her lace-covered breasts, stirring her craving to make love to him.

"You bet, alpha mate of mine. We do it often, whenever and wherever we can."

"Well, hell, Hunter. Why didn't you tell me that before?"

He chuckled darkly. "You'll fit right into the pack, Tessa."

"Are you sure about this?" She motioned to the room. "Shouldn't we go somewhere more private?"

"The room's well guarded with our police friend at the door. It's up to you, but until I've mated you, you're available to any unmated male out there who's willing to fight me for you. So yeah, I'm sure about this. You can't be out of my sight until then."

"But we've already made love. Doesn't that count?" Not that she didn't want to make love to him and like now, but it made her realize she didn't know all the rules of Hunter's world yet, and she could get herself into a lot more hot water. Well, more than she was already, until she understood what was going on better.

He shook his head, then brushed a kiss against her lips, mouth-watering, mind-numbing. Everything about him made her bones and muscles melt like lava beneath his heat. She knew he'd take her for another sensual ride like she'd never known with any man before him, and she was past ready for everything he could give her.

Wanting her like no other, Hunter quickly removed her clothes, desiring to claim her like any wolf would its chosen mate, male and female alike. He wanted the first time to be slow and leisurely now that she was a *lupus garou*. Making love to her all night long would have sufficed, but not with a bunch of reds breathing down their necks. Or Yoloff and his brother still on the loose. And Devlyn would soon be a problem.

Tessa had already covered herself with the thin hospital blanket, her skin raised with chill bumps. As usual, the hospital room felt like a refrigerator.

"Next time I make love to you, we'll have a well-heated room and no huddling under the covers," he said, his brow raised.

Tessa's infectious smile heated his blood, sparking his desire.

He jerked the cover aside and climbed on top of her, then pulled the blanket over them and molded to her soft body, pressing his arousal against her mound. "Not much room, but it should suffice."

"Hmm," she said, yielding to him, wrapping her arms around his back, her embrace every bit as possessive as he felt about her. "Seems like the right amount of room to me. You just need to put that well-honed lance somewhere where it's not so dangerous."

He chuckled darkly.

Everything seemed to fade in the room, the noises in the hospital, the cold air circulating about them, the odor of antiseptics.

Take me, her expression silently pleaded. She moved her legs apart, giving herself completely.

"I know just where to sheathe it."

"Do." She licked his lips. "Mate with me so I'm all yours."

That was all Hunter wanted to hear, yet he couldn't help saying what he knew was in his heart. "You're all mine, anyway."

She cast him one of her impish smiles that said he was being full of himself as usual, which stirred his compulsion to have her even more. He pressed his lips against her sensual mouth, his hand kneading her soft breast and then ran his thumb over her nipple, the rosy crown peaking. Not enough. He could never get enough of tasting or touching her. Of breathing in her subtle arousal.

Her gaze soft and sultry, she turned her head toward the door.

He wanted to groan out loud at her distraction. "You'll learn to ignore the sounds that aren't important," he whispered, then turned her head back to his, lost himself in the exotic sparkles of blue against green in her languid eyes.

He slipped his erection into her wet folds, the heat of her body sparking flames in his. Wanting to fully mate her, possess her, claim her like he'd craved from the first moment he'd seen her checking on Uncle Basil, her determination, her concern for him, her friendliness toward his sister even when the feeling wasn't reciprocated. No matter how much he'd tried to reconcile himself with the notion that he couldn't have a human for his mate, he'd wanted her.

"Ahh," she said, pressing her pelvis against him, working him as he deepened his thrusts. Her eyes closed, her tongue licked her swollen lips, and he captured it, sucked on it, making her mew.

Claiming her felt more than right, like they had been meant for each other since the dawn of time. He'd worried he would notice a difference, that she wouldn't be feral enough, not *lupus garou* enough to satisfy some primal need. But she was perfect, her hot, supple body molding with his, her moves every bit in sync, deepening the bond, the feelings, the ecstasy. Just as driven to satisfy her sexual needs—*and his*—to consummate their relationship, to delve into the unknown and conquer it.

She was alpha all right, but not in the same way as others were. Better—*his*.

His fingers fanned through her hair, the satiny mass a tactile delight as she stroked his back with greedy fingers, her heart pounding, her body trembling with the adrenaline rush of passion and arousal and sex racing through her veins.

Her nails dug into his back, and he silenced her moans with a kiss, but he couldn't do anything about the darned creaky hospital bed. Every time he thrust, he figured all of the hospital staff would hear and know what was going on in the room. He hadn't expected that. But then again, his attuned hearing picked up what humans couldn't.

Thankfully, Tessa was so caught up in the heat of the moment, she didn't seem to notice.

"You're heaven-sent," she mouthed softly against his lips, "… a god from Mt. Olympus, my gold, my treasure."

And she was more to him, a priceless gem, the mother of his future offspring, his legacy, his unwavering and loving companion for life.

He thrust into her tightness, her body stroking him,

drawing him to the zenith of pleasure. He groaned as he found release deep inside of her hot, tight body and sank against her. Kissing her mouth, he loved the feel of her velvety lips, but seeing tears glistening in her eyes, he abruptly stopped.

"What's wrong, Tessa?" he asked, too gruffly.

Already he was mad at himself for being overly zealous, too damned rough, pushing her when he should have seen she needed more time to absorb all the changes she was sure to be experiencing. Hell, what was the matter with him? He loved her more than life itself, and this is how he showed it?

"He can't have me now, can he?" she asked.

Uncomprehending, he stared at her. "Who? Leidolf?"

She shook her head and rubbed her hand over Hunter's arm.

And he relaxed some, figuring her upset wasn't with him. "Yoloff? No, he can't have you."

But he could if the gray somehow managed to kill Hunter, although he hadn't planned on that ever happening.

He maneuvered in the narrow bed until Tessa was lying on top of him. "You're mine, Tessa. Now and for always."

"What about my brother?"

He hadn't wanted to bring up that scenario yet, hoping with the change she would understand how important it was not to let humans know of their existence. But he and most of the others were born with the knowledge that their kind's safety came first. Some of the wolf's wariness was instinctive, but dealing with the brother, that was another matter. Her blood ties were apparently as strong as the wolf's instincts. On the other hand, her brother had *lupus garou* genes also.

"Hey folks," Allan said, knocking on the door. "I hate to interrupt, but I just got word the hospital staff is moving someone in here in just a few minutes. You can stay at my place if you like."

"Thanks, Allan. We'd love that." Tessa scrambled to get off Hunter. As soon as her bare feet hit the floor, she yanked on her clothes.

Not ready to give up the relaxed and satiated feeling that cloaked him, Hunter climbed out of bed, kissed Tessa's lips, and then jerked on his own clothes.

Just as they emerged from the room, an attendant wheeled a gurney toward them, carrying an old man buried under blankets.

"Patrol car's parked this way." Allan led them down the back stairs. "I've got tons of security on the house. 'Brother-in-law' sells the stuff so I get it wholesale. No one will bother you. Jacuzzi's in an enclosed porch. Great for unwinding after a hectic day." He winked at Tessa and sighed. "Never could find a mate after mine died ten years ago. You wouldn't happen to have a widow or two looking for a mate in your pack, would you?" he asked Hunter.

"One, but she's pretty cantankerous," Hunter warned.

"The red's got your people at the hotel. Some of his people brought them with them when they came to get Tessa. If you don't mind, I'll drop by there and say hello. Anything you want me to tell them?"

"We have three newly turned *lupus garous* in the pack, and they have an alpha female pack leader now, too."

Allan smiled. "So that's what you meant when you

mentioned having a heap of trouble. Not concerning the little lady, of course. Three new *lupus garous,* you say?"

Allan grew quiet for the rest of the drive to his place. Tessa cuddled with Hunter in the backseat. Now that they were mated, he seemed different somehow. Less anxious, more… well, like he was riding on top of the world.

"You wouldn't need a cop in your area, would you?" Allan pulled into the driveway of a neat, little red brick suburban home.

"I know the sheriff. If you're interested, I could put in a good word for you," Hunter said.

Tessa wasn't sure the sheriff would want anyone working for him that Hunter recommended.

"Good. It's about time I left this area. I've been here ten years already. Maybe Caruthers could come, too. He and his mate, Greta. That way if anyone from your pack gets in trouble, we can circumvent the situation."

"In California, we lived away from civilization. But I can see where having backup in a more developed area can be beneficial."

"You bet. We have another four on the force here, so we wouldn't be leaving the department shorthanded as far as the grays go. Although Judge Graydon might be a little perturbed with me."

"The one who got me out of jail," Hunter said, squeezing Tessa tighter.

"Yeah. I'm always bailing his brother out on brawling charges. The judge will just have to train another gray cop to take care of his brother." Allan went to the car door and opened it for them. "I understand you're off to see your brother at the prison tomorrow. I'll put in a word for you before you get there."

"Grays work there, too?" Hunter asked.

Allan laughed. "No. But some of the guards were former police officers and friends of mine."

"How's your ankle, Tessa?" Hunter asked.

"A little sore still, but much, much better."

"Then you'll need a lift." He carried her out of the patrol car and she smiled at him.

"I'm not usually the type who likes to be babied, but when you're doing the babying, it's awfully nice."

Preceding them to the door, Allan unlocked it and turned off the security alarm. "Wine, music, guest towels are by the Jacuzzi. Make it a honeymoon. Knock yourselves out. See you in the morning."

"Thanks, for everything," Hunter said.

"No problem." Allan reset the security, locked up, and left.

Hunter headed straight for the enclosed back porch with Tessa cradled in his arms. "I'm feeling like a nice hot soak in the tub. You?" His eyes sparkled like the devil.

"You bet, as long as it's hot."

As soon as they entered the room, a blast of steamy air hit her and she sighed. Perfect for sultry, heated sex.

Hunter flipped on the enclosed patio lights with his elbow, although neither of them needed the illumination to see now, which made her think back to when she gave him the lantern when the electricity was off at her house. *Cad.*

The soft glow of light caressed the dark edges of the room, soothing and seductive. In sharp contrast to the silky ambience created by the soft light and warm wet air, Hawaiian trinkets dangled from the ceiling: plastic purple palm trees, orange flamingos, floral leis, rainbow-colored parrots. The rest of the room was outfitted with silk palm trees, ferns, and bamboo chairs and tables, making it feel like a retail store's version of the tropics. But it didn't matter as long as the hottest male around was firmly entrenched in the scene.

Hunter set her on a chair.

She grabbed his hand and helped herself up. "My ankle's fine. Just a little sore, but I can walk on it."

He drew her into his warmth in a bear-tight embrace and kissed the top of her head. "So you just wanted me to get more of a workout."

"Better you than me."

He grinned, his eyes already smoldering with deep-seated desire. "Sit, while I get some wine for us."

She loved how husky his voice grew when she turned him on. She tilted her nose up and breathed in deeply. And his sex, hmm, she could smell his arousal. She could really get used to her enhanced senses. Well, most of them. The chlorine in the Jacuzzi was a little overwhelming. "I'll get the music."

He gave her another squeeze and shook his head. "Somehow, I don't think you're ever going to listen to me."

As if any man, even one as sexy as Hunter, was going to dictate her every move.

He released her, crossed the tile floor to a full-sized bar, the glass shelves behind it covered in liquor bottles of every kind, then pulled out two wine decanters. "White or red?"

"Red." To go with hot-blooded men, a fiery sunset, and heated exchanges.

"Fuller-bodied, light, medium?"

"Hmm, the fullest." She glanced down at his crotch and smiled to see his arousal straining against the soft fabric of his sweats. "*Definitely* the heaviest."

His mouth curved up as he shifted his gaze from the way her tongue swept over her lips to the bottle, and then he hurried to open it.

She flipped a switch, turning on music with a sensuous beat. The flute and drums surrounded them in a tantalizing instrumental rhythm.

Hunter handed Tessa a glass of wine, took a sip of his, then leaned down to kiss her lips.

"I *really* like this wine on you." She licked his lips and slid her fingers down his sweatshirt, found the ties to his pants and gave a little tug.

He chuckled, drank a couple more swallows of his wine, and reached out to take her glass. She took another sip and handed him hers. Once he set them on one of the glass-covered tables, he ran his hands over her arms in an amative way. "You can tug on something else if you get the urge." He wiggled his brows.

"Ohh?" She trailed her finger down lower, until she traced his rock-hard erection through the soft sweats, making his arousal jump.

Pulling her back against his chest, he began to dance slow to the music, molding his body to hers, his groin pressing against her backside, his large hands caressing her breasts through her blouse, his heat warming her. She closed her eyes as her nipples tingled with his sensuous touch, her body sliding against his in a teasing caress.

He nuzzled his face against her neck. "You're beautiful, you know." He reached up to splay his fingers through her hair. "Every bit of you."

"You are, too," she whispered, caught up in the magic of the moment, pressing her butt harder against him, rubbing, tantalizing him to take it further.

He slipped his hands up her shirt, caressed her lace-covered breasts, tormenting the nipples straining for release. The crotch of her panties was already wet in anticipation, and she was ready to ditch her clothes.

His hands shifted to her belt, and he struggled to unbuckle it. "Ready to get wet?"

"Hmm, already there."

No more belts, she made a note to herself, wanting to shove his hands away and yank off the annoying leather hindrance herself.

He finally managed to unfasten the belt, unzipped her jeans, and slipped his hand into her panties, down lower until his fingers reached her cleft. And stroked.

She shuddered with need, the bones liquefying in her legs, and she slumped slightly against him, ready to collapse.

"Hmm, yes, nice and wet," he murmured against her neck, his arm wrapped around her waist to keep her from sinking to the floor as he continued to stroke her. "Just right."

Wriggling against his fingers to get maximum penetration, she rubbed against his arousal, and he groaned. She smiled.

"Vixen."

"Let's move this to the hot tub," she said, her voice drenched with lust. "But the water *better* be hot enough. After all the cold weather we've been through, I'm not getting in unless it's super heated."

"I'll warm you right up."

"Not in the water if it's not soupy."

He released her. "I guess you're not willing to take a swim in the Pacific with me from time to time then."

She turned around and traced his nipples through his sweatshirt. "Not unless it's by mistake."

Hunter laughed under his breath and walked over to the Jacuzzi and poked his hand in. Hot, but not as hot as Tessa was. He shook the water off his fingers and turned on the jets.

"Perfect temperature." He reached his hand out to her. "Join me."

"I thought I already had," she said, her voice like smooth satin.

She rested her small hand in his, and he pulled her close. He leaned down and kissed a corner of her sensual mouth, then brushed his lips across hers, and kissed the other corner.

"You realize you have to keep Meara and Cara in line whenever I'm not around, don't you?"

He slipped her blouse off and held her arms hostage. Dipping his head, he kissed her mouth, deepening the experience. Wet, wild, tasting of fermented grapes, sweet and delectable, rich and full-bodied.

Her heart beat harder and she barely breathed, enraptured with his touch as much as he was with her.

But then her fingers tackled his sweatshirt, and she hurried to wrestle it over his head. And he smiled.

"You didn't tell me all the details about what I have to do and can't do," she said, nipping his bare shoulder. "Not that it means you can tell me what I have to do and can't do, and I'll blindly serve."

"You can handle it. I have every faith in you."

He pulled her jeans down to her ankles, then ran his hands over her silky panties trimmed in lace. Her eyes were bright and expressive, her brows slightly elevated, her lips rosy and swollen. Already he was at full mast, ready to mate her again.

She yanked off his sweatpants and he kicked them free. "I believe," he said, stripping off her bra and panties, "*you've* had control over *me* since you dragged me from your beach."

She let out a lusty chuckle. "Dragged you. *Right.* It was only a show so you could get your hands all over me."

"Worked, didn't it?" From the moment she'd rescued him on the beach, he'd wanted just that.

He lifted her hot little body and carried her into the Jacuzzi, the steam enveloping them in a warm, wet caress.

"Hmm, after having been so cold, this feels just right." She sank into the tub, the bubbles bumping against the swell of her breasts.

"Better than right." He crouched at her knees and spread her legs, opening her up to him.

A smile percolated on her lips.

If anyone had told him he would've taken a human as a mate, that she would have been a siren in disguise, or he would be sitting with her in a gray cop's Jacuzzi for his mating night, he would never have believed it.

He licked the water off her neck, and she trailed her fingers across his muscles making his erection dance.

"You're all healed. No scratches, bruises, cuts—nothing but blemish-free, golden skin stretched over rock hard muscles."

"And you," he said, taking her hand and kissing it.

"Yoloff didn't bite me hard enough. Nor did you. Nothing remains of the bite marks."

He ran his hand down her leg to her ankle, his chest touching the water, his eyes focused on hers. "And your ankle is all right now?"

Tessa took a deep breath. "Miraculously, yes." She kissed Hunter's neck, her tongue licking a trail down his skin, her warm breath caressing as he gave in to the erotic sensation. His fingers played in her hair while she licked his nipple, then her lips pulled on it gently.

"Tessa," he moaned, trying to hold onto his last thread of restraint, wanting their lovemaking to last.

She looked up with the most innocent expression, and he cast her a devilish grin back. She was no innocent, the vixen, knowing damn well what she did to him with that sweet mouth of hers.

He bent his head and ran his mouth across her bare shoulder, and then the other, loving the feel of her water-speckled skin against his lips. She arched her head back, her lips parted, and moaned, offering herself to him, baring her throat, her body. He took advantage of her need, loving her eagerness that only matched his own, pulled her off the seat and switched places, settling her on his lap, her knees spread, readied for his penetration. And he was damned ready to oblige.

She leaned down and kissed his upturned lips, her hair falling around his face, his shoulders, the strands floating on the surface of the water like a mermaid's silky tresses.

He smiled inwardly—the Navy SEAL had ensnared his mermaid, or maybe just the opposite.

Their tongues mated in a ritual dance as he lifted her

onto his rigid erection. Sweet torture as he penetrated her deeply.

With a seductive moan, she closed her eyes and rocked on top of him, her hands kneading his shoulders, her mouth and teeth nibbling his ear. Blazing desire raced through him, making him lose control of his measured moves.

Unable to last much longer, he kept his hands on her hips, directing her, every thrust he made, bringing him closer to climax. She was everything he'd ever wanted in a mate: clever, strong, determined, loyal. And sexy as hell—even in her pajamas and especially bared to him, skin to skin.

She arched her back and he sensed she was near completion, her lithe body attempting to rock harder, her breasts bouncing with a mesmerizing rhythm. He gave into her, drew her to the top.

"Oh, Hunter," she called out, no longer worried that anyone might hear her cry of jubilation.

He quickly followed, filling her with his seed. "Tessa," he groaned, unable to say anything further. Sweet ecstasy, she was perfect for him—and his forever, this, only the beginning.

She sank down on top of him, her head resting against his neck, and he kissed her flushed cheek. "Time to get some rest, sweet Tessa." He hit the button on the Jacuzzi, turning off the jets, then lifted her off his lap, her body limp with satisfaction, soft, wet, and sensuous.

The sly smile she gave him assured him they wouldn't get much sleep tonight.

❖❖❖

Early the next morning, Tessa turned her head toward the front of Allan's house as she and Hunter grabbed a hasty breakfast. "A car door just shut." She seized her bagel and headed for the front window as Hunter poured himself another cup of coffee.

She couldn't believe how she could hear the slightest sounds, everywhere and anywhere. The heater turning on, a school bus picking up kids, although the bus never came down Allan's street, the whisper of a breeze stirring an oak's branches out front. She hoped she would soon get used to it because for now it was wreaking havoc with her sleep. Not that Hunter's wanting to make love with her throughout the night hadn't something to do with it also. Ahem, well, some of it was her fault also.

"A patrol car just arrived. It's Caruthers."

Hunter joined her at the window and rested his hand on her shoulder in a comforting way. "Time to see your brother."

Trying to squash her nervousness at seeing her brother in prison, she finished her bagel and looked up at Hunter. "Do you always get that much exercise at night?"

His sexy smile hinted he was ready for more. "Not usually."

She gave a ladylike snort. "Then you were just lonely and wanted to cuddle really bad, but things got out of hand?"

He laughed and ran his hands through her hair. "Not usually, as in with other women. But with you, I couldn't keep my hands to myself. Besides, your pheromones are a total aphrodisiac."

"Hmm, well, yours drive me crazy, too, but jeesh, Hunter, I'll be walking bowlegged today, and I'll be yawning the whole time."

"We'll take a nap later."

She shook her head. "Yeah, but will we sleep?"

His grin said that she would have a fat chance at that.

Caruthers knocked at the front door, and when Hunter opened it, the policeman offered them a big smile. "Greta and I are agreeable about leaving here and working on the coast. You might need some backup with three new *lupus garous* in your pack. Allan and the little lady who's widowed in your pack really hit it off last night. From the sounds of it, job or no job, he's joining you, too. I'll drive you to the prison." He relocked Allan's place and then escorted them to his car.

Hunter wrapped his arm around Tessa in a loving gesture.

She glanced up at him, her body warming with his touch, gladdened also that Caruthers and the others would join her mate. "You don't have to worry about your wayward pack. Looks like you've got a whole new one."

"The others will come back."

She couldn't see how he could be so complacent about it. To her way of thinking, they were too disloyal to trust any further. But then again, she hadn't been a *lupus garou* long enough to understand their way of thinking.

"I run a fairly democratic pack," Hunter said. "I'm not an autocratic leader like some are."

"Except when it comes to your sister."

Hunter grinned. "She's my blood relative. And *you* are my mate. Our offspring will have to mind also."

"Ah, so those you love best you keep under your rule."

He kissed her cheek and sighed heavily. "In a pack, it's called being protective."

Tessa glanced at Caruthers. "Is that what your pack would call it?"

"Absolutely. Whatever the boss says." Caruthers winked at her. "Man, does this bring back memories of when I turned Greta."

Tessa folded her arms and Hunter chuckled.

When they arrived at the prison, Caruthers parked in front and gave Tessa a compassionate look. "Just tell them Allan Smith and Jim Caruthers sent you. I'll wait out here for you."

Tessa shuddered. To think her brother was incarcerated in the massive place without any chance of escape unless she could bring the real killer to trial and make him pay for the crime. She hoped to God her brother could shed some light on the case.

Chapter 16

When they arrived at the prison's visiting room, Tessa introduced Hunter to her brother. She tried to keep the tears at bay, but Michael's eyes were as misty as hers, which didn't help. And he looked thinner than before, the orange jailhouse jumpsuit clashing with his red hair.

He scowled at Hunter. "Why the hell is *he* wearing my jacket?"

"He was in an accident, but needed a change of clothes. I'll explain later." Tessa pulled out Rourke's phone.

"What news do you have?" Michael took a seat at the table, opposite them, his voice threaded with hope and despair, although he glowered at Hunter again.

"Hunter is looking into the killing. We've got some pictures to show you." She handed Michael Rourke's phone. "Do you recognize any of these guys?"

Michael considered the photos of the three grays. He pointed to Butch, who had been at his trial, and at the one called Redmond. "They came to our house to check out the circuit breakers." He looked up at Tessa. "They knew what they were doing. They replaced the bad switch and charged us a hefty bill like electricians always do, and left." He rubbed his chin and stared at the table. "Although, they were interested in your photographs." He looked up at Tessa, his expression annoyed. "Not my paintings though. The one asked if you had ever taken a picture of a wolf in the wild."

Her heart hitched. "What did you say?"

"At the wildlife refuge, but never in the wild. You would have told me if you had."

Like she didn't. But as usual he had been too busy painting to pay any attention to *her* artistic endeavors.

"Did these guys have anything to do with Bethany's murder?" Michael asked.

"This one was at your trial when the verdict was read," Tessa said. "This guy called him Butch. The other you named was Redmond. And the one you don't recognize was Jessup. Butch came to the house with the two other men, and I asked him why he was at your trial. He denied having been there. His hair was long, but I know it was him. Why deny it? Why be there in the first place?"

"I wondered why he looked different. Why were they at the house?"

Hunter tensed and she figured he was worried she might say the wrong thing.

"One of them is interested in Hunter's sister. So he tracked her to my place and that's when I met all three of them." She took a deep breath. "I didn't want to tell you this, but you have to know in case anything can shed light on who the real murderer is. A man by the name of Yoloff has been stalking me. Hunter had a run-in with one of his two brothers and in self-defense, Hunter killed him."

Michael's gaze turned to Hunter, and he swore softly under his breath.

"I'm an ex–Navy SEAL," Hunter said, "trained to do work like this. The guy didn't have a chance even though he was armed with a knife. But his brothers went after Tessa, and I didn't have a choice."

Michael's eyes grew big. "Thanks for taking care of my little sister."

She grunted. He was her younger brother, but because he was several inches taller than she was, he called her little.

"My pleasure." Hunter took hold of her hand and squeezed. "We're married. I'll always protect her."

Michael shifted his attention to Tessa.

"Uhm, yeah, whirlwind romance." She hadn't thought Hunter would bring *that* up right now. Besides, they weren't really married as in the marriage license, wedding ring, or marriage vows kind of arrangement. Her cheeks heated and she tried to muddle through. "I found him washed up on the beach after the guy who was stalking me pushed him off a cliff and—"

"Whoa, back up to the guy that was stalking you. I worried someone was, but have you learned who it is?"

She noted her brother's concern for her, but not about Hunter's near-death experience. Michael was probably still pissed off because Hunter was wearing his favorite jacket.

"He broke into our house the day you were taken to prison. Hunter protected me from him. Anyway, Hunter thought maybe this guy wanted you out of the way, and so he murdered Bethany so you would be found guilty of the crime."

Michael pointed to the third man in the photos. "This other guy looks familiar also."

"Jessup's the one who's after Hunter's sister. Where do you remember him from?"

"The driver of the electric truck." Michael frowned and then looked up at Tessa. "I saw him at a number of my art exhibits. Of course, you begin to see the same people at the parties. Avid collectors, people who like mingling with others who enjoy the paintings, philanthropists, novice painters who want to learn how to sell their own works. I remember him because he kept watching Bethany. Do you think he was seeing her behind my back?"

Tessa gritted her teeth. She hadn't wanted to tell her brother Ashton was the traitor. But if any detail could help them solve the case, he had to know.

"Ashton..." Her voice broke. "Ashton's the one who was seeing Bethany when you were at your shows."

Michael's jaw clenched. "I know."

She stared at him. "You knew? Why didn't you say so at the trial?"

"Why? The sheriff would have covered for his son. Ashton would have gotten away with it, *as usual,* and it would have looked like I was lying."

"But what if Ashton killed Bethany?"

Michael rubbed his forehead, then shoved his hands in his lap. "I sure as hell considered it. What if she'd wanted to come back to me? Make it up to me? We'd fought that night. She said she'd done some things she wasn't proud of, although she wouldn't admit she was seeing someone else. I tried to get her to confess, but she wouldn't. She just kept protecting the bastard."

"Then you could have been angry enough to kill her," Hunter said softly.

"I *was* angry, but I didn't murder her. I could have thrashed the guy who'd been seeing her. But I wouldn't have hurt Bethany. I understood how she felt. I really loved her, but I didn't know how to remedy our relationship because the more popular my work was becoming, the more despondent she became over it. To sell, I have to promote. To keep my relationship alive with her, I'd have had to give it all up. But it was my livelihood, my worth." He shook his head. "I didn't kill her. She always walked along the cliffs when she was angry or frustrated. Supposedly, she went there after I left."

"Do you think Ashton might have done it?" Tessa asked.

"Why not? He was always getting away with his petty crimes. What if she had told him she wanted to go back to me and he was so angry, he killed her? He didn't say anything to me about it, but I knew he was jealous of my success."

"If you knew she was seeing Ashton, did you know if she was seeing anyone else?" Hunter asked.

Michael's eyes clouded with fresh tears and his shoulders slumped.

Ohmigod. Had Bethany been seeing someone else? A bunch of different guys?

Running his hand through his hair, Michael stared at the table and nodded. "Ashton wasn't the only one. At least one other guy was seeing her. Maybe two."

"How do you know?" Hunter asked.

"Hell, I don't know. I mean, I don't have any real proof."

"Is that why you said the place was haunted?" Hunter asked.

She couldn't understand why her brother had come up with such a ludicrous story.

"Yeah," Michael admitted. "I felt like a couple of people were watching her house. I thought I saw a man in the shadows of the trees one day at dusk. I wanted to check, but Bethany insisted I was seeing things. Later, I wondered if the guy was her lover, and she didn't want me catching him. It happened again a couple of weeks later. And then another time, I swear someone was actually in the house. A drawer opened in the kitchen. I was half-dressed, but even so I charged into the room and the back door was standing wide open. Bethany said we probably hadn't shut it all the way. So what could I say? Ghosts infested the place? I didn't want to make love to her there anymore. Let her stay with her damned ghosts."

"Did the guy or guys come to your house while she visited you?" Hunter asked.

"Not that I knew of. Why bother? They could see her anytime they wanted to at her place when she wasn't working her shifts at the Lobster Tail."

"If some other guy wanted Bethany and didn't like it that Michael was seeing her, why wouldn't he kill Ashton for seeing her also? Why only frame Michael for the crime?" Tessa asked.

No one had an answer.

"Okay, what about my stalker? He and his brothers pushed Hunter off the same cliff that Bethany had fallen from. Too much of a coincidence?"

Michael looked back at Hunter. "How in the hell did you survive?"

Finally, some reaction to poor Hunter's ordeal.

"Navy SEAL training."

"Oh."

Tessa cast Hunter a look of admiration, then focused on her brother. "Can you think of anything else? Anything that would help us figure out who did this?"

Michael snorted. "Yeah, the treasure hunters."

Tessa made a disagreeable face at her brother. Here he was incarcerated, they were trying to get him out, and he was being flippant about ghosts and nonexistent gold.

Hunter leaned back in the chair. "Treasure hunters?"

Tessa folded her arms. "You know how oral history goes. Supposedly, our great-grandparents had a huge stash of gold, and they hid it somewhere on our land. But it's just a myth, or if it really existed at some time someone else stole it. Our grandparents searched for it, so did our parents. And truth be told, even when Michael and I were younger, we dug all over the place out there, but none of us ever found it. Over the years, we've had tons of offers to take the house off our hands. I figured it had to do with the rumors about the gold."

"Yeah, and you think it was a coincidence our grandparents died in a car accident only a year after our parents did?" Michael asked, one red brow cocked.

"Dad was drunk as usual. And Granddad shouldn't have been driving, although we know Grandmother hated to drive so she was always giving him the wheel. The coroner said his heart had given out before they went off the cliff. So yeah, it's a coincidence, but totally explainable."

"The men who came to the house said they were looking to steal from Bethany's place. If they thought gold was hidden somewhere on your land, maybe that's the reason they were there," Hunter said.

Tessa couldn't believe he'd even be considering it, but then she wondered if he knew about the gold rumors all along. "Did Uncle Basil think there was gold on our property?"

Hunter's lips parted.

Hell, he had. So was that why Hunter had turned her? To get her property? "He kept trying to buy me out." She bit back the bitterness, making it difficult to swallow. Hunter reached for her hand, but she pulled away from him. "Is that why he wanted our property so badly?"

"Leidolf found a couple of newspaper clippings on the guy I killed, pertaining to a dispute Caleb McKnight had with your grandfather over stolen gold. The other was about John Anderson and his killing Caleb McKnight, father of triplets, Yoloff, Ren, and Andreas. So what if they had to do with your family's deaths?"

"I'll kill them," Michael said, his face turning as red as his hair.

The blood rushed from Tessa's face, and she reached across the table and took Michael's hand. "Don't even talk like that."

"I always thought Uncle Basil had some ulterior motive," Michael said. "You sure get to know who your friends are. And here he was insisting we didn't need to stay there because young people our age needed to be closer to the city, especially because of the work we do. Couldn't he see that nature is what inspires our work? Not city buildings and urban sprawl? Not people? But—"

"Wolves?" Hunter asked.

Michael looked from him to Tessa and she quickly said to her brother, "I didn't show him the paintings."

He glowered at Hunter. "Don't you know not to look at an artist's work that's not finished?" He ran his hands through his hair and stared gloomily at the table.

"I just came across them, by accident. Beautiful work, by the way. But back to Bethany's murder, tons of people had been in her house—the three guys who had to do with trying to take off with my sister, and of course the sheriff and his men, the coroner's office, Tessa, Ashton..."

"The sheriff," Michael said, emphasizing him over all the rest.

Tessa straightened. "Sure, because he's investigating a murder."

Michael shook his head. "He was always cleaning up after Ashton, remember? He's the one who reported the murder, except because he's the sheriff, no one considered he might have known who had done the real killing. A sheriff would be above suspicion. Hell, look at how that policeman killed two of his wives and because he was a cop, no one believed there was any foul play. Not until the second one came up missing. But even then, the police force denied he had anything to do with her suspicious disappearance. The family had to have their loved one's body exhumed so the coroner could determine if there was foul play. And of course, this time, the coroner said yes, she was murdered. So you don't think a sheriff could cover up his son's murder and get away with it? Especially when they have me—the perfect patsy for the job?"

"You asked Ashton to watch over me, even knowing what you did about him?" Tessa asked.

Michael took a deep breath. "I figured I kind of deserved it. Sticking with him when I knew he was bad news—getting me into scrapes, causing all that trouble for you. But I also know deep down, the guy's got some decency in him. Hell, our dad was bad enough with being the town philanderer and drunk. But after Ashton's mother took off with another man, his dad changed. Ashton kept reaching out, trying to get his dad to pay attention to him, in a negative way. In any way he could. He didn't have an older sister like you to help him out. And he's damned good with a rifle. He could protect you if need be."

"Because you knew there was a stalker. Why didn't you tell me?"

"I didn't want to worry you."

She frowned at her brother. "You could have told me. And you could have warned me that Ashton was going to be gunning down anything that moved out by our house. He shot Hunter!"

Michael quickly looked at Hunter. "Oh, hell, I'm sorry, man."

"No problem. It was just a graze."

"What made you realize there was a stalker?" Tessa asked her brother.

"I saw footprints outside your window when I was clipping the hedges. And another time I saw someone peeking in the house when I came up with a load of wood, but I was too far away to catch him." Michael looked back at Hunter. "Hell, he looked a bit like you. Long dark hair, same approximate height and build."

"That's why Ashton said he shot him. But Hunter was with me when the man broke into the house on a couple of separate occasions."

Michael considered them both and shook his head. "I'm sorry I didn't tell you. But I'm glad you've got someone who's combat trained to watch over you. I *never* thought you'd get married." He rose abruptly from the chair. "I've got to go. Write, will you?"

"I'll be back. We'll get you out, Michael. You just take good care of yourself."

He gave her a warm hug and she broke into tears, despite struggling not to. "You… you just take care of yourself," she reiterated.

Michael kissed her wet cheek. "I will." He shook Hunter's hand. "Don't let anyone hurt her. Take care of that stalker."

Hunter bowed his head slightly. "Will do."

Michael straightened his posture and gave a half smile. "I don't know what happened, but all of a sudden I began getting some special treatment in here. So don't worry, little sister. Things are already looking up."

"Why would Michael be getting special treatment in prison?" Tessa asked, as Hunter helped her into Caruthers's police car.

She was holding up pretty well, and he was damned proud of her.

"The judge had something to do with it. Maybe Allan and me, too." Caruthers shrugged. "We don't usually mess with humans who are incarcerated in the prison system. Most are there because they deserve it. But since you're one of us, we pulled some strings. Of course, no one in the place really knows why, just that there's a sneaking suspicion the kid's innocent, and he's got some pretty powerful friends in high places."

Tessa brushed away tears and smiled. "Tell Allan and the judge thanks for me."

"I'll do that. While you were inside, that red, Leidolf, came by. He said he'd meet you at The Olive Groves for lunch. He said the rest of your people would be there also. Want me to take you there now?"

"Let's go," Hunter said. "We'll see what Leidolf has to say."

Tessa looked at him.

He cast her an abbreviated smile. "I promise I won't tear into him." *Too badly.* Then he let out an exasperated sigh. "Why didn't you tell me you took a picture of a wolf in the wild and that he was shapeshifting at the time?"

"I didn't say so."

He snorted. "The look on your face revealed the truth. I told you that you couldn't play poker with me."

She'd never get anything past Hunter unless she wore a ski mask, and probably even then her eyes and voice would give her away.

"I'm not sure what it was. I thought it was a wolf. It was really foggy out. And then I saw a man. Or at least I thought so. The photo wasn't clear and no matter how much I tried to enhance it..." She shrugged.

"The man was naked."

"He didn't look like he was wearing any clothes. But it was a long ways off. I just figured my mind was playing tricks."

"He saw you."

"I don't know, Hunter. He was looking in my direction, but I was using a telescopic lens. He couldn't have seen me as far away as I was."

"Hell," Caruthers said. "if he hadn't wanted you so badly, he would have killed you."

The thought she had been living a life of danger all this time without his protection stirred Hunter's blood. "He saw you, Tessa. Believe me. How long before Bethany had been murdered had this taken place?"

"Two days. I showed her the photo and asked her what she could make of it. All Bethany saw was mist. I showed it to Michael also, but preoccupied with his painting, he didn't pay any attention. Said it looked interesting, but barely glanced at it."

But had Bethany's witnessing the photo led to her death?

In Caruthers's patrol car, Hunter and Tessa soon arrived at the Italian restaurant, although Hunter regretted that Tessa was so tense. She would have to see for herself that the pack would accept her as one of their own.

When they arrived at the restaurant, the hostess tried to seat them, but Caruthers motioned to a group of people, both Leidolf's reds and the rest of Hunter's pack, at a large rowdy table. "I'll sit with them."

The waiter escorted Tessa and Hunter to a private booth, and Tessa looked back at the table with his pack mates as if she wished they could sit with them and not have the confrontation with Leidolf. So that was what was worrying her.

Hunter gripped her hand tighter. "I promise I won't kill him for leaving me behind in the jail and going after you."

The smell of oregano, garlic, Italian sauce, and onions wafted in the air, and Hunter's stomach grumbled. Dishes and glasses clinked as servers cleared tables and conversation and Italian music drifted overhead. Nice setting for a romantic dinner for two if Hunter and Tessa could have enjoyed the meal without Leidolf chaperoning.

Leidolf leaned back against the burgundy vinyl seat in the booth at the end of the section, looking self-satisfied and smiled at them. "My lawyer was trying to have you released, but he told me you got yourself out by contacting someone who had a lot more clout. Pays to have a judge back you."

Unable to let go of the irritation, Hunter gave him a dark look.

"I missed you at the hotel last night, but I guess you found a safe place to hole up. Your people are returning with you, and they're dying to meet your new mate. You've got three cops leaving here to watch your backs on the coast, one who wants one of your widowed females, and she's ecstatic. Sounds like your pack is off to a good recovery. Not bad considering the mess you've been in recently." Leidolf unfolded his napkin and placed it on his lap. "Other packs usually don't mix it up much, but I've grown attached to yours, considering one of your people is joining mine. If you need my help any further, just let me know."

Hell, he was attached to Hunter's pack because Tessa still interested him.

"What did you say to the lawyer about me?" Hunter asked.

Leidolf laughed. "He holds a grudge, Tessa. Remember that." He sipped his water. "I told him just what had happened. You were wielding the knife that killed the guy. That's why he released me so quickly. I was only a witness to the whole thing. I'd planned to watch over Tessa until you arrived at the hospital. Imagine my surprise to find you had beat me to it."

Hunter squeezed Tessa's hand in her lap. "So you're returning to Portland?"

"I have to. I've got problems of my own. A red from Texas is stirring up trouble. Thinks he might have what it takes to run my pack. Can you imagine the nerve of the guy?" He winked at Tessa and turned his attention back to Hunter. "But I mean it. If you need my help, just say. I'll come to the coast and give you a hand."

Hunter bowed his head. "Likewise, Leidolf."

Tessa took a deep breath and her shoulders relaxed a little.

"I would have gone to see your brother, Tessa, but thought you might like to spend the time with him alone. With Hunter, of course. Are you any closer to solving the murder mystery?"

"The two who were in the house when you and Hunter came home after cutting up the tree had done some work on our circuit breaker. And Michael said that the guy called Jessup had been driving the truck, and he'd seen him at a number of his art exhibits." Tessa looked over at Hunter. "When Jessup said they'd been casing Bethany's house for valuables, I didn't think they were really thieves, but maybe they were. And maybe they were planning on ripping off the art gallery, but it had too much security so they hoped to find some of Michael's paintings in the house. Easier to break into. Butch was at Michael's trial. Why? To see if he really got time or if he was going to be released? If Michael had been found not guilty, we would have been home and it would have been harder for them to steal anything from the house."

"Or," Leidolf said, "he was calling ahead to the others, who were breaking into your house while you were at the trial. Once you left, he would warn them you were on the way home."

"Was anything missing from your house besides the gun?" Hunter asked.

"I didn't look. I figured Yoloff had only stolen the gun. I never thought anyone would be running around in that weather stealing paintings."

"Do you have anything else of value?" Hunter asked.

"Computers, electronics. My photographs. But again, I would doubt they'd be interested in any of that because of the weather. The ice storm hadn't started yet, but it was on its way."

"Searching for evidence of wrongdoing? Maybe they'd been involved in Bethany's murder, and they were afraid Michael had some proof against them that he didn't know about," Leidolf said.

"Michael mentioned the sheriff could have been covering up for his son, Ashton, also," Tessa mentioned.

Leidolf shook his head. "I'm glad all I have is a simple case of knocking some sense into a red's head if he thinks he's taking over my pack. Keep in touch, and I'll help any way I can if you need me. Your new cops won't be returning with you for a couple of weeks until they settle their affairs here. Your widow is staying with the one cop, but the rest are taking the Ford Escape, making it kind of crowded. I'm gifting you my Humvee, travels in any kind of weather."

"But—" Tessa said.

Leidolf held up his hand. "I've got another back at the ranch. I'll ride home with my people. Maybe Hunter won't hold a grudge against me about the jail situation for too long then." He grinned. "The last time I had to deal with a gray pack leader, Devlyn Greystoke had targeted a red he mated who reminded me of you. She was a redhead also. Bella was her name."

"Devlyn changed a human, too?" Tessa asked.

"No." Leidolf looked at the table for a second, then back up at them. "I was too late for her. She should have mated a red." He shrugged.

"Only a *lupus garou* would do, isn't that right, Leidolf?" Hunter asked.

Leidolf managed a smile. "Sure, that's right, Hunter."

But Hunter suspected it wasn't so. If he had given Leidolf the chance, he might have claimed Tessa for his own, especially since she reminded him of the last one he'd lost.

They finished their meals in silence, and then Leidolf paid the bill. Hunter kissed Tessa's cheek. "Are you ready to meet the rest of my pack?"

No, not now. But that wouldn't be very alpha of her. Yet, Tessa shivered internally anyway. What if they put her to the test? Tried to prove to her that she couldn't be their pack leader's mate? She didn't have a clue what she was supposed to do.

She stiffened her spine as she walked between Leidolf and Hunter. At least while she was wedged between the two alphas, she almost felt alpha herself.

Caruthers and a pretty brunette on his arm Tessa figured was Greta, both in their midforties, were sitting at a long table with several others. Allan, the other cop, and the woman he was interested in, a woman with chestnut hair curled on top of her head in swirls with a quick smile and sparkle in her amber eyes, sat next to them. And three other males, maybe in their late twenties, early thirties, all tall. One with black hair and eyes, who seemed too interested in Tessa, but quickly changed his posture to a contrite expression when Hunter gave him a quelling look. The other two had light brown hair cut short, dark brown eyes and appeared to be twins, except the one was slightly taller.

"Kenneth," Hunter said, motioning to one of the twins, "and Kensington." He waved at the black-haired man. "Adam." He smiled at the woman. "This is Genevieve who seems to have found her new mate. Everyone, this is Tessa, my mate."

All bowed their heads slightly.

"About time," Genevieve said, and hurried forth to give her a hug.

Greta did the same. The men didn't dare.

Hunter shook Leidolf's hand. "Thanks for the Humvee and the offer to help. We'll keep in touch. If you need any of my aid, likewise, give me a call. We have a long drive ahead of us, and I don't want to leave my sister in charge of a couple of new *lupus garous* much longer, so we'll be on our way."

Hunter shook hands with the police officers who would join them in a couple of weeks. Greta whispered to Tessa, "I've been where you are, honey. I'll show you the ropes."

"It's not exactly the same." Caruthers kissed his mate on the cheek. "She's an alpha leader's mate."

Greta grinned. "Like I said, Tessa, I'll help you all I can."

Caruthers shook his head, and Tessa gave Greta and Genevieve a hug, already feeling like one of the pack and it was a damned good feeling, too, but for her brother's continued incarceration. "I look forward to seeing you both soon."

Once Hunter's people were packed into the Escort, Hunter led them in the Humvee.

"I thought they might want to eat me alive, but they were really nice," Tessa told Hunter as he drove out of town.

"A couple of my males would have eaten you all up, but not the way you mean." He gripped the steering wheel tighter, then released it, but still seemed as tense as before. "What do you know about your great-grandfather?"

Here they went around about the gold again. "He was from Colorado originally, but got the gold fever. First he went to California and made it big, then came here. He met my great-grandmother who was working for her father's mercantile. Supposedly, he found a lot of gold here, too. Just had a real nose for it. But all the money in the world wouldn't buy him happiness. Shortly after finding the gold, my great-grandmother died of a fever, and he returned to Colorado. I couldn't find out what happened to him after that."

"What about your grandmother?"

"She was just an infant when her mother died. Her father couldn't take care of her. She went to live with her mother's brother and wife. But my grandmother said her father was generous and had left her aunt and uncle all the gold, enough to make them wealthy. Much of it was put into the bank later on, but some of it was hidden. They never had any children, and Grandmother eventually inherited it all and married a wealthy merchant. They settled where the house is now, where my great-grandparents had once lived in a shack. What happened to Seth?"

"He was killed in a rock slide. Apparently, he must have left your great-grandmother, returned to Colorado, but then rejoined my great-grandfather in California. Three of them died. My great-grandfather, Seth, and my father's twin brother. A fourth man, Caleb McKnight, was the only one who survived."

"The one in the news clippings."

"Right. Did your grandmother have any special abilities?"

"Like you do? Everyone used to tease her that there was no sneaking around Grandmother because she heard everything. She knew things, too. Like when the weather was changing. She explained it was due to her arthritis. As for her sense of smell? She definitely smelled things more acutely than we did. She seemed to always sense people's emotions also, whether they were scared or angry, even when they were hiding their feelings."

"She could smell their fear."

"Yeah, although I thought it was because she was super-observant."

"What about the gold?"

Tessa frowned at him. "There is no gold on the property."

"Seth told my father he'd stockpiled it somewhere in Oregon for people who needed it more than he did. Never in a million years would we have thought Seth had a child by a human. Did you ever find a marriage certificate?"

"No. Lots of records are pretty difficult to locate. No birth record for my grandmother either."

"Apparently in rare cases a human can conceive a child with a *lupus garou*. But in all the years I've lived, I've never met anyone like that, and Leidolf had only met one during his lifetime."

But what if her line had an affinity for getting pregnant by a *lupus garou*?

Hunter must have realized what she was thinking because he smiled at her and patted her leg. "Seth must not have changed your great-grandmother and that's why she died of a fever. Maybe she didn't want to be changed, or maybe he couldn't do it. But you're already one of us, and the babies you have will fully be *lupus garous*."

She'd never thought about that. How was she to deal with being a *lupus garou* and raising offspring like that when she was totally clueless about herself still? Tessa sighed.

Hunter slowed down as wrecking crews waved them past a rock slide. Tessa glanced back to see if the red Escort was behind them.

"Heavy traffic. About five vehicles slipped in between us, but I've given my pack directions if we get separated." He pulled back into their lane past the rock slide. "So what else do we know about Bethany's murder? How come the sheriff found her? Was there a 911 call made?"

"Bethany had made a call to the sheriff, stating that Michael had become violent and she was worried he might return. She said she was taking a walk along the trail by the cliff. The sheriff stopped by to check on her, but when he couldn't find her at the house, he went down the trail and discovered her body at the bottom of the cliff."

"Phone records verified the call was made?"

"Yes."

"What if Ashton had made the call from Bethany's house, told his father he'd killed her by accident, and his father covered up for him?"

"Truthfully, I don't think Ashton killed her." Tessa rubbed her clammy hands on her jeans. "Gut instinct. I think he really cared for her and if he murdered her in a fit of passion, I don't think he'd let Michael go to prison for it."

"Yet, he let him take the rap for minor crimes he was responsible for. On the other hand, what if your brother really did it?"

Tessa glowered at Hunter.

"What if he did? We can't discount that he might be guilty."

"He isn't! What if it's one of your kind?" Tessa choked on the thought. "You... you couldn't have a *lupus garou* convicted, could you? Once the moon appeared, he'd change and you can't have one incarcerated, can you?" Hell, even Ashton was one now.

"If we find one of them is guilty, we'll figure out a way."

She'd figure out a way. If she could just turn into a wolf and bite her brother in prison, the judge would *have* to have him released.

When they finally reached Hunter's house, Tessa figured someone would greet them, but nobody did and her heart began to race.

"Stay in the Humvee. Do not leave until I say so," Hunter ordered, his face dark and threatening.

Before she could respond, he slammed the door shut and strode to the front porch, then disappeared inside. She concentrated on the front door standing wide open and wanted to join him rather than worry about what was happening.

And then his face stormy, he stalked out to the Humvee and jumped in. "Jessup and his pack have taken them."

She hoped Hunter couldn't smell her fear, but she couldn't hide how she was feeling.

"We're to meet them at that burned out pine tree. I'm to hand you over to Yoloff and they'll release my sister and the rest."

Tessa looked behind them, but still didn't see any sign of the Escort.

"I left directions." Hunter pulled out of the drive and headed south on the coastal road.

"You can't face all five of them, Hunter. We should wait."

"They want us alone. I'll do what I can."

Stubborn damn alpha male. He was going to get himself killed and then where would she be? Just when she'd found the man she wanted to love forever. And what about Michael also?

Her skin crawling with anxiety, she looked into the backseat. No weapons. "What about the rifles at the house?"

"They must have taken them. None were there."

The closer they got to where the pine tree was, the more Tessa felt she could lose Hunter for good. She looked into the backseat again. *Nothing*. Leidolf was a neat freak. Not even a hint of dust. But what about the trunk? A tire iron?

"No matter what, you're staying in the vehicle. If they get the best of me, you leave."

"But your sister, and the others?"

"They won't harm them until they're assured they have you. You return to my place, gather the forces, call Leidolf. Hell, have him notify Devlyn of the problem. These guys won't be able to handle all that heat."

"But you can't charge in there and kill them all. Why can't you wait for the others?" She studied the tension in his face and frowned. "You don't think Jessup and the others will wait, do you? You think they'll kill some of them. Rourke and Ashton."

"I would have left you at my place, but I was afraid that they'd be watching and take you. So do as I say, Tessa. You're no match for any of them without having a gun."

They drove the rest of the way in silence and when they reached the designated place, Tessa couldn't stop shivering. She wasn't being an alpha, but she couldn't change into a wolf, which even if she could probably wouldn't have helped much against them. And without a gun, she was totally defenseless and useless.

Hunter pulled up and stopped. Yoloff and his brother stood as wolves near the burned up pine, watching them, waiting. Jessup stood farther away as a human, unable to shapeshift. He didn't have a weapon that she could see. Where were Redmond and Butch? Probably guarding Meara and the others somewhere else.

Hunter squeezed Tessa's hand. "Stay."

"Who are you targeting first? Jessup? He's their leader. If you take him out, maybe the others will tuck tail and run."

"Yoloff and his brother. They're the most dangerous

in their wolf forms." Hunter opened the door. "Lock it after me."

Tessa climbed into the driver's seat and locked the door. Jessup motioned to her to come out of the vehicle, but she ignored him and watched Hunter strip off his clothes, sure of himself, muscular, ready.

Even though Yoloff and his brother stood their ground, she thought they looked a little nervous, their ears flattening and their tails drooping slightly. Hunter didn't take his eyes off Yoloff the whole time while he removed his clothes. Yoloff would die. She knew Hunter wouldn't allow him to live this time. Maybe his brother, too. But she was certain Jessup didn't intend to let Hunter rip him to shreds, if Hunter managed to best the brothers.

And then she saw the rifle leaning against one of the trees. Damn him. What if she could get to it while Jessup watched Hunter's fight?

Hunter shapeshifted, but no one moved until he targeted Yoloff. Then Jessup made a move toward the Humvee. He motioned for her to get out. Like she'd listen to him. Then she had another idea. Could she run any of them over? Probably not because of all the trees. Jessup could easily duck out of her path, she'd ruin the Humvee, and be stuck.

The tire iron. Surely, Leidolf would have one to use in case he got a flat and had to change a tire. Had to be in the trunk.

Hunter ran at Yoloff and Jessup's attention switched to the fight. Typical male. Forget the girl when there's a good fight going on.

She didn't want to take her eyes off the fight either, but she climbed into the backseat and looked into the trunk. Hell, if there was a tire iron, it must be hidden. She glanced back at the windshield.

Hunter and Yoloff clashed, their teeth bared and connecting, the growls reverberating through the woods. They fell to their pads and separated. Her skin prickled with anxiousness, her heart racing. She thought Yoloff's brother might attack next, but he seemed to be waiting for the fight to be decided first. He was probably thinking he wouldn't have to participate if Yoloff killed Hunter first.

But then Hunter did the unexpected. He whipped around and attacked Yoloff's brother, startling him so badly, he dashed off in the wrong direction, close to the edge of the cliff with nowhere to back up, nowhere to run. Hunter rose on his hind legs, his teeth snapping at the gray and with no room to maneuver, the brother slipped off the cliff with a yelp.

Shocked, Tessa stared out the window. Everyone else seemed as stunned. Yoloff didn't make a move toward Hunter and Jessup stood frozen in place. *Yeah, bastard. After Hunter finishes off Yoloff, you're next.*

She climbed into the trunk and began lifting the carpet, looking for the tire iron she hoped was here.

But then Hunter targeted Yoloff, and Jessup went for the gun. Oh, hell. Not finding a tire iron, Tessa scrambled over the backseat and then into the front and started the Humvee.

As soon as Hunter bit Yoloff in the face, Jessup aimed the rifle. Tessa couldn't reach him with the Humvee the way he was standing protected between the trees, but if she rammed the pines, she might be able to distract him enough. She threw the vehicle in drive and roared toward Jessup. He swung around and for a moment, she thought he might shoot her. But instead he jumped back, realizing he was protected by the trees, and turned the weapon on Hunter.

"No!" she screamed, and ran the Humvee into the pine. Because of the constant rain in the area, the roots were shallow enough that when she hit the tree, it toppled, but Jessup got off a round right before it fell.

Hunter yelped this time and she saw the blood on his hip. Ohmigod, no, Hunter. If nothing else, she'd wrestle with Jessup until Hunter destroyed—

Yoloff bit at Hunter and he retaliated, but they were too close to the cliff's edge. *Back up, back up!*

Jessup aimed the rifle again, and Tessa jerked the door open and lunged at him, throwing her body at him, trying to knock him off balance to give Hunter time to take care of Yoloff.

And then her heart nearly gave out when she and Jessup stumbled over the felled pine, falling to their knees as Hunter took another bite at Yoloff's face. Yoloff suddenly went for Hunter's leg. They were both too close to the cliff edge! She wanted to warn Hunter away from the drop-off, drag him from the danger herself. But everything happened so fast she couldn't react quickly enough to do anything.

Yoloff bit into Hunter's leg, and Hunter snapped at Yoloff's neck. But Yoloff's back paws lost purchase on the crumbling soil. He slipped off the edge, pulling Hunter with him.

"Hunter!" Tessa screamed and ran for him, but Jessup grabbed her arm and yanked her back. She kicked and thrashed back and forth, trying to break free, to save Hunter.

"Butch will be pleased," Jessup darkly said, and jerked her toward the edge of the cliff.

Only when she saw the direction he was going did she go willingly to see Hunter, to ensure he was all right. She prayed he was.

Down below, both Hunter's and Yoloff's wolf forms lay still as death. Yoloff's brother was gone. Her heart splintering, she stifled a sob.

"Come on. Time to clean up the last of the loose ends. You'll tell us where the gold is hidden on your property, and we'll let the others go."

With tears streaking down her face, she didn't believe it for a minute, although it wouldn't have made any difference because she didn't have a clue if there was any gold anyway. All that mattered was whether Hunter had made it or not.

Jessup tugged her in the direction of Bethany's house, but she fought him every step of the way, wanting to climb down the cliff to Hunter. He had to have survived the fall like before. He had to have. And she had to go to him.

But Jessup tightened his grip on her, cutting the circulation off in her wrist, her hand numbing. He hurried her faster to the house, forcing her to run to keep up. What about Hunter's pack? Where were they when they needed them most?

Jessup shoved the front door open and yanked her into the house. "She's yours, Butch. Just like you wanted."

"The others?" Butch asked, offering Jessup a beer.

Jessup forced Tessa onto the couch next to Meara

and Cara, their hands and mouths bound, their eyes wild. Ashton and Rourke were bound, but unconscious on the floor. Meara looked at Tessa, trying to read her expression, but Tessa sobbed, attempting to appear so inconsolable that she was useless, and so that they wouldn't tie her up also, while she looked for another weapon. Not that her tears and upset weren't genuine, but she tried to keep a clear head until they were able to destroy the men before they harmed anyone else. And then she had to go to Hunter.

She spied a poker next to the cold fireplace as Redmond took a seat at the dining table. If she could just slip over to it.

"Hunter took care of Yoloff's brother first. Although he worked on Yoloff in the beginning. His tactics threw all of us. Especially, when Hunter forced Andreas off the cliff." Jessup took a swig of beer.

But then Tessa worried that if she got the poker, Jessup still had the rifle and three men against one woman wouldn't do. If she could free Meara, she could shapeshift, whereas no one else could. Tessa had to chance it. She moved closer to Meara and began working on her bindings.

"But Yoloff's gone also?" Butch asked.

"Yeah, Hunter got him, too, only he had the last laugh. He pulled Hunter off the cliff and both hit the rocks below."

"You're sure Hunter was dead? He survived before," Butch warned.

"Yeah, he was dead. Last time, he hit the water and managed to swim to Tessa's beach. Not this time."

Her heart in her throat, Tessa felt the ties loosen on Meara's wrists. Meara quickly yanked them free, then tugged her clothes off. Tessa dove for the fireplace poker and Meara shapeshifted.

As a wolf, Meara targeted Jessup, the leader, and Tessa went for the rifle, poker in hand.

But no sooner had Meara's teeth clamped down on Jessup's arm, making him drop the can of beer, than Butch dove for the rifle.

No, no! Tessa swung the poker at Butch's head and knocked him out cold. But somehow Redmond had managed to slip by her in the shuffle and went for the rifle.

Growling furiously, Meara lunged for Jessup's throat, while he grabbed onto her muzzle to keep her from killing him. Tessa froze as Redmond grabbed the rifle and pointed it at her. He could shoot her, but she wouldn't die. Yet, Tessa couldn't let go of the fear that Meara could. Meara was their only real chance at survival, and Tessa had to protect her. She prayed her *lupus garou* genetics would save her and leapt forward, swinging the poker at the rifle.

Her hands and mouth still bound, Cara had managed to slip behind Redmond and gave him a shove. The bullet fired into the carpeted floor.

Before Tessa could take another swing at Redmond, a different wolf growled low. She turned and saw Hunter, his hip bleeding. *Alive!* Tears filled her eyes and she wanted to rush to him, to hug him, proving he was really real.

His fur smelled foul, like he'd rolled in a bed of rotting kelp. He quickly targeted Jessup, and Meara swung around to get Redmond.

But even over the growling and the sound of a porcelain lamp crashing, Tessa heard a vehicle driving up. Finally, Hunter's people had arrived.

She ran to help untie Cara, but Butch came to and grabbed Tessa's ankle.

Redmond slid down next to her, his throat ripped out. Hunter didn't hesitate to make short work of Butch. Jessup was already dead.

"Hello?" a man called out.

Hell, it was the sheriff.

Still in their wolf forms, Hunter and Meara looked in the direction of the front door, then raced out back.

Tessa continued to work on Cara's bindings.

"What the hell," the sheriff said, his gun drawn.

"A pair of wolves saved us from these men," Tessa said, her voice and hands shaking.

"Ashton?" The sheriff ran over to help his son.

"These men knocked Ashton and Rourke out. They planned to kill the whole lot of us."

The sheriff stared at Butch and Redmond. "Hell, those two were seeing Bethany."

Staring at the sheriff in disbelief, Tessa untied Rourke. All the time he'd said Michael had lied and Bethany hadn't been seeing anyone. What if one of these guys had killed her?

Ashton moaned and rubbed his head. "I thought you said no one had been seeing Bethany, that Michael had made it up. How do you know they'd been here?"

The sheriff appeared flustered.

"How?" Ashton asked his dad again, his eyes slightly glazed, his tone threatening.

"Who the hell do you think you are, questioning me?" The sheriff glanced at the men and added under his breath, "The little whore."

Ashton's face lost all its color. "You were the one

who discovered her body. No one questioned you because you were the sheriff. You said she'd called you because she worried Michael might kill her he was so angry. But she didn't, did she? You used her phone to make the call. You killed her. Why?"

Tessa's skin chilled.

"Because," Hunter said, stalking in through the back door with a limp, his pants leg bloodied, blood on his sweatshirt, his face bruised, his expression deadly, "Bethany reminded him of his unfaithful wife. Isn't that right, Sheriff? Didn't want a two-timing woman to hurt your own son?"

Dying to hold Hunter tight, Tessa's eyes filled with tears of joy that Michael could be exonerated. But the menacing look Hunter gave the sheriff warned her to keep her distance.

What about Meara? Her clothes were lying on the floor next to the couch. Cara's gaze followed where Tessa looked, and Cara left Rourke, grabbed Meara's clothes, and headed outside.

"You must have staged the phone call," Hunter said.

The sheriff reached for his revolver.

His look feral, dangerously challenging, Hunter asked, "What are you going to do? Kill all of us? It's over, Sheriff. Time to be a man and face the judge and jury."

Chapter 17

SEARCHING FOR THE GOLD IN THE AREA BEYOND the house, Tessa tried to settle the way her stomach flip-flopped. Thankful Judge Graydon had obtained Michael's release and agreed to try Sheriff Wellington for Bethany's murder, she still felt badly for Ashton, who was torn between hating his father and still loving him. But now Devlyn Greystoke was speaking privately with Hunter inside her house about Hunter making Tessa his mate without her cousin's permission, and he was pissed.

Tessa hoped to God the two could settle the matter without bloodshed, but she was annoyed they'd dismissed her like she didn't have any say in the matter.

Although, secondary to all that was the fact Hunter was still perturbed with her for biting her brother and changing him. As if she'd go through life without sharing it with her brother.

She took a deep breath of the salty air and of the sea kelp rotting on the beach she normally despised. But if it hadn't blanketed the rock where Hunter had fallen, he probably wouldn't have survived. Where Yoloff and his brother had fallen, the tide had cleaned the rocks, leaving them bare and deadly. The police had eventually found Andreas's body on a different beach, thank God.

She poked around the tree roots of a massive pine, the water and unusually high winds having washed away a ton of soil, the snow long since melted away and something had drawn her attention. Metal? Something shining in the pale light of the moon.

The gold!

Footsteps approached, crunching on the fallen leaves and she looked up to see *him*—Devlyn. Their mutual great-grandfather, Seth Greystoke, was known in these parts as the gray devil wolf, and Devlyn had taken after him. Right now, he looked fearsome enough to hold the title. A strap of leather tied back his coffee-colored, shoulder-length hair, his equally dark brown eyes studying her, no hint of a smile on his stern face, as rugged as Hunter's, and he had the same kind of sturdy jaw. Tall and just as broad-shouldered, his unyielding posture gave her the impression he was a commanding alpha, not one to disobey.

His eyes raked over her and his gaze focused on her hair, a hint of a smile playing on his lips. But then the scowl returned. "It appears I'm too late to take you under my wing, dear cousin." His words were tight and terse.

She stood and brushed the dirt off her hands, faced him, her chin tilted up, although to look him in the eye, she had to anyway. "I'm Hunter's mate," she declared to make it very clear she had no intention of leaving him. Not that she guessed she could, according to what Hunter had said about their kind.

"In our way, I'd be compelled to deal with Hunter, wolf to wolf, for taking you without receiving my permission when he knew damn well I'd ordered him to keep his hands off you."

The thought anyone would have ordered that of Hunter made her smile inwardly, but outwardly with

Devlyn, she steeled her expression. "I'm sure Hunter took your order under consideration, but my life was in peril and *you* weren't here to protect me."

Devlyn bowed his head slightly. "In truth, I didn't believe either Hunter—after what Leidolf told me about him—or you, would mind me. And now Hunter tells me you've turned your brother?" He raised a brow, his look still feral. He *tsk*ed. "I don't envy the task Hunter has cut out for him. But Bella is dying to meet you when she can travel. With triplets on the way, she's confined to her greenhouse and home."

Before Tessa could respond, Devlyn stalked toward her and hugged her soundly. "You and Michael are my cousins. If you ever need me or my pack for anything, we're family and you only have to call. Come see us. You're welcome anytime."

Family. The sound was like the caress of the waves stroking the beach, comforting, encompassing. First, Hunter and his family, and now Devlyn. "We'd be happy to visit with Bella and the rest of your pack."

Even though she hadn't been sure that she could fit in with the world of werewolves and their ilk, as long as her brother was along for the ride, and Hunter was her mate, she was one happy *lupus garou*. She glanced at the kitchen window and saw Hunter watching her, protective as ever. She guessed he and Devlyn had made tentative amends, but she could tell Devlyn wasn't totally satisfied.

Hunter kept an eye on Devlyn through the kitchen window, not liking that he'd hugged Tessa in a warm embrace, even if they were cousins. The word "distant," came to mind. Very distant. And his own mate was a redhead… so, Hunter just didn't care for it one bit.

"Come on, Meara. Change into the wolf so I can paint you," Michael said, following her into the kitchen.

"Hunter," Meara said, waving a magazine, "Uncle Basil advertised in this and said that's where he gets most of the reservations for the cabins. There's nothing in the advertisement encouraging alpha males to come here. I mean, there's no indication that they'll find *me* here. Hunter, are you listening to me?"

Hunter continued to watch Devlyn as he spoke further to Tessa. He'd expected Devlyn to be madder about him taking Tessa for his mate without first getting permission. But Devlyn had revealed how he'd gone after Bella, the alpha leader's chosen mate, and for the most part, understood Hunter's feelings. Although an undercurrent of misgiving was still evident.

"Was he very mad?" Meara asked Hunter.

"Devlyn? No. Everything is as it should be." As long as Hunter had Tessa, nothing else mattered.

"Not until you find me a mate, dear brother." She shoved the magazine at his chest. "Fix the ad or else I will. And you never know what I might offer."

Michael said, "Meara, just shapeshift for a little while. Please? An hour or two? I've never seen a wolf who's as beautiful as you."

She rolled her eyes. "Michael, give it a rest. I've got better things to do than pose for a painting for several hours. Take a picture of me the next time I shapeshift and paint that."

"It's not the same."

Ashton, Rourke, and Cara entered the living room and Michael whipped around, targeting them. "Will you change into wolves so I can paint you? Just think, immortalized forever and—"

"Come on, Cara," Ashton said. "My father's home is mine now. I need to take care of some business there."

"How do you feel?" Cara asked him, her hand stroking his arm.

"Like it's all so unreal. I guess deep down I suspected Dad knew I was seeing Bethany, but I didn't realize how much he hated her."

"That day when you ran after Hunter and Rourke and left us alone—"

"I had to know if they'd discover who the murderer was. I felt terrible I left you, Tessa, and Meara to fend for yourselves, but I had to know." He glanced at Michael and raised his brows. "Bring your paints."

Michael grinned from ear to ear. "You bet." He hurried off to the office.

"Watch them, Cara," Hunter warned.

Hell, having so many new *lupus garous* under several different roofs… He shook his head. Yet, with Ashton's father's arrest, Ashton had finally become more of a man. The notion of being a Navy SEAL was forgotten though. Cara liked his long blond hair way too much, but he was looking into becoming a police officer. And Cara seemed to love him all the more.

Rourke joined Hunter and Meara as the others left the house. "I've got to run by the newspaper office and leave off some reports. We're taking Devlyn to the airport, right, Meara?"

Meara nodded. "He says four of his male cousins are unmated and might like to vacation here." She cast Hunter an interested look.

He grunted.

She stood straighter and folded her arms. "He said they manage his affairs when he's away. Although, Tanner, the one he mentioned most, prefers redheads."

Hunter took his eyes off Devlyn. "*He's* not coming here."

Meara gave him a devilish smirk. "Uncle Basil called and said he'd heard about our bad storms, but couldn't get through. He wanted to know if you took care of Tessa."

"Eliminated the threat. Right."

"Yeah. To her. He figured once the two of you met, you'd keep her safe. Not like he could."

Hunter shook his head. "Uncle Basil could have been less cryptic." He yanked open the back door and headed for Tessa and Devlyn.

Devlyn stepped back, a knowing look on his face, acknowledging the possessive alpha male who wants another to stay clear, no matter the familial connection.

"I found the gold," Tessa said, her face beaming, her green eyes sparkling like crystal gems. "But the greatest treasure of all is finding family and becoming your mate." She reached to take Hunter into her arms, but he moved to do so first.

And with one fell swoop, he lifted her in his arms and headed back to the house. "Meara says your flight leaves soon," Hunter said over his shoulder to a bemused Devlyn. "Better not miss it. And by the way, if your cousins are alphas, they're welcome to stay at our resort. All except for Tanner."

A small smile brightened Devlyn's face, and he even managed a dark chuckle.

"Why not Tanner?" Tessa asked.

"He likes redheads."

Tessa said her good-byes to Devlyn, although Hunter hovered nearby, menacingly threatening. But once everyone was gone, the house was nice and quiet—time to show Tessa how important she was to Hunter.

She headed for the heater and turned it on. No response.

She rubbed her arms while Hunter flipped on a light switch. "Electricity's working." He opened the closet and checked the circuit breaker. "Circuit breaker's tripped." He flipped it back, but as soon as Tessa tried the heater again, it tripped the circuit breaker. Hunter growled. "The brothers Grimm fixed it, right? So much for their being electricians." Hunter lifted Tessa into his arms and stalked toward the bedroom.

"Shoot, Hunter, at this rate you'll never get me out of those pajamas—not until spring at least."

His chuckle was deep and dark and silkily seductive. "In your dreams, sweet Tessa. In your dreams."

The End

Acknowledgments

I want to thank my mother and son and daughter for all their help and encouragement. My mother was always first to offer help when I was stuck, except I would have to remind her that I'm writing a romance, not a werewolf horror story.

And thanks to my Rebel Romance critique partners who always help me over the rough spots—Vonda, Judy, Pam, Tammy, Randy, Carol, and Betty.

And I so appreciate Deb Werksman for being a super editor, for believing in my work, and being such a dream to work with.

Thanks also to my fans, who encourage me to keep on writing.

About the Author

Award-winning author of urban fantasy and medieval historical romantic suspense, Terry Spear also writes true stories for adult and young adult audiences. She's a retired lieutenant colonel in the U.S. Army Reserves and has an MBA from Monmouth University. She also creates award-winning teddy bears, Wilde & Woolly Bears, to include personalized bears designed to commemorate authors' books. When she's not writing or making bears, she's teaching online writing courses. Originally from California, she's lived in eight states and now resides in the heart of Texas. She is the author of *Heart of the Wolf, Destiny of the Wolf, Winning the Highlander's Heart, Deadly Liaisons, Relative Danger, The Vampire... In My Dreams* (young adult), and numerous articles and short stories for magazines.